I HAVE NO SECRETS

I Have no Secrets

Penny Joelson

sourcebooks
fire

Published by Sourcebooks Fire, an imprint of Sourcebooks
P.O. Box 4410, Naperville, Illinois 60567-4410
(630) 961-3900
sourcebooks.com

Originally published in 2017 in Great Britain by Electric
Monkey, an imprint of Egmont UK, Ltd.

Library of Congress Cataloging-in-Publication Data

Names: Joelson, Penny, author.
Title: I have no secrets / Penny Joelson.
Description: Naperville, IL : Sourcebooks Fire, [2019] | "Originally published in
2017 in Great Britain by Electric Monkey, an imprint of Egmont UK, Ltd." |
Summary: Sixteen-year-old Jemma, who has severe cerebral palsy, must grapple
with dark truths that only she knows, and is unable to communicate.
Identifiers: LCCN 2019008889 | (trade pbk. : alk. paper)
Subjects: | CYAC: Secrets--Fiction. | Communication--Fiction. | Cerebral
palsy--Fiction. | People with disabilities--Fiction. | Foster children--Fiction.
Classification: LCC PZ7.1.J575 Iah 2019 | DDC [Fic]--dc23
LC record available at https://lccn.loc.gov/2019008889

Printed and bound in the United States of America.
WOZ 10 9 8 7 6 5 4 3 2 1

For Michael and Zoe

I HAVE NO SECRETS

1

I tense up as soon as I hear the doorbell. I know it's him. I know it's Dan. Sarah's still upstairs getting ready, and I hope she comes down soon. I don't want him coming in here.

Mom calls up to Sarah, and I hear Sarah say she'll be down in a minute. "We've been keeping her busy, I'm afraid," Mom tells Dan, "so she hasn't had much time to get ready!"

"I know she wouldn't have it any other way," says Dan. "She's a gem—and you too. What you do for these kids."

I listen to them chatting away and Mom laughing at Dan's jokes. Everyone loves Dan. Then Mom says she has to get back to the kitchen—she's left things on the stove and she's sure Sarah won't be long.

It's quiet for a moment. I hear the distant clattering of pans in the kitchen. Then I hear Dan's voice, coming closer as he speaks.

"What show are you watching? Ah...*Pointless!*"

I can hear him breathing. Then he whispers, "A little like your life, isn't it, Jemma?"

He's standing behind me now, but I can't see him because my wheelchair is facing the TV. I try to focus on the game show questions and forget he's there, but he gives a long, dramatic sigh.

"Don't know how you can stand it." His voice is low, not loud enough to be overheard. "Watching television must be the most excitement you get." He only speaks like this when no one else is around. He used to ignore me completely, but not anymore.

He moves so he is in front of me, blocking my view of the TV. Grimacing, he leans forward. I get a gulping feeling, a tightness in my throat.

"If I were you," he whispers, "I'd kill myself."

My heart thuds as he rubs his head, feigning thoughtfulness. "Oh, yeah... You can't, can you? Listen," he continues, "if you ever want a little help, I could—"

We both hear footsteps on the stairs. Dan backs away. His face transforms from ugly sneer to fake grin, his features softening as if they have been remolded.

"I'd have done better than that couple!" he says, laughing and pointing to the TV screen. "We should go on this show, shouldn't we, Sarah?"

I get a waft of Sarah's perfume, which is quickly overtaken by the smell of onions frying in the kitchen. "I'm useless at trivia," she says, laughing as she comes into view. "I bet Jemma could do it, though, if she had the chance."

I don't know about that, although I do sometimes get the right answers. It's possible I'd be better than Sarah. She's an awesome aide, but she's not too smart when it comes to general knowledge—or boyfriends.

Out of the corner of my eye, I see her kiss Dan softly on the lips.

My own mouth suddenly feels dry.

The couple playing *Pointless* have been eliminated. They look very disappointed. Dan and Sarah only have eyes for each other. "Ready?" Dan smiles at Sarah. "You look stunning, babe."

She nods and turns to me. Her eyes are sparkly, her cheeks flushed. "Bye, Jem. See you in the morning."

"See you, Jemma," says Dan. He winks at me.

2

"Sorry to leave you so long, dear!"

Mom bustles into the room, and I'm relieved to hear her warm, soft voice. She switches off the TV and pushes my wheelchair into the kitchen, to my place at the end of the table.

I hear the car in the drive. Dad's back from taking Finn to his swimming lesson and picking up Olivia from ballet. Soon the kitchen is noisy and cheerful, as usual, and I push Dan out of my mind.

Olivia is boasting to Mom about how good her dancing was, and I watch as she shows Mom the new steps while Mom tries to get her to sit down at the table. She's nine and has only been here a year. We're all fostered. I've been here since I was two and so has Finn, who's nearly six. I've heard Mom say Olivia was "hard to place." Maybe that goes for Finn and me too, though Olivia's problems are different from ours. Finn is autistic, and right now, he is lining all his beans up neatly on the plate with his fingers. He's obsessed with straight lines.

Olivia is a whirlwind—sometimes a tornado—and she's loud. Finn and I don't speak, so life is very different and much noisier since she came.

"Sit down, Olivia!" Dad says in his "firm but kind" voice, and Olivia finally does. At least she doesn't start one of her tantrums.

Mom serves Dad's lasagna, then starts feeding me my mushed-up version. Dan's words creep back into my head while I'm eating, and I try to shut them out.

"If I were you, I'd kill myself. Listen, if you ever want a little help, I could—"

I can't believe he said it—as if my life is worth nothing!

Olivia is wolfing down her food like she's never eaten before. She's skinny, but she has a huge appetite. Finn isn't eating. He's still lining up his beans, concentrating as if his life depends on it.

"Come on, Finn," Dad coaxes. "Time to eat them now."

But Finn clearly doesn't think his line is straight enough.

"Finn, my love," says Mom gently, "why don't you start with the lasagna?"

I don't think Finn is listening to Mom, but I think he's happy now with his line of beans. In any event, he forks a small amount of lasagna into his mouth.

Mom spoons some more into mine.

"I saw Paula earlier," she tells Dad. "She looks dreadful, the poor woman."

"Still no news?" Dad asks. Mom shakes her head.

"News about what?" Olivia demands.

Paula lives down the street, and her son, Ryan, was murdered last month. He was nineteen, and he was stabbed to death, and no one knows who did it. Everyone's talking about it, though—it's even been on the radio.

Dad quickly changes the subject.

"Finn's swimming like a fish now," he tells Mom. "He's come along so fast."

"And I was really good at ballet!" Olivia says, never wanting to be left out.

"I'm sure you were," says Dad.

"How was school?" Mom asks Olivia. She shrugs.

Olivia never wants to talk about school. It's like it's some big secret for her.

I have no secrets of my own. I've never done anything without someone knowing about it. I'm sixteen years old, and I have severe cerebral palsy. I am quadriplegic, which means I can't control my arms or legs—or anything else. I can't eat by myself. I can't go to the bathroom without help. I can't move without someone lifting me with a hoist or pushing me in a wheelchair. I also can't speak.

I've been this way all my life. I can see, though, and I can hear. Sometimes people forget that; they don't realize that I have a functioning brain. Sometimes people talk about me as if I'm not even there. I hate that.

And sometimes people tell me their secrets. I think it's because it's really hard to hold a one-way conversation. If they are alone with me, they want to talk to pass the time and they end up telling me stuff. They know I won't tell anyone else, so they think telling me is safe. The perfect listener.

Sarah told me her secret. She's cheating on Dan. She's still seeing Richard, her old boyfriend, because he's so sweet and she can't stand to hurt him by breaking up with him. Neither of them knows the other exists. I'm always worried when Sarah has a boyfriend, although I enjoy the way she gossips to me about them. She has this dream of a fairy-tale wedding—she's even shown me pictures of her ideal wedding dress online. I know I should want her to be happy, and I do. It's just that I'd miss her so much if she went off to get married. She's the best aide I've had.

More than that, I don't want her to marry someone who isn't good enough for her. And I definitely don't want her marrying Dan.

3

Sarah's in a great mood when she's back on duty the next morning, though I can tell she has a hangover and is trying to hide it. She's drinking a lot of coffee. She clearly had a good night out with Dan and is singing a track by our favorite band, Glowlight.

She's wheeling me from my bedroom to the kitchen when I hear the clunk of mail landing on the mat. Sarah stops to pick it up and puts the small pile of letters on the kitchen table.

"Oh, look—one for you, Jemma," she comments. As she pushes me into my place, I see that the top letter, though addressed to Mom and Dad, has my name on it too—*Parents/Guardians of Jemma Shaw*. I rarely get mail. I wonder what it could be.

Mom picks up the pile and glances down. Then she quickly moves my letter to the bottom and puts them all on the kitchen counter. Sarah doesn't seem to notice.

Now I am even more curious. Why doesn't Mom want to open it?

After breakfast, Sarah goes to get Olivia ready, and Dad gets up to leave for work. Mom follows him out into the hallway to kiss him goodbye. Their voices are muffled, but I can pick out Mom's words. She says, "There's been another letter. I haven't read it yet, but I think we'll have to tell her."

I strain to hear Dad's reply. "Yes—she is family. Jemma has a right to know."

Family? What are they talking about? If only I could ask. It sounds like they're planning to tell me. I just have to hope that they do.

Dad's gone and Sarah's in the kitchen with me, easing my arms gently into my coat, ready for school. I'm conscious that my letter is still there, at the bottom of the pile on the counter.

Olivia's moaning that she can't find her reading book.

Mom sighs. "When did you last have it, Olivia?"

Olivia shrugs. "Dunno."

"Take a look in your bedroom," Mom tells her.

Olivia heads off slowly toward the stairs.

"Sarah, can you go with her?" Mom asks. "I don't see her book down here."

"Sure," says Sarah. "You're ready, Jemma. That's one down at least!" She hurries off after Olivia.

"Where's Finn's water bottle?" Mom mutters to herself. "I'm sure I washed it yesterday. I bet you know where I put it, Jemma."

As it happens, I do know. I saw it fall off the dish rack and down behind the trash can.

The doorbell rings, and Mom wheels me toward the door. We never know if my minibus or Finn's cab will come first. Today, it's the cab that takes Finn to his special school.

Mom sighs and pushes a spare green water bottle into Finn's bag, which is not going to please Finn, because he always has the blue one. She helps him with his coat and gives his hair a quick comb. He wriggles away as fast as he can and out the front door with his taxi escort, Jo.

"Reading book found," Sarah says, coming down the stairs.

"I hope you said thank you, Olivia," says Mom, though she knows full well that Olivia hasn't.

"It wasn't me who lost it, Lorraine!" Olivia protests. "Why do you always blame me? It's not my fault!"

She stamps her feet, and I'm relieved when the doorbell rings again so I can leave before Olivia starts screaming.

But all I think about as the bus proceeds down the street is the letter. I try to figure out what Mom and Dad were talking about. Family? Mom has an aunt and Dad has a brother, but we don't see much of them because they live a long way from here. Were they talking about their family? Or could it be *mine*—like my birth mom, the one who gave birth to me and then dumped me? Could she have finally decided she wants to see me?

I hope it's not her. I don't want to see her—not ever! She probably only wants to get a look at me and stare. I hope Mom and Dad tell her to get lost.

As soon as Dad is back in the evening, I start waiting for them to talk to me—but they don't say anything. I couldn't even see my letter in the kitchen at dinnertime. The whole pile was gone. Have they changed their minds, or are they waiting for Finn and Olivia to be in bed so they can talk about it? I'm not exactly looking forward to a conversation about my birth mom, but waiting for it is even worse.

Dad does the dishes while Mom and Sarah put Finn and Olivia to bed. It seems like it takes forever, even though I know it is probably just the normal amount of time. But then, finally, when it's nearly my bedtime and I'm watching TV on my own, Mom and Dad both come in. Mom pauses the TV, and Dad turns me around to face the sofa and sits down, looking serious.

He has the letter in his hand. I get a surge of relief mixed with panic.

"We've got something to tell you, Jemma," he says gently. "Something important."

My heart is beating so fast. Suddenly I don't want to hear—I don't want to know.

"We've gotten a letter," Dad continues, "from Social Services." He pauses, as if unsure how to continue.

Mom sits down beside him. "Jemma, I know this is going

to be a bit of a shock, and I will explain why we haven't told you before..."

I wait.

Dad reaches out and touches my hand. "You've got a sister, Jemma."

What?

A sister?

Mom sighs and smiles. "Her name's Jodi."

I try to take it in. The shock is making me breathless. A *sister*. I was so sure it was my birth mom wanting to see me. A sister is something completely different.

"The thing is," Mom continues, "we knew she wasn't told about you. So we thought it might be upsetting for you to know about her. But she found your name mentioned in some papers, and... I'm sorry, Jemma. It's been hard to know what to do."

They knew! All this time Mom and Dad have known that I have a sister. So many feelings are swirling around inside me. The thought of them not telling me makes me angry— but Mom's right. It would have been hard knowing about my sister if she was never going to know about me. I am still in shock, but I'm curious too.

A sister. My sister. I start to wonder what she's like—how old she is...

"The papers Jodi found were her adoption papers," Mom continues. "You and Jodi were split up when you were put into foster care. Your birth mom couldn't cope. She had a lot of problems. She was very young and on her own."

I've sometimes imagined it—my mom giving me up. I could even picture her face, horrified at her own baby, unable to deal with what I was. But there were two of us, two children. That idea had never entered my head. And she couldn't look after my sister either. Does my sister have a disability too? I'm not sure what to make of this—but I know it changes things. It changes everything.

"Jodi's been asking if she can contact you," says Dad, drawing me out of my thoughts.

I get a surge of excitement that quickly sinks when I think what they would have had to tell Jodi—that I can't exactly contact her back.

"She's been persistent, but we weren't sure if it was a good idea," says Mom. "It's so hard when you can't tell us how you feel about it... But we've told her about you, and we've said she can write to you. I hope it's what you want, Jemma. I really do."

My sister! I'm still finding it hard to believe that I have one. I wonder how much she's been told about me. Will she really want to know me once she finds out what I'm like? I am thrilled, though. I can't wait to know more about her. She's going to write to me! My sister is going to write to me!

4

"I still can't believe you've got a sister and no one told you!" Sarah exclaims, as she picks up a book to read to me in bed. "I knew nothing, Jemma. Your mom and dad never even mentioned her."

I definitely believe her—if Mom and Dad had told Sarah about Jodi, she would have let something slip. She'd never keep something like that from me.

"Me and my sister, Kate," says Sarah, "we don't always get along, but I can't imagine growing up and not knowing her. I bet you can't wait for a letter from Jodi!"

Sarah keeps mentioning Jodi over the next couple of days. It's as if she's as excited as I am. I wish I could tell her how nervous it makes me. What if Jodi doesn't write?

At least it means Sarah's not talking about Dan so much. I can almost start to pretend he doesn't exist. In fact, today Sarah isn't talking at all—she's concentrating as she battles to get my rebellious arms into the sleeves of a sweater. My muscle spasms are worse than usual because I haven't been sleeping well. Thinking about my sister has kept me awake. "Tonight's the night," she whispers. I wonder what she means. She's not seeing Dan again, is she? She's seeing so much of him that I'm sometimes scared she's going to run off with him! But of course, she'd never do that.

"I'm breaking up with Richard," she says. "It has to be done. I'm not being fair to him." She runs a brush quickly but gently through my tangled hair. "I can't keep putting it off. I know he'll be heartbroken, though—he's such a softy."

At last Sarah is doing the right thing. It's no good going out with someone just because you feel sorry for them. Now she just needs to dump Dan too! I wish she had more sense when it comes to men. She's had a few boyfriends since she's been here, and they've all been hopeless. Like Jason, who was always borrowing money from her and never paying it back, and a guy named Mario who was only interested in football and a total bore. Next was wimpy Richard. And then Dan came along.

———————

Sarah's in her room getting ready to go out when the doorbell rings. She's meeting Richard downtown, so I know it's not him. I'm in the living room, but the door's open and for once I'm at an angle where I can see into the hall. Dad opens the front door. I hear Dan's voice greeting him.

What's *he* doing here? Sarah is definitely not expecting him.

Dad invites Dan in. I hear the front door shut, then watch them as they talk about the weather. When Dan sees Sarah all dressed up, what's he going to think? He'll get suspicious for sure. I strain to listen, but now Olivia has started one of her tantrums. She's lying on the floor somewhere behind me, kicking and screaming like a two-year-old except twice as loud.

I hear Dad call upstairs, "Sarah! Dan's here!"

He's assumed Sarah is going out with Dan tonight! At least he's warned her. It would be awful if she came down and just found Dan in the hall. I have no idea what she's going to do.

Thankfully, Dan doesn't come into the living room. I think Olivia's screaming is keeping him at a distance. Mom comes to see what's up with her, saying a quick hello to Dan as she passes. She turns my wheelchair around, which is annoying because I'd rather watch what's happening in the hall than look at Olivia, who is lying on the floor at the far end of the room, pointing and screaming. Now I can see what's upset her. One of her ballet shoes is trapped on the candelabra light fixture, near the ceiling. Finn must have thrown it up there. He's got good aim.

Mom calms Olivia and says Dad will get it down. Finn is nowhere to be seen. Mom turns me to face the TV and switches it on. Then she pulls Olivia up gently, hugging her, and holds her hand to lead her out. I hear them going upstairs.

I'm conscious that Dan is still in the hall. Sarah calls to say she'll be down in a few minutes. Then I hear Dan sigh. He walks into the room and goes straight to the TV and picks up the remote, flicking through channels. He's acting as if I'm not even here. I wish I could say, "Hey! I was watching that!" even though I wasn't really.

He settles on the news. I don't want the news. On the screen I can see a casket being carried into a church. A reporter is speaking. It's only when I hear him say the name Ryan Blake that I start paying attention.

Ryan—from down the street. It was his funeral today. I want to know what the police have found out. Mom and Dad think Ryan might have been into drugs. "Police are still seeking witnesses," the reporter continues, "and his parents are pleading for anyone who knows anything to come forward." Dan suddenly turns toward me.

"You don't know anything, do you, Jem?" he sniggers.

I can't stand it when he calls me "Jem," as if he's part of the family or something.

"Here's a secret for you," he continues, "and I know you won't tell anyone." He winks. There's a pause. He presses his face close to mine, so close I can feel his hot breath on my cheeks. "They're never gonna catch me!" he whispers, squinting his eyes and then nodding at the screen. He stands back, smiling, as if he's gloating. "There's something for you to chew on, *freak*!"

Sarah's feet patter on the stairs.

Dan quickly changes the channel to a game show. *Catch him? What did he mean?* It's an attempt to irritate me—it must be...

"Hiya, babe," he says.

"What are you doing here?" Sarah asks. I see her flapping her arms a little, like Finn does. I can tell she's panicking, but she's also gazing longingly into Dan's eyes. She won't cancel on Richard to go out with Dan, will she? She needs to break up with *both* of them. I wish she could hear what I'm telling her in my head.

"You left a glove in my car," he tells her. "I just found it today. I was passing by, so I thought I'd drop it off. Don't want you getting chilly fingers!"

"Oh, thanks! I was wondering where it was," she replies. "But I've got to get going. I'm headed out with Emma and Rihanna. We're going to the movies."

"Out again?" he says.

"Yes, I switched my next night off. It's Emma's birthday," Sarah says quickly. Sarah seems to have her excuse ready— but I guess this is what she's told Mom. "We're having a girls' night out. Becks is coming too. We're seeing that movie you said was for lovestruck teenage girls."

"No way!"

"Yeah, really." Sarah laughs for a little too long. "And I've gotta go or I'll be late."

"No worries, I'll give you a lift," says Dan.

"No, Dan. I'm fine," Sarah assures him.

"It's no prob," says Dan.

"Oh... All right," she replies.

An uneasy feeling grips my chest. I don't want her to go with him. What he said to me... He had to be joking. Dan's horrible, but he wouldn't actually kill someone. Would he? And why did he turn up here this evening? It doesn't feel right. Maybe she's done something to make him suspicious. Was he trying to catch her at it?

Sarah says goodbye to me and touches my hand gently. Her hand is hot. She knows this is a mess, and she briefly meets my eyes with a look that says she knows I know this too. She turns to the door.

"Bye, Jemma," Dan says, winking again. I see his sneering face in my head when he called me *freak* and remember what else he said. I don't trust him one little bit.

They go, and I hear the front door bang shut.

Dad comes in and stares up at the ballet shoe on the light fixture, muttering, "You've got to be joking," under his breath.

5

Mom gets me ready for bed, but I'm barely listening as she chats away about needing to get me some new clothes. What did Dan mean?

If only Mom could see inside my head to the thoughts spinning around. But I know on the outside I must look exactly the same as I always do. Nothing shows. No one knows.

He must have been joking. If he was involved, wouldn't we have heard something? Wouldn't he be a suspect? Even so, I wish I could tell someone. Just so they know what he's like. Just in case.

If he was confessing, he knew he was telling the one person who would keep his secret safe. Maybe he thinks I don't even understand what he says. I just want to know for sure. Because if Dan is a murderer, and he finds out Sarah is cheating on him...

I can't sleep at all, waiting to know that Sarah is back home. My room is downstairs, but at the back of the house, and I listen for the sound of the front door. Finally I hear her come in, but I'm facing away from my bedside clock so I can't see the time. Maybe she'll come in to turn me—I have to be turned in the night so I don't get sore from being in one position. Yes. I can hear her footsteps.

She's breathing quite fast, and her hands aren't as gentle as usual. She catches my eye in the dimmed light and sees that I'm awake. I will her to tell me what happened. Sometimes Sarah seems to read my mind. That's one of the things I love about her.

"That wasn't the best evening of my life," she whispers.

I wait eagerly for more. She sits down on the edge of the bed.

"I can't believe Dan turned up! That glove thing was just an excuse, don't you think? He's getting so serious. He said he couldn't bear to be apart from me." She laughs. "I sat in his car with my fingers crossed that he wouldn't think something was wrong. Then he wanted to actually come into the theater with me, but luckily it was really hard to park so he couldn't."

She runs her hand through her hair. Only Sarah would get herself into this situation.

"I was scared he might hang around so I texted Richard from the lobby to say I'd be late and waited ten minutes before I even dared walk to the bar! You've gotta laugh, Jem."

Sarah is not taking this seriously at all. At least it sounds like Dan didn't catch her.

"When I got there," she continues, "Richard looked so pleased to see me. I just couldn't do it to him."

My heart sinks. Sarah is fidgeting and looks excited about something. Has she changed her mind and decided she wants to be with Richard after all?

"Jem, he got tickets for us to see Glowlight next month! It'll be amazing!" She gives me a sheepish look. "Is it really bad if I keep going out with him until then?"

Glowlight! Well, it's not great to use him for his tickets, but it is Glowlight. Maybe I'd do the same... No, this is wrong. Sarah needs to break up with Richard!

"Perhaps we could just go to the concert as friends," she continues. "But I don't think Richard would like that. I know Dan wouldn't."

She sighs and smooths my comforter down. "I'm such a coward, Jem."

I don't know what I'd do if I were Sarah—though I'd like to think I wouldn't get myself into such a mess in the first place.

6

When the bus drops me off from school on Monday, Mom tells me we have visitors. She pushes my wheelchair into the kitchen, where Mr. and Mrs. Blake are drinking tea. Paula and Mom have known each other for years, but more to say hello in the street than as actual friends. I remember her coming to Mom a few times when Ryan was young and acting up, asking Mom for advice. I think there was a time when she even hoped Mom would foster him.

Since Ryan died, Mom has tried to be supportive, and Paula's been here a few times. Graham—Mr. Blake—doesn't usually come with her, though.

Paula says hi to me and smiles, but her grief is clear in the deep lines on her face and her drooping eyes. Graham shifts awkwardly and taps the rim of his mug with his finger. I can tell that I make him uncomfortable. I notice he's kept his black outdoor jacket on, while Paula has taken off her coat.

He's clearly hoping not to be here long.

"I know he was no angel," Paula is saying to Mom, "but I was so hard on him—always nagging, criticizing, pushing him to change. The last thing I said to him was, 'Get out and don't come back!' Can you believe it? That's what I said!"

She bursts into tears.

Graham touches her shoulder and fidgets again.

Mom hands Paula a tissue.

"I know," says Mom, "but you could never have known what would happen. You were trying to set boundaries. He knew you loved him. He knew that's why you kept after him."

"Do you really think so?" Paula sobs.

When we were young, Ryan used to stick his tongue out at me if he passed me in the street. Then when he got a little older, he called me "Spaz" or "Spazzie" or worse things. He even spat at me once.

I don't miss Ryan, but obviously I feel horrible for Paula. Ryan was a loser, but he was still her son—and Graham's.

I look at Graham. He's like a block of stone. Paula sips her tea. "I can't bear the thought that the monster who did it is walking around free. I might pass him in the street and never know."

Dan's face comes into my mind. *Yes, you might*, I think. *He was here... He was here in this house*, I want to tell Paula. A sound comes out of my mouth, a strained gurgle. Paula glances at me and quickly away again.

I wish I could tell them what he said. Just in case. I don't know if Dan and Ryan even knew each other. They were very different. And Dan doesn't seem like he'd be involved with drugs and gangs and stuff. Or maybe he's just good at hiding it.

"We'd better be going," Graham says gruffly.

Paula turns and gives him a bewildered look. But she pulls herself up from the chair, and Graham helps her put her coat on.

"At least the *Crime Watch* thing might help," I hear Mom say as they go to the front door. "Let's just hope someone calls in and the police get a lead."

So Ryan's murder is going to be on *Crime Watch Daily*! Maybe that will make everything clear. I hope Mom and Dad will let me watch it. I've never seen it, but I know about it—how they reconstruct crimes, and people watching can phone in if they know anything. Maybe there will be a clue that will tell me if Dan really did it—and if he did, then Sarah or Mom or Dad or someone else watching will have to realize it was him.

7

On Tuesday after school, Sarah greets me with a smile even bigger than her usual cheerful one.

"Ooh, Jem! A letter's come from your sister! Your mom hasn't opened it. She's waiting for you. But I hope she'll show me later! I'm dying to know what your sister said."

Sarah wheels me into the kitchen, announcing, "Jemma's home!" to Mom. She doesn't leave. I think she's hoping Mom will let her stay.

"Thanks, Sarah," says Mom.

Sarah shoots me a pretend annoyed look and goes, closing the door behind her. We sit at the kitchen table, and Mom carefully opens the white envelope.

My heart thuds.

"Are you ready for this?" Mom asks. She puts the letter down so I can see it.

"*Dear Jemma,*" she reads.

I didn't know you existed until a few months ago. I found some papers in a drawer that were about me. One of them had your name on it under mine. My name is Jodi, and I am your sister!

Mom pauses and looks up at me before continuing.

In fact, more than that, Jemma. We are twins!

Twins? Mom never told me that.

We must have been born only minutes apart. The thing is, I've always had this weird feeling—like something was missing. When I found out about you I thought, This is it! This explains it. I have a twin sister. We spent nine months together before we were born, and we've been separated ever since.

Missing? I've never felt that. But maybe that's because so much else is missing for me—like legs and arms that work and a voice.

Mom is still reading.

Now I'm going to tell you some stuff about me. I live in Enfield—only a few miles from you! I live with my mom and dad (the ones who adopted me), but I don't

have any brothers or sisters. I've ALWAYS wanted
a sister.

Favorite things. Color—purple. Food—ice-cream
sundae. Sport—field hockey (I play for the school team).
Pet—cat (Mine's called Fluff. She really is like a fluffy
white bundle, and I love her to pieces! She disappeared
last year and was found up in a tree after three days!).
People—my best friend, Ava, my boyfriend, Jack, and
my parents too. They are terrific, and even though I was
angry that they didn't tell me about you and they were
upset that I found out, they've calmed down now and say
they're sorry that they didn't tell me before.

There's so much more I could write, but I'll stop now
because I've got tons of homework.

I know you have disabilities and that you can't
write back. I've been told about that. It's no big deal.
Don't worry, I'll keep writing!

I've put in a photo of me, though our printer at home
is worthless and it came out a little dark. I'll try to find
a better photo—and maybe next time I'll send you a
picture of Fluff too!

I will write again soon.

Love, Jodi

Mom holds the photo so I can see it. It's kind of blurry,

but Jodi has dark hair like mine, and her eyes are a little like mine too. She looks pretty.

"I'll reply for you, Jemma," says Mom. "And I'll encourage Jodi to keep writing. We'll take things slowly, and hopefully one day you'll be able to meet her."

I'm only half listening. I can't take my eyes off the photo. That's my sister—my twin sister!

Mom puts the photo by my bed, and looking at it and thinking about the letter keeps me happy for the next couple of days. I am sleeping better too. It is almost enough to keep me from thinking about Dan. But when Thursday evening comes, I am desperate for Dad to let me stay in the living room to watch *Crime Watch*.

Sarah's upstairs putting Finn and Olivia to bed, and Mom's getting her coat on to go to Weight Watchers. She's been trying to eat healthily, but I know her secret—I see her hide chocolate bars between the books on the highest shelf in the living room.

I'm hoping my limbs stay still and no sounds escape my mouth so she'll forget I'm here. Dad is more likely to let me watch *Crime Watch* than Mom. But she comes to say goodbye to me and then turns to Dad.

"I'm not sure Jemma should see it," she says. "It might upset her."

"She's sixteen," says Dad. "I bet she'd be interested to see it, wouldn't you, Jemma?" He turns to me and back to Mom. "It's not as if she hasn't heard us all talk about it."

I wish I could hug Dad.

Mom still looks uncertain. She glances from Dad to me and back again.

Please!

"All right," says Mom. "Hopefully I'll be back in time, but if not, you'll have to fill me in."

When the show starts, I'm disappointed that Sarah isn't here—but Dad calls her, and she brings a basket of laundry to fold and sits on the armchair.

Mom gets back just as they start showing Ryan's case and hurries in, still in her coat.

"Put on two pounds." She sighs, and I hear the sofa creak as she sits down next to Dad.

"Four weeks ago," the reporter says, "nineteen-year-old Ryan Blake was brutally stabbed to death in Walden Cross. The assailant and motive remain a mystery. Witnesses have helped to make the reenactment that you are about to see."

They show actors, including one I can clearly see is meant to be Ryan, drinking in a local bar, the Hare and Hound. Then Ryan and his friends leave and gradually split up until Ryan is left with one friend, who finally heads for home. Instead of going home himself, Ryan doubles back. No one knows why he did this. He heads down a side street—though they're not sure which one—and comes out somewhere behind the train station.

That was where his body was found.

"Did you see Ryan on Warduff Street or Mackenzie Avenue between 11:00 p.m. and midnight?" the reporter asks. "A man in a black jacket was seen walking along Mackenzie Avenue just before 11:00. This man has not yet been identified. Are you that man, or did you also see him that night?"

I try to think like Hercule Poirot. I've listened to dozens of Agatha Christie audiobooks that Mom's aunt gave me. I need to be observant—to have an eye for anything that might be a clue, even if it seems unlikely. Everyone is a suspect in Agatha Christie. Ryan's friends seem like a shady bunch. Maybe the last friend he was with didn't go home. Maybe he doubled back too. Perhaps Ryan had lied to him—or one of the others—or ripped them off. But there isn't much to go on to figure out a motive. What about the man in the black jacket? Dan has a black jacket, but it's a little different from the one they showed.

Suddenly I remember Graham—Ryan's dad—sitting in our kitchen. His jacket looked like the one on the program. Graham? Is it possible? Could he have gotten so fed up with Ryan that he lost his temper and killed him? One of the crime books I listened to said most people are killed by members of their families. And in Agatha Christie it's often the quiet ones you have to watch. But Graham? Murder his own son?

It's easier to believe that Dan did it. I've seen what he can be like—even though no one else has.

I want to see Sarah's reaction, but I'm facing the TV. I wish she'd say something.

"Police say the alley behind the station is known to be used by drug dealers," the reporter continues, "but no drugs were found in Ryan's blood." They mention that the knife used hasn't been found, and they give the number for people to call.

"Okay, Jemma," says Mom. For a moment I imagine her dialing the number and handing me the phone so I can tell them what Dan said. But of course, she's just telling me that it's time for me to go to bed.

Sarah wheels me out as *Crime Watch* moves on to a series of armed robberies in Dartford.

8

"Listen, dear, I've got something to tell you," Mom says the next evening.

I'm all ears—wondering if it's to do with *Crime Watch*. No one's mentioned it since yesterday, and I've been waiting for news. Did anyone call the program? Do the police have any new leads?

Then I wonder if it's Jodi. Has she written again? "You remember I told you about Carlstone College?" Mom says. "I've arranged for us to go up there next week."

My mind whirls because this is so far from what I was thinking about. *Carlstone College*. When Mom talked about it before, she said I might go there when I'm older—not *now*. Has she changed her mind?

"They have a communications expert coming," Mom tells me. "Professor Spalding. It's a meeting for any interested families, even those whose children aren't at the college. I can't make any promises, but maybe he'll be able to help you.

And we can have a look around, just to see what the college is like."

A while ago, they showed me a leaflet for Carlstone. Mom said they had amazing facilities and might be able to help me much more than the school I'm at. I liked the sound of the college. I thought I might really enjoy it, and they offer many more subjects there. Then Mom told me it's a three-hour drive from here. I'd have to live there, like at a boarding school.

Mom said if I went there, she and Dad would come and visit, and I'd be able to come home some weekends and for school vacations. I was so relieved the next day when Mom said she thought I was too young, and maybe some time in the future we'd all go and have a look at it. But I thought that meant in a couple of years—not a couple of months.

And what about Sarah? If she went with me, it wouldn't be so bad, but I bet students don't get to take their own care-givers. And she wouldn't want to be three hours away from Dan, would she?

I try to focus on what Mom is saying about the commu-nications expert. Hopefully, our visit really is just about seeing this professor. But I can't stop thinking that it might be something more. The worry is gnawing at my brain, joining the other worries and the questions I can never ask.

I feel myself withdrawing like a turtle into a shell. Mom's still talking, but I'm no longer listening.

When Sarah comes to fetch me for dinner, she looks at me for a moment and frowns. "What's up, Jem?"

I don't know how she can tell that something's wrong, but she can and I'm glad. Maybe my limbs are even stiffer than usual when she moves me. I certainly feel stiffer. Everything aches.

"I hope you're not coming down with something," she continues.

She looks into my eyes for clues. I wish they could give her some. She feels my forehead and inspects my arms, legs, and chest for rashes. Then she gets the ear thermometer and takes my temperature. Hopefully once she's figured out I'm not sick, she'll realize how unhappy I am.

Sarah wheels me into the kitchen. Everyone else is already at the table, but the silverware is missing. Finn has removed it and lined it all up neatly on the floor against the wall—a row of forks, then knives, then spoons.

Dad shakes his head at Finn and sighs as he picks them up, and there is a delay while he washes them in the sink. He isn't angry. He understands Finn.

"Something's wrong with Jemma," Sarah tells Mom. I watch Mom's face. Will she make the connection and realize that what she said before has made me worry?

"Are you hungry?" Mom asks me. "Sorry dinner's a little late."

I'm not hungry. And now I feel sick at the thought of eating.

Sarah shakes her head. "It's more than that."

Mom shrugs rather dismissively, and then I wonder if maybe she doesn't want Sarah to know about her plans, because Sarah will lose her job if I'm sent away. Once the silverware is washed and dried, Sarah spoons food into my mouth. I find it hard to swallow. Olivia knocks her cup over. I'm not sure if it is accidental or on purpose, but water spreads in a pool across the table and Dad's "Oh, Olivia" is enough to start her wailing theatrically. Dad tells her to calm down, which brings on a full-blown tantrum. My head is pounding now.

Mom and Dad are both fussing over Olivia. I scream inside my head sometimes, making the kind of noise she's making now, but of course no one ever knows.

Sarah aims another spoonful into my mouth. I cough and splutter. I can't stop coughing. I need a drink. Sarah is distracted, looking at Olivia, and I start to panic. I feel like I can't breathe. It is a moment before she sits me forward in my wheelchair and pats me on the back. She holds the straw to my lips and looks from me to Mom as Olivia finally stops shrieking. "I told you something was wrong. I think she's coming down with something. I'll sleep in her room tonight."

No one understands. When I'm worried and I just want reassurance, I have no way of getting it. Then my worries just grow and grow. Mom and Dad assume it's something physical because it so often is, but all I want is to be able to tell them how I feel.

"Thanks, Sarah," says Mom. "There's a nasty flu bug going around. I hope it isn't that."

Later, Sarah is getting me ready for bed when her cell phone rings.

"It's Dan. We haven't spoken all week. I'd better answer," she says apologetically, "or he might think I'm avoiding him."

She says hello and then puts the phone on speaker and leaves it on the bed while she crouches to take off my socks. I hear Dan's voice as clearly as if he's in the room.

"How was the movie, babe?"

Sarah has taken off one of my socks and started on the other one. She stops, bites her lip, and leans toward the phone. "Great," she chirps.

"Really? What was so great about it?" he asks.

"Why do you care?" Sarah asks. "It's not your kind of movie. You said so yourself."

"Just asking," he says.

There's a pause. "Sorry," says Sarah, "I can't talk now. I'm getting Jemma ready for bed. She's not feeling well. I'll call you later and tell you all about it, okay?"

"Sure—talk later. Love you, babe!"

Sarah puts her phone in her pocket, then laughs. "I'll have to look up some reviews online," she tells me. "I don't even know who's in it!"

9

"Come on, Finn!" Mom calls cheerfully as we reach the gate of the park.

When I woke up this morning, I had this weird floaty feeling, as if nothing in my life is real. I am apparently neither sick nor well. It doesn't surprise me that my body's behaving weirdly. All these thoughts have got to get out somehow. Sarah and Mom keep taking my temperature. "A little under the weather" is how Mom described me. We often go to the park on Saturdays, and she said some fresh air might do me good.

"We'll go and see the ducks first," Mom tells Finn and Olivia.

If I could roll my eyes, I would. I liked being taken to see the ducks when I was six, but right now I've got other things on my mind. If we have to be here, I was hoping we were going to the park café. It's at the top of the hill, and I know it's not easy to push me up there, but from the top you get a view right over the park. I like the feeling of being so high—on top of the world, looking down. From my wheelchair I so often feel low down, looking up at things.

Olivia skips ahead, Sarah's pushing me, and Mom's cajoling Finn—who is walking slowly, flapping his hand in front of his face. I think he likes the patterns of light it makes. Soon we reach the pond, and we stop by the barrier, near a clump of early daffodils. I watch Olivia throw corn at the nearest ducks as if she's trying to murder one. I'm sure she just said, "Yeah! Got it!"

Mom pushes corn into Finn's hand and helps him aim, but the corn just drops onto the sidewalk. He isn't really interested and starts to pull away toward the playground.

"OK, Finn, just a minute," Mom tells him.

Sarah's phone beeps. I bet it's Dan texting her. I see her peering at it when Mom's not looking. I wish she'd tell me what he said.

When we're in the playground, Sarah wheels me onto the wheelchair-accessible merry-go-round and pushes the bar gently so the platform begins to move before she gets on and stands with me.

"Just a gentle spin today, okay?"

This merry-go-round is here because of my mom; she campaigned for it for years, and I was so happy when it arrived. I used to like going fast. It's not often I get to do anything fast. I'm too old for it now, though, and especially not today when my head is already spinning. At least Sarah moves it slowly.

"I'll push!" Olivia says, running up.

"Gently, Olivia," Sarah tells her. But she's pushing too fast so I'm whirling even faster than the thoughts in my head. I want to stop. I want to get off. Now.

"Olivia! Slow down!" Sarah yells. She leaps off and brings it to a halt.

Olivia rushes away toward the playground climbers. "Sorry, Jemma! Are you okay?" Sarah asks, touching my shoulder as she pulls the wheelchair off the merry-go-round. I feel giddy and breathless. I want to go home. Sarah's phone beeps with another message.

She parks me next to a bench where we can watch Finn on the swing. She turns me carefully to make sure the low sun isn't in my eyes. The swing squeaks noisily. Finn would happily swing for an hour, maybe two, if he were allowed.

Sarah takes out her phone again and reads the new message. I wonder if she managed to convince Dan that she really went to the movies.

Olivia runs around, going on everything. She demands that Mom watch her on the monkey bars and then on the climbing wall. She's good at climbing as well as dancing.

I might definitely be too old for playgrounds, but I'd rather be here, with Mom and Sarah and Olivia and Finn, than packed off to some college.

I'm wrapped well in a warm coat and have a blanket over my knees, but I'm starting to feel cold. The fresh air is doing me no good at all, which is no surprise to me. I feel weak and fuzzy-headed. The squeaking of the swing is hurting my ears.

Sarah looks up from her phone. "You're very pale, Jemma."

She goes over to Mom and asks if she can take me home.

Mom comes and looks at me and nods at Sarah. "Yes, you guys go. We won't be far behind."

Sarah pushes me along the sidewalk, past the local stores, the newsstand, and the barbershop.

"Oh, look! See that man coming out of Off-Track Betting?" says Sarah. "I know him—it's Billy."

"Hi, Billy!" Sarah calls as the man walks toward us. He has his head down, but his shoulders jolt and he looks up sharply, then stops and smiles at her.

"Sarah!" he says. "You all right?"

Sarah has mentioned Billy. He's a friend of Dan's. She said Dan calls him "Billy No Brains," which sounded mean to me. Sarah just thought it was funny. My head's really aching now. I hope she's not going to talk for long with him.

"This is Jemma," Sarah tells him. "Jemma, this is Billy." Billy comes around in front of me and smiles at me too. He has a big head, and his smile is so wide it seems to take up most of his face. But he's a friend of Dan's, so I'm sure he can't really be that nice.

"Hi, Jemma. How ya doing?" says Billy. He looks up at Sarah. "Dan's crazy about you, you know. He don't say much, but I can tell!"

Sarah laughs. "Really?"

Thanks, Billy, I think irritably. I don't need him telling her that. *Come on, Sarah. Let's go.*

"He's a good guy, you know. Takes care of his friends. Look, I gotta take off," says Billy. "Nice to see you."

Good.

"I've got to get Jemma home too," says Sarah. "She's not feeling well."

"Say hi to Dan from me," says Billy. "Hope you feel better, Jemma."

10

At last we're home, and I'm glad to be inside where it's warm. My worries slip away, and my head feels better. I enjoy a peaceful five minutes in the living room before I hear a wailing sound from outside. Mom's key is in the door, and the wailing is getting louder.

"Come on, inside," Mom is telling Olivia. I hear Finn run past and up the stairs. I think he finds Olivia's tantrums as painful as I do.

"It wasn't my fault! That boy pushed in front of me!" Olivia says, crying uncontrollably.

"You didn't have to hit him, though, did you?" Mom says.

Olivia has thrown herself on the floor and is kicking her heels and screaming at the top of her lungs, while Mom tries to calm her down. I wish I could kick and yell like that.

Mom and Olivia eventually go upstairs, and the screaming becomes more distant.

By dinnertime Olivia has calmed down. I'm still not

hungry, though. Sarah realizes this when the food she's spoon-ing into my mouth just sits there and doesn't go down.

"Oh, Jem, you're really not well, are you? I'll take your temperature again."

I don't have a high temperature, which she soon finds out. After dinner, she leaves me in the living room with Olivia and Finn. They are changed, ready for bed, and watching TV in their robes. They look cozy and cute, curled up on either end of the sofa. It's *101 Dalmatians*, and I'm half watching too, though I'm not really interested. We've seen it dozens of times.

Someone's at the front door, and I hear Dad go to open it.

And I hear Dan's voice. He's here *again*.

"I was just passing by, and I wondered if I could have a quick word with Sarah," Dan says. "It won't take long, I promise."

I wish Dad would just tell him to buzz off. "I'll call her," Dad says.

He leaves Dan waiting in the hall and goes to look for Sarah. But of course Dan doesn't stay there. I hear his breathing as he comes into the living room. I will him to leave me alone.

"Hiya, Jemma," he says.

Olivia jumps and looks up from the TV. Finn's eyes stay firmly fixed on the screen, as if he's heard nothing.

"What are you doing here?" Olivia asks Dan.

"Just stopped by to see Sarah," Dan tells her.

"You're always stopping by," Olivia comments. "Do you love her?"

I laugh. It comes out as a snort. I'm curious to see how Dan reacts. He doesn't answer right away.

Then, "Yes, I love her," he says as though he actually means it.

Olivia giggles. "D'you wanna see me dance?" she asks.

Dan moves around and I see him nod. "Go ahead." He looks longingly at the door. Maybe he wishes he'd stayed in the hall.

Olivia turns off the TV. Finn continues staring at the blank TV screen while she puts on some ballet music. She takes off her bathrobe and begins to dance in her pink pajamas. Her steps are in perfect time, her toes pointed. Dan claps, and she is delighted with the attention.

Then Sarah comes in.

"Dan wanted to see me dance," Olivia tells her.

"She's good too," says Dan.

Olivia beams, hanging onto Dan's arm. "He loves you," she tells Sarah. "I know cuz he told me."

Sarah smiles at Dan. "What's up? It's not the best time."

He untangles himself from Olivia, pulls Sarah into his arms, and kisses her—as if that is the answer to her question.

Olivia watches, standing right next to them. She giggles loudly again. "D'you want me to kiss you like that, Finn?" She flings herself onto the sofa and pushes her lips toward him teasingly. Finn ducks and dashes upstairs.

"Can we go somewhere more private?" Dan asks. "Just for a minute. I won't keep you from your *work*."

He heads past me toward the door, and I watch anxiously as Sarah follows. She moves quickly out of sight, but I can still hear her in the hallway, telling him we bumped into Billy. They must have moved farther away or lowered their voices because I don't hear any more.

Olivia watches them go too and turns to me, her face sullen. She didn't want them to go off to talk "in private" any more than I did. She starts practicing her dance in front of me. I think she's hoping to dance for Dan again before he goes. I hope he leaves soon.

I watch Olivia dance. She looks almost angelic with her long, wavy blond hair, loose now after her bath. Usually it's tied back in a ponytail or braid.

She was in five different foster homes before she came here. *Five!* I can't begin to imagine that. She's lucky Mom and Dad have so much patience and can cope with her.

I hear Sarah and Dan in the hall. And so does Olivia. She stops midtwirl and dashes out of the room. The front door clicks before she can get there, and her screams pierce through the house as she yells at Sarah for not letting her say goodbye to Dan.

It takes Sarah at least five minutes to calm her down. "Come on, Olivia, time for bed," Sarah finally says. I can still hear the occasional muted sob.

My head is pounding from the screaming. Olivia's music is still playing, and that doesn't help either.

I sit waiting. The music finally comes to a stop. The house

is peaceful at last. I am drifting off. My headache dulls from a throb to a slight pulsing. I'm hoping that when Sarah comes to put me to bed, she'll tell me what Dan said—why he came.

Dad comes in after putting Finn to bed and puts the TV on, turning me so I am facing it.

"*Mastermind* is on," he says. "Let's see how many we can answer."

The first chosen subject is Agatha Christie. I can actually answer lots of the questions. I even get one right that the contestant gets wrong.

Mom comes in eventually and flops down on the sofa next to Dad. He puts his arm around her. Mom's cell phone rings. Dad sighs as she pulls it from her cardigan pocket.

"Hello, Paula," Mom says. "How are you, dear?" There's a long pause. "Really? Well, that's encouraging!"

"What did she say?" Dad asks after Mom puts away her phone.

"The police had a lot of calls after *Crime Watch*. Apparently they've been questioning someone today."

"Let's hope he's the one," says Dad. "It would be good to know he's off the streets."

Sarah is unusually quiet as she gets me ready for bed. Most likely Olivia has worn her out. Or maybe it's what Dan said to

her in private when he came over. It couldn't have been Dan
the police were questioning, could it? Was he telling Sarah
he's a suspect? Sarah is quiet, but she doesn't seem shocked or
upset. Then again, she's under Dan's spell, like everyone else,
so I'm sure he could've convinced her that he had nothing to
do with it. I wish she would talk to me.

Sarah is still quiet when she dresses me on Sunday morning. She doesn't mention Dan. Mom and Dad say nothing more about Ryan or the man the police questioned. Everyone is busy getting ready for Finn's sixth birthday.

Finn doesn't like balloons, but Dad has found some "Happy Birthday" paper decorations with alternating blue and yellow triangles. Finn is oblivious to the specialness of the day and has no interest in the birthday cards, so Olivia opens them for him. Finn is more interested in the colored envelopes and proceeds to line them up neatly across the floor. I watch him, and at one point he looks up at me and meets my eyes. Although neither of us can speak, I feel close to Finn. I always have. I sense that he likes me watching him.

Mom and Olivia bake a cake. I enjoy the bustle in the kitchen and the delicious baking smells, especially the smell of melted chocolate, which Mom lets me taste from a spoon. Olivia is happy and doing what Mom tells her for a change.

Mom is so patient with her, even when she spills sugar on the floor. While the cake's in the oven, Sarah takes Olivia for a walk to the store, and they come back with bags of little candies to decorate it with. Olivia is ecstatic. Once the cake has cooled, Mom ices it with buttercream frosting, and Olivia lines up the candies in neat rows saying, "Finn will like it like that." She puts the candles in a line across the middle.

"It looks great," she announces, and rubs her belly. "Yum, yum!"

"You'll have to wait until later," Mom warns, but once she's left the room, Olivia stays next to the cake, staring at it greedily.

She looks thoughtful, then carefully takes three candies from each row and moves the others to cover the gaps. She stuffs the ones she's taken into her mouth.

Mom comes back before Olivia can do it again. Soon it's time for Finn to open his presents.

Dad showed me his present when he bought it, and I've been looking forward to seeing Finn's reaction.

We all sit in the living room and watch as Finn opens the box with its striped wrapping paper. He pulls out a huge box of matchsticks.

They're not matches you light, but ones people use to make model ships and things like that. There's a picture of a ship on the box. When Dad showed me, I didn't get it at first. I couldn't see Finn making model ships. But then Dad took out a few matchsticks and lined them up. Dad understands Finn.

Finn examines the box, opens it, and tips all the matchsticks out. A huge grin spreads across his face. Finn rarely smiles, and I have never seen a smile as big as this. I catch Dad's eye—his grin is as big as Finn's. Finn gets busy making a line of matchsticks that stretches the length of the living room.

"Don't give me matchsticks when it's my birthday, will you?" says Olivia.

Dad laughs.

We go into the kitchen, and Mom lights the candles on the cake, but Finn is still lining up his matchsticks and won't come. In the end, Mom brings the cake carefully into the living room and Mom, Dad, Sarah, and Olivia sing "Happy Birthday." Finn doesn't even look up, but I feel suddenly happy, with the brightness of the candles and the warmth of my family around me. "You can blow the candles out for him," Mom tells Olivia, and Olivia jumps up and down with excitement.

We go back to the kitchen to eat the cake, which is delicious, and Mom keeps a piece for Finn to have later.

———

Two hours later, Finn and I are alone in the living room. He has moved on from lining the matchsticks up along the wall. He is now arranging them in what looks like a big square around my wheelchair—though I can only see part of it. It definitely has at least two right angles. I sense he is enclosing me completely.

Now and then he looks at me and meets my eyes as if seeking my approval. I have never seen Finn make eye contact with anyone apart from me. I like being the center of his play. I feel alive and connected in a way that is rare for me. I think Finn has completed one square, because he is now starting a second one, right around the first. He has never made anything but straight lines before. I hope Dad will come in—he's going to be so impressed. I hear footsteps, but it's Olivia who comes around in front of me, and my heart sinks.

She sometimes messes up Finn's neat lines deliberately, and I don't think she'll understand.

She gasps. "Wow, Finn! That's amazing."

She gets it! I am stunned and feel a little guilty for assuming she wouldn't. Then I hear her calling, "Everyone, come and see! Come and see what Finn's done!"

That's exactly what I wanted to do. Sometimes it happens like that—I know what I want people to do, and they do it—and it feels a little like I can control things, just for a moment. Olivia is thrilled to be the one who shares the news. Sarah appears first, then Mom and Dad.

They gather around and all "Wow!" over what Finn has done. Dad tells him it's amazing, and the others agree. I see Mom squeeze Dad's hand, and they share a smile. Finn continues, apparently oblivious, but I am sure he is pleased.

In this moment I feel full of love for them all: Mom, Dad, Sarah, Finn—and even Olivia. I don't want anything to change.

12

I was on a high after Finn's birthday until the next morning when I remembered about the college visit on Wednesday. Sarah has already started packing my bag. We're going to stay overnight—Mom, Sarah, and me in a hotel. I am looking forward to having Mom and Sarah to myself for twenty-four hours, even though I can't get rid of the worry about being sent away.

I'm trying to focus on the professor and the possibility of communication rather than the idea of actually going to Carlstone, so I feel calmer. But as the day goes on, I sense something isn't right. I've got a pain in my back and my lower stomach. I might have an infection. That's happened before, and it can get really bad if no one notices.

As Sarah wheels me into the kitchen at dinnertime I hear Mom telling Dad that the police have charged the man they were questioning.

"That's good news," says Sarah. "Who was it? Do they know why he did it?"

"Why who did what?" Olivia demands, coming in. Mom gives Sarah a look as if she shouldn't be asking such things in front of Olivia, which is a little unfair since Olivia just sneaked in and it was Mom who brought it up. I want to know more details too, but Dad changes the subject and starts marveling about Finn's amazing matchstick squares again. It's so frustrating.

Olivia glowers. Everyone tenses. She's like a lit firework that'll go off with a bang at any moment.

Dad tries to distract her by asking her what she'd like for her birthday. She turns to him, her eyes wide with excitement. It's not her birthday for three months, but this doesn't seem to matter as she takes a deep breath and starts to reel off a very long list. A TV for her room, an iPad, a bigger dollhouse. Then Olivia adds, "That's if I'm still here."

Mom and Dad look at her in astonishment. "Of course you'll still be here, love," says Dad. "This is your home. You're not going anywhere."

"I'm not sure I can promise you any of those things for your birthday, though," Mom adds quickly, catching Dad's eye. "You'll have to wait and see."

I suddenly realize that Olivia can rarely have had more than one birthday in the same place. It must be hard for her to trust that she's really here to stay.

At least Dad has successfully distracted her from Sarah's question about the murder suspect. I'm still thinking about it, though. Who have the police charged? If it's Dan, Sarah will hear about it soon. Or is it someone else altogether?

During the night I kept thinking about it until the pain in my stomach got so bad that I was only thinking about that. Now it's there all the time rather than coming and going. I was willing Sarah to notice this morning, because I can usually rely on her to pick up on it when something's not right. But she seemed distracted.

At school, I am uncomfortable all day. Then something happens that stops me from thinking about the pain altogether. About an hour after we get home, Mom asks where Finn is. No one can find him.

Mom is looking upstairs, Dad is downstairs, and Sarah is in the backyard. Olivia is "helping" but clearly getting bored. Dad's searched every closet twice, including the one under the stairs.

Mom comes down. Her hair is all over the place, and her eyes are panicky. "He's not here," she mutters. "He must have gone outside. He's not here!"

Dad soothes her, stroking her back. "He's around here somewhere. I'm sure of it. You know how good he is at hiding. He can't open the front door."

"Maybe he slipped out when someone opened it," says Mom. She puts her hand to her mouth. "I went out the back door to put out some trash. Could he have gotten out then?"

"He's not in the backyard," says Dad, "and you didn't

unlock the gate, did you? He's not tall enough to climb over it without standing on something."

"Finn?" Mom calls. She's trying to sound calm, but there's a rough edge to her voice. "Come on out, dear! You're definitely the hide-and-seek winner."

Mom and Dad are quiet, waiting, listening. There's a sound on the stairs. Mom dashes around the banister.

"Oh, Olivia! No sign of Finn?"

"He's probably gone out and walked into the street," Olivia announces. "He has no idea how to cross streets, does he?"

I hear Mom let out a gasp.

"That's enough, Olivia," says Dad.

"I've been looking for him," Olivia protests. "Looking and looking. Just as hard as everyone else—except Jemma." She's come into view now and gives a glance in my direction.

I am sitting in the living room, facing out toward the hallway. I have been sitting like this the whole time, facing the closet under the stairs—the closet where Finn has been hiding for over an hour. I know he's there. I saw him go in. He must be curled up so far into the dark back corner that Dad's two expeditions inside have failed to discover him.

Dad goes out to walk the streets, though I'm sure he still thinks that Finn is in the house.

"He'll turn up," Sarah assures Mom.

"You're *sure* nothing happened—nothing that upset him?" Mom asks Sarah.

I look at Sarah's face. Although she helps out with Finn and Olivia, her job is caring for me. Mom's not being fair.

"I told you," Sarah says sharply, "he seemed fine to me. He was lining up cars in his room." Sarah looks like she's going to cry. I want to tell her Mom's just worried and doesn't really blame her.

When Dad comes back, Mom wants to call the police. Dad wants to wait. They argue. Mom starts really shouting. It's awful. If only I could tell them. If only Finn would come out. I try to make a noise—gurgling noises that turn into *Ugghh, ugghh*.

Dad then blames Mom for upsetting me. I've just made things worse.

Sarah comes to comfort me. "Don't worry, Finn will be fine," she assures me.

In the end, Dad phones the police.

I know that Finn must be able to hear this. He knows who the police are, though I'm not sure if he understands enough to realize the worry he's causing.

I wonder why he's hiding. He only does it when he's really stressed out. Once he hid when his teacher was off sick and he didn't like the substitute teacher. Perhaps the packing has upset him, and he's worried about us being away. That must be it.

Last time, he was found after twenty minutes. He was at the back of Mom and Dad's closet, behind the shoe rack.

Dad says the police are on their way. Mom calls Social Services too. They have to know he is missing. I feel so sorry for Mom. I'm sure she's worried they'll think she's not taking care of us.

The doorbell rings.

"That was quick," says Mom, rushing to answer.

I hear a voice I don't recognize and strain to hear the words. It's not the police; it's the window cleaner wanting to be paid.

"Sorry," Mom says, sounding frazzled. "Do you mind coming back? We're having a bit of a crisis. You haven't seen a small boy wandering down the street, have you?"

I don't hear the answer. "Oh, look, it's not fair to you. I'll grab my purse," Mom says. She comes into the living room and picks up her bag without even glancing at me.

"That's funny, I'm sure I had more than that," she says to herself. "Ben! Do you have a ten handy?"

"Sure," calls Dad. "Really, couldn't he have waited?"

As Dad goes to the door, Mom looks like she's holding back tears.

When Dad comes back, he persuades her to sit down and have a cup of tea while we wait for the police. He pushes me into the kitchen and Mom sits, head in hands, at the table, while Dad puts the kettle on.

Sarah comes in too, followed by a sulky-looking Olivia.

"Let me do that," Sarah tells Dad, getting some mugs out of the cupboard.

"Can I have a cookie?" Olivia asks, spying the package on the shelf above the mugs.

"Please," Dad reminds her.

Dad pulls down the package and opens it. He stares for a moment at the cookies.

"Can I have one, *pleeeeaaaase*?" Olivia demands.

"I think I'll get out the chocolate chip cookies," Dad says loudly.

That's a little weird. I think the stress has gotten to him. Olivia gives him a confused look. And then it clicks. He's trying to tempt Finn out. Chocolate chips are Finn's favorite. He always has to have three so that he can line them up.

Dad puts three on Olivia's plate, and she beams. "I'll put three on a plate here for Finn," Dad says.

"Oh... The cookies are for *Finn*."

Finn walks into the kitchen and sits down, grabbing all three cookies tightly. He doesn't meet anyone's eyes, but that's not unusual.

"Where have you been?" Mom demands as gently as she can manage.

She knows he won't answer, but I see her shoulders relax with relief as she turns to Dad with a smile.

13

The crisis has passed, and the house has gone from panic to calm. Soon it is as if nothing happened. Everyone's back doing their own thing, and I am back with the pain that has somehow spread while I wasn't thinking about it and is definitely getting worse.

I wish I could focus on something else to put it out of my mind. I try to concentrate on the TV, and then Sarah comes in with a basket of clothes to fold and I watch her as she bends and folds at the edge of my vision. My thoughts go back to Dan and the murder. Sarah looks busy but relaxed. It can't be Dan who's been charged. She would have heard something by now, wouldn't she? But just because they've charged someone, that doesn't mean they've definitely got the right man, does it?

A program comes on about people who are training for the next Paralympics. There's a woman with cerebral palsy who is hoping to compete in archery, and even though I'll never do anything like that, it is inspiring to watch her. She's spent hours and hours each week practicing to get this good, and she looks so determined.

Still, it's difficult to concentrate. The pain won't go away. I try thinking about Jodi instead—about her letter and how amazing it would be to get another one. But nothing's come. I hope she hasn't changed her mind.

I'd love so much to be able to communicate with her. The professor guy who's coming to Carlstone—could he have the answer for me? Even though the college thing is scary, the idea that I might be able to communicate is so huge that most of the time I don't let myself think about it. All through my life, people have tried different things—from pointing at letter boards to eye-gaze technology—but nothing has worked. I remember when I was ten, and we all got excited because a new teacher taught me to say yes and no by blinking. But then I got really sick with an infection. I was in hospital for a long time, and when I felt better, I couldn't control my blinking anymore.

Is there really a chance? I have so much I want to say—but I'm scared to hope. What if by the time I met my sister I could actually do it? When Sarah goes on about Dan, I could inter- rupt her and tell her exactly what he's really like. When Finn hides, I could tell them where he is or tempt him out myself with cookies. And right now I could say that I'm in pain and where it hurts.

I know even if there is a way, it won't be easy. I found it hard enough with the blinking. It took a lot of effort to control it. And all the questions made me feel panicky. I was used to watching, not deciding, and if I didn't respond quickly, people either kept repeating the question over and over, which was infuriating, or just gave up, which was even worse. And of course nobody ever asked me the questions I wanted them to ask.

Sometimes I blinked by accident and gave an answer I didn't intend. I blinked "no" when Mom asked if I'd like ketchup, and ever since, for the last four years, she's stopped giving it to me. I don't like it on everything, but I really do like it on fries.

At least when I could blink I was able to show how much I knew and understood. They were amazed to see that I could read. I had a teacher at school when I was six, Miss Moray, who taught us all as if we were as bright as any other six-year-olds. She went through all the letters and basic words. My next teacher didn't bother with reading at all, but I've always read signs and labels, and Mom often put the subtitles on the TV too. What I found hard was making choices. Mom said she'd always known how bright I was, but I think she was the only one. Even Dad had never seemed sure, although he'd tried hard not to show it.

It's hard to admit, but after I couldn't control the blinking, part of me felt relieved. It was a relief to go back to just watching and not having to decide. But it's different now. I'd give anything for the chance to be able to do it again. I'm older, and there's so much I want to say. I want to talk to Jodi. I want to make my own choices. *Yes* and *no* won't be enough, though, not to tell them about Dan.

This woman I'm watching has been training hard, and she's studying in college too. Her disability is much milder than mine, but it is still impressive to watch. And she's putting in all that effort with no certainty that she'll even make it onto the Paralympic team. It's all about daring to hope, isn't it? You have to dare to think you might win. If I dare to think I might communicate again, it might come true.

But it might not. And the disappointment would be a million times harder.

The pain in my back is getting worse—a constant dull throb.

Sarah's phone rings. It's Richard. Sarah is still upset, thinking Mom blames her for Finn going missing. She's telling Richard about it. "No, no," she says—and I think he might have suggested coming over. "I don't have any time off until the weekend," she tells him. "I'll be fine. It helps to talk to you. You've made me feel much better."

She's no sooner put down her phone than it rings again. She answers without even looking at the screen.

"R–Dan, hi!" She doesn't tell him about Finn. "What, now?" she says. "I can't. I've got to put Jemma to bed soon. And to be honest, I'm worn out. I've had such a crap day..."

I wonder what he's saying. "No, no, you can't," Sarah tells him.

Dan's not like Richard, though. He won't take no for an answer.

Sarah puts her phone down and sighs. "He's coming over," she tells me. "It's not that I don't want to see him; it's just that I'm so tired."

So now I know for sure—the police haven't arrested Dan. It must be someone else.

Mom comes downstairs, and Sarah explains to her that Dan is stopping by. From the abrupt tone of her voice, Mom is clearly not happy.

"He won't be here long, I promise," says Sarah. "I tried to tell him not to come, but he insisted."

"What a day," Mom says, sighing. "I feel like I'm going mad. Oh, Sarah—you didn't borrow money from my purse, did you?"

"What? No, I didn't. Why would I have done that?" Sarah demands.

"I know you buy things for Jemma sometimes, and I thought you might—"

"I wouldn't without asking!" Sarah retorts.

"Forget I said anything," Mom says sheepishly. "I probably spent it without realizing."

Sarah is silent. I feel so powerless. The tension between them hurts me inside and frightens me, but there's nothing I can do. If Sarah's not happy here, if she stops getting along with Mom, then she won't want to stay.

Dan arrives half an hour later. I am still up and in the living room. Mom and Dad are upstairs. I have a partial view into the hall, and I am shocked to see Dan grab Sarah as she opens the door. For a moment I think he's going to hurt her, but he pulls her toward him and kisses her hard. Sarah moves back, laughing awkwardly.

"What's up, babe?" he asks, flinching as if reeling from her rejection.

"Nothing's up," Sarah tells him. She's speaking quietly— but not too quietly for me to hear. "I've told you... You can't keep turning up like this. You know what Lorraine—"

"And I've told you, I can't keep away, babe!" says Dan. "Have you thought about what I said?"

"You know how I feel about you," Sarah says softly. "But I have to be here overnight for Jemma. I can't live at your place."

"Give up the job! I'll take care of you." It's Dan who's speaking quietly now.

My heart lurches. She won't do that, will she?

I listen hard to hear her reply. She starts with a kiss, which doesn't feel like a good sign. I wish Mom hadn't given her such a hard time. She's feeling fed up here, and now Dan's offering her a way out. But what about me?

"I want to be with you, but Jemma needs me," Sarah tells him, and I heave a sigh of relief that comes out as a slight snort. Dan turns toward the living-room doorway and meets my eyes briefly with a look of disgust.

"They'll get someone else, no problem," he says, turning back to Sarah. "There are lots of people wanting aide jobs."

"I like my job," Sarah argues.

"Do you, though? Really?" Dan is shaking his head. "You've got the patience of a saint, babe, but no one does this kind of job unless they have to."

I feel my muscles tighten.

Sarah pauses. "I... Look, let's talk about it more the next time I see you."

"I'll take you out. When're you free?" Dan demands.

"Hang on, I'll check," Sarah tells him.

She's gone to check her days on the calendar, and my worst fear comes true. Dan comes into the living room. He stands close—bends over me—staring at me, screwing up his nose. Then he shakes his head.

"You think she's gonna stay here, don't you? But you just wait—"

At that moment, his cell phone rings and he moves away as he answers it. I can breathe again, though I'm horrified by the way he spoke to me.

"Hiya, Billy! What's up, man?" he says. His voice is quiet but brash, different from the cheerful, friendly one he uses with Sarah, and not that nasty voice he uses for me.

"Yeah! It's all worked out? Behind the grocery store? I know where you mean... Sure thing. See ya."

He puts the phone in his pocket just as Sarah comes back.

"I've got next Thursday off," she tells him.

"That's over a week away! You can stay over, though, right?"

She nods and gives him a nudge toward the door, telling him he has to go now. He jokes that she's always trying to get rid of him, and Sarah rolls her eyes and points upstairs, as though it's because of Mom. Dan whispers something in Sarah's ear and gives her another kiss.

I'm so relieved when he's gone.

"He loves me, Jemma," Sarah says dreamily a little later as she carefully brushes my teeth. She's supporting my head with her other hand in case I suddenly jolt. "And I love him too."

I feel sick. I wish I could tell her he's a disgusting creep. "Big day tomorrow," she says, changing the subject. "Bet you're excited!"

I'd almost forgotten about the college visit. I wonder what the professor will say. Is there really a chance...?

14

"*Have you seen Jemma's red* fleece?" Sarah calls to Mom. It's chaos this morning as Sarah runs around finding last-minute things to put in my suitcase. I seem to need an awful lot of stuff for an overnight stay.

Mom is trying to finish her own packing, and Dad is attempting to single-handedly get Olivia and Finn ready for school. My back and stomach pain are even worse, and I have this kind of fuzzy, giddy feeling. It's definitely an infection. Sarah thinks it's just anxiety about the day ahead. Typical. When I was anxious before, they thought it was physical, and now it's the other way around.

"Here it is," says Mom, handing my fleece to Sarah.

Mom turns to me and looks concerned. "There's no need for you to be worried about today—I promise." The pain in my back has developed into a throb, and it is spreading outward, surging through me.

I feel hot—too hot.

Someone's speaking. Sarah is moving closer.

I think she says, "Something's not right," but the words sound blurry. Her face, close to mine, is blurry too. Everything is spinning.

I am vaguely aware of being lifted out of my wheel-chair, faces bending over me, voices talking. Then the jolting movement of the ambulance, the gurney, the white curtains swishing, bright lights, the IV, the monitor. These are all familiar to me. I've spent a lot of time at this hospital.

Mom is sitting by my bed now, holding my hand. Her hand is warm and safe. I drift off and wake to find the hand holding mine is larger, firmer. Mom has been replaced by Dad. Later it is a smaller, long-fingered hand, as Sarah chats away to me.

Mom jokes about the convenience of living only a ten-minute drive from the hospital. It wasn't something she or Dad thought about when they bought the house years ago, but it has proven very useful.

Mom, Dad, and Sarah set up a rotation. There is always someone by my side. I am so glad they are there. I would completely panic otherwise. Some nurses do stuff without even bothering to talk to me, as if there's no point explaining anything. Whoever's with me will ask and make sure I know what's going to happen. I'd be terrified if some stranger just lifted my arm and started putting a needle in me or something.

Sarah squeezes my hand. She seems agitated. I can feel her pulse faster than it should be.

"You awake, Jem?" she says, seeing my eyes open. "How're you feeling? The pain should be better after all the stuff they're pumping into you."

She gives a nod toward the drip and smiles.

She's right. The pain is better, though I feel very weak and my head feels heavy and peculiar.

"I'm so sorry I didn't realize how bad it was, Jemma," she tells me, giving my hand another squeeze. "Your mom blames me for not spotting it earlier. I feel awful."

Sarah thinks Mom blamed her for Finn going missing and now for this. I wish Mom would stop accusing her.

It's only the next day, when my head is a little clearer, that I realize I missed the trip to the college. I'm not going to meet the professor.

Mom seems to realize what I'm thinking.

"Don't worry, dear. We'll rearrange the trip. I actually spoke to Professor Spalding, and he said he'd be very interested in meeting you."

She isn't saying, "And he's sure he can help." But at least there is still a chance.

I'm dozing, aware that Sarah is holding my hand. She's been here for a long time. When I manage to open my eyes briefly, I see that hers are half-closing. Then suddenly there's a voice. Someone else is in the room.

"Hi, babe," he says. My stomach clenches.

Sarah sits up and turns around.

"What are you doing here?" she asks. It's something she seems to say to Dan a lot.

"I was worried about you—sitting here for hours on end. And I was right to worry, wasn't I? Look at you. You're exhausted."

"I'm okay," Sarah says.

"Yeah, sure," he says, raising his eyebrows in disbelief. "Come on, let me take you for a coffee."

"But I can't leave Jemma," Sarah says, sounding shocked that he would suggest it.

"She'll be all right," says Dan. "It's not like she can run off or anything."

"Dan!" Sarah exclaims.

"Tell you what. I'll stay with Jemma while you get a coffee," says Dan. "That way she won't be on her own, and you get a break. Win, win."

"I shouldn't...but... Oh, babe, would you really do that?" Sarah asks. He leans forward and kisses her. If there was ever a time when I most wanted Sarah's mind-reading skills to kick in, this would be it. With every thought, I urge her to stay. I want her to see it in my eyes. But she's not even looking at me.

"If you're worried at all, press that button to reach the nurses' station," Sarah tells him. "I'm sure she'll be fine, though."

She turns to me, stroking my arm. I stare at her, hoping she will see the distress on my face. I even try to make a sound, but just a horrid *erhhhhh* comes out.

"I'll be back in five minutes, I promise," she assures me.

Then she's gone.

15

Dan doesn't sit down beside my bed and hold my hand—
which is a relief. Instead, he paces around the bed slowly. I
begin to wish he would sit down. I am happier when I can see
him than when I can't, and when he's on the other side of the
bed, I can't see him at all. Now he's back on this side.

Is he really here because he can't bear to be apart from
Sarah, or is he checking up on her?

He fixes me with a sarcastic smile. "Always causing
trouble, aren't you, Jemma? It would be much easier if they
just kept you here. Or..."

He's moved back from the bed, and he seems to be looking
closely at everything—the tube going into me from the drip
with antibiotics, the plugs in the wall.

I can see what he's doing. He's trying to upset me again,
pretending to look for a way to switch me off! At least, I hope
he's pretending.

No! He's crouching by the wall. *He's actually doing it! I*

want Sarah. I need Sarah. A gurgling noise comes from deep in my throat. Dan stands up, holding a plug in his hand, laughing. "What's that? Is that the best you can do for a scream?"

Then I realize the lamp beside my bed has gone off. He's pulled out the plug! I shouldn't have panicked. Of course, I'm not on a life-support machine. I was just so scared of him... I know he wants me out of the way. He wants Sarah to himself.

He pushes the plug back in and chuckles as the light flickers on.

I wish Sarah would come back. It must have been five minutes by now.

He comes nearer, sits down on the chair by my bed. I listen to his heavy breathing. I wait, unsure what he's going to do next. He's still looking around. I can see his eyes on the box of disposable gloves. Now he's looking behind me. Does he have his eye on my pillow? Am I imagining it, or is he still thinking of ways...?

"All okay?"

Sarah's voice is such a welcome relief that I feel myself sink back against the softness of the bed. The thudding in my chest slows down.

"Yeah, Jemma's been just fine," Dan assures her.

"It was so sweet of you to do this," Sarah says, kissing him.

"Anytime," Dan tells her, "no prob." He kisses her back. Dan leaves, giving me a parting smile that makes my heart shudder. Sarah sits down, and soon a nurse comes in to check my pulse, temperature, and blood pressure.

She tuts. "Pulse is higher than it should be," she comments. "I'll get a doctor to check her."

"Dan got your pulse up?" Sarah teases. "You don't have a thing for him, do you? He's all mine, Jemma!"

If only I could tell her...

Mom arrives at that moment and is concerned to hear about my pulse, fussing over me.

"Did you notice anything?" Mom asks Sarah. "Has she been awake or asleep?"

Sarah scowls. Mom is being pretty aggressive with the questions. Luckily, Sarah is saved from answering by the doctor. He takes my pulse again, and it's already going back to normal. My temperature and blood pressure are fine.

"Nothing to worry about," he says, smiling at Mom and then at me.

Sarah leaves without saying goodbye to Mom.

There's a strange feeling when I am finally back home. It's hard to explain, but it's as if things have shifted while I've been away, even though it was only a couple of days. One of the chairs in the living room has been moved around, and there's a small spiky plant in a pot on the hall shelf. It wasn't there before. There's always been a china elephant on that shelf and nothing else, but he's been pushed to the side and the spiky plant is in the middle. Am I getting as bad as Finn—not liking any change?

The second, far more important thing is that Sarah isn't here. Mom gave her extra time off because she'd spent so much time at the hospital with me. Sarah's gone to stay with Dan, like he wanted.

I want her here, and I'm worried about her being alone with him. She has no idea what he's really like. What if she lets something slip about going to the concert with Richard? What if Dan already knows that something is going on?

Finn comes in, and I hope for some sign that he's pleased I'm back. Maybe I should know better, but I've always felt we understand each other. I can hear him moving about behind me, but he doesn't let me see him. Then I hear a sound I've heard before.

Bang, bang, bang.

He is banging his head against the wall—rhythmically, over and over.

"Stop, Finn!" I want to yell. Finn used to do this a lot. But for the last two years he's done it much less. I think me being away and the change to his routine may have really upset him. Perhaps that's why he's staying there behind me. He wants me to know he's angry. I feel so bad. I don't want to upset Finn.

"Oh, Finn! There's no need for that," says Mom, coming into the living room. "Let's find something for you to play with."

My muscles relax as Mom takes the matchsticks out of the cupboard and Finn starts lining them up.

"Look what's come today!" Mom is waving an envelope at me.

I get a gush of happiness as I watch her open it.

A letter! A letter from Jodi. Mom begins reading:

Dear Jemma,

I was so excited when your mom wrote and said she had read my letter to you. I hope you were as happy as I was to find out you have a sister!

She says she really hopes to find a way for you to communicate so you can write back or even talk to me one day. That would be so cool. I looked online, and I found stuff about head pointers and eye-gaze technology—it all sounds so clever! I've been reading up about cerebral palsy too. I really want to understand what it's like.

I've printed out a photo of Fluff this time. I hope your mom will send me one of you.

I hope we will be able to meet one day soon!

Love, Jodi

"She sounds great, doesn't she, Jemma?" Mom says, sighing. "I know she's eager to meet you, and I'm sure you'd like to meet her too, but I still think it's best to take things slowly. I'd like to see Professor Spalding first."

Finn has stopped lining up sticks and is sitting, rocking.

I understand what Mom's saying. It would be amazing to be able to "talk" to Jodi somehow. Even just with a *yes* and a *no*. But I don't know how long I'd have to wait. I want to meet Jodi now.

16

When Dan drops Sarah off the next day, Mom thanks him for the plant he bought. No wonder I didn't like it.

"You're looking so much better, Jem," Sarah tells me, smiling warmly. We're in the bathroom, and Sarah has just emptied my bag. "You gave me a scare, you really did."

I gave myself a scare too. But right now I'm more interested in whether Sarah had her talk with Dan about moving in.

"Your mom was telling me that the professor guy is going to be back at Carlstone College next Thursday," Sarah continues, "just for a day. After that he's abroad for three months. I think we should go for it, if you're feeling well enough."

I'm still feeling tired after my infection, but I do want to meet him. Even if there's only a small chance of anything changing. Now that Mom's fixed on me meeting him before she'll let me meet Jodi, I have an even greater incentive than before. But if he can't help me, will I still get to meet her?

Sarah is pushing me toward the kitchen for dinner when she stops and I jolt in the chair. Her phone is ringing upstairs.

"I'll just get it... It might be Dan. I won't be a sec." She leaves me outside the kitchen. Mom's not in there, but I can see Olivia through the doorway. She's on a stool by the kitchen counter. What is she up to? She climbs onto the countertop and opens a high cupboard, the one where Mom keeps the candy. She has a bag of gummy bears in her hand as she jumps down, and I see her stash them in the pocket of her jeans.

Sarah is back. "It was Richard," she whispers, "about the concert. I can't wait!"

I'm glad she's confiding in me again. It feels more normal. For a moment I imagine that I'm going with Sarah instead of Richard. I'd definitely be just as excited as she is. I've seen concerts on TV, and I think it would be amazing to hear a band live, especially Glowlight.

It is mac and cheese for dinner. I like pasta, but cheese sauce sometimes gets stuck in my throat and makes me cough. Sarah is feeding me. Finn's not eating but is rocking backward and forward in his chair. He's not so enthusiastic about pasta either—maybe because it is so curvy—especially macaroni. Olivia has wolfed hers down.

She looks at Sarah. "Do you like staying all night with Dan?" She giggles.

"Yeah, I had a great time, thanks," Sarah tells her.

"Did you have sex?" Olivia asks.

I cough up some cheese sauce.

"Olivia!" Dad splutters. "You don't ask people questions like that."

"I was just interested." Olivia's mouth turns sulky. I stop coughing. Sarah wipes my mouth with a kitchen towel and gives me a drink. Her cheeks are pink.

"How was school?" Dad asks Olivia.

"Melissa's not my friend anymore," Olivia tells him.

"I didn't know you had a friend named Melissa," Mom comments.

"She was only my friend for one day, and now she's not," says Olivia.

"Why's that?" asks Dad.

"I don't wanna talk about it." Olivia folds her arms.

Dad turns his attention to trying to coax Finn to eat. He has a few mouthfuls.

"I think we should take Jemma to meet that guy," Sarah tells Mom. "She seems to have made a good recovery, haven't you, Jemma?"

"That's great," says Mom, and she actually gives Sarah what looks like a genuine smile. "I think so too."

I'm relieved that the decision is made—and even more relieved to see Mom and Sarah talking normally to each other. Olivia and Finn go off to play while Sarah finishes feeding me and Dad turns on the radio for the news.

I'm not really listening until I catch the name Ryan Blake. Dad turns it up and shushes everyone.

"Jay Wiggins, who was charged last week with the murder of Ryan Blake, has been released after a witness came forward corroborating his alibi. The twenty-five-year-old auto mechanic had been in custody for a week. He described his relief that his name has been cleared, saying that the whole experience had been a 'complete nightmare.'"

Sarah's phone, now in her pocket, rings even before the news item has finished.

"Sorry," she says, taking it out and looking as if she is switching it off.

"Jay Wiggins?" says Dad. "Is he someone Paula knew about? Did she ever mention him?"

"Not that I can recall," says Mom.

"Well, looks like the police got it wrong. Hopefully he's not the only suspect they identified."

Maybe they do have another suspect. Maybe it's Dan. Sarah says nothing about it, of course, as she gets me ready for bed. She starts reading me a vampire romance book. I like it, and it makes for a change from Agatha Christie.

Her phone keeps buzzing as she reads. I get a glimpse of the screen one time it does as she picks it up. I see Dan's name. It's there, and then it fades away again.

17

I doze on and off for most of the drive to Carlstone College. Mom has decided we will do it in a day, so we leave really early. Anytime I open my eyes, Sarah is either texting or looking at her phone. When I wake up again, I'm refreshed, if a little stiff. We've arrived.

Mom lowers the ramp, and Sarah detaches the wheelchair from its clamps and wheels me down.

"Thank God the traffic was good," Mom comments.

"And the sun's come out for us too," adds Sarah.

I share their optimism as I am turned to face the college building. It is modern and bigger than I expected. I'd had an image in my mind from a movie set in an old boarding school. This is nothing like that.

The glass doors open automatically as we approach, and we are welcomed by the smiling woman at the reception desk. She tells us to take a seat and wait.

Sarah wheels me into a space beside some seats, and she and Mom sit down.

Opposite me I can see a sign on the wall that says CARLSTONE COLLEGE: CENTER OF EXCELLENCE FOR AUGMENTATIVE AND ALTERNATIVE COMMUNICATION. I've heard Mom talking about AAC, and I know it has to do with communication systems for people who can't speak, but I never knew what it stood for until now. I don't know what *augmentative* means, though.

Students pass us—some in wheelchairs and others walking. They all look much older than me. I wonder what it would be like to be a student here. I have to admit I get a tingle of excitement at the thought before the fear and worries about everything it would mean take over. I won't think about all that now. Instead, I distract myself by wondering what the professor will look like. I don't have to wait long to find out.

A tall man with thick, curly hair comes striding toward us.

"You must be Jemma," he says, crouching to make eye contact. "I'm very pleased to meet you." He attempts to shake my stiff, curled hand. He has kind eyes, and he is looking deeply into mine. I feel slightly afraid. My eyes give nothing away—I know that.

He turns to greet Mom and Sarah. I'm glad he spoke to me first.

"Follow me," he tells us.

We follow him down a wide corridor. There are ramps

everywhere, and the ride is smooth. The big windows throw squares of brightness onto the clean red floor.

We stop at a door, which Professor Spalding opens and holds for us as we all go in.

The room is like a doctor's office, with a desk, a computer, and chairs. There is a spiky plant on the windowsill. I hope that isn't a bad omen.

"I very much hope I can help you, Jemma," he tells me. "As you know, new communication systems are being developed all the time."

"Yes," says Mom. "We've tried various kinds of AAC with Jemma and also with our son who has severe autism. To be honest, we haven't had much luck with either of them."

Professor Spalding nods. "But you believe Jemma understands cause and effect?"

"Definitely," says Mom. "She was able to communicate 'yes' and 'no' by blinking when she was ten. She was taught to read, and we know that she understands a huge amount. We're sure she laughs sometimes too." Mom goes on to explain more of my history. Then she adds, "I know some of these communication systems can be expensive, but Jemma does have some funds from a medical negligence case. The money pays for her to have her own aide. It's not a bottomless pit, though."

"Hmmm," says Professor Spalding, tapping his pencil on the table. "We can worry about funding later. I'd like to do a few tests that will help me assess the best means of communication for you, Jemma. You must understand that even if we find a way, it will take some time to master. Babies learn to speak by making sounds, babbling, and then gradually learning to express words. Even though your understanding may be good, it will not be easy for you to put phrases together, select words, and so on. You will have to be patient."

Patience is something I know plenty about—though I am feeling impatient now. I wish he'd stop talking and get on with it.

He tries to get me to look left and right. The first time he asks, I am able to do it. He looks so pleased.

But when he asks me to repeat it, I can't. I try. I try so hard. I see the pleasure turn to disappointment as the light in his eyes fades.

He tries to see if I can move anything else—tilt my head, lift a finger, clench a cheek, open and close my mouth. My body sometimes moves. My head jolts. I automatically close my mouth to swallow food, but I cannot do it voluntarily. He asks me to make sounds too, but I can't—not intentionally.

He even tells a bad joke about a chicken, but it isn't funny enough to make me laugh. I can only laugh spontaneously; I can't make it happen.

He soon realizes what I already know. I have no control.

18

"*What makes you so certain* that Jemma's brain is unaffected by her illness?" the professor asks Mom and Sarah.

I can't see their faces, but I know they both believe in me.

"It's an instinct," says Mom. "We both feel it."

"Yes," Sarah agrees.

"My husband too," says Mom. "And the doctors said at the time there was no reason why her brain should have been affected."

Professor Spalding touches his lip and looks at me thoughtfully.

What is he thinking? Does he think I'm brain-dead?

"Can you sniff for me, Jemma?" he asks.

Sniff? I think he's crazy now.

"Breathe in through your nose—as hard as you can," he tells me.

For a moment I panic, and I can't think how. It's not something I've ever thought about. It's also so rare that anyone actually asks me to *do* anything. Then I calm myself. I have to hurry, or he might give up.

I sniff.

"Now breathe out through your nose."

I can do that too—though I'd love to know where he's going with this.

"Now again," he says.

I breathe in and out through my nose. I am pleased to be able to actually respond, but also confused. Everybody knows that I can breathe.

"Hmmm," says Professor Spalding. "Interesting." He pauses.

"I don't think the eye movements are going to be useful," he tells me, turning to Mom and Sarah too. "They are not consistent enough. However, a colleague of mine is developing a new communication tool based on sniffing. It's hard to tell if Jemma would have enough control, but it might be worth a try."

"Communicate with sniffing?" Sarah repeats. "I've never heard of that!"

I sniff again, just to make sure they know I can do it. Professor Spalding continues. "My colleague Alon Katz and his team are based in Israel. When he's here next, perhaps he could meet you and see if it might be suitable. We hope he'll be here in a few months."

A few months! That's so long!

Could I really use sniffing to communicate, though? Would I be able to say the things I want and need to say? I think about Dan. Can you sniff that someone is a murderer?

19

After lunch, Catherine, the assistant dean of the college, shows us around. She has beautiful shiny dark hair and a warm smile, and she is so bubbly and jokey with the students that I sense she loves working here.

"We have students using all kinds of AAC devices," she tells us. She introduces us to some of the students. One girl, who is only able to raise one eyebrow, proudly shows us that she can select words on a computer and move between screens for different categories of words. She raises her eyebrow repeatedly until the pointer reaches the word she wants on the screen, and then she stops. After a second, the word appears on the line below. Then she continues. It's very slow, but eventually she types, I GO MUSIC, and a voice speaks her words.

"Don't let us hold you up, Kaya!" says Catherine.

Then she adds, "Kaya's a total music geek."

I feel a gut-wrenching pull. How amazing it would be to spell out words on a screen like that! Would I be able to do it—by sniffing? Is it possible? We see the bedrooms and bathrooms, which are bright and spacious. Two students share each room, so I realize I'd have a roommate if I came here.

Mom says, "I think this would be a fantastic place for you in a few years. What do you think, Jemma?"

Sarah smiles at me too.

Catherine and Mom start discussing funding applications, but I am thinking about what she said. *A few years!* They weren't planning to send me here sooner. I was worrying for no reason.

On the drive home, I start to feel giddy. Sarah notices I am flushed and gets Mom to pull over. My temperature is up. She gives me medicine. We have to stop three times. I feel every jolt and jerk of the car. Then we are stuck in traffic.

"She doesn't look well," Mom moans. "This was a mistake."

"We didn't know the traffic would be like this," says Sarah. "It's just bad luck."

"I wasn't sure," says Mom. "I thought it might be too soon, but you convinced me."

"You said you felt the same!" Sarah protests, her voice getting louder and higher. "We both wanted to do it. Stop blaming me for stuff!"

"Calm down," says Mom, even though her voice is just as agitated. "I wasn't... Look, we both want the best for Jemma. Let's not fight about it."

Sarah is silent. My skin feels prickly. I feel like crying when they argue.

At last the traffic clears and we are moving, though the horrible atmosphere in the car isn't going anywhere. But I feel worse—hot and sick. My clothes are sticking to me.

When we finally get home, we are greeted by Dad. He looks washed out. He frowns with concern when he sees how flushed I am. He's so pale. And I'm only adding to his worries.

Sarah puts me to bed although the clock on the wall says it's only 6:00 p.m.

"I'm sure you'll feel better after a good rest, Jem," she tells me. "I'll keep a close eye on you. We don't want another stint in that hospital, do we?"

No, we certainly don't. The image of Dan holding up the plug he'd pulled out flashes through my head.

"I'm sorry if today was too much," Sarah says, gently bathing my hot forehead with a cool cloth. "I'm sure you'll be fine after a good night's sleep. The college was great, wasn't it?"

It is a relief to be surrounded by the softness of my bed after the jolting of the wheelchair in the car. I feel better already. My eyes close, but I don't want to sleep. I want Sarah to stay with me. I feel safe with her here, and, while she's with me, I also know she's safe from Dan. It's not much, but it's the only way I can protect her. But my eyes are closing, and I hear her footsteps on the stairs.

She left my door open, and pieces of conversation drift my way from the kitchen. Mom is telling Dad about the day. It takes a while. Then Mom says, "Everything all right here?"

"Not really," I hear Dad say. I strain to listen.

"I dropped them at school and went to work," he tells Mom, "and then I got a call to say Olivia had attacked a boy and I'd have to come and get her. She must have hit him hard... He's lost a tooth."

"*What?*" Mom exclaims. "Have you talked to her about it? Did she tell you what happened?"

"She said it wasn't her fault. I asked if he hit her first, and she said, 'No, you just don't get it,' and she wouldn't talk to me after that. She's been sulking in her room most of the day. They've suspended her until Monday."

I hear breathing close by, and my eyes open. I assume it's Sarah, back to check on me, but it's Olivia I see standing in my doorway. The light in the hall behind her means she is mostly in shadow, but I can see that she is looking toward the kitchen, listening intently to Mom and Dad like I am. I can only see the side of her face, but her eye is glistening; she's close to tears.

She looks like such a sad little girl that I feel sorry for her for a moment. It's hard to believe she hit a boy so hard his tooth came out.

She turns and sees me in bed, and her eyebrows go up.

"Are you sick?" She reaches over and touches my forehead like she's seen Mom and Sarah do. "Yeah, you're a little hot."

She sits silently for a couple of minutes, biting skin from around her fingernails.

"There's no point in telling anyone what really happened because no one believes anything I say," she says finally.

I want to tell her that they will believe her. Even if her teachers don't, Mom and Dad will. I'll believe her. Is she going to tell me? I look at her, hoping so much that she will.

"Dylan found out I'm in foster care, and he told everyone. He keeps being mean about it, like saying it's because my real mom hates me. He teases me till I can't take it anymore. It's so unfair. I didn't mean to hit him that hard. Blood was coming out of his mouth and everything! It was disgusting. But he shouldn't be mean all the time. It's not fair that I'm sent home and he just gets away with it."

Poor Olivia. She shouldn't have hit him, but Dylan does sound really nasty. She should have told someone when it happened instead of lashing out—but even now, if she explained, at least people would be more understanding.

"She's not upstairs!" I hear Mom calling anxiously.

"She was," Dad says, also sounding worried.

"Olivia? Olivia!"

Olivia doesn't move for a moment, but then she calls out, "I'm in here."

"She's in Jemma's room," Dad calls to Mom.

"Thank goodness," I hear Mom say. "What are you doing in there? Jemma's trying to sleep. She's not well. Come here, Olivia. Tell me what's been going on."

As Olivia leaves my room, she bursts into tears.

20

When I wake up in the morning, I am instantly aware that I don't feel feverish. I feel pleasantly cool, and it is such a relief. Dad comes in. I've been turned to face the window. He draws the curtains, and I am pleased to see that the color has returned to his face—a nice rosy pinkness.

"Sounds like you had quite a day yesterday," he says. He eases me into a sitting position with his firm, careful hands and cradles me to keep me upright, his arm around my shoulder, comfortingly.

"Sounds like you did too," I want to say.

Sarah comes in, and Dad explains that she'll have two at home today because I'm not well and Olivia is suspended.

"Maybe Olivia could read to Jemma," he says.

"Do you want to talk about what happened with Dylan?" Sarah asks Olivia as we sit in the living room later. "Your mom says you haven't told her anything."

"No, thanks," says Olivia.

"Why don't you read to Jemma?" Sarah suggests half-heartedly. She's been trying, and failing, to keep Olivia occupied all morning.

"No, can I watch something?" says Olivia. "I'm sure Jemma wants to watch something too."

"Being suspended is meant to be a punishment—not a chance to watch TV all day," Sarah tells her. "Really, I should have you scrubbing the floors or give you some math homework to do."

"No, please—not that!" Olivia has a look of horror on her face, and Sarah grins.

So she reads to me. Her school reading book is about a pony with magic powers. She holds it so I can see the words. I can read, but my eyes flicker a lot so it is hard to look at a page of text. My eyes get tired quickly too. Olivia struggles a little with reading, and I doubt she is as good as most nine-year-olds. The book seems babyish for her.

"Terrific, Olivia!" Sarah tells her when she's finished two tedious chapters. "If you had a magic pony like that, what would you do?"

"I'd ride around the world on him and get him to kick all the bad people with his superhooves—kick them until they're dead!"

I snort. Sarah's eyes widen, and I can see she's trying not to laugh as well. "Oh, Olivia! How would you know who the bad people were?"

"I just would," Olivia says, closing the book with a *snap*.

Sarah's phone beeps.

"Is that Dan?" Olivia asks, boldly trying to see over Sarah's shoulder as she pulls out the phone.

"Don't be so nosy!" Sarah gives her a nudge.

"Who is it, then?"

Sarah sighs. "Actually, it's about a gig I'm going to tomorrow night. Have you heard of Glowlight?"

"You're going to see a band?" Olivia says. "Cool... Can I come too?"

"No, it's not for kids," says Sarah. "I'll play you some of their songs if you like."

"Yeah!" Olivia jumps up, tossing the book onto the sofa.

Sarah finds a song, and the intro starts playing out of her phone.

I sing the words to myself inside my head as Sarah and Olivia bop around the living room. I love Glowlight and wish Sarah would play their music more often.

Mom comes in while we're having lunch. She plops the mail down on the kitchen table and looks briefly through the pile.

"Two for you, Jemma. You're popular today!"

"Why aren't there any for me?" Olivia demands. "No one ever writes to me."

"Most of the mail that comes is very boring, Olivia," Mom points out. "Jemma's letters are mainly hospital appointments.

This looks like one here." She tears it open. "Ah, it's from Professor Spalding."

I wait impatiently while Mom reads the letter and I try to read her expression.

"Good news and bad news, Jemma," Mom says. "Mr. Katz, the guy from Israel, would like to meet you when he's here for a conference—but it's not until July."

July is five months away! It feels like forever.

"I'll read you the other letter later," she says, tapping it gently.

My head buzzes. That must mean it's from Jodi, but Mom doesn't want to read it in front of the others. I can't wait to hear what Jodi says. But Mom said we should wait to see if I can communicate before we meet. Is she really going to make me wait five months? And then whatever they have planned may not even work anyway...

"So what have you been up to?" Mom asks Olivia as she makes herself a sandwich.

"Sarah turned on her music, and we've been dancing for hours," Olivia tells Mom.

Mom frowns at Sarah and then turns to Olivia. "I'm not sure you should be having so much fun when you've been suspended," she tells her.

"She did read to Jemma," Sarah says defensively, "and Jemma enjoyed watching her dance."

Every time I think Sarah and Mom are getting along better, they start snapping at each other again.

"I've been to your school this morning," Mom tells Olivia. "Your teacher has given me some work for you to do, so that should keep you busy this afternoon."

"Bo-ring!" groans Olivia.

When lunch is over, Mom leaves Sarah to help Olivia with her schoolwork and pushes my wheelchair into the living room. She sits close to me on the sofa and reads me my letter from Jodi.

Jodi sounds so chatty and nice. She tells me how she went out for pizza with her boyfriend and he knocked his drink over and it went all over the pizza so it was a soggy mess! And how her team won their last three field hockey matches and might win the championship. She says Mom sent a photo of me, and she can see our hair is the same color. Again, she is asking to meet me.

"Jemma." Mom sighs, looking up at me. "I really thought it would be better to wait for you to meet Mr. Katz and try his communication system before you met Jodi. But that means such a long wait for both of you. I'll talk to your dad, see what he thinks." My heart is racing. I'm sure Dad will agree. I'm sure both of them know how much this means to me.

All night, I can't stop thinking about Jodi. Over breakfast I try to figure out if Mom has spoken to Dad yet. And then, when the others have left the room, she finally says, "Jemma, I've spoken with Dad, and I've had a word with Beth too."

Beth is my social worker, and she's always eager to be helpful. I hope she agrees with Mom.

"Beth suggested I talk to Jodi first, so I've had a little talk with her on the phone."

Even though I know it's ridiculous, I get a twinge of jealousy that Mom got to speak to Jodi first. I wonder what she sounds like.

"I wanted to make sure she understands about you. I don't want her to put too much pressure on the meeting, for either of you."

I know that Mom is just being Mom—cautious as usual and wanting to explain everything carefully—but I wish she would hurry up and get to the point! None of this matters to me. Jodi is my sister. I have to meet her... I must.

"But Jodi sounds nice," says Mom finally. "I think you'll like her. She insists that she does understand. We've arranged for you to meet next weekend—on Sunday."

21

*"**Love will find a way,**"* Sarah sings as she gets me dressed. She doesn't have the most tuneful voice, but she makes up for it with enthusiasm. I'm still reveling in the news about meeting Jodi next weekend, and I love the Glowlight song that Sarah is singing. The concert is tonight, and she's extra smiley, clearly excited.

She wheels me out of my room for breakfast, and something rustles beneath my wheels. Sarah gasps.

"Oh, Finn!" she says.

She turns me sideways so I can see that the hall floor is lined with neatly torn strips of newspaper, carefully arranged in rows. Finn is at the other end of the hall but comes back swiftly, looking annoyed that my wheels have moved a few strips out of place.

Dad comes downstairs. "Finn!" he exclaims. "I hope that's not today's paper. I haven't read it yet!"

The little strip near to my wheel with *Sat* on it gives him his answer. The paper is Dad's weekend treat—he doesn't have time to read one during the week. In fact, he often doesn't end up reading it on the weekend either, but I think he likes it being there. Dad looks annoyed for a second, then laughs and Sarah joins in.

Then, when Mom goes to sit down at the table for a coffee, she jumps back up again, shouting "Oww!" and clutching her bottom. From the chair, she picks up the spiky plant. Finn must have had enough of it. I bet he's moved the china elephant back to its normal spot too. The plant is squashed and misshapen, and I think Finn and I are both glad when Mom throws it in the trash.

Sarah is getting all glammed up for the concert. She paints her nails with gold nail polish. Then she does mine. It isn't easy as my hands like to curl up and my fingers are reluctant to stay straight. Muscle spasms make my arms and hands move about sometimes too. But Sarah is patient.

"Try to keep them still until they dry," she tells me. No amount of effort will give me control of my limb movements, but somehow my nails dry without too much smearing. I like the way the glint of gold catches my eye every time my head or hands move.

Now Sarah is doing her makeup. I watch as she carefully applies gold eye shadow, black eyeliner, and black mascara.

"I'll do yours in a minute," she tells me.

She looks so glamorous—like a model. She hardly ever

wears any makeup except on dates. I wonder what I will look like with makeup on.

Sarah carefully applies foundation to my skin with a sponge. It feels soft and cool.

"I'm not sure it's quite your color, but it's close enough," she says, turning me toward the mirror.

She looks at my eyes, thoughtfully. I soon have a sparkle of gold eye shadow above my eyes. The mascara is a disaster, though, as I jolt and end up with smears of black on my cheek. As Sarah rubs at it, I look like I have a black eye.

"If your mom came in now, she'd think I'd been beating you up!" says Sarah. There is an edge to her voice despite the jokey tone.

The mascara cleaned off, Sarah starts again with more foundation. I wonder if she'll bother with mascara, but she does.

"Your eyelashes are longer than mine," she says jealously.

I feel the soft grease of the lipstick as it brushes my lips.

"Look at you now!" She moves me around so I can see myself more clearly in the mirror.

I look so different. My head is still at a funny angle, my mouth gaping and not quite symmetrical, but I look older. I wish I could look like this when I meet Jodi. I look like someone about to head off to a Glowlight concert. I wish I was. I wish so much!

Sarah leaves me in the living room with the TV on while she finishes getting ready.

Dad comes in, on his way up to read bedtime stories to Finn and Olivia.

I hope he'll say something nice about my makeup, but he doesn't even notice! Now I know how Mom feels whenever she gets her hair cut. Sometimes she says she's tempted to shave her head, just to see if he realizes.

"You like Glowlight, don't you?" he says. "I'll put some on for you."

He turns off the TV, and soon the sound of Glowlight fills the room, the song with the cool drum intro at the start. Mom calls to him to turn it down.

"We like it loud, don't we, Jemma?" says Dad. "But we'd better keep your mom happy." He smiles at me and then looks closer. "Jemma! Is that makeup? You look great!"

I love the music. I absorb it—every note, every beat. I imagine I am there, with Sarah. My eyes close. Maybe this is better than really being there because in my mind I can clap and dance. I'm not in a wheelchair. I am just like everyone else.

The image of the band goes in and out of focus, and the figures around me start to blur. The notes suddenly go off-key. I look down and see my wheelchair. I'm not dancing. And then the person in front of me turns around. A face looms closer.

"If I were you, I'd kill myself." Dan's menacing grin. His cold eyes.

"I know you can't, so I've come to give you a hand to put you out of your misery."

Then I feel my chair being pushed. *I need Sarah!*

Where is she? I can't see her.

I wake with a start.

Mom is standing over me, frowning. I'm breathing fast, but my breaths come slower as I take in that it was just a bad dream, that I'd nodded off.

"What has she done to you?" Mom exclaims. "All that makeup!"

Sarah comes in. I get a wonderful whiff of her perfume.

Mom takes Sarah to one side and speaks quietly to her. I try to hear what they're saying. Sounds like Mom's complaining about my makeup, saying it will take forever to clean off.

I wish I could tell Mom I enjoyed being made up and to lay off Sarah for once.

"Enjoy the concert," Mom tells her.

"Thanks... Bye." There is still frostiness in Sarah's voice. She turns to me and smiles. "Bye, Jemma! I'll tell you all about it tomorrow!"

I hear the front door close. She's gone.

22

In the morning, Mom gets me ready.

"Looks like Sarah's sleeping in," she tells me. "Must have been a late one. I didn't even hear her come in."

I realize I didn't hear her either, though I have a blurry memory of hearing a car outside.

At about ten thirty, Olivia comes running down. "Sarah's not here! She's not in her room!"

"You shouldn't have gone in," Dad scolds her. He goes up to look and comes back confirming Olivia is right.

"Told you." Olivia pouts.

"She must be staying with one of the friends she went with to the concert," says Mom.

"She could have let us know." Dad sounds irritated. "I'll text her, just to make sure she's okay."

He does, but an hour later, he's had no reply. "Probably still asleep," he says.

I'm trying not to panic, but I don't believe Sarah has gone

back to Richard's. She sounded really certain when she said she doesn't want to be with him anymore, so why would she?

Could Dan have found out about Richard, found out that Sarah was going to the concert with him? I feel like my worst fears are coming true.

Hours go by. I keep wishing Sarah would walk through the door, bubbly, pretending not to be hungover, full of what a great concert it was.

She doesn't.

Mom tries phoning Sarah but says her phone seems to be switched off. "She probably turned it off for the concert and forgot to put it on again," says Mom. "Or left her charger at home."

By 4:00 p.m. Mom and Dad are both looking anxious. "I don't even know who she was going with," Mom comments. "Was it Dan? Do you think we should try to call him? Or her friends...that Rihanna? Who's the other one—Emma, isn't it? But how would we get hold of them? All their numbers will be in Sarah's phone."

"Should we call the police?" says Dad.

"Let's give it a few more hours," says Mom. "She's probably still hungover at Dan's or a friend's house, something like that."

Mom doesn't sound sure that she believes what she's saying, even as she says it. I am even less sure.

A few more hours go by. Mom says she'll try looking at Sarah's laptop—see if she can find a number for Dan or one of her friends—but she comes down saying she can't get into anything without Sarah's password. She finds the phone number for Sarah's sister, Kate, which Sarah gave her for emergencies. Dad phones Kate after dinner, but there's no answer. Then he phones the police.

"They took the details, but they didn't sound that interested," he tells Mom. "She's an adult. It's not like when we lost Finn."

"It isn't like her to go off and say nothing, though," says Mom.

"I did tell them that," says Dad. "I'll keep trying Kate. Sarah doesn't have any other family, does she?"

"No, her mom died years ago," says Mom. "I don't think there was anyone else."

I'm facing toward the doorway, and I can picture Sarah coming through, smiling and laughing. Then I see her at the concert, like she was in my dream. But as I try to fix the image of her in my mind, it fades. *What happened, Sarah? Where are you? Did you get to the concert? Did Dan find out? Just come home, Sarah. Please.*

23

I wake with a moment's calm on Monday, and then my stomach drops when I remember that Sarah is missing. She's still not back. This is seriously worrying. And the police aren't even looking for her yet.

Mom gets me ready. She is gentle, but her face is weary, her eyes droopy. I don't think she's had much sleep.

The glint of my sparkling nails keeps catching my eye. It feels like it was just moments ago that Sarah was putting the polish on me.

"Don't worry, Jemma. I'm sure Sarah will be home soon," Mom tells me.

It doesn't feel right for me to head off to school and act like everything is normal. Olivia doesn't want to go either. She tries hiding the car keys, but when Mom quickly finds them, she starts screaming.

"Dylan will kill me for breaking his tooth!" she yells.

"If you're worried about anything, tell a teacher," Mom

says. "I'll come in with you and explain about Sarah. I'll tell them today is a difficult day for you."

"I'm not going! I'm not going!" Olivia cries.

The bus is here to pick me up. I am wheeled out, leaving Olivia still in a tantrum.

We drive away from the house, but the same series of images runs through my mind. The frosty look Sarah gave Mom. The front door slamming as she left. Sarah at the concert, blurry figures around her. Is one of them Dan? Sarah and Richard—he's thrilled to be with her; she's worrying Dan will call. Sarah and Dan, him begging her to live with him. Sarah's phone beeping, always with Dan's name.

A new thought hits me. Could she have planned this? Could she have run away with Dan?

The next image is Dan's sneering face as he watched Ryan's funeral on TV and told me no one would catch him. If she has run away with him, she's not safe.

At school, I have swimming. It's a pain being changed and dried and changed back again, but it is always worth it. I am held in the water by Sheralyn, my volunteer helper, with the aid of some floats.

My arms and legs stretch out in the water. I feel free floating and uncurling as if I'm moving through air. In my chair I feel heavy and unwieldy; it's hard for people to move me. In water, a nudge is enough. I am as light as air, and nothing presses into me at awkward angles. The water is so soft—softer even than my bed and so gentle. It feels delicious, the strongest sensation I experience apart from eating, and far more pleasurable.

I lie on my back in the pool and stare up at the paneled ceiling. I can see my reflection repeated in a number of mirrored tiles all at once as if there are three or four of me. The mirror reflects reality, but not quite. That is how things feel with Sarah—real, but not quite. She can't really have disappeared, can she?

The water is warm, but I get cold quickly. Sheralyn comments that my fingers are going white. It is time to come out. I like Sheralyn. She is very gentle. She's training to be a teacher and says she wants to teach "people like me." She's good, but she sometimes forgets to talk to me. Sometimes while they are changing us, the volunteers start chatting to each other and forget that we are people who need to be talked to as well.

On the way home from school in the bus, I try to picture Sarah sitting in the living room. Running into the hall when I come through the door. I pray, even though I don't know if I believe in God.

"Please, God," I say in my head, "please let Sarah be home." She is not.

Later, after dinner, Mom is putting Finn and Olivia to bed, and I'm keeping Dad company in the kitchen while he does the dishes. The phone rings, and he quickly dries his hands on a towel and grabs it.

I hold my breath. My heartbeat thuds in my ears. "Oh, hello, Kate," says Dad. "You got my message?"

Maybe Kate knows something. Maybe Sarah is with her. I listen eagerly, but Dad takes the phone out of the room.

Mom comes running down the stairs. "Who is it?" she says. "Any news?"

"Kate just saw the message now," says Dad as they both come back into the kitchen. "She's not spoken to Sarah for about a month, but that's not unusual. They're not that close. She didn't sound too worried, though. She said Sarah's sometimes a little impulsive. She went missing for a few days when she was a teenager. She'd gone off with some boy she liked and didn't bother to tell anyone."

"She's not a teenager now, though," Mom says doubtfully. "She's a woman in her twenties with a job and responsibilities. If she wanted to go off with Dan, why wouldn't she just tell us? What do you think, Ben?"

Dad shrugs. "It's hard to believe she'd go and leave all her stuff here."

"Go where?" Olivia has appeared in the doorway in her nightie. "You're talking about Sarah, aren't you? Where's she gone? Tell me."

"Bedtime, Olivia," says Dad. "We're sure Sarah will be back soon."

24

Sarah's been missing for three days. Mom and Dad are talking a lot in hushed whispers.

"Kate suggested we try her laptop again. She gave a few suggestions for passwords," Dad tells Mom.

"I'll try," says Mom. "One of her friends must know where she is."

The one person they need to contact is the one they won't even think of looking for. They need to speak to Richard.

Dad puts on a Disney movie for us when we're all back from school. I don't feel like watching it. I want to do something. I want to help find Sarah.

Mom spends a while in Sarah's room. She comes down sighing.

"I checked and I'm sure all her stuff is still there, like we thought—her iPad, her clothes, her jewelry," Mom says. "I tried a few passwords for the laptop, and would you believe it was 'Jemma' and her birth date?"

I am Sarah's password! I get a painful ache in my chest. I wish they'd realize that I am also the real-life password to the information they need.

"Good job!" says Dad, impressed.

"I searched her contacts and Facebook friends, but I can't see Dan there, which is strange. She doesn't use email much," Mom tells Dad. "I guess it's all texts these days. But she'd sent messages to Rihanna and Emma. I've emailed both of them to see if they were with her on Saturday or if they know how to get in touch with Dan. The emails don't mention the concert, but one to Rihanna mentions what a bitch I've been to her lately." Mom's voice cracks slightly. "I know we haven't been getting along very well. But things weren't bad enough for her to walk out on us, though."

"I don't think so," says Dad.

I think about Dan trying to convince Sarah to leave me. She was tempted, I'm sure. She wasn't as happy here as she used to be.

The police arrive just after dinner. Two officers walk into the kitchen. They are both tall and with their uniforms, the kitchen seems instantly too full. I see the man glance at me and then quickly look away, while the woman smiles as if she's ignoring the tense atmosphere. It's like the room itself is holding its breath.

"I'll put the television on for the children," Mom tells them. I wonder if I am going to be sent off to the living room with Finn and Olivia.

"Have you found Sarah?" Olivia asks the policewoman.

She shakes her head. "We're trying our best," she says, and then introduces herself to us as Officer Sahin.

"You should look harder," Olivia tells them. "Dad found Finn with some chocolate chip cookies. Maybe if we get something that Sarah really likes, that'll make her come back. I know! She loves Glowlight. Maybe if we put their music on—or maybe we can even get the band to come here and put an announcement on the TV. She won't want to miss that."

"Thanks for your help," Officer Sahin says, smiling. "It's nice to hear your ideas."

"So will you do it, then?" Olivia demands.

"Come on, Olivia," says Mom.

Olivia hesitates. She'd love to stay, just as I would, but she loves TV too and follows Mom. Finn goes with them. The police officers sit down at the kitchen table. They smile at me, but seem unsure whether to speak to me.

"You must be worried about your aide," says Officer Sahin.

I certainly am. My head jolts back, and an *ughhh* noise comes out of me.

"Is she compos mentis?" the man, Officer Hunt, asks Mom quietly as she comes back in.

"Oh yes, but she can't communicate. I wish she could. Sarah talks to her a lot."

"Not much use to us, then," Officer Hunt mutters, screwing up his nose.

I wish I could kick him.

Mom looks at me and then makes coffee for the police officers. She leaves me where I am. She's decided I should be in on this, maybe because Sarah is my aide or maybe she feels bad about what the policeman just said.

Officer Hunt starts asking Mom questions. It's all background stuff—how long Sarah has been here, how the care is paid for. I have a question of my own: How is this going to help find her? Mom tells them about Dan, that she's been trying to get ahold of him.

Finally, Officer Hunt begins asking questions about the night Sarah went missing. But of course all Mom knows is that Sarah was going to the concert. She doesn't know who with; she doesn't think it was Dan. Emma and Rihanna replied to Mom's email, but they didn't know about the concert and haven't heard from Sarah either. They also didn't know much about Dan.

"Most missing people reappear within forty-eight hours," Officer Sahin tells Mom. "Now that three days have passed, this is, of course, more concerning, but please try not to worry. We will pass the details to the Missing Persons Bureau, but we have classified her as 'low risk.' The most likely thing is still that she has gone off of her own accord, that she's with her boyfriend or some other friends."

"I really don't know," says Mom. "Dan seems like a good person to me. I don't see why they'd go off together without telling us."

"We will try to trace Sarah's phone," says Officer Hunt, "and also speak to Dan. It's a shame no one knows his last name."

It seems odd to me that he isn't on Facebook and Sarah's friends don't know him.

The doorbell rings while the police are still talking, through.

Mom goes to get the door, leaving the kitchen in silence. I recognize the voice, even though I've only met him a few times. It's Richard. Is Sarah with him?

"Is Sarah in?" I hear him ask Mom.

"Oh...Richard," says Mom. "No, she's not—"

"Her phone's been off since the concert," Richard interrupts. "I'm kind of worried that she's not been in touch. Maybe I did something to upset her."

"She went to the concert with you?" says Mom.

"Yes! Who did you think she went with?" says Richard. Then he pauses. "Wh-what's wrong?"

Mom lowers her voice as she explains to him what's happened. I can't hear his reaction, but the next moment Richard comes into the kitchen, blinking likes someone who's come into a bright room from somewhere dark.

He looks from Officer Hunt to Officer Sahin and back at Mom. He shifts around on his feet. Then he glances back toward the front door as if he wishes he could make a fast getaway.

Mom explains to the police about Richard being with Sarah at the concert. Richard begins to babble.

"We met downtown, went to the concert, and afterward I drove Sarah back here. She got out of the car, and I watched her walk up the sidewalk to the front door. She had her key out. I didn't wait for her to go inside. I drove off. Oh my God! How could something happen to her at the front door?"

"Do you remember what time you dropped her off?" Officer Hunt asks him.

"Let me think. It must have been about eleven thirty."

"Are you sure she didn't come in and then go out again?" Officer Sahin asks Mom.

"I didn't hear the door, and it doesn't look like she changed clothes or anything. I really don't think so."

I know she didn't. I'd have heard the front door. But what Richard is saying sounds so unlikely—he brought her back, and she *disappeared* before coming inside. Can that really be true?

Officer Sahin turns to Richard. "And you didn't have any kind of a fight? She wasn't upset?"

"No, we had a great time. She's always smiling, Sarah. I don't think I've seen her upset in the ten months we've been going out! We've never fought... I can tell you that."

I see Mom's eyebrows shoot up to her hairline. Her mouth drops open. She's not sure what to say. As far as she's concerned, they broke up three months ago, when Sarah started going out with Dan.

Officer Hunt turns to Mom. "I thought you said her boyfriend was named Dan."

"Dan?" Richard repeats. "Who's Dan?"

Mom's hand covers her eyes as if she wishes she could hide. She slowly takes a breath and then looks at Richard.

Richard's mouth is taut as Mom explains about Dan. His eyes are still, staring at her and then at the wall. "I don't believe it... I don't believe it." His eyes are glassy now.

He's being so dramatic that I begin to wonder if he knew already.

I'd been worrying so much that Dan would find out about Richard, but what if Richard found out about Dan? Does that change things?

"You appear to be the last person who saw her," says Officer Sahin.

25

There is still no news about Sarah. Four days. That's double the time they said missing people usually turn up in.

Finn is doing his head-banging thing more and more, and Olivia is having even more tantrums than usual. Mom's put the TV on for them, and they're quiet for the time being, watching a kids' show about aliens. I'm in the kitchen keeping Mom company while she cooks dinner. She seems to like having me close to her at the moment. I don't think she likes being alone. Or maybe she's worried about how I'm feeling without Sarah.

Someone rings the doorbell, and Mom hurries to open the door. I hear Paula's voice.

"Lorraine! I heard about Sarah. The police came to speak to us. What do you think has happened to her?"

"Come in, Paula," Mom says. "Have a cup of tea." As she leads Paula into the kitchen, Mom catches my eye with a look that says she could have done without Paula turning up.

"The police think she's gone off somewhere of her own accord," Mom says, pulling out a chair.

Paula sits down.

"You don't mind if I continue?" Mom asks, pointing to the chopping board full of waiting carrots.

"They said that when I first reported Ryan missing," says Paula. Mom stares at her and then glances at me.

But Paula doesn't seem to take the hint. "I said to Graham, it's strange that the police should come to us. Only a few doors apart. And so soon after my Ryan..."

There's a loud snap as Mom chops a carrot with extra force. I see her breathe in and compose herself. "Paula, I'm not sure what you're—"

"Do you think they're linked? It can't just be a coincidence."

Paula gives me an awkward glance. She's clearly wondering if she should be saying all this in front of me. I swallow. I want her to keep talking. Even though what she's implying has happened to Sarah is making my chest hurt, I want them to realize there is a connection—Dan and Sarah, Dan and Ryan. Dan.

But looking from Mom to Paula, my heart sinks. The desperation in Paula's eyes. Mom will just think it's Paula's grief, that she's trying to make things fit together so she can have an answer.

"They're speaking to everyone who lives on this block,"

Mom says softly but firmly. "Richard says Sarah got out of his car just outside the house around eleven thirty on Saturday night. The police want to know if anyone heard or saw anything."

"Yes," says Paula. "That's what they asked us. But we both take sleeping pills, you see. Don't get a wink otherwise—not since...you know. Do you really think she just took off?"

"I don't know what to think," says Mom. She pours tea for Paula and then goes back to chopping the carrots loudly. "Have you gotten any news yourselves, about Ryan?"

Paula sighs deeply and runs her finger around the rim of her mug. "Nothing," she says. "I got my hopes up when they charged that Jay. He was Ryan's regular dealer, and they had a falling-out about money or something. But Jay was out of town—he proved it. The more time that goes by, the less likely I think it is that they'll get him." She looks up. "Though perhaps now..." The doorbell rings again.

"Goodness, we're popular tonight!" Mom exclaims. She turns down the heat under a pan on the stove and excuses herself. The smell of hamburger frying wafts over me as she goes out into the hall.

Paula meets my eyes briefly for a moment and looks as if she might say something, but then thinks better of it. People do that a lot.

Mom's voice is loud with surprise as she opens the front door.

"Oh, Dan..." I hear her say.

26

I can't believe he's here. I feel suddenly cold, so cold. Mom is talking to him as he follows her into the kitchen. "We wanted to call you," she's saying, "but we couldn't find your number."

"Call me? Why? Has something happened?" Dan asks as he comes into the room. "I—" He stops when he sees Paula. He doesn't look at me at all.

"Paula, this is Dan, Sarah's boyfriend," says Mom. She runs her hand across her forehead. Her eyes are wide with shock. If Dan's here, that means Sarah hasn't run off with him.

Paula nods.

"Dan, this is my neighbor, Paula," Mom continues. Dan nods back. Does he realize who Paula is?

"What's going on?" he asks. "Sarah's phone has been off. I came over to see her."

"Oh, Dan," says Mom, her voice shaking. "She isn't here. We haven't seen her since Saturday. Haven't you heard from her at all?"

"No. What's going on?"

Dan turns his head to look at Mom, and I can't see his face. I wish I could. I bet his expression would give him away.

Paula stands up, her chair scraping the floor noisily in her haste. "I'd better be going," she says. "I do hope she turns up."

"Turns up?" Dan repeats. He looks at Paula, and I see a crease spread across his forehead. I watch him closely. He definitely looks surprised to hear that Sarah is missing. There are beads of sweat on his forehead. Does he really know nothing, or is this all an act?

"I'll see Paula to the door, then I'll tell you everything, Dan," Mom says.

For a moment I am alone with Dan. I wish he'd say something, confide in me. I watch him. His hands don't keep still. He's rubbing his fingers together.

Mom is back. Phlegm clogs my throat, and I cough.

"Dan, the police have been looking for you," Mom tells him.

He seems nervous now, his feet shifting back and forth. His eyes flash in alarm. "What? Why?" he asks.

"You haven't seen or heard from her then, Dan—not since Saturday? We thought she might have been with you."

Dan shakes his head. "No."

"Sarah was at a concert on Saturday night and didn't come back here. No one's seen her since. Sit down, Dan—this must be a shock. I'll make you coffee."

Dan moves toward a chair and leans on the back of it, but he doesn't sit down. "A concert? I thought she was working last weekend."

It's Mom's turn to shift around awkwardly.

I look at Dan. I'm sure this is an act. He's challenging Mom to confirm what he knows—that Sarah was two-timing him.

"She went with a friend...actually, her ex, Richard. I think he must have gotten tickets for the concert a long time ago. She probably felt she had to go. You know what she's like!"

"Right," says Dan, with an edge to his voice. "So I assume the police have been questioning him?"

"Yes," Mom says. "He was the last person to see her, but I don't think they... They want to speak to you too. You'll call them, won't you?"

Dan's gaze is steady. "Of course," he says.

27

I spend all the next day wondering what will happen when Dan talks to the police. He has to call them, doesn't he? But one thing we know now is that Sarah hasn't run off with him. Could she have left on her own? Would she really do that? Or has something else happened, something I can't stand to even think about?

When I get home from school, I'm surprised to find Sheralyn, my swimming volunteer, waiting for me. Mom says when she told the principal at my school what had happened, she said Sheralyn might be able to help out because she's worked as an aide before. It turns out she's still registered with the agency Mom uses, and she was eager to help. I'm glad it's Sheralyn, but at the same time, having her here only makes me want Sarah back more, if that's possible. Sarah has been missing for five days.

Sheralyn decides to take me for a walk to the shopping center. Maybe she's trying to take my mind off things, but

I hate the place. Too many people staring. They either look appalled or desperately sorry for me. There's always some kid with a finger up one nose pointing at me with the other hand and saying, "What's wrong with her?" Sarah used to bring me here a lot, but I think she sensed all the comments were upsetting me and we stopped coming so often.

As we reach the center, I recognize a man who is walking toward us. It's Dan's friend Billy. I see him look and recognize me, but he just walks straight past. It's the total opposite of what he was like before. Of course, he doesn't know Sheralyn, but would it hurt to stop and say hello?

As we reach the more crowded shopping area, I start thinking about my sister. She doesn't live that far away. What if she was here now, walking around the stores? I wonder if I would recognize her from the photo. I'm looking at every girl and wondering if she could be her. That girl with dark hair looks too tall. This one has a kind face, but her hair is too light.

Ahead there is a woman with blond hair, tied back in a ponytail, walking away from us. My heart suddenly skips a beat. *Sarah.* She looks like Sarah. She really could be... She could be Sarah! She's walking faster than us. She's disappearing into the crowd. *Wait!*

She doesn't wait. She's gone. It couldn't have been Sarah, could it? If she's run away, she wouldn't still be around here. She'd be worried about being spotted. I don't think she walked quite like Sarah either. I have a lingering hope, though. Maybe it was her. Maybe she's on her way home. Perhaps she's stopped at the store to buy some flowers—or something to give Mom, to give all of us, to say sorry for all the worry she's caused.

She doesn't need to say *sorry* to me. I'd forgive her for getting us all so worried if she only came home.

"Hey—wait!" a woman calls. Sheralyn stops and swings me around. The woman has short gray hair. She must be sixty or seventy. What does she want?

"Here, take this for the poor lass," the woman says.

She holds out a ten-dollar bill.

I can't see Sheralyn's face, as she is pushing me, but I hear the shock in her voice.

"No... Really, that's very kind, but—"

"Please, dear," says the woman. "I insist. Take it." The money has gone from the woman's hand.

I'm not a charity. Sarah would never have done that. She would have explained that I am well looked after, that I have what I need. I don't need strangers giving me money in the street. I'm not a desperate homeless person.

"Sorry, Jemma," Sheralyn says quietly as the woman disappears in the crowd. "That was so embarrassing. I didn't know what to say. I'll donate the money to charity."

When we get back, I am still feeling upset about the woman treating me like a charity case. Mom's upstairs with

Finn and Olivia, but Sheralyn takes over with them and Mom comes down. She's holding something—a letter!

"Jemma, I've got another letter for you from Jodi," she says.

I can feel my heart beating faster as Mom begins to read.

Dear Jemma,

This is just a short note to say I am so excited about meeting you on Sunday! I can't wait, and I can't think about anything else! Your mom was so great on the phone. She's told me all about you. I hope you are as excited as I am! I'm counting the days and the hours and the minutes!

Love, Jodi

Mom folds the letter and looks at me.

"Jemma, I'd forgotten we arranged this. I wonder if we should postpone it."

"No!" I want to yell. I know everything with Sarah is awful, but I want to meet Jodi so much. I need something good to happen, and this is going to be it. I must meet my sister.

"Then again," says Mom, "we don't want to let Jodi down. This is such a big deal for both of you. Maybe it will take your mind off things."

Mom sighs. I'm relieved. I just hope she doesn't change her mind again.

When I get back from school the next day, Olivia's already home, and she's jumping up and down with excitement. My heart races. Is it Sarah... Is she back? I've been full of excitement myself all day about meeting Jodi on Sunday, but Olivia can't be excited about that.

"Guess what?" she says, bounding up to me. "I took a photo of Sarah to school, and I showed it around to see if anyone had seen her—and Ruby Jones says she saw her in the supermarket!"

"Don't get your hopes up too high, Olivia," Mom says gently. "It was probably someone who looks like Sarah."

So Sarah is not back. I get a pang of guilt for feeling happy about meeting Jodi when Sarah is still missing.

"It was her," Olivia insists. "Ruby said she was sure!"

"It might have been Sarah that Ruby saw," Mom acknowledges. "It also might not."

"It was her," Olivia insists again.

I wish it was. I wish so much that it was Sarah who Ruby saw in the supermarket and who I saw in the shopping center.

During dinner, the phone rings. Dad answers it. "Oh, Kate! Hello," he says. "Any news? How are you coping?"

"Tell her Ruby saw Sarah," Olivia demands. "She'll want to know. You must tell her."

"Shhhh! Wait," Mom whispers. "Let's find out why she's called first."

"You have? Really?" says Dad. "Do any of them seem likely?"

Likely? What could that mean?

I can't see Dad's face, but I can see how eagerly Mom and Olivia are watching him. Finn is tapping his fork on his plate. *Tap, tap, tap,* over and over.

I wish he'd stop.

Dad says something about a card. And then "That's typical."

"What's she saying?" Olivia demands. "Have they found Sarah or what? Tell her about Ruby. Ruby saw her!"

"Shhhh!" Mom tells her, putting her finger to her lips.

"That sounds like an excellent idea," Dad continues after listening for a few moments. "Of course we'll help in any way we can. Just let us know."

He puts the phone down. Mom looks at him questioningly.

"Why didn't you tell her?" Olivia shouts. She stands up and kicks her chair over.

"Stop that, Olivia!" Dad says firmly. "Sit down and listen if you want to know what Kate said."

Olivia hesitates, but she does want to know. She picks up her chair and sits down.

"Kate's started a social media campaign, and she's already had a few people contact her with sightings," Dad tells Mom.

"See? I told you Ruby saw her!" Olivia interrupts. "I told you, and you didn't believe it."

"The first few didn't sound likely," Dad continues, "but

now there've been three quite close together—all within ten
miles of here—that do sound possible. The most interesting
news is that the police say Sarah's debit card was used two
days ago to withdraw a hundred dollars—and the ATM is in
Watford, not far from those three sightings."

Sarah has taken money from an ATM. That must mean
she's alive, doesn't it? Or is this Dan trying to throw people
off the scent?

"Goodness," says Mom. "Was there a security camera at
the ATM?"

"The camera near it wasn't working, and they couldn't
see anyone matching her description on the other nearby
cameras—though they're still going through the footage. The
police think it's a good sign. Her phone was last used at the
concert itself, so that hasn't been much help. Kate is certainly
hopeful, though."

"It was her," says Olivia firmly.

"Kate's put Sarah's details on the Missing People web
page. If someone doesn't want to be found, they can still leave
a message on there, just so family and friends know they are
okay. Kate is getting some posters made, and she's asked if
we'll help put them up around here."

"I'll help!" says Olivia.

If Sarah has been seen, if she's used an ATM, then it truly
sounds possible she chose to leave. I want her to be alive,
even though it's hard to bear the thought that she left us like

that—that she was so unhappy. I can't take this much longer, this limbo.

Later, Mom gets out the nail-polish remover and takes off my now-chipped nail polish. I keep thinking about Sarah putting it on me so carefully, so kindly. I can see her sparkly eyes, her excitement about the concert. I don't want Mom to take it off. It connects me to Sarah, and, without it, I feel like Sarah is even farther away. But soon the nail polish has gone and only the strong smell of the remover lingers, making me cough. I wonder if anyone will ever paint my nails again.

28

It is a week since Sarah went missing. *A whole week.*

Kate has come with a stack of posters, and we are going around the streets putting them up. I've never met Kate before. She doesn't look like Sarah. She is much shorter, and her face is narrower. Her hair is dark, and Sarah's is fair. She has lines on her face. She looks much older than Sarah.

"Hi, Jemma, nice to meet you," she says, smiling a little awkwardly. I jolt at the way she speaks. Her voice is so similar it could be Sarah's.

Dad wasn't sure about all of us coming, but Olivia was determined to help.

I am "parked" in front of a streetlight where the first poster has been attached. It is weird seeing Sarah's face smiling down. Is she smiling somewhere now? I can't picture what she's doing, where she might be. It's just a blank. Kate seems so confident that the sightings were really Sarah and that she's alive. Could it be true? Could it?

Dad asks Kate if the police have followed up on the sightings and the ATM.

"They're still not sure if it was her," Kate admits, "but there's no proof that it wasn't either."

"And Ruby Jones saw her too!" Olivia pipes up.

"Yes, so you said," says Kate. "Any sighting might help. It's good that she told you."

Once the posters are up, I am disappointed to see most people going past without even looking at them. If they look at all, it is such a quick glance that they can't really take in her face—can they?

Sheralyn is with me and is supposed to be watching Finn too. To make him feel useful, Dad has given him a wad of posters to hold, while Olivia is handing Dad pieces of tape. Sheralyn is watching Olivia. No one apart from me has noticed that Finn is now lining up his posters neatly on the sidewalk against the fence. He has more than I thought—at least ten faces of Sarah staring up from the ground—and I can see what's going to happen. It's not that windy, but it will only take a little bit of a breeze. *Please, Sheralyn... Look back! Look at Finn!*

She does—but too late. A gust lifts the corner of one sheet, then another, and suddenly they are all fluttering up into the air, spreading across the sidewalk.

Finn lets out an anguished cry and starts flapping his arms, his neat work undone.

"Oh! Finn!" Sheralyn exclaims.

He makes no effort to pick up the posters, just watches as Sheralyn, Dad, and Olivia quickly try to gather them. Some are flapping into the street like injured birds. Olivia runs to the edge of the curb.

"Olivia—not in the street!" Dad yells, and to my relief, Olivia stops.

A car runs over a poster, and even from here, I can see tire marks on it.

"I could have gotten that one!" Olivia tells Dad angrily. Mom and Kate are farther down the street. I can't see them, but I hear Kate's voice. They must have seen and come back to help. I only see Kate when she steps into the street and retrieves the poster with the tire marks. She stands on the sidewalk in front of me, staring at it and brushing it with her hand, as if the tire marks might rub off. Tears run down her face.

As we head home, it begins to rain—just to make everyone more miserable—and no one has an umbrella. Although they are in plastic sleeves, the posters will be dripping and bedraggled before anyone even sees them. Mom and Sheralyn struggle to get my shower-proof cape over me, but I am already very wet. The chilly dampness has seeped through to my skin, making me shiver. Raindrops tickle my face like insects, and I wish I could wipe them away.

When we reach the house, Mom says Kate can't go all

that way home on the train when she's soaked through. She insists on lending her some clothes and invites Kate to stay for dinner.

Once I am in dry clothes, Sheralyn leaves me in the living room with some music playing, saying she's going to take a shower. Kate, Mom, and Dad are in the kitchen, and I wish she'd taken me in there.

I'm sitting here, almost asleep, when Olivia slips in, unusually quietly for her. She goes over to Mom's purse, which is on the sofa, opens the zipper, and starts digging in it. I wonder briefly if Mom has asked her to fetch something from her bag—but it's unlikely. Olivia keeps glancing toward the door, so she's obviously doing something she shouldn't.

She doesn't seem to have realized that I'm here. I watch as she pulls out Mom's wallet and takes out a ten-dollar bill. She folds it and presses it quickly into her pocket. She zips up Mom's bag, then glances up at me. She meets my eyes, but then looks quickly away and hurries off.

What does Olivia want ten dollars for? Then I remember Mom saying money was missing from her purse. It was Olivia all along.

"Sarah was a little on the wild side as a teenager. She had a string of hopeless boyfriends," Kate tells us over dinner.

"Not much change there," I want to say.

"And like I said," Kate continues, "I tried to warn her about this one boy, and she got annoyed and went off with him for a few days."

"But she hasn't gone off with Dan—or with Richard," Mom points out. "They've both been here and are clearly worried about her."

"I know," says Kate.

There's a silence, and I feel them all thinking about the other possibilities that no one wants to mention—the bad things that could have happened to Sarah.

When Kate leaves after we've eaten, I miss her voice. I miss her voice that sounds so much like Sarah's.

29

We pass one of our posters as Mom drives me to the Family Center where the meeting with Jodi has been arranged. I had imagined we'd meet in a café or something like that, but Mom says this will be more private, and Jodi will have a social worker there to support her if she needs someone to talk to afterward. Whatever I feel after this meeting will have to stay inside me. I can't share it. I hope it will go okay.

I am starting to feel sick as we go over bumps in the road. I'm relieved that it's not a long drive, and I am soon out of the car and being pushed by Mom up the ramp of a modern building that looks like a preschool.

Mom speaks to someone at the reception desk, and we are directed to the back of the building. Is Jodi here already?

We've arrived first and have to sit in a room similar to a doctor's waiting room. It's all making this feel so formal. Mom pulls me near her and squeezes my hand. I am grateful. I know she is nervous too. Then, after a few minutes, a woman with an ID on a lanyard comes bustling up to us, smiling.

"I'm Donna," she tells us. "I'm a social worker. Jodi is on her way. Would you like to come through to the room we've set up for you?"

Mom nods.

"Can I get you a coffee while you're waiting?"

"Thanks, that would be great," says Mom.

"Would you like anything, Jemma?"

"No, she's fine," says Mom. *Fine? I'm not sure about that!*

The room is cozy with armchairs and a striped rug, but the pale lime-green walls and shiny plastic floor make it still look like a doctor's exam room. There is a landscape picture on the wall of fields and farm buildings and a scarecrow. It looks like a beautiful day—the sky is so blue, and there are lots of shadows on the ground. I stare at the picture. It is calming.

"I hope she won't be long," says Mom, looking at her watch and bringing me back to now. I wish I could have stayed with the picture. I've been excited so far, but I'm suddenly feeling really shaky inside.

It is a few minutes before Donna brings the coffee.

She goes out, leaving Mom clutching the mug as if for warmth, though it's not cold in here. She's anxious too—wondering if she's done the right thing, whether this is a good idea. She couldn't change her mind now, could she?

Donna is back, smiling. "She's here! She's just stopped in the restroom. A little nervous, I think!"

"I'm sure Jemma must be nervous too," says Mom.

"You shouldn't worry, though," Donna tells me. "We won't get in the way, but we'll both be here, on hand if needed." She winks. It reminds me of Dan winking, though it is a very different wink. I'm sure this wink is saying "good luck" rather than "I'll be back to kill you sometime." It makes me slightly uneasy, though. Mom and Donna move their chairs toward the far wall so Jodi and I will have some space. I can't see them now because I'm facing the door.

Then the door opens slowly, and a girl comes in. She glances past me toward Mom, and I hear Donna say warmly, "Come on in, Jodi. This is Jemma."

Jodi walks toward me and stands still. We stare at each other. She is a prettier than her photo, with dark hair and a fluffy black sweater. The shock is—she looks far more like me than I'd realized. Our hair, dark eyes, small noses, and pale, thin lips are so similar. My face looks as if it has been squashed in sideways. It is distorted, my features out of alignment. Yet I can see myself in her. We are so alike! She is shocked too. I can see it. Her mouth has dropped slightly open.

I wish she'd speak, and I wish she'd sit down. She's standing too still for too long. I think she's frozen.

"Oh...Jemma," she says at last.

I love it. I love hearing her say my name.

My sister saying my name! I wait for more.

Her face creases up. She bursts into tears.

"I'm so sorry, Jemma. I can't do this!" she sobs.

Her hands cover her tearstained face. I hadn't noticed the makeup until now when I see it smearing down her cheeks.

I want to reassure her, to tell her to sit down, not to worry. I realize my delight in seeing the likeness between us has had the opposite effect on her. She is horrified to be so like someone so deformed. I'd normally be angry, but I can't be. I'll forgive her anything if she'll just talk to me. She's my sister. My sister.

Donna rushes over. "Jodi, why don't you sit down for a minute? I can understand this being a little overwhelming. I'll get you a tissue."

But Jodi doesn't sit.

"Jodi?" Mom tries.

"Stop crying, stop crying, please!" I want to beg her. But suddenly the door has opened and shut, and in a blur, she is gone.

30

Donna hurries after her, and a few moments later, Mom follows.

I am alone. I don't think I've ever felt as alone as in this moment. I only had a sister for about two minutes, but now there is a gaping hole in my life. She's gone. If this is what she meant about a missing piece, I understand now. I'm missing her. But I was not her missing piece. Like Mom feared, I was not what Jodi was looking for. She's had a glimpse, and I don't fit the gap in her puzzle.

I'm not alone for long, of course. Mom rushes back in and hugs me. My face is wet. I realize it is Mom crying, but when she finally lets go of me, my face gets wetter still. I am crying too.

"Donna's talking to her now," Mom says. "She might calm down and come back in, but it's possible she might not. I'm so sorry, Jemma."

We wait. Mom strokes my hand. We wait more.

I stare at the picture, the sunshine and the shadows. She

will come back. She'll calm down. Donna will talk to her. She'll come back in.

We wait...and wait. Mom looks out into the corridor. "They're still in that room," she tells me. "That has to be a good sign. You still want to see her, Jemma, don't you?" Mom looks at me closely. "Maybe we should've waited until you could communicate. It's not fair to you. It would've been easier for Jodi too."

Maybe Mom's right—but who knows how long that's going to take, and if it will ever happen. I don't want to wait for that. I want to see Jodi now. I can't stand that she's so close—across that corridor—and yet so, so far away.

Come back, Jodi! Please come back.

The door across the corridor bangs. The bang echoes down the hallway. Mom hesitates, unsure whether to go out to see what's happened or to wait. Our door opens. Donna comes in. She is alone. My heart sinks.

"I am so sorry," Donna says, her voice low and grim, the opposite of the buzzy chirp she met us with earlier. She goes on, talking about how bad Jodi feels, but I am feeling too sad to listen.

"Is she still here?" Mom asks hopefully. "Maybe I can talk to her."

Donna shakes her head, and my heart sinks down my legs and under my wheels. She's gone. It's as if she's closed the door on me.

She came, she took one look, and she went. That was my sister.

Back at home, I'm in a daze as Dad wheels me into the living room. I can see he has been playing Connect Four with Olivia while Finn lines up matchsticks along the wall. Finn is wearing a helmet because he's been head-banging so much lately. Mom tells Dad what happened with Jodi and then says she has a migraine and needs to lie down.

"I think we need to build a nest for Jemma," Dad tells Olivia.

"A nest?" Olivia asks. "What do you mean?"

"Jemma's had a hard morning and needs some TLC. We'll stack up as many cushions as we can find into a nest, and Jemma can sit in it and feel soft and safe and warm."

"Can I sit in it too?" Olivia asks.

"After Jemma's had a turn, you certainly can," says Dad.

Dad got into this "nesting" years ago when I was about five. He used to make nests for me all the time. It's been a long time since he's made me one. I thought I'd grown out of them, but the thought of him doing this for me fills me with warmth and love, and I realize I'm yearning to be snuggled and safe.

Olivia and Dad get busy with cushions.

I count as they pile them up. They get up to ten in the end. Olivia stands back as Dad eases me gently into the nest. Even Finn pauses for a moment and looks up as I am lowered into the softness.

"How's that?" Dad asks.

I am held, nestled, caressed by the comforting cushions—though I can't be left alone in it in case I roll or cushions fall over me and I can't breathe.

"Is it my turn now?" Olivia asks.

"Let Jemma have some time in it first," Dad tells her. I expect her to protest.

"She does look cozy," Olivia acknowledges. I'd smile at her if I could.

My nest is so comfy, and I can feel Dad's warmth and even Olivia's too—but I'm still so sad inside. I'm missing Sarah so much, and I want my sister to come back. I want Jodi.

An hour later, I am back in my wheelchair. Olivia had a turn in the nest after me. Finn showed no interest, though I think he would be in it in a shot if no one was here. Dad has gone upstairs to check on Mom.

Finn is still lining up matchsticks, while Olivia is lining up all the dolls on the top floor of her dollhouse and then knocking them one by one out the window, saying, "*Wheeeeeee!* *Thump*—you're dead!"

I half watch her, but not closely, because my mind is elsewhere. I am thinking about Jodi. Her face is imprinted on my mind—her likeness, the connection between us. Did Jodi feel it? Maybe she did, and it was so strong it overwhelmed her. I wonder what she's doing right now, how she's feeling.

I realize after a while that I can't see Finn or Olivia. I'm not sure if they've left the room or are out of sight behind me, but then I hear an unhappy grunting sound that must be Finn.

The sound is coming from behind me. Finn suddenly lurches past.

"Get back here," Olivia says, but Finn is wriggling toward the door. He scrambles past me, hotly pursued by Olivia. She tries to grab him, but he is out of the room in a flash. Poor Finn. I want to protect him. If I could move my legs, I'd love to give Olivia a gentle sisterly kick. If I could talk, I'd ask her what's bothering her, and maybe she'd tell me, like she told me about Dylan.

Olivia holds her head up high and struts out.

As I sit alone thinking, I start to feel achy. I hope it's just the worry making this happen and that I'm not getting sick. That's all I need.

There's a sudden piercing scream from upstairs. "What's happened?" I hear Dad demanding.

"Finn head butted me with his helmet!" Olivia screeches. "I think he's cracked my head open!" She is wailing.

Maybe Finn can stand up for himself after all.

Later in the evening when Finn and Olivia are in bed, Dad wheels me into the living room. We find Mom in there, curled up in my nest, looking cozy, eating a bar of chocolate.

31

I feel wiped out, and I don't want to go to school. The bus arrives, and Sheralyn comes with me because today is swimming.

The pool is not as warm today as it should be. I float, but I don't enjoy it. I feel shivery. Last week at swimming, Sarah had only been missing a day. I was sure she'd be back when I got home. Now I'm scared she's really not coming back. I thought with the posters and Kate's campaign and the debit card that she might be found, but there's been no more news.

Back at home, the phone rings while we are eating dinner. If the phone rang during dinner, the rule used to be that no one answered it. The person could leave a message. Now that rule is constantly broken. The phone rings much more often than it did too. Dad jumps up and answers it. "Yes," he says.

Then I see the color drain from his face as he listens. I can't swallow. It's Sarah. It has to be about Sarah. Mushed carrot sits in my mouth, and a little spills out. Sheralyn doesn't notice. She's looking at Dad. We all are—apart from Finn, who is busy trying to line up the carrot sticks on his plate.

"One minute," says Dad. He gives Mom a look and goes out into the hall with the phone.

"What's happened?" Olivia demands. "Is Sarah dead? Did someone murder her? How did they do it? Was it a knife or a gun, or did they strangle her?"

"Olivia!" Mom bellows in horror. "Be quiet!"

"I want to know!" Olivia protests.

Some mushed carrot has dripped onto my pale, cream top.

I am sure I hear Dad swear out in the hall. I don't think I've ever heard him swear before. The news must be bad.

"Ooh, yuck! Look at Jemma!" Olivia cries, screwing up her face.

Sheralyn and Mom both turn to me quickly.

"Oh... Sorry, Jemma," Sheralyn says, anxiously glancing from me to Mom, who has already jumped up to grab a kitchen towel.

"Here," Mom says, passing it to Sheralyn.

Dad comes back in. He looks pale, and his eyes look deeper than usual and darker.

"What's happened?" Olivia demands. "Is Sarah dead?"

Finn bangs his head on the table.

"Should I take them upstairs?" Sheralyn asks. Finn goes with her, but Olivia refuses.

"I suppose you'll have to know sometime." Dad sighs.

"That was Kate on the phone. The police have found a body. They haven't identified it yet, but we have to prepare ourselves. They think it might be Sarah."

I feel panicked. I was half expecting this, and yet I wasn't. I wasn't at all.

Olivia begins to cry.

"It might not be her," Mom tells us.

Dad hugs Olivia, who clings to him as she sobs in his arms.

I wish someone would hug me. Then Mom touches my shoulder and turns me to face her.

"Oh, Jemma," she says gently, and she squeezes my hand. I am so grateful, so relieved that she can sense my pain.

"Where...where did they find...the body?" she asks Dad.

"In Fox Woods," Dad says. "Kate's coming tomorrow to identify her. I'm relieved that they didn't ask us to do it." I see him shudder.

Olivia pulls away from Dad, her eyes red and face wet. Dad's shirt has a big wet patch too.

Mom goes and gives Olivia a squeeze, her eyes meeting Dad's. They know they can't promise us that it will be okay.

Later, when Olivia and Finn are in bed, I hear Dad talking to Mom. He says the police told Kate the circumstances "look suspicious."

They've found a body; Dan must have killed her. However much I try to think of a different explanation, I keep coming back to it. He killed Ryan, and now he's killed Sarah. And he taunted me with it. I can rage all I want. I can hate him more than anything, but it makes no difference. He knew he could do what he wanted.

I knew all along what he was like. And now it's too late.

32

When the doorbell rings after dinner, I'm sure it's him come to taunt me again, the keeper of his secret. Mom and Dad are upstairs, so Sheralyn goes out of the living room to answer it. I hear her say, "Can I help you?"

But it's not Dan; it's Richard.

He jabbers nervously. "Is Lorraine here? I... I'm Sarah's... I don't even know what to call myself—boyfriend, friend, ex-boyfriend—one of those... Who are you?"

Olivia sneaks out into the hall to see what's going on, just as Sheralyn explains that she is taking Sarah's place as my aide.

"I'll call Lorraine. She's upstairs," Sheralyn tells him. "Lorraine! Sarah's boyfriend is here," she calls loudly.

"He's not her boyfriend... Dan is!" Olivia blurts out. "He hasn't been her boyfriend for a while! Why are you pretending to be Sarah's boyfriend?"

"I'm not pretending. It's complicated," Richard explains. He sniffs.

"Anyway, Sarah's dead!" Olivia blurts out.

There's another loud sniff and Richard tries to speak, but Olivia interrupts him. "You're crying. Men don't cry."

"Olivia! Go back in the living room," Sheralyn tells her.

"Won't!" Olivia says with her usual stubborn tone.

"Please, Olivia—now!" says Sheralyn.

"I'm just telling the truth, so why should I be punished?" Olivia protests.

It's Mom to the rescue as she comes downstairs and invites Richard through to the kitchen.

"I'm sorry to drop in like this," he says. "The police came around. They've been asking more questions..." Richard's voice disappears into the kitchen. I strain to catch anything—try to tune out all other sounds—but it's no use.

My bag needs emptying. If Sheralyn takes me to the bathroom, there's a good chance I will hear something. I want her to notice, but she is still busy arguing with Olivia.

"I'm going upstairs," Olivia says finally. She seems to expect Sheralyn to protest, but Sheralyn says nothing and Olivia storms out and up the stairs.

I see Finn's clenched hand on the sofa relax as she leaves the room.

"I'll take Jemma to the bathroom, and then I'll be back," Sheralyn tells him.

As she pushes me in and turns me, I see that she hasn't fully closed the door. I strain my ears to hear.

"We don't know for sure that it's her," says Mom.

"They think I k—" says Richard. He swallows. "They think I've done something to her. They keep asking me—am I sure she got to the door, what did I do when I got home, can anyone confirm I was there?"

"No one saw you get home, then?" Mom asks.

"I live by myself," says Richard. "Nobody saw me go into my apartment." He's babbling now as his voice chokes up. "I love Sarah so much. I'd never hurt her. I'm not like that. I'd never hurt anyone."

"I'm sure you wouldn't," says Mom. I can hear Richard crying again.

"Anyway," says Mom, "we'll have to wait until the body's been identified. The police can't have any evidence against you or they'd have arrested you, wouldn't they?"

Sheralyn is taking longer than usual. She must be eavesdropping too. Now that the conversation seems to be ending, she wheels me back quickly to the living room.

The police must be questioning Richard for a reason. Even though I want to believe him, Poirot says I should never rule anyone out.

33

The minutes crawl by the next day at school when all I can do is think about Sarah.

Kate phoned early this morning. She said she didn't think she could cope with identifying the body on her own. Mom was busy with us, so Dad said he'd go. I can totally understand her asking, but I do feel sorry for Dad. I know how he felt about it.

Sheralyn is at school and the rest of us are home now, waiting for them to come back, waiting to find out if it's her.

Olivia is not happy because she's had to miss ballet. I don't think Finn's aware enough to know he's missed his swimming lesson too. Mom has decided we should play Pairs to take our minds off things. I say *we*, but Mom and I are playing together, and Mom is mostly playing for Finn too. The cards are all laid out facedown in rows, and we take turns to pick two and see if they match. Mom is useless, which is frustrating because I have a good memory and could do much better than her if I could just pick the cards myself.

Finn is not very interested at first, but he suddenly begins to pick out matching pairs by himself. I've never seen him play a real game like this. Mom has to restrain him until it's his turn. He is beating Olivia, and I can see the tension building in her face. Finn has no interest in winning, of course. I don't think he knows what that means. He's just enjoying matching cards. Olivia will not cope well if she doesn't win, least of all if she is beaten by Finn.

Mom can see this too. She gives a brief lecture, supposedly to everyone, about winning not being everything and how not everyone can win.

Finn gets another pair. Then another. Olivia picks two cards. They match. *Phew!* She has another turn. This pair doesn't match. She throws those cards down and then kicks the rest of them so that they are all out of position.

"Olivia," Mom says sternly.

"I'm not playing this dumb game!" Olivia yells and storms out. I hear her feet thudding loudly as she thumps her way upstairs.

Mom sighs. She begins to put the cards in the box, but sees that Finn is still playing with them. He turns all the cards faceup and proceeds to match them into pairs and line them up. He is trying to make order out of the chaos.

The game had actually distracted me from thinking about Sarah, but now Mom's looking at her watch.

The doorbell rings. I see Mom jump.

Dad has his key—unless he forgot it. I wonder who it is.

I am facing the wrong way. I have to wait for a voice. "Hiya, any news?" a voice asks softly. Of course it's Sheralyn. I'm glad she's here.

As Sheralyn comes into the living room, I hear Mom's cell phone ring.

"Well?" says Mom.

It must be Dad. I wait, ears straining. "Oh, goodness," she says next.

Mom comes into the living room while Sheralyn is taking off her coat.

I see Mom's smile, but it is a small, sad smile. "It isn't her," she tells us. "The body isn't Sarah."

Mom flops down in the armchair, still clutching her phone to her ear, speaking into it. "See you soon, dear," she says.

I'm not sure if I'm crying or if my eye is just watering, but I can feel the wetness running down my cheek.

Finn stands up, looking almost as if he's going to say something. He turns and looks carefully at his lines of pairs. Every card is now matched, but one is slightly out of line. He straightens it and then claps his hands.

Has he heard what Mom said? I'm sure he has.

Sheralyn turns to Mom and then reaches out to give her a hug. Then Mom goes out into the hall, calling up the stairs for Olivia to come down.

"The body isn't Sarah," I hear Mom tell her.

"Where is she, then?" Olivia asks. "Where's Sarah? Why doesn't she come back?"

"If it turns out she's gone off somewhere on a whim," Kate says as we sit around the kitchen table with Mom and Dad later, "I will never forgive her for putting me through this—never."

That sounds weird to me. She has to be relieved that the body wasn't Sarah. But she and Dad just looked exhausted when they got back.

Kate starts to cry. "When they pulled back the sheet, I was so expecting it to be her, and then...and then..."

"It must have been awful," says Mom. She looks at Dad. I can't see his face, but his head nods slowly.

Mom goes over to Kate and puts a hand on her shoulder.

"That poor girl," says Dad. "The police don't know who she is."

Dad shudders. Mom goes over and gives him a hug. She kisses him, and he hugs her back. I can see the love between them, and it warms me inside, like the hot chocolate Mom's just made me that is the perfect temperature. People usually make it too cold because they're so worried about it being too hot!

Dad sits down and sips his coffee.

"Thank you for coming with me," Kate tells Dad. "It would have been much worse on my own. I just want to find her. I think she's alive and she's gone off somewhere to straighten her head out."

"I hope you're right," says Mom.

Soon after Kate leaves, I hear a sudden sobbing sound. It's Mom crying. I think she still blames herself for Sarah going missing.

Poor Mom. I wish I could comfort her and tell her it's not her fault.

And I need her to stay strong. If Mom goes to pieces, she might decide she can't look after us anymore. Then what would happen?

34

Mom's resting upstairs, and Dad and Sheralyn are looking after us. It's evening now, and Dan stands awkwardly in the hallway. Dad was wheeling me out of the living room when the doorbell rang, so I'm facing into the hall, wondering what Dan is doing here.

"I heard about the body they found," he says. "Thank God it wasn't her."

"Yes, Dan, it's a huge relief," Dad agrees.

"So there's no news at all—no more sightings or anything?" Dan asks.

There's something intense about the way he's asking this.

"No, nothing." Dad sighs.

I give an involuntary grunt, and Dad glances back toward me. "If only Jemma could speak," he says. "I often wonder what she'd be able to tell us."

"Yeah... I bet she knows all sorts of things," says Dan. He meets my eyes with a stare that makes me shudder.

Dad nods. "Lorraine took her to a specialist who thinks there might be a way for Jemma to communicate, but we've got to wait to be able to try it."

"Really?" There's a distinct edge to Dan's voice. His eyes flick over to me again. He watches me, and something clouds his expression. His lip twitches as if he is about to say something.

"Is there anything else?" Dad asks.

"No, no, I'll let you get back to what you were doing. I hope you don't mind me stopping by. It's just... I'm finding it tough, all this, you know."

"I'm sure you are. We all are," says Dad as he walks Dan out.

Dad comes back, sighing, and pushes me into the living room. I realize I must have been holding my breath because it all comes out in a rush. Dan's face when he found out about the specialist. He looked like he was suddenly seeing me differently. Like I might not be so powerless after all. He already wanted me out of the way. If he thinks I could tell his secret, what will he do?

The next morning there is something else for Mom to worry about—me. Maybe it's just exhaustion after everything with Jodi and the body and what Dad told Dan, but my back's aching again, and I worry it's another infection. I'm not sick enough to go to the hospital, thank goodness, but my temperature's up and I am too sick to go to school.

I think I'd rather be at school, to be honest, because I

don't want to be a strain on Mom, and at least at school there would be other things to think about. Here I can only think about Dan and Sarah and Jodi. I keep imagining Dan waiting outside the house. Figuring out when he could get me alone. I'm scared of Dan, and I'm scared I will never see Sarah or Jodi again.

I'm in bed. Mom checks me every ten minutes and takes my temperature. If it gets too high, I will have to go to the hospital. Every part of my body aches.

"I'm so sorry, Jemma." Mom sighs. "Life's the pits at the moment, isn't it?"

She's right. I feel so low—the lowest I can remember feeling. There's no point to anything anymore. I used to be content to watch, but now I don't like anything I'm seeing. Not being able to tell what I know is unbearable. I can do nothing, and Dan is running around free. I'm a complete waste of space. I'm a burden to everyone. I can't tell anyone about Dan. I couldn't protect Sarah. My own sister wanted to know me until she actually saw me, and then she changed her mind. What is the point of me being alive?

I feel so achy, so weak. They'll have to send me to the hospital soon.

Then I have a thought—a ludicrous thought. That would be Dan's chance, wouldn't it? That was how he got me on my own before. If Dan killed me and got caught, then they'd figure it all out.

I feel a weird elation, and my heartbeat races.

Maybe all these thoughts have finally made me crazy.

I'm getting hot and sticky. Mom takes my temperature again. She tuts. "It's too high, Jemma. This is no good. I'm going to call the hospital."

On this trip to the hospital I am aware of everything—every corner turned, every bump in the road. I don't want to live anymore. Not having a sister was okay. Having one but not seeing her is horrible. It was bad enough not being able to communicate, but having something I desperately need to say and not being able to say it is too much to take.

———

I am woken by a cough, a man's cough. It's not Dad. I'd recognize Dad's cough. I'm in the hospital—I can smell the disinfectant. There's a man standing close to me. Is it Dan? Has he come already? I can't see. I am facing the wrong way, but I can't see anyway. I try to focus, but my vision is blurry.

Right now I want Mom. *I want Mom!* A hand squeezes mine. It is a warm, soft hand.

"It's okay, Jemma. I'm here," Mom says gently.

"Ah, Jemma, you're awake" comes a man's voice from the other side of the bed. He has a strong accent. It's definitely not Dan.

"I'm Doctor Sargent," the voice continues. He speaks

slowly and loudly, as if I might not understand. Mom turns my head so that I can see a blurry white coat. The doctor is leaning over me. "You're doing poorly," he continues as if I don't know that, "and we've had to give you some medicine. Don't worry if your vision is a little fuzzy. It's a side effect, but it should settle down."

I am relieved to have an explanation for the blurriness.

Mom stays a long time, and I don't know how long she's been here already. I sleep and wake and sleep and wake, and she's still here. Now I wake and think she's gone, because I can't feel her hand, but I hear a snorting sound and then another. Mom's hand has slipped from mine, and she's actually asleep. She's snoring. Poor Mom. This is too much for her.

Dad comes eventually and takes over. Then Sheralyn for a while. They rotate. I mainly sleep. I dream about Dan.

"If I were you, I'd kill myself. Listen, if you ever want a little help, I could—"

In my dream I am able to nod, and then he is holding a pillow. It is coming down toward my face. I think, *This is it. This is the end.*

35

I've been here overnight. I know I will have to wait for Dan to find out I'm here, but I'm sure it won't take him long. Someone else comes—someone I'm not expecting.

It's Paula.

"This is so kind of you," Mom tells her. "I wouldn't leave Jemma with someone she doesn't know—but you know Paula well enough, don't you?" Mom looks at me and squeezes my hand. "It's just for a while. I have to go to Olivia's school."

I wonder briefly what's happened with Olivia. Has she hit someone else? Then my thoughts turn to Paula. My vision is clear again now, thank goodness. Paula's chunky-knit sweater does not disguise how thin she's getting. Her cheekbones are almost poking out of her face, and her hands look so bony there is barely any flesh on them. I hope she's not going to hold my hand. She shifts from one foot to the other anxiously.

It's taken courage to offer to do this, and I admire her for that, but I'm not sure I want her here. Actually, I'm sure I don't.

"It's no bother at all," Paula tells Mom. "You've been so kind to us. I'm glad to be able to do something for you."

"I've brought a book, if you feel like reading it to her," Mom tells Paula.

Paula nods.

Then Mom leaves.

Paula picks up the book and turns it over. I realize at once that she's not going to want to read it. It's not the vampire romance, though I'm not sure Paula would like that much either. It's a murder mystery! I hope she doesn't think Mom is too insensitive for suggesting it. Paula sighs and puts it down.

"Your mom says you understand everything, so I'm sure you do. I wish they'd catch Ryan's killer. I want to know what happened and why, and I want whoever did it locked up. Is that too much to ask, Jemma?"

She sounds like she's caught in a loop, like she's said the words so many times. I wish I could speak to her. I could change things.

"Between you and me, there's something I haven't told the police, Jemma, and I don't know what to do," she continues, leaning forward and speaking quietly. I had slightly lost concentration as she rambled on, but now I am alert.

"Before it happened," Paula tells me, "Ryan asked me to hide some stuff for him. I know I shouldn't have. I should've at least asked what was going on, but he clearly didn't want to tell me. I know I was stupid, but I did what he asked. I wanted to keep him out of trouble."

She pauses, and I want to ask, "What stuff?"

She edges even closer, and her voice is lower, almost a whisper. "It was jewelry, Jemma—diamond rings, gold necklaces—and I think Ryan might have stolen them," she says. "I didn't want the police to know he was a thief. They already knew he was a drug user. They might have written him off, not bothered to look for his killer. So I hid the things. I'm sure I shouldn't have, but I promised him and I hid them— and when the police came looking for clues, I didn't tell them. I couldn't cope with Graham finding out what I'd done, and I didn't want to get myself in trouble too."

I watch Paula. Her eyes look straight through me as if I'm not even here, and she's constantly rubbing her fingers together as she talks. It reminds me of Dan when Mom said the police were looking for him. It looks as if this guilt has been eating her up.

"It didn't occur to me at the time, but now I'm worried that the stuff belonged to the person who killed Ryan. What do you think, Jemma? I wish you could tell me. I bet you could figure it out better than me."

Maybe I *could* figure it out. I need to think...

"The thing is, I don't know what to do now," Paula continues, sighing. "Should I go to the police and tell them?

I'm scared I might get arrested for withholding evidence. I could say I just found them, but the police did such a thorough search, they might not believe me. How will Graham cope if I get thrown in prison? That's why I haven't even told him."

Paula suddenly sits up straighter. "I'm sorry, Jemma. I shouldn't be talking to you about this, should I? It's terrible of me. You're sick. You don't want to hear about Ryan—especially when you have Sarah to worry about too. Let's talk about something else."

But she clearly can't think of anything. She glances briefly at the book, but I can see she can't face picking it up. So we sit silently and she twiddles her thumbs.

I think about Ryan. I didn't know him well, but it sounds likely that he did steal the things Paula found. Why would someone kill him for that? Maybe he owed money for the drugs, and he stole the things intending to sell them. Could there be any link with Dan and Sarah? Maybe Ryan stole the jewelry from Dan, and that's why Dan killed him. Then Sarah found out, and he had to kill her too. The black jacket comes into my head. Could Graham have been involved? Could he have found the jewelry and confronted Ryan? Or could Graham have stolen it and Ryan found out? Then I remember Dan's face when Dad said I might be able to communicate.

Paula's phone beeps, and she pulls it from her bag in relief and continues to look at it, touching different areas of the screen for what feels like a long time.

36

Sheralyn takes over from Paula, and Mom comes back after lunch. I'm not feeling much better. I feel so, so tired.

Mom smiles as she sits down, and I notice she has big bags under her eyes. I want her here—but I also wish she could go home and get some sleep.

"I'm sorry I couldn't be here," she says. "I hope you were okay with Paula. Olivia's getting herself into all sorts of trouble at school." Mom is digging around in her bag as she speaks. "I've persuaded them to give her another chance, but I'm not sure she'll be able to stay there if she keeps starting fights. More parents have been complaining."

Mom's bag is bulging. An old shopping list, a pen, and a lipstick fly out, and she hastily retrieves them from the floor.

I hope Olivia isn't going to get herself thrown out of her school. I wonder what she did. I wish I could tell Mom what Olivia told me about Dylan.

"Here it is," Mom says finally.

It's a letter. I see right away that it is Jodi's writing on the front. My heart starts thudding, and my stomach churns. I don't know what to expect or how to feel. Jodi has written—but what has she said?

"I hope you don't mind that I opened it first," Mom says. "I didn't want to bring it if it was going to upset you. Not with you being so sick."

Mom pulls the letter out of the envelope.

Dear Jemma,

It's really hard to write this, but I hate thinking how upset you must be with me. I'll understand if you hate me and never want to see me again. I want you to know, though, that's not how I feel about you.

I want to explain what happened—or try to at least. I think I had a kind of image of you in my head, and I guess you didn't look anything like I was expecting. I know your mom sent a photo, but until I saw you, I had no idea how much you looked like me. I know we're twins, but I just wasn't expecting it for some reason. You must have seen that too. We are so alike!

You also—this sounds really bad, but I want to be honest—you look much more disabled than I expected. I knew you were in a wheelchair and that you can't speak, but it was a shock to see you.

I flinch as Mom reads this. She's referring to the strange shape of my head, my gaping mouth. I don't want to be a shock to look at, but there's not much I can do about that.

Mom continues.

I thought I'd just be able to start talking. I had so much I wanted to say that I wasn't worried about you not talking back. I'm quite a blabbermouth usually! No one else can get a word in. So I thought I would be okay.

I froze up, Jemma, and everything I wanted to say went out of my head. I felt so stupid standing there unable to speak. I don't know where the tears came from, but once I started, I couldn't stop, and I felt even worse so I had to just get out of there.

I want you to know that I do want to try again. You are my sister, and I want to know you and for you to know me.

Please, please forgive me, and let's start over— please!

Love, Jodi

My sister still wants to know me.

The warm feeling spreads through my body. I can even feel it in my legs and arms, and I can't feel much there usually.

"I can see that's brought some color back to your face!"

Mom exclaims. She strokes my cheek gently and touches my forehead. "Yes, it's not fever—just a healthy glow."

"When can I see her again?" I want to ask Mom.

She doesn't tell me, but I will forgive her for that because I am so happy about the letter. I wish I could hold it, smell it, keep it. I don't want Mom to fold it and put it in her bag. I wish she'd stick it on the wall beside my bed so I can look at it and read it over and over.

I try to remember the words as Mom puts her bag back on the floor.

You are my sister, and I want to know you.

That is all I need. I say it over and over in my head. From her to me, and me to her. I feel it. I live it. I don't want to die. I don't want Dan to kill me anymore, even if it would help the police catch him.

I feel the strength returning to my body all day.

I want to see Jodi. I need to get well.

37

Mom calls Jodi and arranges for us to meet her on Sunday.
It's only two days to wait, but once I'm home, all I can think
about is Sarah. Her absence is like a wide-open window
through which a cold breeze constantly blows. I cannot feel
warm and safe and happy, even knowing I will soon meet my
sister again. What has happened to Sarah?

Mom still looks stressed out—and worse, she says Sheralyn
has a bad cold and won't be able to help for a few days.

After dinner, Finn and Olivia go upstairs. Dad's not back
yet because he has a late meeting at work. Mom pushes me
out of the kitchen, saying she'll turn the TV on for me while
she gets them ready for bed. As we reach the living room, the
phone rings.

"Back in a minute," she tells me, sighing, and rushes off
without even turning the light on, let alone the TV. I expect
her to pick up the phone in the hallway and bring it back in

here, but she must have taken it into the kitchen because her voice gets more distant.

She must be speaking quietly. I can't hear what she's saying or figure out who she's talking to. I hear the phone click, but it rings again almost immediately. I only hear "yes," "no," and "I should think so." Then "I'll let you know if I hear anything."

I can't believe Mom has left me here in the dark. I'm trying to hear her, but I get a sudden sense of someone behind me. I can hear breathing—loud breathing—as if someone is panting by the living-room door. My heart races. I'm not imagining it. Someone's here.

Has Dan gotten in? Was he waiting outside? He didn't come to the hospital, but he's here now! He's used Sarah's key to get in. He could have been in the house for hours—just waiting for the right moment.

The breathing is coming nearer.

"Mom!" I want to scream. "Get off the phone! Get in here now!"

He is right behind me. I feel my wheelchair jolt.

What is he going to do?

My chair jolts again. The breathing is still close, but... What's happened? The sound of breathing is right underneath me—under my chair!

There is a *bang*, *bang* against the right wheel. I suddenly realize it's Finn! Finn is under my chair, panting and banging his head against one of the wheels. I try to steady my breathing.

This whole Sarah thing must be affecting him badly. He's under my chair, wanting me to keep him safe, to make everything okay. He is trying to tell me how bad he feels. I wish I could do something—make everything better. I wish I could bring Sarah back.

At last I hear Mom's footsteps. But she doesn't come in. I hear her feet thump, thump up the stairs. She thinks Finn's up there. She's forgotten about me altogether.

She's gone up. Finn's breathing has slowed down, but I can still hear it. Mom's feet are soon on the stairs again because she hasn't found Finn.

"Finn! Finn, dear! Are you down here?"

She approaches the living room and turns the light on. She gasps.

"Jemma!" As she comes around in front of me, I am shocked to see she is sobbing. Tears are rolling down her cheeks. "I've left you here in the dark! I completely forgot! I'm so sorry. I'm so sorry, Jemma. I'm losing it. And I can't find Finn."

She collapses on the sofa, crying. I can't stand to see Mom like this. If Mom falls apart, Social Services will take us all away. It's a terrifying thought. She has to get it together. She can't let that happen!

At that moment, I hear Dad's key in the door.

He hears her sobbing and is by her side in seconds. "What's happened?" he asks softly. "Have they found her?"

"No, no—it's not Sarah, it's Jemma. I forgot her," Mom

sobs. "I left her in the dark when the phone rang. I left her in the dark for about twenty minutes! And I can't find Finn!"

Dad sees him right away. "That's easy, dear. Look, he's under Jemma's chair!"

"My God," Mom exclaims. "Finn, what are you doing there?"

Finn doesn't come out.

"If Sheralyn can't help, we've got to get the agency to send another aide," Dad says.

"Other families have to get by without aides," says Mom.

"Yes," says Dad, "but we wouldn't have taken on the other two if we didn't have help with Jemma."

"I didn't want to get someone else. Sarah... I thought she'd be back," says Mom, wiping her eyes with her sleeve.

"I'm sure she will," says Dad, though he doesn't sound convincing. "But in the meantime we need someone."

38

Dad has ordered Mom to take it easy, and the agency aide arrives after breakfast. She is smiley and bubbly, although her voice is a little loud.

"Hey, this must be Jemma!" she says.

"This is Rosie," Mom tells me.

"I can see we both like purple!" Rosie says, beaming at me. She points to my cardigan and her purple top. "We're going to get along just fine!"

Sarah chose that purple cardigan for me. I feel a pang.

Mom smiles at Rosie. "That's great. I'm so glad you could come so quickly," she says. "Let me tell you a little about Jemma."

"It's okay," says Rosie. "The agency filled me in. And I have lots of experience. You can leave us to get to know each other."

"Good," says Mom. "Just call me if there's anything you need."

There's an awkward silence as Mom heads off upstairs.

"I hear you like books," Rosie says. "I thought I could read to you, okay?"

I am relieved, although she's speaking strangely—not like she was with Mom.

She goes to her big purple backpack, which is on the sofa. "I always carry books with me!" she says. "Hang on a second—let me see what you might like."

I wish she'd just get the book that's on my nightstand, the one Mom's reading to me.

"Hey, this is a great one!" says Rosie. The singsong enthusiasm in her voice is already getting to me, but I will give her a chance. I look to see what book she's holding. The size of it and the brightly colored cover make me swallow hard. It's a fairy-tale picture book. *The Little Mermaid.*

This has to be a joke. No—she's wheeling me close to the sofa so she can sit beside me.

"I know you'll want to see the pictures!" she tells me, holding the book so it rests on my lap.

No one has told her I have a brain. She also hasn't thought to ask. I hope Mom will look in soon to see how she's doing and set her straight.

Mom doesn't come. I have to endure *The Little Mermaid* read in a patronizing voice with every picture pointed out. "Look, there's the mermaid!" "Look, there's a crab!" I don't even like the story of *The Little Mermaid.* Finally, it's over. "Do you like music?" Rosie asks me.

"I bet you do! I've brought some with me, specially." This sounds encouraging—though if it is Glowlight, I won't be able to stand it.

She pulls out her phone and swipes a few times. "Here we go!" I listen as the music begins. It's a baby song—"The Wheels on the Bus." This is utter humiliation. I am not a toddler in a teenage body; I am an actual teenager. I am sixteen!

She begins to wheel me around with dance-like movements, jerking me uncomfortably and singing along.

This is a nightmare.

Then I hear a laugh. It is a raucous, jeering kind of laugh. As I am spun around, I see Olivia standing in the doorway, laughing hysterically. The humiliation can't get any worse.

"Hey, do you want to join us?" Rosie asks her. "We're having a great time here!"

"You might be," says Olivia. "I don't think *she* is."

"No?" Rosie stops still. She turns me around to face her and looks at me closely. "It's hard to tell," she admits.

"She's not stupid," Olivia says.

"Of course not," says Rosie. "But she—"

"She's sixteen. She likes teenager stuff, not baby stuff."

"Thank you, Olivia!" I want to shout.

"Are you sure?" Rosie asks. "I thought bright colors and simple rhymes would be the right thing. I mean, how do you know what she likes or what she's thinking when she can't speak?"

"I just know," says Olivia. "I know lots of stuff, actually. I like teenage stuff too. I almost am a teenager."

"Really?" Rosie is looking more and more uncomfortable. "So how old are you?"

"Nine," Olivia says, "but I'll be a teenager in only four years. I know tons of things that teenagers know—tons."

"Okay," says Rosie. "So what do you suggest we do? What would you and Jemma—you teenagers—like to do now?"

Olivia looks thoughtful. I wonder what she's going to come up with.

"Watch TV?" she says. "We can watch *Fuzz Heads*. There's this really hot boy on it."

"Hot boy?" Rosie repeats, wide-eyed. "I'm not sure..."

"Mom lets me watch it. Even Finn watches it, and he's six," says Olivia.

"I'm not sure your mom will be happy to pay me to sit and watch TV," Rosie says doubtfully.

"I'm sure she will," says Olivia. "I promise you."

I don't like *Fuzz Heads*, but I am begging Rosie to agree.

"Okay—just for a few minutes," Rosie says.

"Yay!" says Olivia, plunking herself on the sofa.

When Mom comes down with Finn, I can see from her expression that she is not pleased we are watching TV.

"I read to Jemma and played her some music," Rosie assures Mom.

"Yeah—she put on nursery rhymes!" says Olivia.

"Nursery rhymes?" Mom exclaims. "Why would you do that?"

"I didn't know…" Rosie says. "I thought—"

"No, you didn't think!" Mom yells.

I am shocked to hear Mom raise her voice like this. It is so unlike her.

"You have to leave. Now," Mom tells her, pointing to the door. "Jemma is an intelligent young woman, and I cannot imagine how she felt. This is outrageous."

"I'm so, so sorry," Rosie says, her singsong voice gone and a feeble whisper coming out. "I really didn't mean—"

"Just go," says Mom.

Although I don't particularly like Rosie, I actually feel sorry for her in that moment—and surprised at Mom reacting so strongly. I'd have expected Mom to be upset and to explain, but I thought she'd give Rosie a second chance.

Once Rosie is gone, I see Mom grab a chocolate bar from between two books on the shelf and wolf it down.

After dinner, there's a call from Kate. Dad answers, and he looks shocked when he comes back into the kitchen.

"They arrested Richard yesterday," Dad tells us. "They've been questioning him, and they've applied for permission to hold him longer."

"*Richard?*" Mom says. "He seemed so nice and so genuinely upset when we told him she was missing."

"He was kind of a mess, if you ask me," said Dad. "I'm still surprised, though."

The police have the wrong man! I am sure of it. And while they're busy questioning Richard, they won't be thinking about Dan.

39

Last night I dreamed that Sarah came back—walked through the door as if nothing had happened. She said she'd lost her memory, and she had no idea where she'd been for the last few weeks. She put me to bed as usual and turned me in the night. She was smiling like she always did, and I knew that everything was going to go back to normal. Everything was going to be okay.

I woke this morning and had that sinking feeling I always get when I realize Sarah is still missing. I don't think everything is ever going to be normal again. Then I remember that today is not a normal day, not even a "normal without Sarah" day. Today I am meeting Jodi. I'm trying to wipe that first meeting out of my mind and just think about her last letter. The same thing can't happen again, I'm sure. This time we are meeting in a café. My social worker, Beth, and Donna, the social worker who came to support Jodi last time, are going to be there too.

The waiting was so awful last time that Mom has decided we should be a few minutes late in the hope that Jodi will already be there. Either that or we are just running late anyway!

Mom maneuvers my wheelchair into the café. It's big inside and not busy. I see Jodi with Donna and Beth, at a spacious table in the corner. She's here. My stomach wobbles. Donna sees us and jumps up to move chairs so I can get near the table.

"Hi, Jemma. Come and join us. Come and meet Jodi for real this time," she says.

Jodi gives me a quick smile and then turns away awkwardly. She looks stiff and terrified. I wonder if she is going to run off again.

Everyone says hello. Beth hugs me—I haven't seen her for a while. She looks from me to Jodi and smiles, talking in her low, soothing voice. "I feel quite emotional seeing you together. You can certainly tell that you're twins! I can imagine what a big deal this must be for both of you."

"I'm so glad you decided to come," Mom says to Jodi.

"It was hard." Jodi nods. "I was just...overwhelmed."

She looks quickly at me and back to Mom. "I hope she doesn't mind me saying that?"

I wish so much that I could smile at her, reassure her, tell her it's fine. It's enough that she's here.

"Don't worry so much," Donna tells her. "You'll be fine."

"I don't know what to say," Jodi continues, giving me

another brief, awkward glance. She fidgets anxiously on her chair. "Like last time, I could think of all sorts of stuff to talk about before I got here, but now here I am, and it feels so much harder…"

"You're getting yourself worked up," says Donna. "Don't upset yourself. Just start talking."

Jodi's face crumples. She looks even more like me for a moment. She's going to lose her nerve. I can see it in her eyes. She's going to get up and leave.

"Why don't you come closer and hold Jemma's hand?" Beth suggests. "I think Jemma would love that, and you don't need to talk at all unless you want to."

Jodi's shoulders seem to relax. She smiles gratefully at Beth, stands up, and moves her chair closer to mine.

She looks at me, her eyes still frightened, but there is warmth in them. I can see it. I can feel it.

"I'd like to hold your hand, Jemma," she tells me.

She touches, and then she squeezes gently. Her hand is soft and smooth and warm. It is the same size as mine, although mine is bony and clenched.

I feel a weird sense of connectedness. It is different from anyone else who has ever held my hand. This is my sister, my twin.

A waitress comes and takes our order for drinks. Jodi orders a smoothie, and Mom orders me an apple juice, asking for a straw.

Jodi says nothing, but I don't mind. Mom was right. I want her to talk at some point—I want to know all about her—but right now it is enough that my sister is holding my hand.

40

"What are your hobbies?" Beth prompts Jodi. "Maybe you could tell Jemma about them."

I'm so glad Beth's here. Donna is nice, but Beth's calmness and suggestions are definitely helping.

"Oh...well..." says Jodi. "I told Jemma some stuff already in my letters... I like reading." She starts off looking at Beth and then at Mom. "My favorite authors are John Green and Suzanne Collins. I've been reading *Paper Towns*. It's about a guy who goes on a road trip to find a girl. It's amazing."

"We read to Jemma a lot," Mom tells Jodi. "We'll have to look for that book."

"I can lend it to you," says Jodi.

"That would be wonderful," says Mom. "Maybe you could even read some to Jemma yourself?"

Jodi's face lights up. "Yes—I'd love to!"

I like the sound of the book. It's not the kind of thing I usually listen to, but I'd love Jodi to read it to me.

"I like sports too," Jodi continues. She's still talking mainly to Mom, but I can forgive her because at least she is talking now.

"I play field hockey at school. Maybe you could bring Jemma and come and watch one day."

I know nothing about field hockey, but watching Jodi play would be really cool. If I wasn't disabled, would I have been athletic too? It's not something I've ever thought about.

"That's great," says Mom. "I'm sure Jemma would love to."

The waitress comes at that moment with our drinks. "Do you want to give Jemma her drink?" Mom asks Jodi.

Jodi frowns. "No, I...I don't know. I don't want to spill it down her or something."

"Don't worry. Just watch me," Mom tells her. Jodi lets go of my hand, and Mom comes closer, pushing the straw carefully into my mouth.

"I could hold the glass now, if you like," says Jodi.

Mom passes it to her.

Jodi's face is close, very close to mine. I like that she's giving me my drink, the way she's focusing every ounce of her attention on me.

Mom slides her chair a little farther away and begins to chat to Beth and Donna.

"I'll tell you something else I like," Jodi says, putting my glass down carefully on the table. She clasps my hand in hers and continues. "Do you want to know my favorite band?"

For the first time, she is talking directly to me and not partly through Mom.

"I totally love Glowlight," she continues. "Have you heard of them?"

My heart almost stops beating. She loves Glowlight, just like me. And Sarah—poor Sarah. I wish I could speak. I wish I could tell Jodi all about the concert, about Sarah going missing.

"I wanted to go to their last concert a few weeks back, but I couldn't get tickets. I'd love to see them live one day."

She is still talking. Now that she's started, she can't stop. She's telling me about other bands she likes, some I've heard of and some I haven't—but I am thinking only of Glowlight. I can hear their lyrics in my head.

"Should I tell you more about me?" she says.

"Yes!" I want to say.

"So, I was adopted when I was eight months old, but I've always known. Maybe you've been wondering why my mom and dad didn't adopt you too," Jodi says anxiously.

"Don't worry, that's pretty obvious," I want to tell her.

"I think it's because we had different needs. That's right, isn't it, Donna?"

"Sorry—what?" Donna says. She's been talking with the others and not listening in, which pleases me.

Jodi repeats her question.

"Yes, Jemma. Jodi's parents never met you. You went to separate foster homes because your needs were very specialized. People who want to take in children who need special care like you need special skills—like your mom." She smiles at Mom. "You both have parents who love you. That's what matters, isn't it?"

I wish we had been able to stay together, though I realize what she's getting at. If we had, no one would have adopted both of us. At least on her own, Jodi had a good chance. And Mom and Dad are long-term foster parents, so it's not really different from being adopted. I couldn't ask for better parents than them.

"I think it's awful that we were split up," Jodi says to me. "My mom said the social worker told them they should tell me about you, but they decided not to. She said she realizes now they did the wrong thing. Anyway, I bet there's tons you want to ask me and tell me! I can't imagine how frustrating it must be not being able to speak. I think I'd lose my mind. I mean, I'm not saying you have, or that you're crazy or anything. You know that, don't you? I just mean it must be hard. I hope they get something figured out for you soon."

But she's right. I feel like I *am* going crazy inside—and she doesn't know half of what I need to say.

Mom stands up and comes nearer. "How's it going?" she asks.

"Great," says Jodi. "Thank you so much for giving me another chance." Jodi is reaching into her bag. She pulls out her phone. "Can you take a picture of us?"

"What a great idea!" says Mom. "I'm sure Jemma would like one too. I'll take one with my phone."

Jodi pulls her chair around beside mine, clutching my hand. Mom clicks away. I am delighted. I will have a photo of me and Jodi. I hope Mom will put it by my bed. I'm sure she will.

———————

It's horrible saying goodbye to Jodi, and I want them to arrange another day to meet, but Jodi says we will and I believe her. And there is another nice surprise when I get home. Sheralyn's back. She's feeling better, thank goodness, and Mom is still looking so tired. Sheralyn isn't Sarah, but she's a great improvement over Rosie. Sheralyn reads to me. She has a nice reading voice, but she's not as good as Sarah. Sarah gave each character a different voice, and she read with such expression that I used to wonder if she'd ever tried acting.

I think she would have been good.

Mom printed the photo of Jodi and me, and now it is by my bed. I thought it might bother me that Jodi is beautiful and I am not, but when I look at the picture, all I see is the likeness. She is what I was meant to be—what I really am inside. Seeing her, I feel as if I am that beautiful. It makes me feel stronger. It's hard to explain, but I never imagined before that if I wasn't disabled, I might have looked so pretty. Now I can imagine it, and instead of feeling sad that I am not the same as her, I feel happy. I almost look as if I am smiling in the picture, and Jodi is definitely smiling.

Olivia comes to look at it.

"I wish I had a sister," she says.

I feel sorry for her. I want to say, "But I'm your sister, Olivia. We're a family—you, me, Finn, Mom, and Dad."

Olivia picks up the picture and holds it close to her eyes. I want her to put it back. I feel protective of it, and I'm scared she's going to scrunch it or even tear it.

Sheralyn comes in.

"Maybe I've got a sister too, like Jemma," Olivia says.

"Maybe," says Sheralyn. She sounds doubtful.

"Can you find out?" Olivia demands. "I want to know."

"I'll ask your mom," says Sheralyn, "but I think someone would have told you if you have a sister."

Olivia puts the photo on my nightstand, but she's laid it down flat so I can't see it. I panic. I feel an urgent need to see it, to keep it visible—as if Jodi might cease to exist or cease to be my sister if I can't see the picture of the two of us. I might wake and find it was all a dream. Sheralyn is my lifesaver. She notices and stands the picture up for me.

"Come on, Olivia—off to bed now," says Sheralyn.

41

I've been on a high since meeting Jodi. I enjoyed swimming at school yesterday, especially because the water was warmer than last week. Then in the changing rooms I overheard my teacher asking Sheralyn if there was any news about my aide, and I felt pangs of guilt. How can I even be happy for a second when Sarah is still missing? Last night I heard Dad tell Mom that Richard has been released, and I'm relieved about that, though Kate still thinks he did it. She thinks they just didn't have enough evidence to charge him. Everyone's so focused on Richard that they're missing the truth. They're not thinking about Dan.

Today, Sheralyn's gone to school. I'm ready for school, but my bus hasn't shown up. Mom phones and discovers it has broken down.

Finn's ride came, and luckily Dad was still here so he's taken Olivia. Mom says she'll take me to school herself.

She is pushing me out the front door when the phone rings

inside. She sighs, pulling me back a little and then pushing me forward. I can't see her face, of course, but I can tell she's not sure whether to take the call or not.

She pulls me jerkily back inside, and I hear her footsteps down the hall—running to pick up the phone. "Oh!" Mom sounds like she's walking toward the front door. There is real surprise in her voice, so much so that I actually wonder for an instant if it is Sarah herself calling.

"I wasn't expecting to hear from you. We got your letter, of course, but July... It's so far away..."

Professor Spalding! Why is he phoning?

"Really?" I hear Mom say. "Is he? When would that be?" There's a long pause. It seems to go on forever. Then finally she says, "Yes, I'm sure that would be fine." And there's silence again, but I can hear that she's taking notes.

A few minutes later, Mom is back, pushing me out the door again.

"Well, it's good I took that call, Jemma," she says. "The researcher from Israel who has created the sniffing technology decided at short notice to come to a conference here this week, and Professor Spalding says he wants to meet you."

What? I can't believe this. He's actually here?

"Mr. Katz would like to try his sniffing equipment with you. He wants us to meet him tomorrow!"

The waiting room at the University Hospital for Neurology and Neurosurgery is big and busy. Hospitals to me always mean long waits. Mom gets a coffee from the machine, so she is clearly thinking the same.

"I don't want you to get your hopes up too high, Jemma," Mom says quietly. "If this doesn't work, don't worry. We'll keep trying until we find a way. Technology is developing and changing so fast."

From a look at her face, I can see the hope in her eyes. I heard the high-pitched excitement in her voice after she hung up the phone yesterday. She does believe it; I'm sure she does. But do I? What if I can't do it, or I can't master it quickly enough and they decide it won't work? Will they give me a chance to practice?

Nurses with lists have been calling people, but then I see a man in a suit with dark hair, tanned skin, and a beard come into the waiting room and look around.

He spots me. I see his eyes stop and his bushy eyebrows go up. He walks confidently toward us.

"Jemma Shaw?" he asks, looking at me and then Mom. He has a strong accent and a serious expression. I wish he'd smile. Maybe he doesn't think this will work either.

Mom stands up quickly and introduces us.

"Alon Katz," the man says, nodding at each of us and then holding his hand out to Mom. "Please follow me," he tells us.

He heads off through the double doors and along a corridor, into a small room.

"I am sorry it is a little tight for space in here," he says as Mom awkwardly parks me between a chair and a desk.

She sits down on the chair beside me and squeezes my hand as Mr. Katz picks up glasses from the desk and puts them on. In front of him is what looks like a thin plastic tube with some pieces sticking out of it.

"This is it," he tells us. "This is the sniff controller. It is still in the research phase, you understand. We have had success using this equipment with patients suffering paralysis following accidents, even with some who were thought to be in a vegetative state. We have not tried it on someone with cerebral palsy, and my colleague Professor Spalding thought you would be an interesting case for me."

I can't see Mom's face, but I wonder if she is as surprised as I am. I expected some complicated machine or something— not just a plastic tube.

"We attach this with these sensors just inside the nostril," he explains. "The other end can be attached to whatever a person is trying to control—a computer, a communication device, even the movement of a wheelchair."

"Really?" says Mom. "It looks so...simple."

I see what I am sure is a slight smile behind the beard of Mr. Katz.

"First, I will check your ability to control your sniffs,"

he says, approaching me. He has the tube in his hand. "This won't hurt," he tells me, "but it may feel a little odd at first, having something in your nose. The sensor is tiny, though."

He leans very close into my face. I can feel his breath, hot against my cheeks. One hand is on my chin, holding my head steady. I wish my head would stop pulling away from him. He might think I'm objecting, but it's just my body not behaving. I want to try this. I really do.

He stands back. My nose does feel strange—a little tickly. I hope I don't sneeze the thing out.

"We will attach it to this computer," says Mr. Katz, fiddling with the other end of the tube. "Now, you see this on the screen? This line here will move when you sniff. Try a small sniff, Jemma—in through your nose."

Oh, marvelous. I feel so nervous I think I've forgotten how to sniff!

"In through your nose," he repeats gently.

I must. I can do it. He must see I can do it. I sniff. The green line bounces on the screen. *I did it!* I made that happen. I do it again, even though he hasn't told me to. I want to see the line move.

"Good...good," he says slowly. "Now try a bigger sniff."

I do it—and right away the line soars up the screen.

"There." He grins, and I think this is the moment he is sure. The little sniffs might have been accidental, but this time he knows it is for real.

"Another big one, please," he asks. The line soars again.

"Now a small one."

This is easy. I can do this—I really can. I can make things happen!

I practice this a little more, and then Mr. Katz presses a few keys on the keyboard. The screen with the line disappears. I feel disappointed. I could have kept doing that all day. I was making the line move. I was doing it myself. I don't want to stop now.

There is something else on the screen.

"On this screen you will see two words," he tells me. "YES on one side on the green background and NO on the other side on the red."

He points to the words. I want to say, "I can read. I don't need you to point," but I try to stay calm.

"You will see the cursor here is constantly moving from one word to the other, every few seconds? I will ask you a question. You will sniff when the cursor is on the answer you wish to give. Okay? Big sniff when the cursor is where you want it."

This is my chance to communicate. *This is it!* What is he going to ask me?

"Do I have a beard?"

What?

It takes me a moment to take his question in. He is very still. So is Mom. I can hear them both breathing. I must stay calm. I can do this. I already know I can.

I wait for the cursor to move. I do a big sniff.

"YES," says a loud woman's voice.

I lurch inside. I didn't expect the computer to actually speak the word. The YES on the green side of screen is flashing too. But it is the voice that I can't get over.

"Good. Let's try another one. Is the wall in this room red?"

The cursor is on NO. I am worried it will move to YES before I manage to sniff. I sniff quickly.

"NO," says the voice.

I am ready for it this time, but I am still enthralled to hear it.

I have a voice.

42

Mr. Katz asks a few more questions—pointless questions like "Is the sky blue?" and "Do dogs have six legs?" Then he asks, "Do you like the sniff controller?"

I do a big sniff for "YES." Then two more. "YES. YES." Mr. Katz smiles a big smile.

He turns to Mom. "Would you like to ask Jemma something?"

"Gosh," says Mom, coming around to face me. "There are so many things I want to ask. I can't think…"

Mom hesitates.

"Meeting Jodi…" she says finally. "Are you glad you met her? Please be honest, Jemma."

"YES," I sniff.

Mom stares at me, her eyes open wide as she takes in the fact that she's asked me a question, and I have answered it. I can't quite believe it either.

Her lip quivers, and she rubs her eye. Her mouth opens and

then shuts again. Then she smiles. "Good. I'm so relieved," she says. "I hoped so much that it was the right thing."

"YES," I sniff.

I wish the voice of my *yes* had as much enthusiasm as I feel. I sniff "YES" and "YES" again just to be clear.

"Now let's try a letter board," says Mr. Katz. "I understand from Professor Spalding that you can read, Jemma, but don't worry too much about correct spellings."

Things are moving fast. Am I ready for a letter board?

I watch as a screen with three panels appears. One is the alphabet spread across four rows. The next is numbers. The third panel is an empty green block. Underneath these three is a wide white block. YES and NO was one thing, but how can I possibly control this?

"This is very basic software that you can use to spell out words," Mr. Katz explains. "The sniff controller can be linked to any communication software on a computer or tablet, so if this works, a speech therapist can help to identify the best software for you."

Mr. Katz points at the screen. "As with the YES and NO screen, the cursor moves between the blocks, as you see. If you want a letter, give a big sniff when you reach the letter block. The cursor will then move from row to row. Give a small sniff when it reaches the row you want. The cursor will then move along that row, and you can select a letter with another small sniff. What you type will appear in the white box below. In the green box you will see predictive text, but don't concern yourself with that for now."

I am starting to feel panicky. This is meant to be basic? I'm not going to be able to do it. It's too hard—I can't take it all in. And what if I spell the words wrong? "Let's try a letter," he suggests. "See if you can select the letter *C*."

I try to remember how to do it. I am relieved when he reminds me.

I wait as the cursor moves between the screens.

I sniff. It isn't that different from picking yes or no. "Choose the row with a small sniff."

C is in the first row. The cursor goes past before I can sniff, so I wait for it to go through the rows and back to the first. This time I do it!

"Now another small sniff when you reach *C*," says Mr. Katz.

I've done it! *C* has appeared in the white box.

After a few minutes, with Mr. Katz's patient instructions, the word *CAT* is visible at the bottom of the screen. It is slow, but I am writing words, real words, for the first time in my life.

"Do you want to type something yourself?" he asks me. "Maybe tell us how you feel about the sniff controller."

I panic now. What do I say? What are the best words to express how incredible this is? Amazing? Brilliant? These feel right, but they will take forever. Good? Great? Slowly I begin to sniff out the word *GREAT*. I type *G R*, but sniff too late for

the next *E* and get *F*. I've typed *GRF*. What do I do now?
How do I correct a mistake?

Mr. Katz sees I have stopped sniffing. "If you make an
error, select this eraser symbol to get rid of the last letter,"
he tells me. "And this"—he points—"is the space bar, if you
need it."

Yes, now I can do it! I erase the *F* and sniff the *E* instead.
Then *A*, then *T*.

"If you select the red speaker button—bottom right,
here—then it will speak your words," says Mr. Katz.

It takes a few sniffs to get there, but then it happens. The
voice says, "GREAT."

"You are doing so well," says Mr. Katz. "I think *you* are
great, Jemma!"

"So do I!" says Mom. Then I hear sniffing—and it's not
me. There is a sob. Mom is crying.

I begin to type *DONT CRY*. It takes about five minutes for
me to get the right letters. Mom watches. I select the speaker.
Mom cries harder.

"Sorry, Jemma," she says between sobs.

"Let me fetch you a glass of water," says Mr. Katz,
handing Mom a tissue.

He leaves the room, and only now do I wonder what
happens next. When can I have one? It might take a while to
order it, I guess. Will it have to come from Israel? I need to
type something now while I have the chance.

I am about to sniff toward the *D* when Mr. Katz comes back in with a glass of water and gives it to Mom.

"You have worked very hard and must be tired," he tells me. "It is best not to do too much the first time." He presses something on the computer, and the screen disappears. He pulls the tiny sensor tubes from my nostrils.

"No!" I want to scream. I find myself sniffing as if to select *NO* through my nose, but of course I am disconnected now.

"I know you have waited a long time for this moment, Jemma," says Mr. Katz.

"All her life," says Mom.

"And I am sure you are impatient to have the system at home."

Yes, I am! He's switched it off now, but maybe he'll let me take it home with me.

"I'll have to ask you... How much does it cost?" Mom says.

I freeze. What if it is too expensive? What if I can't have it at all?

Mr. Katz smiles. "You will be surprised," he tells Mom. "This is unusually cheap to make. As you can see it's low-tech. It's really just a plastic tube. It doesn't rely on advanced technology of the kind used for eye-gaze sensors or vocal cord hummers, although it can be connected to many devices running all kinds of software."

So it's not too expensive! When can I have it? "However,

it is still, as I say, in the research phase and has not gone into production yet," Mr. Katz continues. "This equipment is just a prototype."

My heart sinks. How long will I have to wait?

Can't I just have this one?

"So how soon would Jemma be able to have one at home?" Mom is asking exactly what I want to ask. I can see the disappointment on her face too.

Mr. Katz's feet shift as he wrinkles his forehead. "I have seen, Jemma, that you can use the equipment successfully. I will speak to my team and find out if I can leave this one with you. If so, I would require you to report on your use of it as a participant in our research project. We're leaving in two weeks, but someone on the team can bring it over to you and set it up before we go."

The significance of this slowly sinks in. I had an opportunity to say something here and now, and I've missed it. I've got so much that's so important to say. Instead of typing *CAT*, I should have typed *DAN KILLED RYAN*.

43

Mom and I have lunch in the hospital cafeteria. She leaves me by a table where I can see her and goes to get the food. I watch her pull out her purse to pay, and she has a puzzled expression. She searches her bag.

"I must be going mad," she tells me, plunking down a tray. "I'm sure I had twenty dollars in my purse. Lucky they take credit cards."

I think about Olivia. Has she been taking money again?

Mom sits down next to me. "That sniff controller's amazing, isn't it?" she says as she spoons soup into my mouth. I am conscious of people watching, but I don't care. I wish I could tell them—all of them. *I can communicate now. I can talk!*

Mom phones Dad and tells him all about it. She sounds so excited. Then she listens while Dad speaks. I wish I could hear what he's saying.

He greets me warmly when we get home. "Such wonderful news, Jemma. You'll be bossing us around and telling us what's what soon!"

I wish!

"All okay here?" Mom asks as she pushes me into the kitchen. Dad follows.

"Yes. Dan phoned," Dad tells her.

"Oh?" says Mom.

Dan—what did he want?

"Yes, he just wanted to know if we'd had any news about Sarah," says Dad. "He's very worried, like we all are."

"It must be hard for him all alone," says Mom. "At least we have each other for support."

I cringe inside as she says this. The only thing he's very worried about is getting caught.

"Yes, I think he sees himself as a family guy. He said he was eager to settle down with Sarah, start a family with her," says Dad. "He asked how the kids are doing, and I told him the good news about Jemma. He sends his congratulations. He was very interested in how it works. He said to tell you, Jemma, that he'd love to come and have a talk with you sometime."

"It's nice to have something positive happening," says Mom, sighing.

Panic surges through me as I take in what Dad said. He has told Dan that I can communicate! Dan is never going to let me tell his secret. No wonder he's very *interested*. His message to me was a threat, I know it. I feel like I was at the top of a hill, happily looking at the wonderful view, but someone has left the brake off my wheelchair and now I'm rolling down, down, faster and faster, heading straight toward a busy street. It doesn't sound like Dad told him I might have to wait two weeks. Dan won't take the risk. He won't wait. He'll have to kill me now, won't he?

I'm scared. I will for someone to stay with me at all times, but later I find myself alone in the living room watching TV. Finn and Olivia are upstairs. Mom is cleaning the table from dinner. I'm not sure where Dad is.

I don't feel safe on my own. I can't stop thinking about Dan. I am alert to every little sound, though it's not as if I can do anything. I thought this sniff controller was going to change my life. I thought I had a future ahead of me, that I was going to have the chance to get to know my sister. I was stupid. The sniff controller is amazing, but Dan can't let me use it, can he?

If only I'd told Mom about Dan while I was trying it. Then someone could have done something, and I wouldn't be so frightened now. I missed my chance. I know he's going to come. I can feel it.

I try to watch the game show on TV. I force myself to concentrate, but I don't know any of the answers. Ten, maybe fifteen minutes pass. Maybe he won't come yet. Maybe he'll wait until I'm in bed.

Then I hear a car pull up somewhere outside, a car door

slam. Is that him? Could it be? I wait, look at the TV. He'll
have Sarah's key—he could slip in, so quietly. A minute or
two passes. There is a sound behind me. The living-room door
clicks shut. That door should be open. I hear another sound.
Someone took a breath. I can't see toward the door, only
the TV, but I know. Someone is here, in this room, standing
behind my wheelchair.

My heart beats faster. I find myself sniffing, picturing the
letter board and spelling *HELP* as if a miraculous imaginary
sniff controller might respond by blurting out, "HELP! HELP!"

Nothing's happening, but I can definitely hear breathing—
very close behind me. What is he waiting for? *Come around in
front of me. Let me see you.*

He's moving—as if he's heard me. *I want Mom!*

I want Mom! I am as helpless as a baby.

A knife glints in my face.

44

The knife—a small, sharp blade—is so close to my face that it is blocking my view of anything else. I've not seen a knife like this except on TV. I think you'd call it a switchblade.

As my eyes focus, I see that the shape of the person behind it is small. The knife is held in a small purple-gloved hand. These can't be Dan's hands or gloves. The knife moves back a little. It isn't Dan.

"I know you saw," Olivia says quietly. "I know you saw, and I know you'll tell on me."

Olivia. Where did she get the knife? Why is she waving it at me?

"I know you saw," she says again.

I have no idea what she's talking about.

The knife is in front of my eyes. It wavers in her shaking hands. I wish she'd drop it. It's so close. It's almost scratching my cheek. I can't control my head movements. If my head jolts the wrong way, that knife will slice me.

My head jerks suddenly, as if it's heard my thoughts. I tipped away from the knife and not toward it, but I know that was pure luck.

"I've got to make sure you can't go telling on me." There is venom in her voice though she speaks barely above a whisper. The knife is steadier. "If you tell anyone I stole Lorraine's money, they'll throw me out of here." She's breathing hard. I'm in shock. It's about the money she took from Mom's purse. She didn't think I'd ever be able to tell anyone. But now she knows I will.

"I like you, Jemma," Olivia continues, "even though you don't do anything." She screws up her face. "But I can't let you tell. I'll do it quickly, okay? No one will think it was me."

She pulls the knife slowly back, ready. She can't be serious. But I can see the determination in her pressed-together lips. She means it. She's going to do it. *Mom! Mom! I need you!*

"*Olivia!*"

Suddenly Dad is there. "What the—? For God's sake, Olivia. Where did you get that knife?"

Olivia jumps, and the knife jolts wildly in front of my face. I think I feel it scrape my cheek.

"Give it to me," says Dad.

Olivia is shaking, harder and harder, but she doesn't let go of the knife.

"Olivia. Give it to me now," Dad says again. His voice is low, calm, and serious.

She drops the knife. Dad quickly grabs it and shuts it. Olivia is sobbing now, wailing. She curls up on the floor and rocks like Finn.

Saliva gathers in my mouth. I can't swallow. Would she have done it? Could she really have stabbed me? I don't know. It's hard to believe she would.

Dad's face is white with shock. He stands, paralyzed for a moment, staring down at Olivia on the floor.

"Lorraine!" he yells loudly. "Can you come in here?"

Mom runs in. "What's happened?" Her voice is high, panicky.

"I found Olivia holding this knife out as if she were about to stab Jemma."

Dad flicks the knife open and shut again for Mom to see.

"*What?*" Mom exclaims. She comes around in front of me, looking at me anxiously and then at Olivia.

"Olivia! Calm down. What on earth were you thinking?"

Olivia is still sobbing loudly and doesn't look like she's about to calm down.

"We need that sniff controller," says Mom. "We need Jemma to be able to tell us what's going on."

And she has no idea how much I need to say!

Mom sits on the floor and puts a hand on Olivia's shoulder. Olivia pushes her away. Dad is holding the knife, staring at it with a bewildered expression.

"That's not ours, is it?" Mom asks him.

"No," Dad says firmly.

"Just tell us one thing, Olivia," says Mom. "Where did you get this knife?"

Olivia sobs for what feels like minutes before she finally says, "I...f-found...it. I f-found it in the y-y-yard."

"In *our* yard?" Dad says. "Where exactly?"

"My ball...went into the bushes right at the back, and... and...something was sticking up in the mud behind the shed, and I p-pulled it."

"When was this? Why didn't you tell us?" Dad asks.

"Weeks ago. I...I wanted to keep it," says Olivia. "Just in case."

"In case of what?" Dad demands. Olivia shrugs, but says nothing.

"Why *Jemma*?" Mom steadies her voice. "Why were you pointing it at *her*?"

Olivia's shoulders are shaking. She begins to sob again.

"Come upstairs with me," Mom says firmly.

I wonder if Olivia will tell her the truth.

As Mom leaves, I hear Sheralyn coming down. "Is everything okay?" she asks. "I heard shouting..."

Dad goes out into the hall, and I can hear him telling her what's happened.

"That is one messed-up kid!" says Sheralyn.

"I know," says Dad. "I don't think we realized how bad it was. I'm not sure what'll happen now."

I wonder what he means, what will happen to Olivia. It's only when I am lying in bed later, unable to sleep, that I think about the knife. How did a knife end up buried in our garden?

Could it possibly have been the knife Dan used to kill Ryan? Dan goes into the garden to smoke sometimes. Olivia might just have found the most important piece of evidence, and she has no idea.

Olivia is staying in her room, and Mom has taken some breakfast up to her. She says Olivia won't get out of bed and won't talk.

Finn is eating his cereal slowly and deliberately. He seems to be checking carefully that each wheat square has four sides before it reaches his mouth.

Dad doesn't go to work.

"I'm going to call Mr. Katz and find out when the sniff controller is coming," he tells me as he feeds me breakfast.

It's hard to swallow. I feel stuffed so full of things I need to say that there is no room for food.

I'd like to hear the call, but once I've finished eating and been wiped up, Dad goes into the living room with the phone.

He comes back looking pleased. "Thank goodness. They say it's coming tomorrow," he tells me. "Someone named Mr. Fogel is bringing it."

Tomorrow.

When Mom comes down, Dad tells her about Mr. Fogel. And he says that Olivia's social worker will be over in half an hour.

Mom decides I should go to school, that it is best to keep things normal. I think they want me out of the way while they deal with Olivia.

When I get home, Olivia has gone. Mom explains that her social worker has found her somewhere else to stay for a while.

"I don't know if we'll be able to have her back here. She won't say what happened," Mom says, shaking her head and sighing despairingly. "I still can't believe it. I'm so sorry, Jemma. It must have been terrifying."

Finn is home. He isn't playing or lining things up either. He just sits rocking. I hope he is okay. I hope Olivia will be okay too.

45

The next morning, the hour and a half between Finn leaving for school and the time the sniff controller is due to arrive passes so slowly I wonder if the clock on the living-room wall has stopped. I'm starting to get a headache.

At last there is a ring at the door. He's here!

Mr. Fogel introduces himself and tells me it's great to meet me. He says it with such enthusiasm it's like I'm a celebrity or something. He says I'll be set up in no time.

"No time" turns out to be another hour. First he has to download the communication software onto Mom's tablet. From the frown on his face, I think he's having problems. What if he can't get it working? I hope I'll be able to sniff okay—be able to work it. What if the other day was a fluke, and this time I can't do it at all? I try to practice while I wait. My headache gets worse.

"When you have a moment, I've got some forms I need you to sign to say you're happy for Jemma to be part of our research project," says Mr. Fogel. "And then we'll go through the records we need you to keep." He switches his gaze to me. "I wanted to try this out with someone with a disability like yours, and it's great to have the opportunity."

I wish he'd get on with it. He has no idea about the urgency.

"Here we go. Sorry it's taken so long," he says finally.

He puts the sensors into my nostrils and turns the screen so that I can see it.

"Now, I know you've worked with this—but haven't had much chance to practice yet! We'll start with the YES and NO screen. Big sniff when the cursor is on your choice of word. Are you ready?"

I am flummoxed for a moment. I wish my head would stop thumping. How do I tell him I'm ready? Then I realize. A big sniff!

"YES," speaks the voice.

"Great! Good job. Can you see the screen clearly enough?"

"YES," I sniff.

Then we switch to the letter board. He gets me to spell a few words, which I do, slowly and carefully. I guess it may seem slow for someone listening, but I can do it! The thrill of it surges through me all over again. It's like a kind of magic.

"Would you mind if I asked Jemma some things in private?" Mom asks.

"Of course," says Mr. Fogel. He smiles at me as he heads off toward the kitchen.

"Jemma," Mom says softly. "Do you know why Olivia was threatening you?"

The seriousness of what I have to say brings me back down to earth.

"YES," I sniff.

"Please tell me," says Mom.

I hesitate. I want to answer Mom, but I am not sure she is asking the most important question. I need to talk about Dan—and Sarah. Is it wrong to answer the question I want to answer rather than what Mom is asking? Will it confuse her? I feel panicky. I'm not used to having to make decisions like this!

I begin to spell. I select *D*. But when I try *A*, I miss and get *B* so I've typed *DB*. How do I erase a letter? I panic. Then I remember there is an eraser key.

I select it. Now I'm back to *D*. I wish I could do this faster. At last I have sniffed *DAN*.

"Dan?" Mom repeats, clearly confused.

I ignore her. I have to think how to do a space... Yes, I've selected a space. I need to explain, but I want the fewest words. I spell *RYAN*, hoping she will get what I mean. Sometimes I pass the letter I need and have to wait for the cursor to go around again. I know Mom is watching. I don't know what she's thinking. I have to concentrate. I select the microphone, and the voice says, "*DAN RYAN*"—although I know Mom has already read what I've typed. Hearing it aloud, I feel suddenly overwhelmed. My head spins.

"Dan Ryan?" Mom repeats. Her eyes are wide. "Is this to do with Olivia?"

"NO," I sniff.

"You're telling me something else. Am I right?" Mom asks.

"YES," I select, with relief.

Mom pulls her chair close to me. "Jemma, what are you trying to tell me about Dan and Ryan?"

"KILL," I slowly sniff.

"What? Dan killed Ryan?" Mom asks. "Is that what you're saying?"

"YES," I sniff.

"How do you know this?"

"TOLD ME," I sniff.

"Who told you?"

"DAN," I sniff again. Then I keep sniffing because I don't want another question. Mom waits patiently.

"KILL SARAH TOO."

Mom's eyes are even wider. "Jemma, wait. I need to call the police. I don't want to make you tired—I know it's a lot of effort. We'll speak to the police together."

Mom phones the local police station and explains. When she says, "Jemma has important information," I feel relieved. I just hope I can explain clearly and that they'll believe me.

"They'll be here in half an hour," Mom tells me. "Do you want to rest?"

I am aware that I haven't answered Mom's question about

Olivia. Although I'm tired and my head is spinning, that feels important too.

"OLIVIA," I sniff.

"You want to tell me about Olivia?" Mom gives me an encouraging smile. "I'm all ears, Jemma."

"MONEY," I sniff.

"Money?" Mom frowns. "PURSE," I sniff.

Mom hasn't gotten it yet. She's frowning as she tries to piece it together. I'm not being clear enough—this is so hard!

"Olivia took money from my purse?" Mom says at last.

"YES," I sniff.

"I thought money was disappearing. I had no idea it was her. But why was she threatening you with a knife?"

"I SAW," I sniff.

"She thought you would tell me?" Mom asks. "She was scared?"

"SENT AWAY," I sniff.

"She was scared she'd be sent away? What a mess!" says Mom. "But we can't keep her here after what happened."

"SAD," I sniff.

"Yes, Jemma, I'm sad too. Do you know why she took the money?"

"NO," I sniff.

Mom suddenly holds her head in her hands. She has tears in her eyes.

I feel bad. I didn't want to make Mom cry. "Social Services weren't sure about placing her here, but I convinced them. I thought we could help her." It is Mom sniffing now. "Maybe this wasn't the right place. And everything with Sarah means we've been giving her a lot less attention than she needs. What useless foster parents we are. We're supposed to be keeping you all safe!"

No! I don't want Mom to feel useless and sad! "YOU GOOD," I spell. "LOVE YOU."

"Thank you, Jemma. I love you too—so much. I'm going to phone Ben. I think he needs to be here. I still can't take all this in."

I'm thinking about Olivia, about how terrified she was of being sent away—so terrified that she pointed a knife at me. And now her worst fears might come true. I'm sure she didn't mean to hurt me. I'm sure she wouldn't do it again. When she first came, Olivia never really felt like part of our family, but now she does. Since she's confided in me about things, I've started to feel like a big sister to her, and now that I'd be able to talk to her, I could be that even more.

"OLIVIA STAY," I tell Mom.

"What? I'm not sure, Jemma. Not after what she did..."

"STAY," I repeat. "FAMILY."

Mom sighs and wipes her forehead. She looks like she has a headache, and I think her hands are shaking.

My own headache is getting worse. I wish someone would

give me some painkillers. We wait. Then I suddenly realize I can actually ask for some!

"HEAD PAIN," I sniff.

"Of course. I'll get you some painkillers," says Mom. I am stunned at how easy this is. *I can communicate!*

I really can! And I don't have to stay in pain with no one knowing. This is huge!

46

While we wait for the police and for Dad, I have a break from
sniffing. It takes a lot of effort. The painkillers start working.
My headache is still there, but easing off.

Mr. Fogel seems unsure what to do once Mom has explained
what's going on. He tells Mom he feels he should stay a while
longer in case anything goes wrong with the sniff controller, but
he doesn't want to be in the way. Mom reassures him and makes
him a cup of coffee. He comes to sit with me in the living room
and tells me more about his research, how he is a neurobiologist
specializing in olfaction—which he says is all things to do with
the nose and sense of smell. They came across the idea of sniffing
as a means to control things purely by chance. I am fascinated.

"I never imagined one day I'd be sitting with someone
who is using the sniff controller to give a crucial witness statement to the police!" he says, giving me a big smile.

Then Mom turns on the TV, and Mr. Fogel and I watch a
program about people who want to move to Australia.

Mom phones Olivia's social worker to tell her what I said. She's in the kitchen, but I can hear snippets. It sounds like Olivia can't come back. I feel sad.

Dad's home. Mom starts crying when she tells him about Olivia. He hugs her, and then he comes and hugs me too, so tightly I worry he might pull out the sensors in my nose.

"I think I'm still in shock," Dad says.

The police arrive. They're the same two that came when Sarah first went missing. Dad takes his newspaper into the kitchen for Mr. Fogel to read while he waits. So I have Mom, Dad, Officer Hunt, and Officer Sahin in the living room with me. Mom explains to the police how the sniff controller works and that I have just gotten it and haven't had much practice.

"Can you tell us what you told your mom?" Officer Sahin asks.

It is very slow, but now I see how I can use the predictive text, which makes it slightly quicker. Even so, by the time I've spelled a word, Officer Hunt is already fidgeting impatiently.

"DAN KILL RYAN," I sniff.

Officer Sahin has been watching the screen, but she looks startled as the voice finally speaks my words.

"And you know this because?" she asks.

"TOLD ME," I spell again.

"Who told you?" she asks.

"DAN," I sniff. "WONT CATCH ME."

"Dan won't catch you?" Officer Sahin asks.

I thought I was doing well—I'm definitely getting faster—but I'm frustrated now. "NO," I sniff. I try to think how to be clearer.

"Ahh—are you telling us what Dan said?" asks Officer Sahin.

I am so relieved that she has understood. "YES," I sniff. "THEY WONT CATCH ME."

I can't believe I have managed to say a whole sentence. Suddenly, I remember the knife. I didn't tell Mom that.

I sniff quickly before Officer Sahin can ask another question.

"KNIFE." Is that clear? She looks unsure, but Dad's eyes light up.

"I think I know what Jemma means... Can I...?" Dad begins.

"I'd rather we ask the questions if you don't mind. We have to make sure we don't ask anything leading," says Officer Hunt.

"Oh, okay," says Dad.

"You know something about a knife?" Officer Sahin asks me. "Can you tell me more about it?"

"OLIVIA KNIFE," I sniff.

Officer Hunt looks confused. I'm not explaining clearly enough. I wish I could talk more in whole sentences, but sniffing each letter is so much effort.

Dad can see I'm struggling, and he ignores Officer Hunt's

request to keep quiet. "Olivia found a knife in our garden," he says. "I'll get it."

I hear his footsteps leave and come back a few moments later. "Here."

I can't see because of the angle, but I assume Dad is giving Officer Hunt the knife. I hear the rustle of plastic. "Just put it straight in here," says Officer Hunt.

"KNIFE RYAN," I sniff.

"Does it look like the kind of knife that stabbed Ryan?" Dad asks.

"I couldn't comment on that," says Officer Hunt.

"DANS KNIFE," I sniff.

"Do you know that?" Officer Hunt asks.

"THINK," I admit.

"Jemma, when did Dan tell you he killed Ryan?"

There's a tone in his voice as if he's not sure he believes me.

When did he tell me? I can't remember! It was weeks ago. Is it okay to say that?

"WEEKS AGO," I sniff. I feel I need to explain more, although it is taking a lot of effort.

"Do you know anything about Sarah's disappearance?" Officer Sahin asks.

What can I say? "DAN," I sniff.

"You know Dan is responsible—or you think he might be?"

"THINK," I sniff.

"Do you know of any reason why Dan might be responsible?"

"RICHARD," I sniff.

Officer Sahin nods thoughtfully.

All the energy has drained from me. I need a break. I hope there are not too many more questions.

"TIRED," I sniff.

"Okay," says Officer Sahin. "I think that's enough questions for now."

"What happens next?" Dad asks. "I mean, Jemma can't sign a statement or anything."

"We'll need you to bring Jemma to the station so we can film her answering these questions," Officer Sahin explains. "The video evidence can be used in court if needed. You have been very helpful, Jemma—very helpful indeed."

"Good job, dear," says Mom, stroking my arm.

"TIRED," I sniff again.

"You look washed out," Mom says, stroking my cheek. She turns to Officer Sahin. "I really don't think she can answer all these questions again now."

"How about you rest and come to the station after lunch?" Officer Sahin suggests.

"Thank you, we'll do that," says Mom.

"GET DAN," I sniff.

"We'll certainly be making further inquiries," Officer Sahin assures me.

I've done it! I've told them—although I wish I didn't have to do it all over again for the video. At least they are taking me seriously. The police will arrest Dan, and they'll find out what happened to Sarah. I feel ecstatic at being able to communicate something so important. "Do you want to lie down?" Mom asks when they've gone.

"YES," I sniff.

"It's so nice to be able to ask you what you want rather than decide for you," she says as she wheels me into my bedroom.

But lying there on my bed, I couldn't sleep. My head felt like it was full of bees buzzing around and around. I couldn't switch off until I knew the police had locked Dan up.

I heard Mr. Fogel leave and wished I'd said goodbye to him and told him how grateful I was—though I could hear Mom and Dad thanking him again and again.

By the time I'd been to the police station with Mom and gone through all the questions again, I felt like I had nothing left. I wish I'd managed to ask if they'd arrested Dan yet, but answering the questions had used up all my energy.

As we left the police station, we passed a police car arriving. Maybe Dan was in it. I wish I could have seen. Back home, I was able to ask to lie down again.

Mom took out the sniff controller tube, and that time I fell asleep instantly.

Now I'm awake, and I have no idea how much time has

passed. I can hear Mom's voice. I think she's in the kitchen on the phone. I try to listen, but I can't hear what Mom's saying or figure out who she's talking to. Is it the police?

Mom doesn't come. I'm lying here, waiting and waiting.

Finally her head appears around the door.

"I was feeling impatient, wondering what was happening," she tells me, "so I called the station." She smiles. "They've got him, Jemma! The police have got Dan. They're questioning him now."

I'm so relieved. *They've got him!* I wish I could have seen his face when he opened the door for them.

But what about Sarah?

47

Mom sits me up gently and moves me into my wheelchair. She pushes me into the living room before connecting the sniff controller. It takes a few tries to get the tube up my nose right. "We'll get some kind of clamp so we can attach the tablet to your chair," she tells me as she props it up on a tray so I can see it. I am impatient, eager to ask about Sarah.

"SARAH?" I finally sniff.

"No news yet," says Mom, "but give them a chance, Jemma. Would you like a drink? I'm going to make myself a cup of tea."

"WATER," I sniff. It still feels incredible to be able to ask for things.

I think about Dan, imagining him being questioned. I hope he's squirming in his chair, stuck for words. I'd love for him to know what it's like when you can't speak. I hope he's scared too—really scared.

Mom brings the drinks, sits down near me, and helps me drink the water from a straw.

"It must have been terrible for you," she says as she sips her tea, "knowing all that and not being able to tell us."

"YES," I sniff slowly.

"And we were all taken in by him, apart from you."

"YES," I sniff. Though I know if I had been able to talk, Dan would never have shared his secret with me.

"SARAH?" I ask again after dinner.

"I'll phone the station and see if there's any update," Mom tells me.

"WANT," I sniff.

"What do you want, Jemma?" she asks. "HEAR," I continue.

"Of course," says Mom. She fiddles with the phone, turning on the speaker.

I wait while Mom gets through to Officer Hunt.

"We wondered if there was any news about Sarah," Mom says.

"Well," says Officer Hunt, "we've talked to Dan Harris, but unfortunately we've found no reason to hold him."

"Oh?" says Mom.

"He has an alibi for the evening Ryan was killed, and we have no other evidence against him. There is nothing to indicate he is connected with Sarah's disappearance either. He has an alibi for that night too. So we've had to let him go."

"Goodness," says Mom.

My breath comes fast. I don't believe it. The police have

made a mistake. Dan must've lied about his alibis. I know he did it. I know!

"But Jemma was so sure," Mom says quietly. "I don't believe she was making it up."

"It wasn't exactly your average witness statement," Officer Hunt says. "She's never spoken before. Maybe she got overexcited, started making up stories. Maybe it's all jumbled in her head."

He doesn't believe a word I said! He'd rather believe Dan. *Making up stories...jumbled in her head.* How dare he say that?

Mom glances at me, and I think she's wishing she hadn't put the speaker on. I hope she doesn't turn it off now.

"TRUE," I sniff to Mom. "WAS DAN."

"I think Jemma believed what she told you to be true," Mom tells Officer Hunt. "Dan may have been joking with her, but I'm sure Jemma heard what she says she heard."

"You know her best, of course, but like I said—it's a weird situation. Perhaps she just wanted something dramatic to say. She's a teenager, after all."

Even Mom is speechless at this. I can speak, but I don't know what to say either.

"What about the knife?" Mom suddenly asks. "Was it the one that killed Ryan?"

"The knife will be tested," Officer Hunt tells her.

"And Sarah?" asks Mom.

"Sarah remains on the missing persons list. Hopefully, in time she will make contact. We'll keep you informed."

Mom gets off the phone and looks at me. "Are you all right, Jemma?"

I am seething. I want this tube out of my nose, but I don't feel like sniffing, not even to say that. How can he have an alibi? It must be a lie. Why can't the police see through him? They'd rather believe him than me—just because I'm in a wheelchair and he's standing on his own two feet. I know I'm right. The way Officer Hunt spoke about me was utterly humiliating.

"Jemma?" Mom asks again.

I don't answer. I'm not sniffing again, not ever.

I have nothing more to say.

48

"Jemma's had a shock," **I** hear Mom saying. It's the next morning, and she's on the phone to Mr. Fogel. "I'm not sure if she's stopped trying to sniff or whether the sniff controller has stopped working," she tells him. There's a pause. "Okay," Mom says. "I'll contact you in a few days. We'll see what happens. Thank you."

Mom has to realize. She doesn't really think it's broken, does she?

At breakfast Dad tries to encourage me to speak. I don't. I won't. Breakfast is very quiet. No Sarah and no Olivia either. I miss her. In a weird way, I even miss her tantrums.

After breakfast, Finn has his box of matchsticks and is lining them up against the kitchen wall when he accidentally steps on the box and the matches spill. He is horrified, frantically trying to pick them up and put them back, but he's trying to do it too fast and some of them spill out again.

This is how I feel—like everything's spilling out, all over

the place. Like Finn, I want life to all be straight lines for a change.

"Here, let me help you, Finn," Dad says gently. Finn doesn't react, but he doesn't stop Dad either. Soon the matches are all back in the box, and Finn goes back to lining them up.

"Jemma," Dad says, sitting beside me and touching my arm. "You told the police what you knew. It isn't your fault that Dan lied to you. What he did was very unkind."

Unkind. I still can't believe it was a lie—not when I think about what he said when he learned there might be a way for me to communicate.

"Don't let that spoil things. You can talk to us, Jemma! It's incredible. Don't let Dan or the police take that away."

They're not taking it away. I just don't want to do it anymore. That's all.

By the evening there is no further news, and I am still not sniffing. Dad phones Kate, but she has nothing to report.

"Talk to me, Jemma," Mom begs as she clears up from dinner. "Tell me how you're feeling. I know it must be tough."

She has no idea how tough. And no, I'm not talking, not to anyone.

"What would cheer you up?" Mom asks.

Dan in prison, finding Sarah, everything getting back to normal—but that's not going to happen, is it? Nothing will cheer me up.

By bedtime I have still not sniffed at all.

"What about Jodi?" Mom suggests gently, putting an arm around my shoulder. "Would you like to see her?" My sister. I don't feel like talking, but maybe...

Jodi. That's different. Now that Mom has said it, I know she's right. Mom has said the only thing that might possibly make me feel a little better.

But she's given up on waiting for me to answer. She stands up to walk out of the room.

"YES," I sniff.

49

I am waiting for Jodi. Yesterday passed so slowly, and now she's late and I'm scared she's changed her mind. Apart from sniffing "YES" to seeing Jodi, I have kept quiet. Dad has attached the tablet to my wheelchair with a clamp so I can speak whenever I want to, but I still don't feel like talking. I'm not even sure I'm going to talk to Jodi. I want to see her, though.

We wait. Where is she? She was supposed to be here half an hour ago.

Mom looks at her watch. "I'll text her in a minute if she still hasn't arrived," she tells me.

Then I hear the bell, and Mom goes to answer the door.

"Hi, Jodi," I hear her say.

"So sorry I'm late!" Jodi replies.

"Don't worry. Jemma will be delighted that you're here," says Mom. "Come in."

"I'm a little nervous," I hear Jodi say. "This sniff thing...

How does it work? Will I need to do anything?" I don't want Jodi to be nervous.

"It's easy," says Mom. "Jemma does it all! We'll show you. She might not say much, though."

Finally they come in from the hallway. Mom points Jodi toward the sofa.

She turns me so I'll be facing Jodi, who sits down a little awkwardly.

"Hi, Jemma. So sorry I'm late! The bus took *forever*. The traffic was terrible."

"I'll get you a drink," Mom tells her. "What would you like? Tea? Coke?"

"Coke, please," says Jodi.

Mom goes out. Jodi leans toward me. "Now, show me how this thing works," she says. "I'm so excited that you can speak!"

Her excitement is infectious. My wonderful sister is here, and I can talk to her. I want to... I really do.

"HAPPY," I sniff slowly.

"Wow! That's so cool," she says, watching patiently as the letters appear and the voice finally speaks. "I'm so happy to see you too, Jemma!"

There's an awkward pause. I guess it's my turn to speak. What do I say? My mind goes blank.

Maybe Jodi will say something else—but she doesn't. I have to say something. Now I understand what Professor

Spalding meant about learning to speak. Even though I can think clearly and my thoughts just come into my head with no effort, with speech I have to decide what to say and choose the words. And then with AAC I need to find the shortest words, to use the least effort to express what I want to say. I feel panicky. I say the only thing that comes into my head.

"SAD SARAH," I tell Jodi. It takes me a long time to get all this out.

"Sarah's sad? No, you're sad about Sarah? You must miss her so much."

"YES," I sniff. Jodi gets it—she understands me! There's another pause. Jodi's not saying anything.

I realize I should ask her something, but I can't think what.

"Actually, I've had quite a week myself," she tells me. "I broke up with Jack. We'd only been going out for a month, but I really liked him. He went off with another girl from my class."

"IDIOT," I sniff, and Jodi bursts out laughing. It's awesome that I can make her laugh.

"NEW BOY," I sniff.

Jodi smiles. "I need a new boyfriend? Yes, actually there is a boy I've got my eye on... He's a year older than me."

"GOOD LUCK," I sniff.

"Ha! Thanks!" Jodi grins. "I'll let you know how it goes! Is there anyone you like, Jemma?"

I am about to sniff *no* but then I remember.

Actually, there is.

"LEO GLOWLIGHT," I tell her.

"You like Glowlight too! You're right. He's awesome!" Jodi laughs.

A strange snort comes from my throat. I think I am actually laughing too!

"LOVE YOU JODI," I sniff.

"I love you too, Jemma," Jodi tells me. "It's so cool that we can really talk now!"

Mom comes back with a Coke for Jodi and an apple juice for me. She's taken a while—maybe she was just giving us some time to talk. She puts the straw in my cup and holds it up.

"I can do that," says Jodi.

"I'll leave you to it, then," says Mom, smiling. "Just call me if you need anything."

Mom's gone. Jodi holds my cup and eases the straw into my mouth. I sip.

She puts the drink down. She is quiet again. I'm tired from all the sniffing, but I don't want to stop. I'm just not sure what to say.

"FIND SARAH," I sniff.

"It must be awful not knowing what's happened," says Jodi. She strokes my hand. "I wish there was something I could do to help, but I think you'll have to leave it to the police."

"NO GOOD," I tell her.

She laughs. "It's their job. I'm sure they're trying their best."

"WE FIND HER," I sniff. "YOU ME."

"But...how?"

"TRY," I sniff.

"Okay, then." Jodi sighs and leans forward. "You must've known Sarah so well, better than anyone, maybe. Think about everything you know, Jemma. Tell me if you can think of anything—*anything*—at all that might help."

I think hard. I love it that Jodi is listening. But what do I know that I haven't already told the police?

"SARAH LOVE DAN," I sniff. I'm pleased that I'm already getting faster at it, though it still takes me a long time.

"Okay..." Jodi says, frowning.

"DAN BAD MAN," I sniff.

"But he didn't kill Ryan," says Jodi.

"DID," I sniff. "AND HE GOT SARAH."

"Come on, then." Jodi smiles. "How are we going to prove it? What else do you know?"

I try to remember everything I know about Dan, every time that he came to the house. The things he said to me flash through my head, making me shudder. What do I know that could help? There has to be something, but I just can't think.

Jodi sits waiting, fiddling with a pretty ring on her finger. Her phone starts buzzing. She looks at it and switches it off. "Nothing important," she says, smiling. I have a sudden memory—Dan standing here, his cell phone ringing. Billy—it was Billy. Could he know something?

"DAN FRIEND BILLY," I sniff.

"Do the police know about him?" Jodi asks.

"NO," I sniff. I don't know for certain, but I don't think so.

"What do you know about Billy?" she asks.

I remember what Sarah called him. "BILLY NO BRAINS."

Jodi laughs. "Oh yeah?"

"BIG HEAD BIG BRAIN?"

"Big heads don't always equal big brains, Jemma." Jodi laughs.

"DAN PHONE BILLY," I continue.

"You heard him? What did he say?"

I try to remember. It wasn't anything that interesting, or it would have stuck in my mind. Then it comes to me. "BEHIND THE GROCERY."

"Interesting," says Jodi. "What do you think he meant was behind the grocery store?"

"DONT KNOW," I sniff. This is hard work. I can't keep sniffing like this. It's wearing me out. But then I have another thought. "YOU ME GO."

"Go where?"

"STORE," I sniff. "NOT FAR."

"You really think this might be important?"

"YES."

Jodi smiles at me. "Okay, then."

50

She goes into the kitchen and asks Mom if she can take me for a walk. Mom sounds pleased, and a minute later she comes in with my coat.

"Don't be out too long. It still gets dark so early. Oh, and if you pass the grocery store, would you mind picking up a few onions for me?" Mom asks her. "Here, I'll give you the money."

"Sure," says Jodi. "I've never pushed a wheelchair before," she adds, suddenly sounding nervous. I hope she's not going to change her mind.

"Jemma's well strapped in," Mom tells her. "Going up and down curbs is the only tricky thing. Come outside, and I'll give you a demo."

Soon we are off! I am out with my sister. I jerk the first couple of times we go down a curb, but then Jodi gets the hang of it. She seems to be enjoying it. She starts to run, pushing me fast so the wind zooms past my face. This is great!

I direct her to the grocery store so we can get Mom's onions there and investigate. Left, then second right. Then all the way to the other end of the block and left. She stops at each junction, and I tell her which way to go. It's not complicated, but I hope I'm doing it right. I've only been there a couple of times—and I've never given directions before.

To my relief, the store comes into view. This part of town is kind of run-down and dingy. There are some row houses, but it's mostly apartment buildings, warehouses, and office complexes. Some of the buildings look derelict and have boarded-up windows. Others have scaffolding around them. There are very few people around. I start to feel nervous. The tablet attached to my wheelchair might look very tempting to a thief. And I got so carried away with the idea of coming here that I didn't actually think about what we'd do when we got here.

Jodi stops outside the store. "What now, Jemma?" I don't know what to say. Jodi turns me right and left so I can see in both directions. It doesn't help much. Jodi stops, and I stare at the door, thinking. Then I remember what Dan said. "BEHIND," I sniff.

"Okay, here we go," she says.

Around the back, there are dumpsters. Lots of dumpsters. Some of them are overflowing.

"Hmmm," says Jodi. She turns me slowly so I can see all the way around.

There is the delivery entrance, a few spaces for cars to park. Not much else that could hold a clue.

"Should we go?" Jodi asks me.

I am about to sniff "YES." This was a stupid idea, and I wish we'd never come. What Dan said to Billy was the only thing I could remember, and I thought it might mean something. That was ridiculous, wasn't it? But I am reluctant to leave.

"TURN," I say.

"Okay."

Again Jodi turns me. There's a passageway between two tall buildings. It looks dark and uninviting, but I think we should investigate. It's hard for me to get Jodi to stop in the right place so she'll see where I mean.

"Well?" she asks.

"TURN," I repeat.

She turns me twice more, and I am starting to feel dizzy before we are finally pointing in the right direction.

"THAT WAY," I sniff.

"Okay," she says. "We'll have a look, and then we'll go." The buildings tower above us as Jodi pushes me along the alley between them, their flat roofs merging with the gray-black of the late-afternoon sky. I feel very small. There is no sidewalk, so I hope no cars choose this moment to enter. We come out into a narrow yard with a row of run-down garages. A few have closed doors, but some doors are hanging off and some garages have no doors at all. The nearest open one has stacks of bricks inside, and another has a pile of wooden planks.

Jodi pushes me nearer. There is a smell like dirty toilets. It's getting darker too.

"I don't like it here," says Jodi. "Can we go now?"

I don't like it here either, but I'm reluctant to leave. I can't exactly ask Jodi to look in those creepy garages. "YES," I tell her. "SORRY."

"It's okay," she says. "It was worth a look, if you thought it might be important. I'm not sure what we were looking for, though."

She is pushing me back toward the passage when I hear a sound behind us—a clang of metal. Jodi doesn't seem to hear, and I can't turn to look. We're moving so I can't tell her to stop. It was probably nothing.

We're nearly at the gap between the buildings when I hear voices—men's voices. They're coming from the alley we are heading to—and they are getting closer. Jodi instinctively pulls me back and around the side of the garages so they won't see us. I suddenly feel very vulnerable. What if they find us?

I want to know what's happening, but Jodi doesn't dare risk putting her head out in case she is seen. I hope I can keep quiet. I can't help making sounds sometimes. The more I think about trying to keep quiet, the more I worry that a sound will come out. I try not to think about it, to focus on listening as the voices come nearer.

"I don't like it," says one man. "It's gone on too long." The voice sounds familiar. It could be Billy. It sounds like him, though the tone is anxious, not relaxed like when I met him. It could easily be a stranger.

"Quit whining," says another voice.

That's Dan. Now I'm sure it's Billy too. I can barely breathe.

"You've gotta let her go, man!" says Billy, pleadingly. "We can't just keep her..."

"I told you to shut up! I'll figure it out, okay?" says Dan.

"What do you mean?" says Billy.

"Don't know why you're scared after what you..." I don't catch the end of the sentence. They're moving away from us now. I hear the clink of keys.

Then the sound of one of the garage doors lifting and going down again.

I've got to get Jodi to call the police. She's got to do it quickly. But my breathing's gone all weird, and I can't sniff. I get a surge of panic.

Jodi whispers to me. "Is that them? Were they talking about Sarah?"

"YES." The word appears on the screen, but I am careful not to select the speaker button. It's hard to sniff accurately. I have to slow down, even though I want to get the words out fast. "POLICE."

I can see Jodi hesitating. Maybe she's wondering if it's safe to call from here, or if it is even more dangerous to move in case they come out and spot us.

Jodi takes out her cell phone. "Police," she says quietly when the call connects. There's another pause. "We think someone's being held prisoner. Behind the grocery store on Redding Road, in one of the derelict garages. We're too scared to move. Two of us. My sister's in a wheelchair." She listens, then hangs up.

"They're coming," she whispers.

I'm starting to feel shivery. *What if Dan heard?*

What if he finds us here?

We wait. The buildings around us seem to creak and groan. Apart from that, it is quiet. Did the police believe Jodi? Did they realize the urgency?

At last! There is the crunch of tires and the sound of an engine. The police car pauses at our end of the gap, headlights lighting the gray alley. Jodi runs out. I can't see what's happening. I hear the car doors opening, footsteps.

There's a muffled scream—a woman's scream. Then I hear the voice.

"Police!"

I hear shouting, banging. I'm terrified. I can't see Jodi. I can't see anything. The police car is in the way.

It feels like forever, and my heart is thudding like a drum. What's happening? *What?*

Then I hear the voice again. "Ambulance needed, garages on Redding Road, behind the grocery store."

A gurgling noise comes from my throat. *No!* Then I hear, "Woman in her twenties, conscious but injured."

She's alive! Sarah's alive!

Jodi is back. She pushes me out into the open, which is now action-packed, like something from a movie. There are more flashing lights. A police van is here now too. A man is in handcuffs, being put in the back. I can't see well, but I think it's Billy.

"Move back," a policeman tells us. Then suddenly Dan is in front of me. He's handcuffed too. His eyes meet mine. His mouth drops open in astonishment.

I feel hot and cold all at once. *I got you, Dan. I got you!*

And then I realize I can say something. At last, I can say something to Dan. I start to sniff.

"FREAK."

Dan's shoulders jolt in surprise, and his eyes are wide. He turns away, and the policeman blocks my view as Dan's put into the van. An ambulance arrives, and there is hardly space for it to park. The paramedics jump out, and I wait. I desperately want to see Sarah. But she doesn't appear. They're taking forever. How badly hurt is she? The police are saying we should go home. A policeman offers to come with us, but Jodi says no, it's not far to walk. They say they'll take statements from us later. They are talking to Jodi as if I am not there.

"We came because of Jemma," Jodi says. "Something she

overheard. She thought it might be important and wanted to check it out."

"Well, it was a really risky thing to do," says the police officer, "but you did well, both of you."

When we reach home, Jodi rings the bell and Mom opens the door, smiling. "You were gone a while. Everything okay?"

Jodi doesn't speak. I think the shock of everything has suddenly hit her.

"Did you manage to get the onions?" asks Mom.

"NO," I sniff. "GOT DAN."

"You did what?" Mom asks as we make our way into the kitchen.

"We forgot the onions, but the police have Dan," Jodi tells Mom. "Because of Jemma."

Mom's mouth opens, but she can't speak.

"FOUND SARAH," I tell her.

"Is she...?" Mom asks.

"She's alive," says Jodi.

Mom listens to our story. A police officer arrives at the door. I recognize him from the garages. He says he is Detective Sergeant Bell, and he wants to ask me and Jodi some questions. He wants us to come to the station so they can videotape my answers. I have done so much sniffing today that I can barely stay awake. I ask how Sarah is, but all the detective can say is that she's been taken to the hospital, which I already know.

At least at the police station Sergeant Bell questions me as if he believes everything I'm saying. He's very different from Officer Hunt.

When we're finished, Mom drops Jodi off at her house and takes me home. I am able to tell her I want to sit in the living room with some gentle music on. I think if she hadn't been able to ask me, she would have put me to bed, but my mind is whirring far too much to sleep.

I can't believe what just happened. What Dan did... It makes me sick. Keeping Sarah locked up in a garage all these weeks, and coming around here pretending he was worried about her. And what if Jodi and I hadn't been there at that moment? I think how we nearly turned back. We were about to. I shudder. Poor Sarah... I can't imagine what it was like locked in there. She must have been desperate. She must have wondered if she'd ever get out.

Then I think about what I did. I can hardly believe that either. Dan thought I was powerless, but I wasn't. I knew I wanted to communicate, but I never really thought about the power it would give me. I feel different—as if I have a new inner strength. Even so, I realize there are some things you just can't control—no one can—like the way other people behave.

———

We have fish and french fries for dinner, and I manage to sniff, "KETCHUP." Mom looks at me in surprise before mashing some ketchup into my fries. Mom fills Dad in on everything that's happened. Dad shakes his head in disbelief.

I watch Finn lining up his fries in neat rows on his plate. The next minute, he's pushed the plate away and is banging his head on the table.

"Finn! Stop that," Dad tells him. "What's the matter?"

I look, and I can see what's wrong. Finn is one fry short. As he leaned over the plate, a fry attached itself to his sweater and is still hanging below his elbow.

I have to swallow my mouthful, and then I sniff, "FINN."

His head jerks up in surprise at the computer voice saying his name. He looks bewildered. He doesn't seem sure where it's coming from.

I select the speaker again. "FINN. FINN." Until he looks at me. "FRY SWEATER," I tell him. Finn looks at his sweater and suddenly sees the french fry. He pulls it off and puts it back in line on his plate.

"Nice job, Jemma," says Dad.

This is the first thing I have said to Finn. He glances up at me, meeting my eyes for just a second. He's smiling.

The next day Mom is supposed to come with me to school to show my teachers how the sniff controller works. I feel completely drained after yesterday, though, and tell her I don't feel up to going to school.

"Don't worry," says Mom. "Stay home today and rest. I'll come and show them another day."

It is late afternoon when the phone rings. Mom answers it and then runs into the living room.

"Jemma, that was Paula. The police have gotten the DNA results back from the knife. Someone tried to clean it with bleach, apparently, but there were still tiny specks of blood. It was the knife that killed Ryan!"

"DAN," I sniff.

"No," says Mom. "Dan's alibi for that night was backed up by security cameras. He was miles away at a casino, or something. But what they have discovered is that a hair found on Ryan's clothing belongs to Billy. He's the main suspect now, Paula says."

"WHY BILLY," I sniff. That doesn't make sense.

If Billy killed Ryan, why did Dan make me think he did it?

"I've no idea why Billy did it," says Mom.

"SARAH?" I ask.

"I've spoken to Kate," says Mom. "They're keeping her in the hospital for a few days, but it sounds like she'll be okay."

I am so relieved. I just want her back here.

52

Sarah is coming! There's been a weird atmosphere at home these last few days—such a mixture of things, like one of Mom's "everything goes in" stews. We're all pleased and relieved that Sarah's been found, that she's alive—but shocked too, and horrified at what she's been through. I am less shocked than Mom and Dad because I knew what Dan was like, but I still feel dreadful thinking about all those days Sarah was locked in that garage. If I only I could have told them sooner, if only I could have warned Sarah, she might not have had to go through all that.

Kate wanted Sarah to go and stay with her, but Sarah wanted to come here. I am worried about what state she'll be in, how she'll be feeling, but I can't wait for her to be back. Once Sarah is here, things will feel a little more normal again.

I hear the bell. My heart starts beating so fast.

Sarah. *Sarah!* But the voice isn't Sarah's. It's Paula.

"Jemma," says Paula, as she comes into the living room. "Thank you so much! It's because of you that they got him, that evil man."

"Do they know why did Billy did it?" Mom asks her.

"He's a thief," Paula tells us. "The police have connected him to a string of thefts from jewelers. I suspected my Ryan had gotten himself into some kind of a mess. They think he was helping out with raids and decided to keep some of the stuff himself. And Billy found out."

Mom is shaking her head as she takes all this in.

Paula keeps talking. "And I'm thinking that if Dan knew what Billy had done, he might have used it to make Billy help him kidnap Sarah."

There's a pause as all of this sinks in. "SARAH COMING," I sniff.

"Really?" says Paula. "That's wonderful! The poor girl. It's dreadful to think..."

"Yes, she should be here soon," Mom says, looking at her watch. "It's because of Jemma that they found Sarah too, of course."

Mom smiles at me.

"Anyway, I won't stick around if you're expecting Sarah," Paula says, standing up. "I just wanted to fill you in—and to thank you, Jemma. I'll be off."

Paula has only been gone two minutes when the doorbell rings again.

So many times I've imagined her walking through the door. And here she is.

I knew she might look different after going through something so horrific, but this doesn't stop the shock when I see her. She looks thinner. Her hair is lank, her skin spotty, and her eyes have a scary emptiness. She does manage a tiny smile when she sees me. She opens her mouth as if to speak, but she coughs. The cough is chesty and hollow, and it sounds like it will never stop.

"Jemma, it's so good to see you," she finally croaks. "Thank you...for everything." Her voice is sad and small, and even though I know she's pleased to see me, it feels as though part of her is somewhere else.

Now is my chance—my chance to communicate with Sarah for the first time. "LOVE YOU SARAH," I sniff.

She manages a slightly bigger smile. "Wow. Look at you talking!"

There's a silence. No one really knows what to say. She knows—she must know—we care about her so much. But you can't just fix something like this.

Sarah turns to Mom. "I'll go and have a shower, if that's okay," she says. "I had showers at the hospital of course, but I don't feel clean. I can't..."

"Have a shower, dear. Take as long as you want," says Mom.

She disappears upstairs. It is Sarah, but it isn't. Things aren't going to be the same. And of course I knew that, deep down. It will be good that I can speak, though. I want to help her feel better.

Sarah doesn't come down for about an hour. I wait and wait. She looks better, but her face still has an emptiness.

"Cup of tea?" asks Mom.

"Thank you." Sarah nods.

Mom goes into the kitchen to make it, and Sarah sits down with me.

"I can't believe I was so wrong about him," she says quietly. "I guess you knew, Jemma. I bet you've got more sense than me."

"I KNEW," I tell her.

"I should have stuck with Richard, sweet Richard. I don't know what got into me."

Mom comes in at the end of this. "Dan was a charmer," she says. "Anyone can fall for a charmer."

"He said I was his and his alone, like he owned me." Sarah looks shaky.

"Don't talk about it now unless you want to," says Mom, touching Sarah's shoulder gently.

Sarah takes a sip of tea and then coughs that chesty cough again.

"Have they given you something for that cough?" Mom asks.

Sarah nods. "I've got antibiotics. It was freezing and drafty in that garage."

"How could he do it—treat you like that?" Mom's voice
is bitter. "He deceived us all, you know."

I wasn't taken in, but I don't bother to point this out.

"You're welcome to stay here and rest up," says Mom.
"Take all the time you need to recover. It must've been a
horrendous ordeal."

"Thanks," says Sarah. She rubs her eyes. "Look, I don't...
This, this is so hard... I hope you'll all understand, but..."

I brace myself as Sarah pauses. But *what?*

Sarah sighs. "I need space and time to figure things out.
I wanted to come here because this is my home, but I'm
only staying a few days. Then I'll go to my sister's. I need
time to think."

"WANT YOU STAY," I sniff. "I LOOK AFTER YOU."

Sarah gives a little gasp. "That is so sweet, Jemma. I love
you. This... It's nothing to do with you, I promise. I don't
know. I just need space."

As I try to take in this awful news, Sarah tells us that
Richard visited her in hospital yesterday.

"He feels so bad about not seeing me go into the house
after the concert," she says. "I tried to say he's got nothing to
feel bad about... I was cheating on him!"

"I don't think you or Richard should worry yourselves
about that now, not after everything." Mom sighs. "What
happened when you got out of the car after the concert?"
she asks. Then she puts her hand over her mouth. "I'm

sorry, I shouldn't have asked. I'm sure you don't want to talk about it."

"It's okay," says Sarah. "I got to the front door, and just as I went to put the key in, a hand went over my mouth. Dan was holding me tight, forcing me to walk, and he bundled me into a car and drove me to that garage. He'd found out about Richard, and he was angry—so angry! But I deserved it, didn't I?" Sarah breaks into sobs.

"You can't think that!" says Mom, just as I sniff, "NO."

"Dan may have felt angry, but that could never make it okay—what he did," says Mom. Her fists are clenched.

Sarah bursts into tears. Mom is by her side in a second. She puts her arm around Sarah and grabs some tissues from the table. I try to think of something I can say.

But I guess sometimes there is nothing you can say.

It's just being there that's important.

I can't take in that she's leaving. Is she going to come back? I have wanted her back so much. I know the most important thing is that she's okay—and that she does what she needs to do right now. I'm trying not to think about myself in this, but I don't want her to go, not now. Not right away.

Later, I am lying in bed and overhear Mom and Dad talking in the kitchen. Sarah has gone to bed early.

"I can't stand thinking about it," Mom says. "Her being locked up in that garage all that time. At least she says he didn't lay a finger on her."

"No, just left her there to rot," Dad says sourly.

"Acted like he was doing her a favor by bringing a little bit of food and water. Expecting her to be grateful... Can you imagine?" says Mom. "I'm not surprised she wants a break."

"Maybe we need a break too," Dad says. I feel a flash of alarm. What is he saying?

"We've had such a tough few months," Dad continues. "Jemma could go to that college. I'm sure she'll do well now she has the sniff controller. Someone else could take Finn."

"No!" says Mom.

I am relieved that she sounds so horrified.

"You know how he hates change—and Jemma too," says Mom. "They need us."

"We're only good for them if we are in a good state ourselves. And I'm not sure we are," says Dad.

Then I hear Mom crying.

I knew things weren't going to stay the same, but Mom and Dad? I thought they'd always be here. How wrong could I be?

53

All night, my mind tosses and turns even though my body can't. I thought my world was going to be back to normal now that Dan is in custody. I thought my home, my "nest," would be safe—with Mom and Dad and Sarah and Finn and the chance to get to know my sister Jodi too.

I can speak. I told Mom to let Olivia stay, and they've sent her away. I told Sarah I wanted her to stay and I love her—but it made no difference. So what is the point?

I am awake when Mom comes to turn me. I realize Sarah may never do it again—never turn me, never read to me, never paint my nails, never confide her secrets. In the morning, Mom puts my sniff-controller tubes up my nose, but I have nothing to say. I can't stand what's happening, and I don't even answer when Mom asks me if I am okay. Sarah doesn't come down for breakfast. Mom takes up a tray with coffee and toast.

"Talk to me, Jemma," Mom says gently when she comes

down. "You can tell me how you feel and what you're thinking now. Let me try to help."

I know I am being mean, but I don't feel like communicating. It is an effort to do it, and I don't even know what to say.

"Are you upset about Sarah?" Mom asks me.

I rouse myself to sniff *Y* and then select *YES* from the predictive text.

"I know," says Mom. "We got her back, and now she's going again. It's so hard, isn't it? But we'll get by. This is what she needs—and whatever happens, she's part of our family. And we'll make sure you always have the care you need, Jemma."

She's looking at me as if she's waiting for a response. I want to ask, "Are you going to stop fostering?" but I'm too scared. What if she says yes?

I watch as Mom empties the dishwasher. I feel like I have been emptied too.

"Come on, I'm taking you somewhere," says Mom.

"WHERE," I sniff.

"Wait and see," says Mom.

I am soon in the car with Mom. I want to know where we're going. We drive for about ten minutes. I am shocked when she parks outside the police station. I can't believe there are more questions. I've told the police everything I know. Mom lowers the ramp and wheels me out of the car, pushing me toward the entrance.

"WHY HERE," I sniff. "GO HOME."

"You'll see," says Mom.

Mom speaks to the woman behind the screen, and a police officer comes out.

"Mrs. Bryant! Jemma! I'm so glad you're here."

I recognize his voice before he comes around in front so I can see him. It's Officer Hunt, the one who said I invented my story. He's the last person I want to see. He may be glad I'm here, but I'm not.

"Come this way," he says.

"NO," I sniff, but Mom ignores me. Officer Hunt smiles at her as he holds a door open and she pushes me through.

He's got nothing to smile about as far as I'm concerned.

He leads us into a room and moves a chair aside to make room for my wheelchair. He holds a chair out for Mom and then sits down opposite us and strokes his chin.

"GO HOME," I sniff.

"I can understand why you're not eager to be here," says Officer Hunt. "But I asked your mom to bring you for a reason. I have something important to say to you."

I had something important to say to you last week, I think. *But look how that turned out.*

"I wanted to apologize to you, face-to-face," he says. He's looking straight into my eyes, and he looks serious. "This crime has been solved thanks to you. I know you heard some things I said on the phone to your mom, things I should never have said. I'm sorry if I upset you."

"YOU DID," I sniff. I'm not letting him off that easily.

He smiles awkwardly. "You found Sarah—and Dan and Billy are locked up now, thanks to your help."

"I SAID DAN," I remind him. "NO LISTEN."

"Yes, you were right—and in more ways than you know."

What does he mean? I am interested now. "Although Dan didn't actually kill Ryan Blake," he goes on, "we now believe Dan got Billy to do it for him."

I begin to sniff. "DAN MADE."

Officer Hunt nods. "Exactly. Dan made Billy do it. Billy has finally agreed to help us with our investigation. He says he was working for Dan, and Ryan was too. He told us that when Dan found out Ryan was keeping some of the stolen goods, he was furious. He wasn't going to allow it—and told Billy to kill him."

"Sounds like Dan was a complete control freak," says Mom. "And yet he could be so charming..."

Officer Hunt nods solemnly. "Billy is not the brightest guy around. Dan had him wrapped around his finger. Billy admits that he panicked after stabbing Ryan and went running to Dan, who took the knife and said he'd deal with it. He must've been visiting Sarah and took the opportunity to stash it in your backyard. We've charged Dan with conspiracy to murder."

"I'm just glad you've got him," says Mom, "and Billy too."

"Jemma," says Officer Hunt. "I'm sorry I didn't believe you. I was wrong."

I am shocked. He actually means it.

"But you didn't give up. You were determined to prove your theory right. And you did! We'll do our best to make sure Dan and Billy are both locked up for a long time. I hope you can forgive me, Jemma."

I am stunned. I don't know what to say. His eyes look desperate now, pleading with me to let him off the hook. I didn't think he cared, but now I believe he does.

"OKAY," I sniff.

"Thank you," he says, his shoulders sinking with clear relief. "That means a lot."

54

I've realized something important. Being able to communicate doesn't mean that anyone's going to listen. The one thing I didn't want to have happen is happening, and there is nothing I can say to stop it.

"I know you're upset that I'm leaving." Sarah sighs. "And... Look, I want to be honest with you. What's happened—it's changed everything for me. I'm sorry, Jemma, but it's only fair to tell you. I don't think I'm going to be coming back to work here."

Out of the corner of my eye I glimpse the dark shapes of her suitcases in the hall. She's already said goodbye to Finn, though I don't think he has any idea what's going on.

"It's not easy for me, and I know it must be very upsetting for you," Sarah continues, "especially after you rescued me so amazingly!"

"YES," I sniff.

"I want to explain. I want you to understand," she tells

me. "I haven't changed the way I feel about you. I still care about you. I still love you, Jemma."

"GET BETTER COME BACK," I sniff.

Sarah shakes her head. She looks like she's going to cry. "It's just that... What's happened, it's made me realize that I've been hiding here, in a way. This isn't actually my family, though I've kind of been pretending that it was."

She wipes a tear from her eye. "One day I'd like to have my own family and maybe be a foster parent like Lorraine. I think being here has been an excuse to not grow up, and what's happened these last few weeks has made me grow up—fast. Do you understand, Jemma?"

Of course I do. What she's saying does make sense. I've just been fighting it. I want her to stay so much. I don't reply.

"And maybe," she continues, "it's not so good for you to be so dependent on me. I know you need care, but other aides might be just as good or better—or different anyway, and give you different experiences."

I'd love to tell her about Rosie. I don't want other aides, even though Sheralyn's been okay. I want Sarah.

"I don't want to stop you growing up and experiencing new things. And this sniff controller—it's amazing! It's going to change your life completely. You will have so much more control."

I know she's right. You can't always keep things the same. I think about Jodi... New experiences can be good. I think about my future now I can communicate, all the possibilities. But...

"Tell me you understand. Please?"

Part of me wants to, but the rest of me refuses.

I know it's selfish, but I want her to stay.

She strokes my hand. She looks at the sniff-controller screen—but I am not sniffing.

Then she looks at me, and I see the pain in her face. She has been through so much. Suddenly, I see I am hurting her, and I don't want to do that.

"Please, Jemma?"

Sarah waits patiently while I sniff each letter. "YES," I sniff. "LOVE YOU SARAH."

Then as she hears the words spoken, she leans forward to hug me as best she can. I feel the wetness of her face as she kisses my cheek. I am crying too.

She lets go. Then she gets a tissue and gently wipes my eyes. "I'll keep in touch, Jemma, I promise. Your dad says you'll be able to text and email with this thing. It'll be great!"

She gives me her warmest smile and walks toward the door.

"BYE SARAH," I sniff.

And then she is gone.

55

Nine Months Later

I'm being pushed in my wheelchair, and I am surrounded by people. I have never seen so many people, and they all seem so tall and so close that I feel as if my chair and I are going to disappear under the crowd—flattened on the sidewalk. I'm trying not to be scared.

My new aide, Alice, is pushing me. I was anxious before she started, but I was surprised to find I actually liked her right away. I had wanted it to be just me and Jodi, but the good thing is that with Alice pushing me, Jodi can walk beside me. Now and then she squeezes my hand. I catch the glint of her midnight-blue nail polish and look with pleasure at my own matching nails. I think of Sarah—that day when she did my nails, the awful things that followed. It feels so long ago now.

I didn't realize it would be so far. We seem to go on and on. I'm glad it's not raining.

"I cannot *believe* we're really here!" says Jodi.

I've talked so much to Jodi. We meet up every weekend. Mom and Dad decided not to take a break from fostering, to my relief. They asked me if I'd like to go to Carlstone College in a few years, and I would. Mom's finding out about applying for a place, but I don't know if I'll get funding. In the meantime I've started going to a mainstream school for part of the week. I was really nervous, but Jodi encouraged me to try it. I wanted to go to her school, but the school district said a nearer one was more suitable. So I tried it—and I love it! It's not easy, but I have a teaching assistant to help me and everything is so interesting. At first I was going two days a week there, and now I'm going three.

I have new communication software, and I've had lots of training with a speech therapist who specializes in AAC. She's been amazing, and now I can select words and phrases from categories rather than spelling everything out. It's still very slow, but faster than typing each letter. I know it will take time, but I want to do my exams and go to college—just like Jodi plans to do.

I am also going on a sailing trip for teenagers with disabilities. Alice loves water sports, and she told me she used to help on sailing trips as a volunteer. I searched the internet using my sniff controller and found out more about it myself, and I've already been on a day's sailing class. It was amazing! Beats the local park any day.

And Olivia came home! Mom and Dad were eager to have her, and I told the social workers I wanted to give Olivia a chance too. It was weird how much I missed her in the weeks she was away. Her social worker has organized some therapy for her. She's a little quieter than she was, but not much, and she still has tantrums. She talks to me sometimes, though, and it's wonderful to be able to talk back. She's still going to ballet lessons too. Olivia never explained why she took the money. She said she didn't know and that she just wanted it.

Finn seemed happier when Olivia came back. He is doing better, though it's not always easy to tell with him. He hasn't done any head-banging for months, at least. Mom hopes one day he'll be able to communicate too.

I've had a few emails from Sarah. She's still living with her sister, and she says they're getting along really well. I miss her, but I'm glad—because I have my sister, and Sarah is with hers too. She finally broke up with Richard. I hope she'll find someone who will be right for her one day.

Next month is Dan's trial for kidnapping her. He's pleading not guilty, but the police have plenty of evidence against him. Dan and Billy's trial for Ryan's murder will be soon too. They may show my video in court. If they do, it will be the first time someone has given evidence using a sniff controller.

I suddenly realize we have arrived. This place is massive! Jodi is speaking to someone who's wearing a hat and looks like he works here. She's pointing to my wheelchair and asking which way to go.

We go up in an elevator. First stop is the accessible bathroom. Now we are back with Jodi and searching for the where we want to be. So many people!

Jodi leads the way through an entrance labeled BLOCK C, and Alice pushes me quickly after her. We're at the front of a balcony in a wheelchair space with seats on either side. I can't believe how vast this place is. It's a huge oval shape, and I can see rows and rows of people below and across the other side who look as small as insects!

"You okay, Jemma?" Alice asks, moving around to face me.

"THIRSTY," I sniff. "DRINK."

Alice reads the words as they appear, and I don't bother to press the speaker. It is so noisy in here that I don't think she'd hear—even with the volume on full. "Of course," says Alice. She rummages in the bag for my drink and opens it. It's taken a while, but I'm getting used to being able to ask for what I want.

Once I've had a drink, Alice gently puts small earplugs in my ears. "NO!" I sniff. I am worried I won't hear well.

"You'll need them!" Alice tells me, and Jodi nods in agreement.

"Seriously, Jemma. It's *so* loud!" she warns me.

"EXCITING!" I sniff.

Jodi smiles back.

Then suddenly, there they are. They look so small on that

faraway stage, but the screens are big so I can see their faces clearly. Glowlight! It is really them. I see Leo! My heart thuds. He is gorgeous.

The music starts. It is like a musical thunderstorm.

The beat is so loud and the vibration so strong I can feel it in every bone of my body. Then the voices. It is so loud—so incredible. I sing along in my head. I catch a glimpse of Jodi's ecstatic face. She squeezes my hand.

I am here at a Glowlight concert with my sister. She is glowing.

I am alight!

AUTHOR'S NOTE

When I began to write this book, I had not decided how Jemma was going to be able to communicate, although I knew she would need to by the end! Advances in technology have made communication possible for many more people with disabilities. However, there are lots of people who do not have access to this technology or are unable to use it for various reasons.

The device that Jemma uses in the book is inspired by a real invention, developed by researchers at the Weizmann Institute in Israel. Trials have shown that some people with severe disabilities and people with locked-in syndrome, for whom other systems have not worked, have been able to use this device. And as a relatively inexpensive product, it has the potential to make AAC technology accessible for more people than ever before. It has not yet gone into production, but my hope is that by raising awareness, this book may help

persuade a company to take this up and make it commer-
cially available. I dream that one day everyone who has the
potential to communicate will have access to the equipment
they need.

A CONVERSATION WITH THE AUTHOR

What inspired you to write *I Have No Secrets*?

I enjoy reading thrillers myself, and I had this idea for a story in which the protagonist knows the identity of the killer but can't tell anyone for some reason. The character of Jemma sprung into my head. I think she came from my experience of volunteer work with people with disabilities. I was very shy as a child, and this led to an interest in people for whom communication is difficult for more physical reasons.

Why was it important to you to write a protagonist with cerebral palsy (CP)?

Although I set out to write a thriller, and the character with CP was secondary to this, once I'd decided on a character with CP, I realized how little representation there is in fiction. I wanted people with CP to see themselves in books and for other people to increase their awareness through reading. I also wanted to represent Jemma as an ordinary teenager who happens to have a disability.

CP affects people in different ways. What gave you the idea to make Jemma struggle to communicate with people as a key part of the plot?

Jemma's inability to tell anyone what she knew was central to the idea for the plot. I therefore needed her disability to be severe enough for her not to be able to communicate. I was, however, determined from the start that this would be more than a "plot ploy" and use it as an opportunity to explore Jemma's life and family relationships too.

What kind of research did you do to write this book?

It was vital to me to reflect Jemma's experiences as accurately and authentically as possible. I researched by talking to people—most importantly people with disabilities, including those with severe cerebral palsy and those with other disabilities but who use AAC (Augmentative and Alternative Communication). I also talked to relatives, caregivers, and other people who work with people with cerebral palsy.

I read books and researched online, and it was an online search that led me to a possible way for Jemma to communicate. Once I had a first draft, I got lots of feedback from people with direct experience and made changes accordingly. When one man with severe cerebral palsy said he thought his parents would understand better what it was like to be him through reading my book, I felt reassured that I was on the right path.

Why did you choose to write about a foster family?

When I was doing voluntary work, I met some wonderful foster parents who took in children with multiple and complex needs and disabilities. I thought a family like this would be a perfect setting for Jemma's story.

You've worked as a support teacher for children who are hearing impaired, as a reading recovery teacher, as an adult education teacher, and as a teacher of adults recovering from and experiencing mental health issues. What impact did those teaching experiences have on your writing?

I think my teaching experiences have helped me empathize with people who have all kinds of barriers to overcome in order to learn and in order to live life in the way they want. I recognize the frustrations and the need for people to listen, to have patience, to offer support, and to not be afraid to ask for and receive support. I think my writing is impacted by every person I meet, and I enjoy connecting with people as a teacher and hearing their stories too.

What were the easiest and hardest parts about writing *I Have No Secrets*?

The easiest part was Jemma's voice. Because she spoke so

clearly in my head and felt so alive, it was easy to write from her perspective. The hardest part was the writer's block that I experienced from time to time when I wasn't sure how to bridge the gap from one part of the plot to another. I sometimes didn't write anything for weeks.

What is your writing process like?

I am a plotter—I like to have the framework of the story worked out before I've gotten very far with it. I tend to write best first thing in the morning. I write mainly on a computer at home but sometimes write by hand in the garden or go to a library or café.

What did you edit *out* of this book?

I had written more about Sarah's relationship with her own sister, which was cut during the editing process.

What would you like readers to take away from the novel?

I mainly hope readers will have enjoyed the read, but I also hope they will feel more aware and more confident about interacting with people with disabilities.

I hope readers will see that life can have value even for someone who can't communicate, but that communication gives power and autonomy, and we should do everything we can to give people a voice and to listen to one another too.

READING GROUP GUIDE

1. Discuss the contrast between the way Dan speaks to Jemma and the way he speaks to everyone else. Why do you think he speaks to Jemma the way he does? Which voice do you think is the "true" Dan?

2. What makes Sarah a good caregiver for Jemma?

3. How did you feel toward Richard? Did you suspect he might be guilty? Did you hope that he would get together with Sarah in the end?

4. Finn, like Jemma, faces communication challenges. What role do you think he plays in the story?

5. Why do you think Olivia acts the way she does? How do you think her story might continue?

6. Can you imagine Jodi's expectations about meeting Jemma and why she reacts the way she does when they first meet?

7. When a passerby offers Jemma's caregiver money, why do you think Jemma feels so upset?

8. Has the book changed the way you feel about the life or experiences of someone who can't communicate or move independently?

9. Do you know anyone who has difficulty with communication or uses alternative means of communication like sign language or AAC? Can you think of any ways in which you could support them more?

10. Have you ever felt burdened with someone else's secret and felt that you wanted to or needed to share the secret?

11. Sarah was two-timing Dan. Do you think she deserved what happened to her?

12. How do you think Jemma's life will be changed by the events of the story going forward?

13. Why do you think Jemma's foster parents decided to foster her and the other children?

14. Imagine Jemma's family going on vacation. What would they need to think about to ensure all needs are met and they have a good trip?

15. What was the most moving moment of the story for you?

ACKNOWLEDGMENTS

First, I would like to thank my lovely agent, Anne Clark. I couldn't ask for a better agent, and your commitment to this book has been wonderful. I am so lucky too to have brilliant editors in Stella Paskins and Liz Bankes at Egmont. Your skillful editing, enthusiasm, and excitement about the book have been amazing. Thank you to the whole team at Egmont! And thank you to the team at Sourcebooks, too, for all your work on the U.S. edition.

I am eternally grateful to all those people who took the time to answer my questions and to read the manuscript and give feedback at various stages. Any errors are my own and not the fault of anyone acknowledged here.

For help with cerebral palsy and AAC information, I am especially grateful to Jonathan Kaye, Ellie Simpson of CPTeens, and Debbie Simpson, Natasha Bello, Julie Bello, and Kate McCallum from 1Voice, Kate Caryer from Communication Matters and Unspoken Theatre, and Jenny

Herd from Communication Matters. Thanks also to Carl Ritchie, Joan Ritchie, and Kevin Robinson who answered police-related questions for me.

From the Weizmann Institute, I would like to thank Lee Sela and Noam Sobel for answering many questions about their recently developed communication device.

I would not be the writer I am without fabulous City Lit, where I started out as a student and now teach. From there, I formed my own Friday writing workshop, with talented writers Jo Barnes, Angela Kanter, Vivien Boyes, and Derek Rhodes. Your constructive criticism and support have meant so much to me. I'd also like to thank my young adult beta readers, including those found for me by Janis Inwood, librarians at Southgate School, where I was educated, and Jessica Pliskin, whose excellent suggestion really helped.

My family—every one of you, I thank you for your support—and especially my husband, Adam, for all his love and for putting up with my mind being elsewhere a lot of the time (and for his helpful suggestion, gratefully received and ignored, that I should write about zombies). Final thanks go to our children, Michael and Zoe, to whom this book is dedicated. I know you are annoyed at not being old enough to read it yet—but you will be, one day, and I enjoy watching you grow so, so much.

ABOUT THE AUTHOR

Penny Joelson was born in London, where she still lives with her husband and two children and teaches creative writing. She began working with people with disabilities when she was a teenager, which gave her the inspiration and insight for *I Have No Secrets*. Find Penny on Twitter @pennyjoelson.

ALSO BY RUTH RENDELL

THE INSPECTOR WEXFORD SERIES

From Doon with Death
The Sins of the Fathers
Wolf to the Slaughter
The Best Man to Die
A Guilty Thing Surprised
No More Dying Then
Murder Being Once Done
Some Lie and Some Die
Shake Hands Forever
A Sleeping Life
Death Notes
The Speaker of Mandarin
An Unkindness of Ravens
The Veiled One
Kissing the Gunner's Daughter
Simisola
Road Rage
Harm Done
The Babes in the Wood
End in Tears
Not in the Flesh
The Monster in the Box
The Vault
No Man's Nightingale

DARK
CORNERS

∽∽∽∽∽∽∽∽∽∽∽⥥∽∽∽∽∽∽∽∽∽∽∽

A Novel

Ruth Rendell

Scribner

New York London Toronto Sydney New Delhi

Scribner
An Imprint of Simon & Schuster, Inc.
1230 Avenue of the Americas
New York, NY 10020

First Scribner hardcover edition October 2015

SCRIBNER and design are registered trademarks of The Gale Group, Inc., used under license by Simon & Schuster, Inc., the publisher of this work.

For information about special discounts for bulk purchases, please contact Simon & Schuster Special Sales at 1-866-506-1949 or business@simonandschuster.com.

The Simon & Schuster Speakers Bureau can bring authors to your live event. For more information or to book an event, contact the Simon & Schuster Speakers Bureau at 1-866-248-3049 or visit our website at www.simonspeakers.com.

Manufactured in the United States of America

10 9 8 7 6 5 4 3 2 1

Library of Congress Cataloging-in-Publication Data is available.

ISBN 978-1-5011-1942-2
ISBN 978-1-5011-1944-6 (ebook)

DARK
CORNERS

1

For many years Wilfred Martin collected samples of alternative medicines, homeopathic remedies, and herbal pills. Most of them he never used, never even tried because he was afraid of them, but he kept the lot in a cupboard in a bathroom in his house in Falcon Mews, Maida Vale, and when he died, they went, along with the house and its contents, to his son, Carl.

Carl's mother recommended throwing it all out. It was junk, harmless at best, possibly dangerous, all those bottles and jars and sachets just taking up room. But Carl didn't throw it out because he couldn't be bothered. He had other things to do. If he had known how it, or one particular item among all the rest, would change his life, transform it, ruin it, he would have emptied the lot into a plastic bag, carried the bag down the road, and dumped it in the big rubbish bin.

Carl had taken over the former family home in Falcon Mews at the beginning of the year, his mother having moved to Camden when his parents divorced. For a while he thought no more about the contents of his bathroom cupboard. He was occupied with his girlfriend, Nicola, his novel, *Death's Door*, which had just been pub-

lished, and with letting the top floor of his house. He had no need of those two rooms plus kitchen and bathroom, and great need of the rent. Excited though he was about the publication of his first book, he was not so naïve at twenty-three as to suppose he could live by writing alone. Rents in central London had reached a peak, and Falcon Mews, a crescent looping out of Sutherland Avenue to Castellain Road in Maida Vale, was highly desirable and much sought after. So he placed an advertisement in the *Paddington Express* offering accommodation, and next morning twenty prospective tenants presented themselves on his doorstep. Why he chose the first applicant, Dermot McKinnon, he never knew. Perhaps it was because he didn't want to interview dozens of people. It was a decision he was bitterly to regret.

But not at the beginning. The only drawback Dermot seemed to have was his appearance—his uneven yellow teeth, for instance, his extreme thinness and round shoulders. But you don't decide against a tenant because his looks are unprepossessing, Carl told himself, and no doubt the man could pay the rent. Dermot had a job at the Sutherland Pet Clinic in the next street and produced a reference from the chief veterinarian there. Carl asked him to pay each month's rent at the end of the previous month, and perhaps the first mistake he made was to request that it be paid not by transfer into his bank account, but in notes or a cheque in an envelope left at Carl's door. Carl realised that these days this was unusual, but he wanted to see the rent come in, take it in his hand. Dermot put up no objection.

Carl had already begun work on a second novel, having been encouraged by his agent, Susanna Griggs, to get on with it. He didn't expect an advance payment until he had finished it and Susanna and his editor had read and accepted it. No payment was promised on paperback publication of *Death's Door*, as no one expected it to go into paperback. Still, what with being both a published author with good prospects and a landlord receiving rent, Carl felt rich.

Dermot had to enter Carl's house by the front door and go up two flights of stairs to get to his flat, but he made no noise and, as he put it, kept himself to himself. Carl had already noticed his tenant was a master of the cliché. For a while everything seemed fine, the rent paid promptly in twenty-pound notes in an envelope on the last day of the month.

All the houses in Falcon Mews were rather small, all different in shape and colour, and all joined together in long rows facing each other. The road surface was cobbled except for where the two ends of the mews met Sutherland Avenue and where the residents could park their cars. The house Carl had inherited was painted ochre, with white window frames and white window boxes. The small, overgrown back garden had a wooden shack at the end full of broken tools and a defunct lawn mower.

As for the alternative medicines, Carl took a couple of doses of something called benzoic acid when he had a cold. It claimed to suppress phlegm and coughs, but it had no effect. Apart from that, he had never looked inside the cupboard where all the bottles and jars lived.

DERMOT MCKINNON SET off for the Sutherland Pet Clinic at twenty to nine each morning, returning to his flat at five thirty. On Sundays he went to church. If Dermot hadn't told him, Carl would never have guessed that he was a churchgoer, attending one of the several churches in the neighbourhood, St. Saviour's in Warwick Avenue, for instance, or St. Mary's, Paddington Green.

They encountered each other in the mews on a Sunday morning and Dermot said, "Just off to morning service."

"Really?"

"I'm a regular attender. The better the day the better the deed."

Carl was on his way to have a coffee with his friend Stacey Warren. They had met at school, then gone to university together,

where Carl had read philosophy and Stacey had taken a drama course. While she was still at university, her parents had been killed in a car crash, and Stacey inherited quite a lot of money, enough to buy herself a flat in Primrose Hill. Stacey wanted to act, and because of her beautiful face and slender figure was given a significant part in a TV sitcom called *Station Road*. Her face became known to the public overnight, while her slenderness was lost in a few months.

"I've put on a stone," she said to Carl across the table in their local Café Rouge. "What am I going to do?" Other customers were giving her not very surreptitious glances. "They all know who I am. They're all thinking I'm getting fat. What's going to happen to me?"

Carl, who was very thin, had no idea how much he weighed and didn't care. "You'll have to go on a diet, I suppose."

"David and I have split up. I'm finding that very hard to take. Have I got to starve myself too?"

"I don't know anything about diets, Stacey. You don't need to starve, do you?"

"I'd rather take one of those magic diet pills that get advertised online. D'you know anything about them?"

"Why would I? Not my kind of thing."

The waitress brought the two chocolate brownies and the slice of carrot cake Stacey had ordered. Carl said nothing.

"I didn't have any breakfast," she said.

Carl just nodded.

On his way home, still thinking about Stacey and her problem, he passed the bookshop kept by his friend Will Finsford, the one remaining privately run bookshop for miles around. Will had confided that he lay awake at night worrying about having to close, especially as the organic shop down the road had not only gone out of business but had had the bailiffs in.

Carl saw him rearranging the display of bestsellers in the window and went in.

"D'you have any books on losing weight, Will?"

Will looked him up and down. "You already look like you're wasting away."

"Not for me. For a girl I know."

"Not the beautiful Nicola, I hope?"

"No, for someone else. A friend who's got fat. That's a word I'm not supposed to say, isn't it?"

"You're safe with me. Have a look along the shelves, health section."

Carl found nothing he thought would be suitable. "Come over one evening, why don't you? Bring Corinne. The beautiful Nicola would love to see you. We'll ring you."

Will said he would and went back to his window arrangement.

Walking home, Carl realised it wasn't really a book he wanted. Stacey had mentioned pills. He wondered if any slimming medications were among his father's stash of pills and potions, as Carl had come to think of them. Wilfred Martin had always been thin so was unlikely to have used that sort of thing, but some drugs claimed to serve a double purpose, improving the skin, for instance, or curing indigestion.

Carl thought of his father, a rather taciturn, quirky man. He was sorry Wilfred was gone, but they had never had much in common. Carl regretted that his father had not lived to see *Death's Door* published. But he had left Carl the house, with its income potential. Had that been his way of offering his blessing on his son's chosen career? Carl hoped so.

The house was silent when he got in, but it usually was whether Dermot was at home or not. He was a good tenant. Carl went upstairs and saw that the bathroom door was open. Dermot had his own bathroom in his flat on the top floor, so had no reason to use this one. Probably I forgot to close the door myself, Carl thought, as he went into the bathroom, shutting the door behind him.

Wilfred's pills and potions were in a cupboard divided into five sections on the left-hand side of the washbasin. Only the topmost

section was for Carl's current use; he didn't need much space, as his toothbrush and toothpaste and roll-on deodorant were on the shelf above the basin. Surveying the collection of bottles and phials and jars and packages, tubes and cans and blister packs, he asked himself why he had kept all this stuff. Surely not for its sentimental value. He had loved his father, but he had never felt like that about him. On the contrary, he regarded the pills and potions as mostly quack remedies, rubbish really, and quite useless. A lot of the products, he saw, taking small jars out at random, claimed to treat heart problems and safeguard against heart failure, yet his father had had two heart attacks and died after the second one.

No, nothing here would encourage weight loss, Carl told himself. Best throw it all out, make a clean sweep. But what was that in a large plastic zip-up bag in the second section from the top? Yellow capsules, a great many of them, labelled DNP. *The foolproof way to avoid weight gain!* promised the label. Behind the bag of capsules was a box full of sachets also containing DNP but in powder-to-liquid form.

Taking the plastic bag out, he noted that, farther down, the label advised using with care, and not to exceed the stated dose, etc., etc. The usual small print. But even paracetamol containers said that. He left the bag of capsules where it was and went downstairs to look up DNP on the computer. But before he got there, the front door-bell rang and he remembered that Nicola—beautiful, clever, sweet Nicola—was coming to spend the rest of the day and the night with him. He went to let her in, telling himself he must give her a key. He wanted her as a more permanent part of his life. With Nicola, his new novel, and a reliable tenant, life was good.

For the time being, he forgot all about the slimming pills.

2

A T FIRST, BEING a landlord seemed trouble-free. Dermot paid
his rent on the appointed day with the minimum of fuss. That
is, he did for the first two months. The thirty-first of March was
a Monday, and at eight thirty Carl was, as usual, eating his breakfast when he heard Dermot's footsteps on the stairs. Generally they
would be followed by a tap at the door, but this time they were
not. The front door closed, and Carl, getting up to look out of the
window, saw Dermot walking down the mews towards Sutherland
Avenue. Maybe the rent would come later today, Carl thought.

Carl seldom saw a newspaper except for selected bits online, but
he bought a couple of papers on April 1 to see if he could spot the
jokes. The best one he had ever heard of—it was published before he
was born—was the story that the arms of the Venus de Milo had been
found washed up on some Mediterranean beach. Still, today's made
him laugh, and by the time he got to his mother's flat, he had forgotten all about the missing rent. It was her birthday as well as April
Fool's Day, and Carl was invited to a celebration lunch along with a
cousin and two of his mother's close friends. His mother asked him if
she should have invited his girlfriend, and he said Nicola would still
be at work in the Department of Health in Whitehall. It was a lovely
sunny day and he walked halfway home before getting on the 46 bus.

But there was still the matter of the late rent, with no envelope from Dermot. Carl woke up early the next morning worrying. He disliked the idea of confronting Dermot; he found he had broken into a sweat just thinking about it. He was drinking a mug of strong coffee when he heard Dermot's footsteps. If the front door opened, Carl told himself, he would make himself go out and ask for the money. Instead, Dermot tapped on the kitchen door and handed over an envelope. Smiling and showing his horrible yellowish teeth, he said, "Did you think I was playing an April Fool's joke?"

"What? No, no, of course not."

"Just a mistake. He who makes no mistakes makes nothing. See you later."

Carl felt great relief, but just to make sure, he counted the notes. And there it was, as it should be: twelve hundred pounds. Not nearly enough, his mother had said, considering today's prices, but it seemed a lot to Carl.

He filled a bowl with muesli because he was suddenly hungry, but the milk had gone sour so he had to throw the contents of the bowl away. Apart from the milk, though, things were going well, and it was a good time to get back to work on his new novel, a more serious venture than his first. Carl looked at the notes he had made about Highgate Cemetery, the research he was doing for his first four chapters. Perhaps he should have made another visit to the cemetery yesterday, but he thought he had enough material to write his first chapter. The only interruption was a phone call from Stacey. It surprised him the way friends unloaded their trivial (it seemed to him) concerns.

"I'm so sorry, Carl." She seemed to think the simple apology was enough to permit a long misery moan about her weight.

"I'm working, Stacey."

"Oh, writing, you mean?"

He sighed. People always said that, as if writing were quick and easy. Should he mention the DNP? No, it wouldn't shut her up. On

the contrary, it would fetch her round here, and as much as he liked her, he needed to work. Instead he listened, making sympathetic noises, until he told the white lie those who work from home sometimes have to employ.

"Got to go, Stacey. There's someone at the door."

He still couldn't write. It was absurd and something to feel a little ashamed of, suddenly to be happy, to be carefree, because he'd received a packet with twelve hundred pounds in it. Money that was rightly his, that was owed to him. Now he came to think of it, the rent money was his sole secure income. He couldn't count on more book money for a long time. The rent brought him relief and happiness.

He definitely wouldn't be able to write today. The sun was shining and he would go out, walk up to the big green space that was Paddington Recreation Ground, lie on the grass in the sun, and look up through the branches at the blue sky.

3

I T WASN'T APRIL Fool's Day or even May Day but May 2 when the next rent payment arrived.

Carl wasn't as nervous as he had been the previous month. Nicola had spent the night with him, but he had said nothing to her about the rent's being late in April. After all, it had come and all had been well. She had gone to work on May 2 before Dermot left the house, so she wasn't there to see Carl listening for his tenant's footfalls on the stair or to see Carl's surprise when the front door closed without Dermot's tap on the kitchen door. Perhaps the rent would come later in the day, and this in fact happened.

They encountered each other in the hallway, Carl leaving the house to do some food shopping and Dermot coming in at five thirty from the pet clinic.

"I've got something for you." Dermot handed over an envelope.

Carl thought it strange that Dermot should have carried that envelope containing twelve hundred pounds about with him all day, but still, it wasn't important: Carl had got his money. He wouldn't have to break into his meagre and dwindling savings to go on a week's holiday with Nicola. They would only be going to Cornwall, not abroad anywhere, but he was looking forward to their stay in Fowey.

Stacey had phoned again in some despair before they left, but on his mobile this time. He told her he was going away but that she must come over to see him when he got back. They'd go out to eat and he would see what he could do to help with her weight problem. Why had he said that? It must have been the DNP that had come into his mind. He dismissed it. He couldn't help anyone lose weight.

He and Nicola went to Fowey with the couple who had introduced them, and who were still special friends partly for that reason. They had a good time, and by the time they got back to Paddington station, Carl had asked Nicola to come to Falcon Mews: "I mean to live with me. Permanently." He felt good about Nicola. They cared about the same things—books, music, the outdoors. She loved that he was a writer. He loved her.

"I'll have to go back to my flat and tell my flatmates, but then I will. I want to. I'd been going to ask you, but . . . well, I must be sort of old-fashioned. I thought it wouldn't be right for me to ask and not you. Me being a woman, I mean."

She moved in three days later.

THE DAY BEFORE Nicola moved in, Stacey came round. She and Carl planned to go out to eat at a nearby restaurant. Before that, Stacey used his bathroom to renew her makeup. Perhaps because of her acting and her modelling, she made up heavily, especially around her eyes.

After a few minutes, Carl went upstairs to fetch himself an antihistamine pill for his hay fever. He left the bathroom door ajar. Stacey followed him in. She was one of those people who, when someone told her of a mild illness or problem, always claimed to suffer from the same complaint. "Funny you should say that because I've got hay fever too." He opened the cabinet and found the antihistamines on the top shelf.

Stacey was standing behind him, telling him about her symptoms and peering over his shoulder. "Where did all this stuff come from? Do you use it?"

"It was my dad's. I sort of inherited it—you know, when I got the house and the furniture and everything."

He reached into the cabinet and brought out the package with the yellow capsules. "This is supposed to make you lose weight. I expect he got it online."

"Did your dad use it?"

"He can't have. He was so thin he was practically a skeleton."

She took the package from his hand and looked at it. "DNP. Dinitrophenol. One hundred capsules." Then she read the instructions and looked at the price marked on the package. One hundred pounds.

Carl took the bag from her and replaced it on the shelf, but not at the back.

"I could order some online. But—well, you've already got these. Would you sell me fifty?"

Sell them? He knew he should just give them to her, but the hotel he and Nicola had stayed in, in Fowey, had been pricey, the restaurants they had visited in various other Cornish resorts as expensive as London—the kind they never went to in London— and the holiday, though the costs had been shared with Nicola, far more expensive than he had expected. Fifty pounds for these pills wasn't all that much, but it would be a help. And Stacey could afford it; well, she certainly could if she lost that weight and kept her sitcom job.

"OK," he said, as he counted fifty out into a tooth mug and handed her the packet with the fifty remaining in it.

He went downstairs, realising as he did so that Dermot was closing the front door on his way out. As he came down the stairs, could he have heard Carl's conversation with Stacey? Perhaps. But what did it matter if Dermot had?

By now Stacey had finished her makeup and joined Carl. They were going up the road to Raoul's in Clifton Road. Outside on the pavement she handed over the fifty pounds.

HE FORGOT ABOUT the transaction, not least because Nicola had moved in and he wondered why they had waited so long; it had been two years since Jonathan had first introduced them. But Carl's novel wasn't going well and he struggled to produce two or three paragraphs a day. Nicola asked about it, and he always said everything was fine. He had no idea why this writer's block had arisen.

May was a fine warm month in London, and because staring at his computer was useless and unprofitable, Carl had taken to going out in the late morning while Nicola was at work and picking up a copy of the *Evening Standard*. He chose the *Standard* rather than any other daily paper because it was free.

He stared at today's front page. There, in full colour, was a three-column photograph of Stacey. She looked beautiful, not smiling, but in a soulful pose, her long, thick blond hair draped about her shoulders in a theatrical head shot. Described as twenty-four years old, with her face familiar from her starring role in *Station Road*, she had been found dead in her Primrose Hill flat by a friend who had a key. Police said foul play was not suspected.

It couldn't be—but it must be. Carl broke into a sweat. The phone was ringing as he let himself into the house. It was his mother, Una.

"Oh, darling, have you seen the news about poor Stacey?"

"It's in the *Standard*."

"She was so lovely before she put on all that weight. There was a time when I thought you might marry her."

His mother belonged to a generation where women always thought in terms of marriage. Useless to tell her, though he often had, that even girls seldom thought about marriage anymore. The subject only came up when they became pregnant, and often not even then.

"Well, I can't marry her now, can I? She's dead."

"Oh, *darling*."

"We were friends. That's all."

His mother's words hardly penetrated as he thought about Stacey. He couldn't believe she was dead. She had eaten for comfort, he supposed. Her addiction to food had been the opposite of anorexia. When food was around, especially butter and cheese and ham and fruitcake and anything in a rich sauce, she would declare that she mustn't touch the stuff, she shouldn't dream of touching it, but she couldn't resist. As he watched her grow larger, visibly, it seemed, increasing each time he saw her, he stopped seeing her, only going over to her flat in Pinetree Court, Primrose Hill, when she begged him not to desert her, please, please to come. Then it seemed to him that she would stuff down food in front of him to annoy. That couldn't have been her motive, but it seemed like it, especially when mayonnaise dribbled down her chin, fragments of carrot cake or macaroons stuck all over a close-fitting angora sweater, and her once-beautiful breasts were transformed into vast mounds of sticky cake crumbs.

They had never been lovers but they had been best friends. Now she was gone.

"A man and a woman can't be friends," said his mother. "I wonder if that's what was wrong, that she ate for comfort."

"You mean if I'd married her, she'd have stopped eating?"

"Don't be silly, Carl."

He imagined himself married to Stacey and walking along Sutherland Avenue beside her, an increasingly ridiculous sight. He was thin, which had nothing to do with what he ate or didn't eat and everything to do with his thin mother and thin father.

He sat down in front of the computer and touched the tiny switch with its blue light. The screen showed him its usual picture, a green hill and a purple mountain behind it. Dermot had once come in just after Carl had switched it on and started singing some hymn about

a green hill far away without a city wall. Now every time Carl saw the screen he thought about that stupid hymn and sometimes even began humming it. He had meant to move the mouse on to *Sacred-Spirits*.doc and try to get back into his novel, but instead he went to the Internet, telling himself he had never checked on those yellow capsules he had sold Stacey. The little arrow hovered over *Google*. He typed in the letters DNP, but went no further. He was afraid.

Shutting his eyes—he didn't want to know, not yet, maybe never—he shifted the cursor to exit.

4

F OUR DAYS BEFORE Carl read the story of Stacey's death, Lizzie Milsom entered Stacey's flat. Leaving the keys to one's home outside the property was imprudent, and quite difficult to do so when the property was a flat. Still, Stacey Warren did it, and a good many of her friends knew about it.

The four flats in Pinetree Court all had different-coloured front doors. The door to the ground-floor flat was blue, while those to the first- and second-floor flats were yellow and green respectively. A staircase went down to the basement flat, where Stacey had told Lizzie the front door was red. Stacey lived on the first floor; she secreted her two keys on a single ring inside the cupboard underneath the flight of steps that led up to the front door. The cupboard, which had no lock, held the four tenants' waste bins. Beneath the loose brick in the floor, in the hollow space, were Stacey's spare keys.

Because Stacey had told her she would be out that morning, Lizzie Milsom lifted up the loose brick and helped herself to the keys. She then went into the entrance hall, and went up the stairs to the first floor. Once outside Stacey's flat, she stood still and listened. Silence. All the occupants would be out at work. She intended to find some small object of no great value, such as a piece of pottery or a paperweight or a ballpoint pen—the kind of thing a friend

might give you for a Christmas present—and take it away with her, having first substituted another valueless object in its place. The latter she had brought with her: a black-and-white plastic napkin ring. Doing this—and she often did it—gave her a sense of power. People thought their lives were private and safe, but they were not.

She inserted the key in Stacey's yellow front door and let herself in.

Lizzie wasn't beautiful, but she was the kind of girl people called attractive without specifying whom they were attractive to. She had lovely, caramel-blond hair, thick and long, large, innocent brown eyes, and pretty hands with nails she kept nice with different-coloured varnish that was never allowed to chip. Her figure was good. She would have liked to dress well but couldn't afford it.

She and Stacey had known each other for years. Their parents' homes had been so near each other that they had walked together to their Brondesbury school, which was just down the road. This wasn't the first time Lizzie had been in Stacey's flat, but it was the first illicit visit. She searched through the living areas, looking for some trinket or useless article, and after a while decided on a small diary, unused and three years out-of-date but with Stacey's name printed inside the front cover. The napkin ring was substituted and the diary went into Lizzie's bag.

The rooms in Stacey's flat were large. That is, the living room was large and Lizzie assumed the bedroom was too. She devoted half an hour or so to exploring and searching through cupboards and drawers. She had no intention of taking anything else, and what she had taken she would bring back. But she was more inquisitive than most people and, once in a place that wasn't hers, was consumed with curiosity. She was also a consummate liar. In the unlikely event of someone's entering the place she was exploring, she was always ready with the excuse—she called it a reason—that the owner had asked her to check that she or he had turned off the gas or not left the iron on.

She passed an interesting twenty minutes investigating Stacey's

desk drawers, where she found a wad of twenty-pound notes, a bunch of leaflets advertising weight-loss remedies, an unpaid electricity bill, and an envelope containing photographs of a naked Stacey taken in the days before she got fat. Lizzie told herself she wasn't a thief and helped herself to only two twenty-pound notes, while anyone without principles would have taken the lot. She proceeded to the kitchen, found a half-full bottle of Campari in the fridge, which was otherwise empty of food and drink, and took a swig from it. It made her choke and she wondered what it could have been diluted with. Stacey had a lovely big bathroom, large enough to accommodate an elliptical cross-trainer and a rowing machine. "She doesn't get much use out of them," said Lizzie aloud.

She nearly gave the bedroom a miss. She wasn't interested in sorting through Stacey's underwear or trying out her moisturiser. But the Campari had gone to her head and she thought a lie-down might be a good idea. She opened the bedroom door and stopped short. Stacey, in a lacy nightdress and velvet dressing gown, lay on her back on the floor beside her emperor-size bed. A small plastic packet, empty of whatever it had contained, was beside her, and a glass of what was possibly water. Pale yellow capsules were scattered across the pale yellow carpet.

Lizzie knew Stacey was dead, though she couldn't have said how she knew. She didn't scream. Privately she believed that women who screamed when they saw or found a dead body only did it for effect. They could easily have controlled themselves. She made no noise at all.

She knelt down on the floor and felt for Stacey's pulse. But she didn't need that; she only needed the coldness of the skin on Stacey's face and the icy dampness of her hands to know that Stacey had been there for a long time, probably since the evening before. Lizzie also knew that she had to call the police, or maybe an ambulance, and that now Stacey was dead, she really needed no explanation for being in the flat. It would only be a tiny bit awkward. She tapped

out 999 on her mobile, and the speed with which it was answered amazed her.

"Police," she said when presented with options. "I've just found my best friend dead."

Stacey wasn't Lizzie's best friend, but a small lie was necessary. She would have felt cheated if she had told anything in the region of the truth. Saying she had come into the flat with her own set of keys, keys that Stacey had given her, was only a way of supporting the best-friend statement. She mustn't overdo it.

The operator asked her if she would stay in the flat until the police arrived, and she said of course. She sat down, because in spite of her bravado, she felt quite shocked and afraid that she might fall if she stayed standing up. While she waited for the policeman and perhaps others to come, she replaced the diary in the living room and took back her napkin ring. Best do that—suppose they found her DNA on it?

Alone with her thoughts and feeling stronger, Lizzie sat in an armchair in the living room and wondered what would happen to the flat. It had been Stacey's own, free of mortgage, bought with an inheritance from her parents. Stacey had been proud of her financial independence, certain she could carry on with her acting, with big parts in TV serials, once she had lost weight. Her parents had died in a car crash on the M25 when Stacey was at university. She had been staying with her aunt Yvonne Weatherspoon and her aunt's children when the accident happened and remained with them throughout her time at university. Lizzie wondered if she should phone Yvonne to tell her about Stacey's death, but thought better (or worse) of it. Let the police do that. She didn't have her number, and although she knew Stacey's aunt slightly, she had never got on with her.

In contrast to Stacey, Lizzie lived in a rented bedsit in Iverson Road, Kilburn. The rent was high for what it was, and the place was small, damp, and in dire need of redecoration. She thought about it while she sat in Stacey's flat, thought too how little she wanted to

return to it. Her job as a teaching assistant at a private school paid badly, although it had its advantages. To be able to walk to work was one of them, and a free lunch was another. She wasn't supposed to have a free lunch, or indeed any lunch at school at all, but no one noticed her eating from one or more of the many untouched plates she removed from the children's cafeteria. She also ate an evening meal at her parents' once a week, not because she wanted to, but bearing in mind—never for a moment forgetting—that her father paid half her rent. Well, her father *and* her mother, her mother told her she should say, though Lizzie couldn't see why, as her mother didn't work—or wasn't, as she preferred to put it, a wage earner. A breadwinner, said Lizzie's father, who had been, until he retired, quite well-off.

Lizzie was thinking rather wistfully of the shepherd's pie and queen of puddings her mother would serve up tonight when the doorbell rang.

The police had arrived.

5

CARL HAD NEVER attended an inquest and had no intention of going to this one. That it would happen, and quite soon, loomed large in his consciousness. He thought about it all the time, though unwillingly, because he would have preferred to forget it and dismissed the whole Stacey business from his mind. If he only knew when it was, he could go away somewhere, perhaps to Brighton, or to Broadstairs, where he had once spent a week with a girl-friend. But leaving town wouldn't help him avoid seeing a paper or watching the TV news. Besides, like everything else in his life, he couldn't afford another trip.

Dermot settled the matter for him. He tapped on the living room door on June 1, the day after rent-payment day, handed over his money (a cheque this time) in the envelope, and said he was on his way to "the Stacey Warren inquest." He expected he'd see Carl there, he said.

Carl thought quickly. His nerves wouldn't stand the idea of Dermot's hearing all the evidence, even taking notes, and then coming back here and telling Carl in detail what had happened. He wanted to ask why Dermot was going. He had hardly known Stacey, having met her only once. Carl wanted to tell him that Stacey and her

death weren't Dermot's business; she had been *his* friend, not Dermot's. But Carl had no reason to be rude to Dermot, especially as the month's rent had come on time.

"You mustn't think," Dermot said after Carl had told him he wouldn't be going, "that I'm taking time off work for this. It happens to coincide with my midday break." Dermot smiled, showing the yellowish teeth. "A piece of luck."

Halfway down the path, he turned. "I'll look in on the way back, tell you what happened."

He returned several hours later and seemed to have plenty of time to spare, readily accepting the tea Carl felt constrained to offer. Dermot settled on the sofa Carl thought of as "Dad's sofa" with his tea and a Bourbon biscuit and described the evidence of the doctor and the biochemist in detail.

Dinitrophenol capsules had been lying all over Stacey's bedroom floor, and the same substance was partially digested in her stomach and intestines. The doctor was unable to say if the dose she had recently swallowed was her first or the latest of many. Dinitrophenol—or DNP, as it was called, Dermot said—was known to bring about weight loss, but only if the dose was great enough. A heavy dose or series of doses raised the body temperature far above the danger level and increased the heart rate. Its side effects might be skin lesions, cataracts, damage to the heart, and—here he paused—death. The coroner asked a police officer who had been present at the medical examination where this substance could be obtained and was told it could be bought on the Internet.

"The coroner asked this police officer if it wasn't against the law," said Dermot, "but he said it wasn't, and then he added, 'Not yet.' Meaning it would be one day, I suppose."

Carl thought he shouldn't ask but he had to know. "Did the coroner say anything about where Stacey got this batch of pills?"

Dermot gave Carl a penetrating look. "I said, apparently it's obtainable on the Internet. All right if I have another biccy?"

Carl pushed the plate in Dermot's direction.

"The coroner called Stacey 'this poor young woman.' He looked quite sad. He said her death should be a warning to all women who were unwise and foolish enough to put the slenderness of their figures before their health."

"I suppose the verdict was accidental death?"

"That's right. My goodness, look at the time. I must be off. See you later."

So the coroner had assumed Stacey had bought the pills online. Everyone would assume that. While Carl was disappointed to have his fears about the DNP confirmed, he felt relieved that buying or taking the drug was not against the law, and that therefore, in selling Stacey fifty capsules of it, he had done nothing illegal.

NICOLA WAS DUE home at about six. She used the tube: Westminster to Baker Street, then changed to the Bakerloo Line for Maida Vale. Dermot walked from the veterinary practice in Sutherland Avenue, and this evening he arrived before she did. He was in Carl's living room, and the door was open so there was no avoiding him. He was carrying a large carrot cake in a box.

"Eating all Carl's biscuits the way I did this afternoon, I thought I owed you this."

"Oh, well, thanks."

"I'll just have a tiny piece and then I'll leave you in peace. Sorry, didn't mean to make a pun." Dermot cut himself a generous slice. Addressing Nicola as Miss Townsend, he said he supposed she wouldn't approve of biscuits and rich cake.

She looked doubtfully at him. "Why not?"

"Well, working at the Department of Health like you do."

How did he know where she worked? she wondered. Strange.

She smiled her "beautiful Nicola" smile, with a radiant brightness that illuminated the whole of her pretty face. Fortunately Dermot McKinnon could not see beneath the smile to what she was really thinking.

CARL AND DERMOT were in a café in the Edgware Road, seated at a table covered in animal-print plastic. Dermot had ordered two cappuccinos without asking Carl what he wanted. Carl didn't protest. He was wondering what Dermot's motive in following him in here might be. Silence fell, broken by Dermot asking, while running his fingers across the leopard's spots, if Carl had read in the papers that visitors to zoos shouldn't wear animal-skin prints because they caused excitement inside the cages. Carl hadn't read about it and wasn't interested. The cappuccino, which he had never tasted before, was rich and thick and not much like coffee.

"If I remember rightly," said Dermot, "there was some of that DNP stuff that Stacey Warren took among your dad's medicaments."

An odd word, Carl thought, *medicaments*. "Was there?"

"Perhaps you didn't know what it was?"

"I didn't." Carl wanted to tell Dermot that he had some nerve, snooping about.

"If you've still got it, you ought to throw it away, you know. I expect there'll be a big story in the papers tomorrow. I expect it will be all about how people shouldn't use DNP and how it ought to be banned. I mean, the law ought to be changed, with a heavy penalty for anyone who gives it to—well, to someone else."

THERE WAS INDEED a big story the next day. The front page of the *Daily Mail* had a glamour photo of Stacey and a picture underneath of yellow capsules in a glass jar labelled DNP.

Carl saw the *Mail* on the rack outside a newsagent. Initially he wasn't going to buy it and walked away, then went back when he feared perhaps he might regret not doing so. He read the story as he walked along. It said that as a result of Stacey's death from "DNP poisoning," dinitrophenol would soon be banned, which could happen without a new law but through something called an "order."

"You shouldn't believe stuff you read in the paper," Carl said to himself, and from the stare a passing woman gave him, he realised he had said it aloud.

6

Lizzie Milsom kept hold of Stacey's keys, both sets. No one seemed to know she had them. The police were not long in Stacey's flat, and when they had finally gone, three days after the discovery of the body, Lizzie let herself in once more and walked round the rooms, examining pieces of furniture and equipment, looking at the lovely prints of tropical birds that adorned the walls and confirming that all Stacey's possessions were a lot nicer than anything she had. If she lived here, she wouldn't have to convince herself of her power by borrowing little knickknacks. She would be powerful already, and confident.

Someone must now be the owner of the flat in Pinetree Court, Lizzie thought, but surely Stacey hadn't left it to anyone? People of twenty-four didn't make wills. It would probably go to her aunt Yvonne, or a cousin, or even someone who had never heard of Stacey. Lizzie thought she would stay awhile, perhaps a few days. No one could get in, she was sure of that, for Stacey had told her there were only two sets of keys: the set Stacey carried in her handbag, and those in the outside cupboard. The concierge might have a set, but Lizzie wouldn't worry about that.

She knew she must be careful that no light in the flat was visible from the street below or the car park at the back. The bedroom and

bathroom windows looked down onto a kind of tree-shaded yard whose purpose was unclear. The living room was more of a problem, as it fronted on Primrose Hill Road, but the blinds could be pulled down to cover the window and the curtains drawn to make doubly sure. It was June now, and light till nearly ten, so Lizzie felt pleased with her solution to the problem. She would change and go out, taking both sets of keys with her. It was a pity Stacey had been so overweight—conditioning had made Lizzie never use the word *fat*—as her clothes would no doubt be a size 16. Yet there Lizzie was only half-right, for investigating the left-hand side of the wardrobe as well as the right, she found that ever-hopeful Stacey had kept all or most of the clothes she had worn in her slim days.

Lizzie and Stacey had been the same size in those days, a 10. Lizzie was still a 10. She hunted enjoyably through the clothes and finally laid out on Stacey's bed a jade-green jacket, a short jade-green skirt, and a green-and-pink top studded with tiny pink pearls. Why not have a bath before getting dressed? Stacey's bath was snow-white, wide and deep, a seemingly inexhaustible flood of hot water flowing into it. At home in Kilburn, Lizzie had to rely on a feeble shower that was inclined to splutter, cough, and sometimes stop altogether. Soaking in the hot water, to which she had added nearly half a bottle of Jo Malone nectarine-blossom bath oil, she thought how nice it would be to luxuriate like this every day. Stacey's towels were not towels but bath sheets. Lizzie wrapped herself in one of them and, having sprayed herself with nectarine scent and dressed in the green ensemble, decided to leave her face fashionably free of makeup. Turning off the lights, she went down in the lift. It was a pleasant summer day, mild and windless. She got into the tube at Swiss Cottage and went the four stops to Willesden Green.

"I've never seen that before," said her mother when she opened the door. "Is it new?"

Lizzie said it was, not exactly a lie. The outfit was new to her.

Her parents' house was one of the few in Mamhead Drive not divided into flats. Because it was big, with a large garden, Lizzie had always been proud of it without wanting to go on living there after she came down from university. Tom and Dot Milsom had bought it in 1982 for what Tom now called a derisory sum and stayed there with no intention of ever moving. Lizzie wandered into the enormous living room, pursued by her mother with cups of tea and cakes on a tray.

"Dad out on a bus?"

"Gone down south today. Having a look at some houses in Barnes, he said. I hope he's not thinking of moving."

"You know he never gets off the bus except to come back," said Lizzie, thinking of Stacey and refusing a cake her mother called a "millionaire's macaroon." Lizzie smoothed the silky stuff of which Stacey's skirt was made and asked her mother what she thought of the tragedy in Pinetree Court.

WHEN HE RETIRED at the age of sixty-five—as he put it himself, quite a successful man in a small way—Tom Milsom had never been on a bus. With one assistant, later his partner, he ran a business in commercial photography from a shop in Willesden he referred to as an office. It was so near his home in Mamhead Drive that he could walk to work, and when he was called out on a job, for a wedding photo, for instance, or—something of a comedown, this—platters of chicken tikka and lamb biryani for an Indian restaurant chain, he drove there in the elderly silver Jaguar he kept in pristine condition. His photographic equipment he carried with him in the car, and very occasionally, when it needed servicing or a minor repair, he took his camera and adjuncts on the tube. Going on a bus he never even considered. But when the free bus pass for those over sixty came in, without actually using it he thought it a waste not to. So he put it in his pocket and forgot it.

Traffic in central London, traffic anywhere in London, had become what Dot called, using one of her favourite expressions, "a nightmare." And there was nowhere to park except on the residents' parking in Mamhead Drive or Dartmouth Place, where people didn't need to park because they had garages of their own. "Gold dust" in London, as Dot put it.

Like many men of his age, Tom thought that when he retired, he would find enforced leisure wonderful. He would be free, he would be on a perpetual holiday. What had slipped his mind was how, on the holidays he and Dot had taken over the years, he had been bored stiff trudging along the narrow back streets of little Spanish towns or going on conducted tours to ruined temples in Sicily or trailing up wooded hills in Turkey for the sole purpose of looking at the view from the top. Dot hadn't been bored or, at least, had never said she was—but then nor had he said so. She said it was a lovely change from the housework. Tom had no hobbies. He knew nothing about golf; he didn't even watch it on TV. He didn't care for the cinema, which had nothing on it you couldn't get on telly. He had never been much of a reader and had never learned to like classical music. Looking back to those holidays, what he mostly remembered was how slowly the time passed; that when he looked secretly at his watch, thinking it must be eleven thirty by now, he saw it was just ten past ten.

Again like most men, unless they were accompanying a woman, he seldom if ever went to Oxford Street. Dot, who wanted him out of the way one day while she turned out the living room, suggested he go out and buy himself some socks. Possible shops in Willesden she dismissed. Why not go to Oxford Street, where Marks & Spencer—which she, like the rest of the country, called M&S—had their flagship store?

"Go in the car," she said. "It won't take you more than half an hour there and back."

As if saving time were one of his priorities. "You wouldn't say that if you were a driver."

Instead of the car, he took the tube, Willesden Green to Bond Street on the Jubilee Line. On a Tuesday morning, Oxford Street wasn't crowded. He bought his socks and walked back towards Bond Street station. If half-empty of people, Oxford Street carried a load of buses, so many that Tom fancied their weight would be too much for the road surface and any minute it would crack and sink under this scarlet mass of metal. Where did they all go to? Or come from? Why did they come here, queuing up like animals in a line heading for a water hole? He paused at a bus stop and saw that many buses, six and more if you counted the night ones, were scheduled to stop here. The first on the list was a number 6. He was standing in front of the timetable, which was on a pole and encased in glass, when a bus came looming out of nowhere and bearing down on the bus stop, its light on. The number 6 was on the front of it, and so was its destination: Willesden.

That was the beginning of it, the start of his new occupation. He refused to call it a hobby. Climbing aboard, he waved his pass at the driver, who mimed a touching of this card in a plastic case onto a round, yellow disk that squeaked when contact was made. It was easy, it was rather nice. He got a seat near the front and settled down to be driven home for the first time since he'd come to live in Willesden Green.

That was a year ago, and in that year he had ridden at least half of London's buses, been everywhere and become an expert. This afternoon he was coming back from Barnes and in the Marylebone Road had changed on to his favourite number 6. A most interesting afternoon it had been, and outside, the sun had come out brilliantly.

Most parents would be delighted to come home and find their grown-up daughter paying an unsolicited visit. Dot evidently was, plying this vision in jade green and rose pink with cups of tea, plates of cakes, and now something that was obviously a gin and tonic. Since

her late teens, when Tom had expected Lizzie to change, to grow up and behave, he had viewed his daughter with a sinking heart, only briefly pleased when she got into what she called "uni." But her degree in media studies was the lowest grade possible while still remaining a BA. Gradually, as she moved from one pathetic job to another, ending up with the one she had now—teaching assistant, alternating with playground supervisor of after-school five-year-olds killing time until a parent came to collect them—he felt for his daughter what no father should feel: a kind of sorrowful contempt. He had sometimes heard parents say of their child that they loved her but didn't like her and wondered at this attitude. He no longer wondered; he knew. Walking into the house in Mamhead Drive, he asked himself what lie she would tell that evening, and how many justifications for her behaviour she would trot out.

Dot never seemed aware of her lies and prevarications. Dot and he had talked about it, of course they had, but such discussions usually ended with Dot saying that she couldn't understand how a father could be so hard on his only child when that child was so devoted to him. As if to prove it, Lizzie now got up and kissed him, letting her scented face rest for a moment against his cheek.

Believing he had chosen a subject for conversation unlikely to lead to lying, exaggeration, or fantasising, Tom said that Stacey's death had been a sad business. "I remember her of course from when she was a child in the neighbourhood. You and she used to walk to school together. You and Stacey were good friends." His wife brought him a glass of wine. "You'll miss her."

"Oh, yes, I do," Lizzie said. "So much. You don't know how much I wish I hadn't been in her flat and found the body. I don't think I could ever set foot in there again."

"I don't see why you should have to," said Tom.

"Oh, no, I don't have to. I shan't."

She was lying. He could always tell. He could tell by the tone of her voice and the look on her face, a combination of piety and vir-

tue. They sat down to supper, Lizzie picking delicately at the mushroom omelette that was one of her mother's specialities. Dot wanted to know who owned Stacey's flat now, and Lizzie said she had no idea. She wished she did. It was a lovely flat, luxurious and spacious.

"That's an estate agent's word," said Tom.

"I couldn't think of another one. What would you say?"

"Roomy."

Lizzie went into detail about how beautiful the flat was, the carpets, the sleek black-and-white furniture, the Audubon bird drawings, and this time Tom knew she wasn't lying. Lizzie's love of and knowledge of bird artists and birds themselves was her only intellectual interest. He thought—he couldn't help himself—about the place in Kilburn she lived in and on which he paid half the rent. Nobody would call it beautiful or luxurious, but she was the sole occupant, which was more than you could say for most of her friends, people who shared or had just one room or still lived at home with their parents. He felt hard done by, a state Lizzie's presence usually left him in. She was telling her mother about the shopping spree in Knightsbridge she had been on that had resulted in the purchase of the green suit among other garments. He thought of the portion of her rent he paid and then, looking at her face, knew that the Knightsbridge story was also a lie and she had spent nothing.

STACEY'S FLAT IN Pinetree Court was in darkness when Lizzie got back. She had left the heating on low, and it was pleasant to be lapped in warmth. She turned on the television to a police drama and went into the bedroom, where she took off the green suit and wrapped herself in the dark blue silk dressing gown she found in Stacey's cupboard. Another cupboard, in the kitchen this time, was well stocked with all kinds of wines and spirits. Lizzie made herself a tequila sunrise and settled down in front of the screen with her golden drink.

7

"IS EVERYTHING ALL right between you and Miss Townsend?" said Dermot, passing Carl outside his bedroom door the next morning.

Carl thought this a fearful impertinence. "Of course it is. Why do you ask?"

"Just being friendly. To tell you the truth, I thought you and she would have put things on a more permanent level by now."

"What does that mean?"

Dermot smiled, baring his awful teeth. "Well, once it would have meant marriage, wouldn't it? More like getting engaged these days."

Carl thought quickly. It wouldn't do to make an enemy of Dermot. "It takes two to make an engagement," Carl said rather gruffly.

Dermot shook his head. "I hope I haven't upset you. I wouldn't do that for the world. The way Miss Townsend looks at you, anyone could tell she's crazy about you." He hesitated. "How about a coffee? Your place or mine?"

"I'll make the coffee," said Carl, wishing he had said no. "You won't mind instant?"

"To be perfectly honest with you, I prefer it."

When Dermot had finally drunk his coffee and gone back upstairs, Carl decided that now was the time to tell Nicola about

Stacey. It was Saturday, and she was spending the weekend with her former flatmates. He tried the landline, but there was no reply. Strangely, he couldn't bring himself to try her mobile number. Was it because she would almost certainly answer it?

He needed to talk to Nicola about Stacey, but for some reason, he couldn't. At least not on the telephone. The last time he had gone to dinner with his mother, her friends Jane Porteus and Desmond Jones had been there, and as soon as he came in, Jane had begun talking about Stacey and her horrible death. It would be the same with Nicola.

He asked himself why he didn't want to talk about Stacey. He had done nothing wrong; in fact he had been doing her a favour as far as he knew. It wasn't his fault that she had taken an overdose of the pills. She could have checked them on the Web. The label had advised using care. All he had done was give her—well, sell her— fifty slimming pills that in some circumstances, for some people, caused nasty symptoms. "And death," an inner voice reminded him. Death could be caused by taking DNP. He had by this time been to several dinitrophenol websites, which all mentioned death as a possible result of taking the stuff. Not inevitable, of course, but possible. He had to accept that, painful though it was.

Really, the whole situation was his father's fault. He had died after a heart attack, and one of the websites had said DNP could damage the heart. Could it be . . . ? No, Wilfred had been an old man, and old men died from heart attacks. Young women didn't.

Carl jumped suddenly out of his chair. It was a fine day, another fine day after many in this month of June, and he would go out, walk in the sunshine, think about *Sacred Spirits* and how best to get into it. He had made a false start with this book, and he must begin again. He must find the kind of creative inspiration he had felt when writing *Death's Door*.

He made his way through the little streets of St. John's Wood, then turned down Lisson Grove. The June sunshine fell gently on

his face, the kind of warmth sunshine should always bestow; not a punishing heat or a mildness spoilt by the wind, but steady and promising a permanence. He thought, Why can't I just appreciate things as they come? Why can't I enjoy the moment? I have done nothing wrong. But that inner voice said to him, "You sold those pills to that girl and you never emphasised to her that they had side effects. You never even told her to google them. You wanted the money. You didn't warn her."

Nothing, he told himself as he let himself back into his house. There is nothing to be done. Put it out of your mind. Nothing will bring her back. Sit down at that computer and write something. Anything.

Close to thirty children must have been in the play centre that afternoon, but on a fine day like this it wasn't so bad looking after kids. Only another half hour to go and then Lizzie could get back to the beautiful flat in Primrose Hill Road. The playground had been quite a big area when she was a child herself, but over the years it had become smaller as more and more children reached school age, more and more classrooms were needed, as well as a bigger gym and a science lab, though what little kids needed a lab for she didn't know. Now the children actually bumped into each other running about. Lizzie wasn't supposed to have a whistle for the little ones, but she had and blew it often, trying to bring them to heel. Like dogs, said her mother, who didn't approve.

It was worse when it rained and the children had to stay indoors. Another thing Lizzie wasn't supposed to do was feed them anything but their tea, which consisted of wholemeal bread and Marmite, and apples. Lizzie gave them crisps and sweets called star fruits to shut them up. It cost her a fortune, but it was worth it, especially now she had no gas or electricity to pay for.

On the dot of five thirty, when the parents would start coming

for them, she shooed them indoors and counted them. She dreaded one's going missing. Not because she cared—if anything, she disliked children—but because of the trouble there would be and the loss of her job. But they were all there today, and they all wanted to get home. So did Lizzie.

It wasn't far to Primrose Hill Road from West End Lane, just a short walk along Adelaide Road, and halfway along she sat down on a seat, tore up the four slices of wholemeal bread she had taken from the children's snacks, and scattered the crumbs on the pavement. Pigeons appeared at once and began gobbling up the bread. People said pigeons were grey, but Lizzie knew better. One was red and green, another was silver with a double streak of snowy white, and a third, perhaps the handsomest, jet-black with a metallic emerald sheen to its feathers.

By this time, she had got into Stacey's habit of keeping a set of keys in the recycling cupboard, not because she expected someone else to try to gain entry in her absence—there was no one—but because she was inclined to forget things and knew well that if she inadvertently shut herself out of Stacey's flat, she would have no means of getting back inside. Not for her the services of a locksmith when she couldn't identify herself as the owner or legal occupant of the flat. No relative had come forward as far as she knew, no other friend who might possess a key. In putting the spare set in the recycling cupboard, in the hollow under the loose brick in the floor, Lizzie calculated she was safe. The only alternative she could think of was to carry the keys with her at all times, maybe on a chain round her neck. She disliked the idea because it spoilt her look when wearing Stacey's clothes.

UNA MARTIN WASN'T much of a cook. She relied on smoked salmon and the kind of pasta dishes you bought ready-made and just had to put in the microwave. Her son didn't notice what he ate and seemed to be glad of anything he got. Una assumed that he and Nicola lived on ready meals and takeaways.

"I've been wondering," she said as she and Carl began on their first course (there was no second), "who's going to get poor Stacey's flat? I mean, what happens to property if it's not left to anyone and no one comes forward to claim it?"

"It goes to the Crown," Carl said, guessing. He didn't really know.

"I've never been in her flat. I expect it's very nice."

"Yes, it is." Carl helped himself to more pasta. "I've been a few times."

"Now if only you'd married her, it would be yours."

Carl sighed. "I don't need a flat. I've got a nice house. There was no prospect of me marrying her. You got this crazy idea into your head, and I don't know where it came from. Stacey was just a friend."

"There's no such thing as a man and a woman just being friends."

"Is there any more wine?"

No answer was forthcoming.

"There was an aunt," he said, remembering.

"What on earth do you mean, darling, there was an aunt?"

"Stacey Warren had an aunt."

"How do you know?"

"She lived with her after her parents died."

"So you're saying that this aunt, whoever she is, would inherit that beautiful flat? What's her name? Where does she live?"

"I don't remember."

But Una pursued the matter exhaustively. Who was the aunt? How would they find her? How long would it take?

While she talked, Carl sat eating everything that was left. It was a change for him to think about Stacey from a different aspect, not from the point of view of her death and whose fault it was. He also remembered where Stacey had kept her spare set of keys, though he was sure they wouldn't be there any longer.

Una lived in Gloucester Avenue in Camden, which was not far from Primrose Hill Road, but some way from the part of it where Stacey's flat was. On a whim, he made a detour on his way home

and, looking up at what had been Stacey's windows, saw a faint light on. Someone was in there. Perhaps a solicitor? An estate agent? At twenty minutes to ten at night? It wasn't his business. He had come to check on the keys in the recycling cupboard.

No one was about. He shifted the recycling bin a few inches, surprised to find it half-full of newspapers and packaging. The keys were there all right, underneath the floor brick. Suppose he went up in the lift and let himself into the flat—he had never done so in the past—and found Stacey in there, not as she had been in recent months, but a slim and beautiful ghost, waiting for him, waiting to accuse him of killing her.

Don't be a fool, he said to himself as he made his way out onto Chalk Farm Road, where the pubs were spilling out and noisy crowds sat at the tables on the pavement.

8

Tom Milsom got off the number 98 bus at Marble Arch and, having walked a few yards to the top of Park Lane, hopped onto the 414. It was amazing how you could get on and off buses and on again all for free. Well, not really free; you'd paid for it in taxes all your life. But he wondered if there was any other capital city in the world where, so long as you were over sixty, you could ride on any bus without paying. He felt a surge of affection for his country, so cruelly maligned by many people. The words of the hymn came into his head, "I vow to thee, my country, all earthly things above," and tears pricked the back of his eyes, but they were tears of warmth and love.

He went to the upper level. Most people of his age didn't, but you saw so much from the top of a bus, especially when charging down the sloping part of Park Lane. He looked down at Grosvenor House and the Dorchester and the beautiful houses that remained, and there, walking along the pavement, was his next-door neighbour Mrs. Grenville, holding the hand of a man who wasn't her husband. Tom thought it should have been a woman observing this bit of scandal; gossip was wasted on him.

It was three in the afternoon, and the bus was three-quarters empty as it made its way down into Knightsbridge. To his surprise,

it stopped right outside Harrods. No use to him, he thought. He might as well stay on and go to the bus's destination, Putney Bridge. Another bus was bound to be waiting there for him, one he had never before been on, never even heard of, and if it didn't take him all the way home, it would take him somewhere he could pick up a number 98 or even a 6, which passed the end of Mamhead Drive.

CARL WAS FORCING himself to write three or four paragraphs every day, but now as he read his new pages, he admitted to himself that they weren't very good. The prose was laboured, heavy, lifeless, the obvious result of pushing himself. But it's about a philosopher, he thought, it's bound not to have the witty lightness of *Death's Door*. Perhaps he should look on his efforts as a practice run, a trial exercise to get himself back into novelist mode? He produced a few more lines and interrupted himself by remembering that today was the last of the month and tomorrow the first of July, rent day. Of course the rent wouldn't come; it never came the day before now, though apologies sometimes did.

So he wasn't surprised when Dermot tapped at his door. Letting him in, Carl awaited the excuses. But there were no excuses, only smiles and the handover of a brown envelope.

"What's this, then?"

"Your rent, Carl. What else?"

"You never pay me the day before, or the day itself, come to that." Carl opened the envelope and took out the so-desirable purple notes. "Still, I'm not complaining."

"Look at it this way. It may be the first time, but it may also be the last."

"You don't mean you're leaving?"

"Oh, no. No, no."

Dermot gave Carl another of his ghastly smiles, the yellow blotches on his teeth looking worse than usual. Carl noticed that a

large pustule had appeared on Dermot's chin. Carl listened to him mounting the stairs, and then asked himself what that had meant. That stuff about Dermot's payment being the last.

It meant nothing, he told himself. Dermot thought he was being funny. Put it out of your head. It was nonsense.

But that "No, no" rang out and echoed in his head. He looked again at the contents of the envelope. Perhaps there were twice as many notes this month? But he had counted them the first time and there were not. He wanted to get back to *Sacred Spirits*, but concentration was impossible.

"Oh, no. No, no" surely meant that Dermot wasn't giving up his flat. It had been a firm denial. Suddenly Carl saw that, firm or not, it had nothing to do with the contents of the envelope being Dermot's last payment. He had plainly said it might be the last. Could he have meant instead that at the end of next month, there would be no envelope and no money? He couldn't mean that. A tenant had to pay his rent. Carl would have to ask Dermot what he had meant. Carl couldn't go another four weeks with the suspense of not knowing.

But a week went by without Carl's doing anything about it. From his living-room window he saw Dermot going off to work, and on the Sunday morning leaving for church. Some respite from the nagging anxiety came with the idea that Dermot had only meant that this was the last time the twelve hundred pounds would be paid in cash, and that in future he intended to pay by cheque or direct debit. The relief lasted only a few minutes. If he had meant that, he would have said so.

Carl had rarely been to the top floor since Dermot had arrived. Now he determined to go up and ask for an explanation of their last bizarre exchange. What had it meant? Ten days had passed since he had encountered Dermot. Almost never in the course of their association—you couldn't call it a friendship—had as much as ten days gone by without their seeing each other, even if only on the stairs.

He left it another two days. There was still no sign of Dermot. But he wasn't ill and confined to bed, and he hadn't done a moonlight flit. Carl could occasionally hear footfalls on the bare boards of the top-floor flat, and once a burst of religious music indicated that Dermot's front door was open. On the third day after he had come to his decision, he climbed the top flight and thumped on the door.

"Goodness me," said Dermot from inside. "Whatever's wrong? Has something happened?"

"Just open the door, will you?"

The door came open, but slowly, rather reluctantly, as if it had been bolted on the inside. There had never been bolts on that door before Dermot came. From the kitchen came a strong smell of sausages and bacon frying. Stepping back to let Carl come in, Dermot said in the pleasantest, friendliest tone Carl had ever heard from him, "Now I do hope there isn't going to be trouble, Carl. We have had such an amicable relationship up till now."

"I just want you to tell me something."

"If I can. You know I always bend over backwards to keep a peaceful atmosphere. Now what can I tell you? No, wait, let me make us a nice cup of coffee."

"I don't want any bloody coffee. I want you to tell me what you meant when you handed me the last lot of rent. You said it was the first time and it might be the last. I said, 'You're not leaving, are you?' and you said, 'Oh, no. No, no.'"

Dermot smiled his ghastly smile. "Let me just pop into the kitchenette while I turn off the burner." He came back still smiling. "There, sorry about that. I couldn't have my lunch ruined, could I? Yes, back to our last conversation. I don't quite see where I went wrong. I said I wasn't leaving, and I'm not. Does that satisfy you? Not leaving. Staying. Happy again?"

Carl felt rage rising inside him. Dermot was playing with him. "Correct me if I'm wrong, but we have an agreement, signed by

both of us, and witnessed. Right? And that agreement states that you pay me a certain sum each month while you occupy this flat. Right again?"

Dermot had put a spoonful of instant coffee into each of two mugs and picked up the electric kettle. Through a window in the side of the kettle Carl could see the water boiling. Dermot held it close to Carl's face, and Carl flinched, jerking his chair back. Smiling, Dermot poured water onto the coffee.

"Ah, but don't you remember who the witness was? I do. It was Stacey Warren. A sheet of paper taken out of your printer, written on by you and witnessed by a woman who's now passed away. Valueless, I'd say, wouldn't you?" Dermot took a gulp of the strong black coffee he had made. It would have choked Carl but it had almost no effect on the other man. "So, yes, I'm staying, but I'd say it's probable I'll never pay you rent again."

"But you can't live here rent-free."

"I think I can," said Dermot calmly. "Shall I tell you why? It's DNP. Dinitrophenol. I think you should know that while I'm a believer, a pretty strict follower of the Christian faith, a churchgoer, as you may have noticed, I haven't any of what some people call honour. Now I know you had a cabinetful of DNP. It came from your dad, I heard you say, and I had a good scrounge round through all his medication. If you didn't want that happening, you should have locked your bathroom door. The first time there were a hundred capsules, the second time fifty. You sold fifty of those poisonous pills to Stacey Warren, didn't you? As a matter of fact, I was passing your open bathroom door when the transaction—the sale, I mean—took place."

Carl would have expected someone in his situation to turn white. They did in books. In his own book. Conversely, his face had flushed, and he could feel the skin burning.

"It's not against the law. It's not. You can't make it against the law," he said in a tremulous voice, a voice that didn't sound like his own.

Without a word, Dermot got up and walked out of the room. He was back quickly, carrying a page cut from the *Guardian*. "You want to read that. You can keep it. I've got copies."

"Killed by DNP," the line under the pictures said, photographs of a girl and a young man and a number of yellow capsules. The police believed that the man had given the pills to the girl with the specific intention of killing her. He had used DNP as a poison. Carl read in the article that the drug could kill even if doses of it had safely been taken previously. One woman had taken it for two years before she died. Another's death had been mysterious until tests found that the pills by her bed were DNP. The drug was available online, and selling it wasn't against the law, but it could too easily be lethal. Two MPs had expressed concern, and one said it might be helpful to have DNP brought under the Misuse of Drugs Act.

Carl laid down the paper. He was sweating and could feel the drops of perspiration on his upper lip. "This means nothing. The drug is not illegal."

"So you're not worried. In two weeks' time I pay your rent and you won't mind if I chat to a few people about what you did. Fifty pills. That's a lot. More than enough to kill. Perhaps you intended her to die? And what about your reputation as a brilliant young writer, such a promising new talent?"

Carl stood up. "So you want to chat to people about me? That's rich. And who are these people?"

"Sit down a minute. There's the press, of course. The anonymous tip here and there. And I've been doing my homework. Stacey Warren had an aunt, and this aunt has a son and a daughter. As it happens, I know the aunt quite well. Mrs. Yvonne Weatherspoon was devoted to Stacey and had her to stay when her parents died. She brings her cat to the clinic where I work, and it would be the easiest thing in the world to have a little chat with her about poor Stacey's death. In fact, she's due to bring the cat in for her shots tomorrow."

Carl knew very well that you should never say "How dare you?"

to anyone, least of all someone who was threatening you. It sounded ridiculous. But he did say it. "How dare you threaten me, you blackmailer?"

But Dermot seemed calm and in command of the situation. "I've been threatening you for the past ten minutes, as you very well know. I can't threaten you with police arrest. But it's nasty stuff, isn't it? Mrs. Weatherspoon is a very strong-minded woman—do they still use that expression? You probably know better than I do. A strong character is what I mean. Once she knows where poor Stacey got the DNP, she will, as they say, take it further. The *Hampstead and Highgate Express*, for a start, and maybe that paper that operates around Muswell Hill? They may even send their photographer round to get a picture of you. Stacey was well-known. You're a novelist. The gossip columns will love it."

"I don't want to talk any more about it. You have to pay the rent and that's all there is to it."

Carl was barely out of the room when he heard his tenant putting the coffee cups in the sink and tipping the contents of the frying pan onto a plate.

Without that rent, what was he going to live on? It would take him months, if not years, to finish *Sacred Spirits*, and already he had no confidence in his work. But this was all hypothetical. He would have his rent and let that criminal bastard, that blackmailer, do his worst. He would ignore him. He would get back to his writing.

This brave stance buoyed Carl for a while. But when he sat down at the computer again, he found that nothing would come. All he wrote, without really knowing that he was doing so, were the words that kept running in a continuous loop through his head: *It's not against the law, it's not against the law, it's not against the law.*

9

THE SUTHERLAND PET Clinic was within easy walking distance of Falcon Mews. Dermot could be there in less than ten minutes. Like Saint Matthew, who was a kind of tax collector, he sat at the receipt of custom, but unlike the saint, since there was no animal welfare in the Holy Land, he made appointments and received payment for neutering, injections, operations, checkups, and, sadly, euthanasia. It was not unknown for Dermot to bow his head and weep a little when Jake or Honey had to be put to sleep. That was the terminology he preferred; he had been known to admonish a cat or dog owner who spoke of "putting down" an animal.

The area of his job he liked best was as a salesman, such as when he was called upon to advise a client about which variety of cat food he would recommend for sixteen-year-old Mopsy or kitten Lucy. Which artificial bones would he suggest for the incorrigible biter Hannibal or breath deodorant for ancient Pickwick? His finest contribution to the social life of the clinic was the Pet of the Month competition he had invented. This was popular. Owners submitted their pet's details to him with a photograph and some instances of bravery or achievement, and he judged which was the top dog or cat. Up on the wall for the rest of this month was a charming photograph of Pippa, a cuddly British Blue whose howls at midnight had

alerted her owners to the presence of a burglar in the house. The announcement of the competition winner he timed—so that he couldn't forget it—for his rent day. This of course would no longer be a factor, so he would have to fix on some other way of remembering to reveal the result.

The day after his encounter with Carl, Dermot was sitting behind his desk at the clinic, contemplating the list of clients expected that day, when Yvonne Weatherspoon arrived with Sophonisba, her Maine coon, in her cat box. Her appointment was for nine thirty and it was now twenty past. Sophonisba, always called Sophie, was due for a flea and worm check.

Close on fifty but retaining her fine blond good looks and slender figure, Yvonne had already confided in the sympathetic Dermot about her niece's death, hugging Sophie and squeezing out a tear or two.

"You know who I'm talking about, don't you, Dermot?"

"Ah, yes. That poor young lady Miss Stacey Warren, the beautiful actress. What a sad event that was."

"Well, we were very close, you know." Dermot did know, but continued to listen with great interest. "She left me her flat. Well, she didn't actually leave it to me, but I am her next of kin, her heir. I'm not going to live in it. I've already got a lovely house of my own, what the government calls a mansion, and dear Sophie wouldn't put up with moving. Cats hate a change of home, as I'm sure you know."

"Yes, indeed."

"I'm going to hand it over to my son. Gervaise. He and poor Stacey were very close."

"He's a very fortunate young man."

Further conversation was terminated by the appearance of Caroline, the head vet, come to fetch Yvonne and Sophie. The cat, no doubt aware of what was in store for her, set up a howling, and Dermot, left to his thoughts, said a thank-you to God, but in a whisper, because the deity could hear everything.

The thanks to the Almighty were not for the outcome of his interview with Carl, but for the news imparted by Yvonne Weatherspoon. Carl already knew about Dermot's acquaintance with Yvonne, but not that her son was moving into Stacey's flat. And this knowledge would confirm to Carl something that Dermot was sure Carl had doubted: that at almost any time, and in an intimate manner, Dermot could impart the details of the DNP sale to Yvonne. Perhaps, if he could fix it, he could also tell Gervaise, he who had been so close to "poor Stacey."

Carl had called him a blackmailer. Dermot hadn't liked that. Not at all. He didn't see himself that way. You could almost say he was the reverse of a blackmailer, because instead of taking money from Carl as the price of his silence, he was withholding it. He had never disliked Carl and didn't now. To dislike anyone would be unchristian. To love your neighbour as yourself was a tenet of Dermot's faith, and he was proud of loving himself a lot. In any case, there was nothing in the Bible about blackmail. Or reverse blackmail.

The street door opened and Mr. Sanderson came in with his dalmatian, Spots. Not Spot, but the plural—"Because he's got lots of them," the dog's owner had once said. "I counted, and there were a hundred and twenty-seven."

Very privately, Dermot thought all the clients were mad.

CARL WAS FORCING himself to write. He read and reread what he had written and tinkered with words, but with no noticeable effect. He was writing stiffly: the little dialogue he attempted was stilted and strangely outdated, and his characters spoke to each other as if they lived in the middle of the last century.

The reason for his failings was obvious. His mind was full of Dermot's threat to withhold the rent or ruin Carl's reputation. The rent was due on July 31, though in the usual course of things it would not be brought to him until the first or second day of August.

Would it be brought at all this time? Would Dermot carry through on his threat? Carl had avoided his tenant since their conversation, but he often heard his footsteps on the stairs. He thought about him constantly, and if he could manage to fall asleep at all, he woke in the small hours and stayed awake for the rest of the night, tossing and turning and no doubt disturbing Nicola, creating all possible variations on what would happen if the rent didn't come, what he would do and what Dermot would do.

Carl had said nothing about Dermot's threat to Nicola, reasoning that if he told her, he would also have to tell her about selling the DNP to Stacey. He should have told her long ago. She knew that something was worrying him. Would she understand? Nicola was almost indifferent to money, seldom bought clothes the way other girls did, never used makeup. Unlike the other women he knew, she was always reading books—books made of paper, not in cyberspace—and listening to what he called classical music and she called real music. That was one reason he had been attracted to her. She had loved *Death's Door*. She was his biggest fan. So why hadn't he told her about Stacey?

The longer he waited, the more difficult it became. Once, anticipating her return from work at six thirty, he found himself wishing she hadn't moved in. He reproached himself for that, telling himself that this dread would pass, that it would one day be gone but he would still have her.

"I don't believe you've got any food in the house," she'd said the previous evening. "I think you've lost weight, and you can't afford that." A note of anxiety came into her voice. "You look as if you've been ill, which you haven't, I know."

"I've been a bit under the weather," he said, in Dermot mode.

On the way back from doing the shopping together, he thought he might tell her. He'd make her promise not to tell anyone, and once he'd got that undertaking from her, he'd confide in her, tell her everything he'd done, starting with the collection of medicines

and remedies he had inherited from his father. She had, of course, seen them in the bathroom they shared, but they had never discussed them. Then he'd go on to talk about Stacey and her weight, her despair, and how she had begged him to let her have the yellow capsules. If he put it like that, Nicola would see how impossible it'd been for him to refuse.

"You're very quiet," she said now. "You really are worrying about something, aren't you? I've sensed it for a while."

"I'll be all right."

"As soon as we get home, we'll have a glass of that Chablis. We could both do with it. I've had a bit of a rough day."

Not compared to his day, Carl thought, or the eleven or twelve days he'd lived through since Dermot had threatened him. And as he thought of Dermot, as they made their way into Falcon Mews, his tenant approached from the other end. He was walking jauntily, in Carl's eyes, and carrying tulips.

"Snap!" said Dermot, and to Nicola, "What a coincidence. Long time since we've seen you round this neck of the woods."

Carl muttered to himself that he had never before seen a man buy flowers for himself, but Dermot didn't hear because Nicola was telling him how nice it was to see him. She was out all day and their paths never seemed to cross. They let him go into the house first. Carl was thinking with longing of that glass of Chablis. He seldom bought wine. He had let Nicola buy two bottles, explaining in the shop that he couldn't afford it, though he still had some money from this month's rent. But was it the last he would receive?

Nicola put the food in the fridge and poured the wine generously. "Waiters and barmen always fill your glass only half-full. Have you noticed? It never used to be like that."

He didn't say anything. He could hear Dermot pacing around two floors up. It sounded as if he was leaping up and down. Carl took his wine into the living room.

"Shall we have some music, Carl? I've bought you a new CD."

"Not yet. I've got something to tell you."

The face she turned to him was aghast. It was the only possible word.

"No, no. Nothing that's going to affect you. For God's sake, don't look like that." He set his glass down, hesitated, and then picked it up again to take a great gulp of his wine. Seated now on the sofa, he patted the cushion beside him; when she sat down, he took her face in his hands and kissed her with a gentleness that surprised even him. "There. I don't know what you'll think. And better not say a word to Dermot after what I tell you; I mean, if you felt like going up there and having it out with him."

"What is it?"

"It has to do with Stacey Warren. You didn't really know her, did you?"

"I'd met her, of course. She was your friend. Is that what's been bothering you? Her death?"

He waited for her to say how fat Stacey had become, but she didn't.

"Nicola, you know those medicines—well, I suppose you'd call them quack remedies—my dad left in the house? Stacey came to see me one day, and she found these pills. Well, capsules. They're called dinitrophenol." It sounded better using that word, as Nicola might have read the name in the newspaper. "I didn't know anything about the pills, but she said they could help her lose weight. She asked me if she could have some."

Nicola took a sip of her wine.

"There were about a hundred in the packet. I let her have fifty." An idea came to him. "Would you like to see them? I've still got the rest."

Nicola nodded. They went upstairs and she followed him into the bathroom. He took the packet of yellow capsules out of the cupboard and she held it in her hand. "You gave her fifty?"

There was no point in telling her at all if he failed to tell her the

truth. So why was it so hard? He looked into her beautiful, gentle face. It would be fine; she just wanted clarification. "As a matter of fact, I sold them to her. A pound each, that's the price that was listed on the package." Nicola nodded, but gave no indication what she was nodding about. She handed back the capsules and walked out of the room. He went after her, but she moved slowly. On the stairs, she turned and said over her shoulder, "And she died? Did she die because of the dinitro-whatever?"

"They said at the inquest that it contributed to her death. Come back and finish your wine, and then we can make supper."

"Where does Dermot come into it?"

Carl saw now that bringing his tenant in would make things much worse. Should he tell her that Dermot was threatening him? Instead, he repeated the phrase: "The pills are not against the law."

"Then they should be."

"Maybe." He began to reel off the stories he had taken from the newspapers of people who had used DNP and lost weight but been OK. Their temperatures had risen dangerously and they had felt ill, but they'd got thin and now they were absolutely fine. "Please, can we have another drink?"

"Not for me."

"What's wrong, Nic?"

There was no need to ask. The tears were falling silently down her cheeks. He had never seen her cry before. "Why are you crying?"

"You know. Of course you do. I love you, or I thought I did. But I don't think I can love someone who did what you did. Gave her pills—sold her pills—that you must have known were dangerous. It's horrible."

Carl shook his head. "I'm not hearing this."

"Yes, you are. Don't you see it was bad enough giving her the stuff, let alone selling it to her?" She wiped her eyes with a tissue. "I can't believe you've kept all this a secret from me. I should never have come to live here."

"Don't go, Nic. Please don't go."

"I've nowhere to go to. The girls have let my room in the flat. I'll have to sleep in the spare room."

Carl had never felt such despair. It enclosed him in its cold emptiness. He drank about half the second of the bottles of wine they had bought—no, Nicola had bought. He went into the kitchen and ate a slice of bread and a hunk of cheese. It seemed that he lived on bread and cheese these days. Later, after he had slept awhile on Dad's sofa, he heard Nicola getting ready for bed, using the bathroom, fetching herself a glass of water. He held his breath, hoping against hope that she had changed her mind and gone into their bedroom. But, no, she hadn't.

The spare-bedroom door creaked a little when it closed, and now he heard the creak before the click of the lock.

10

T HE FLAT IN Pinetree Court could never become her permanent home; Lizzie knew this from the moment she'd moved herself in there. She had known it when she discovered Stacey's body. But the trouble was, she was getting accustomed to it. It had begun to feel like hers. She even cleaned it, which was the first time she had ever cleaned anywhere. Her mother came round and hoovered and dusted her place in Kilburn, but the flat in Pinetree Court was so beautiful, so luxurious, that Lizzie couldn't bear the idea of its getting dirty, so she did it herself.

She wondered why no one had taken the place over. It was weeks since Stacey had died, and it must by now belong to someone. It must have been *left* to someone. Perhaps the person it had been left to didn't want to live here because he or she had a place of his or her own. Lizzie tried to think who besides Stacey's aunt Yvonne this person might be. Stacey had once been Carl Martin's sort of girlfriend, or had been till she got so obese, but though Lizzie had known Carl years ago, they had not had any contact recently. She couldn't go up to him in the street and ask him what was happening to Stacey's flat. And he probably wouldn't know anyway.

But what about that chap who lived in the top half of what

she had heard from Stacey was Carl's house? Lizzie liked walking through the mews, imagining what it would be like to live there. One time she'd seen that chap come out of the front door. This was before she'd started at the school and when she'd been doing old Miss Phillips's typing. Imagine being called miss in this day and age! One day Lizzie had to take Miss Phillips's pooch, a fat pug, to the vet's, and there was that chap from Falcon Mews on reception. Was he a vet, then? No matter; she would think of a reason to go into the clinic and ask him whether by any chance he knew if Carl now owned a flat in Pinetree Court.

Lizzie was going out to dinner with a new man. She'd met him at a coffee bar near Stacey's flat. He seemed posh, promising, though she couldn't yet call him her boyfriend. His name was Swithin Campbell. She was meeting him at Delaunay's in the West End, and afterwards he would bring her back here in a taxi and she would ask him in for coffee or something out of one of those exotic bottles of Stacey's. Lizzie had never before met anyone called Swithin; she had only heard of it in connection with St. Swithin's Day. Sometime in July it was, and if it rained that day (it always did), it would keep on raining for forty days, or so her father said.

Lizzie never went to hairdressers. She had thick, glossy, caramel-coloured hair that only needed washing. She put on what she judged to be Stacey's best dress, more a gown than a dress, in a gorgeous blue-green. It was called teal, Lizzie thought, and the neckline was encrusted with what looked like turquoises. She had bought nail varnish in the same colour on the way back from the play group but decided against it. Men only liked red varnish.

At ten to seven, she went downstairs to walk to Chalk Farm tube station. She was trying not to spend money on taxis.

Tom Milsom had had a lovely day, down to Holborn on the number 98, lunch in a nice pub where they served good fish and chips,

then back on the 139, which didn't go where he thought it would, but dropped him outside a tube station on the Jubilee Line. The train took him to Willesden Green. Then it was just a short walk to Mamhead Drive.

Dot had wanted to come with him, but he had put her off, he hoped not unkindly. He said she would be bored, but in truth he enjoyed his bus trips so much, he wanted to keep them to himself. He didn't want to talk but to look and, he supposed, to learn, to discover how little he really knew of London. Now he *was* learning, and that was something she wouldn't understand. She and Lizzie tended to laugh at this new interest of his, but to him it wasn't funny. It was marvellous, and serious.

Next week he would be more ambitious. He could take the number 6 to halfway down the Edgware Road, then get on the 7. Lizzie had once told him that she went on that bus to the Portobello Road. It was such a trendy place to go to that he hadn't liked to tell her he had never been there, that he barely knew where it was. The number 7 bus driver would, though.

"You're very quiet," Dot said when he got in. "Thinking about your exciting trip, are you? I'll come with you one of these days."

"No, you won't," Tom said hastily. "You don't get your pass till you're sixty."

The following day he took the number 16 to Victoria. The building works going on around the bus station, the chaos and the crowds, even though it was only half past three in the afternoon, made him resolve not to come here again until the underground improvement works were finished.

Coming home, he got on the 16, which went to Cricklewood Broadway, from where he could transfer to one of the three routes that would take him to Willesden. But at the Edgware Road stop, a big, burly man got on, slapped his pass onto the card reader, and shouted out when it didn't beep. The driver took the card from him and read it; it was out-of-date and the driver told the fat man he

would need to renew it. The queue getting on the bus began muttering angrily. The man with the out-of-date pass shouted insults at the driver, calling him a black bastard. That was enough. The driver said to get off, everyone must get off because he was calling the police. The man with the out-of-date pass yelled that he wasn't getting off, and the driver said good, that suited him. Tom escaped through the exit in the middle of the bus and walked the short distance to the next stop, where he got on the number 6.

He smiled. When he got home, he would tell Dorothy about the row on the bus. She always enjoyed a bit of a fight so long as no one came to blows.

For once, as Lizzie put it to herself, she hadn't drunk very much, just a gin and tonic and two small glasses of wine the whole evening. She wanted to make a good impression on Swithin, and she noticed how little he drank.

He had at their first meeting seemed an intelligent man, but he hadn't much conversation, and long silences fell. She tried to fill the gaps by telling him about her father's bus rides, making his small adventures as amusing as she could, but Swithin appeared to have no sense of humour. Like most of her friends, Lizzie believed that if a man took you out for an expensive dinner in a place such as this, he would expect you to have sex with him afterwards. You didn't necessarily have to. She looked across the table at him and smiled mysteriously. He began talking about the Scottish referendum.

Taking her home in a taxi, he accepted her invitation to come in for coffee. She had only once tried Stacey's espresso machine and looked forward to using it again. She wanted to see the impression it made on him. She wasn't disappointed.

"You own this place, do you?" Those were almost his first words as he walked into the living room.

She said she did.

"At current prices it must be worth close on a million."

"Not quite that." She went to make the coffee. When she came back, he was looking at Stacey's paintings of tropical birds and examining a table of pale yellow wood with a grey inlay. Lizzie didn't much like it; it was the kind of thing her mother would have called too modern.

"Is it a———?" Swithin uttered a name that sounded like a town in Slovakia.

"Oh, yes. It was very pricey." She knew she shouldn't have said that. It wasn't the sort of word to use in connection with valuable furniture. "I didn't buy it, my mother did."

He gave her a strange look. They drank their coffee and he talked about house prices. When he had emptied his cup, she expected him to move towards her along the sofa, but he got up instead. "Very good coffee."

There was nothing to say to that. He gave her a kiss, a light peck on the cheek, and quickly departed.

In the weeks she had been in Pinetree Court, few callers had come to the door. The post, what there was of it, was deposited in the boxes in the entrance hall. Meters were read in cupboards outside and by the front doors. So when the doorbell rang the following morning, Lizzie jumped. She wasn't going to answer it or even guess who it might be. It rang again. It will ring twice, she thought, and then they'll give up and go away.

The sound of a key turning in the lock brought a cold shiver. She waited in the little hallway as a man she recognised as the concierge stepped into the flat. With him was a tall, handsome man of about her own age whom she vaguely recognised.

"Who might you be?" said the concierge.

Lizzie did her best to make her voice bold. "I'm a friend of Miss Warren's. I'm looking after the place."

"Miss Warren passed away some time ago. The apartment is now about to be occupied by this gentleman, Mr. Weatherspoon."

Of course. That was who it was. Aunt Yvonne's son. "Hi, Gervaise."

"Well, if it isn't little Lizzie," said Gervaise Weatherspoon. "How did you get in?"

"I've had a key for *years*."

The concierge plainly didn't believe her, something Lizzie resented, as for once what she said was more or less true. "I'll have that key, thank you, miss, and then we'll say no more about it."

She gave him the key meekly because she had just remembered she didn't need it. The other one, the one in the floor of the recycling cupboard, was known to her and her alone. She favoured Gervaise with a radiant smile. "Will you be living here?"

"One day." His smile matched hers. "First I'll be going on an archaeological visit to Cambodia and Laos."

Gervaise asked for Lizzie's phone number so she could give him details of the flat's phone and energy suppliers. The concierge looked disgruntled: he could help Mr. Weatherspoon with that, he said. But Lizzie took no notice and wrote down her mobile number and the landline at the Kilburn flat. Gervaise's request had given her an idea and done her a power of good. Never mind that she was going to be an hour late for school.

"I'll be in touch," she promised.

Lizzie packed every bag she could find in the flat. Seeing no reason to leave any of Stacey's clothes behind, she stuffed them into suitcases from Louis Vuitton, Marks & Spencer, and Selfridges. Then she phoned for a taxi.

While she was waiting for it, a knock came at the door. She thought it was the taxi, but, no, it was the concierge, with an enormous bunch of white lilies, feathery gypsophila, and pink rose-

buds. The card accompanying it was addressed to "Darling Liz" with love from Swithin. Liz indeed. No one had ever called her that.

Taking the flowers with her, she removed the extra key from underneath the brick in the floor of the recycling cupboard and put it in her handbag. Then she stacked the luggage on the pavement to wait for the taxi to take her to Kilburn.

11

Rent day, the last day of the month, had gone past. By August 2, Carl knew he wouldn't be paid.

He wasn't yet destitute. The second instalment of the advance he had received on publication of *Death's Door* had taught him to be careful, if not frugal, and though nearly all of that had gone, he had saved a little more from the July rent that had come in. He probably had as much as four hundred pounds in his current account. But if Dermot's August rent failed to appear—and plainly it was not going to—the demand for council tax did. *City of Westminster* it said across the top of the letter, and underneath that, the sum. He could pay it in instalments, of course, but was that much help?

That afternoon, he sat down at the computer, went to the document called *SacredSpirits*.doc, and read with mounting disgust what he had written. It was hopeless, useless. Tinkering with it was a waste of time. After staring at the text in despair, he deleted all ten pages. He must forget this philosophy theme, this learned stuff he was obviously useless at, and think seriously of something he could do, such as a sequel to *Death's Door*. If that wasn't feasible, he could create a new detective, a woman, perhaps. He would begin by making a list of characters, looking up names online and finding new ones in the surname dictionary.

But his heart wasn't in it. All his heart could do was sink. He missed Nicola so much. Her old flatmates had found room for her. She was gone. And there was Dermot. Suppose he really did stay in the flat and never paid the rent again? Perhaps Carl could tell him to leave because he wanted to sell the house. But he knew this wouldn't work. Dermot would refuse to go.

Another course would be to force him to pay the rent and leave him to do his worst. Dermot would no doubt tell this woman Yvonne Weatherspoon the tale of Carl's "medicaments" and the sale of the DNP to Stacey. And why should it stop there? Dermot might not lead an involved and widespread social life, but he met a lot of people. He talked (chatted, he would call it) to a host of pet owners, for example. He would carry out his threat to go to that newspaper that sold widely in Hampstead and Highgate. He would say he had a story for them and go to their office to give an interview. He might even approach one of the tabloids, the *Sun*, say, or the *Mail*. Stacey was known to the public. It would be a juicy story: "Author Kills Actress." Carl would never have a serious literary career again.

He was making himself feel sick. He leaned over his desk, putting his head in his hands, but this did nothing to help. He ran, choking, into the kitchen and threw up into the sink.

The footsteps behind him could only be Dermot's. Carl kept his head bent, ran the cold tap, switched on the waste disposal unit, hoping the noise would drive his tenant away. It didn't.

"You're not very well, are you?" Dermot used his deeply concerned voice. To Carl it sounded as if he was enjoying himself. "Don't you think you should see your doctor? I'll come with you if you like."

"Go away. You're ruining my life."

"No, no. It's you who's doing that."

Carl drank some water from the tap. He wiped his mouth on the tea cloth.

"I came down to ask you if you would like to go out for a drink. Maybe something to eat as well?"

In this instance, to respond with "Are you joking?" was a genuine question.

"No," Dermot said. "I thought it would be a good idea to get to know each other better."

"I don't want to know you better. I don't want to know you at all. I want you out of my life. Now go away, please. Please go away."

When Dermot had gone, Carl sat down at the kitchen table, found Nicola's mother's number on his phone's list of contacts, and rang it. There was no answer. He remembered his own mother telling him that not so long ago your name didn't come up when you made a call. The person you called didn't know who it was, so they had to answer. As things were now, Nicola might be sitting in her mother's house, also in a kitchen for all he knew, and deliberately not answering because she could see *Carl* on the screen. He thought, I don't even know where her house is. Aylesbury, I think, but I don't know the address.

As he was leaving, the postman brought ten copies of Carl's book. When he'd originally been shown the jacket design, he hadn't liked it, but had accepted the corpse and the blood and the weeping woman. It looked no better now under the bright-coloured glaze, and he dumped the box on the hall table and left it there. A moment that should have been glorious—the delivery of copies of his first published book—was just a disappointment, like everything else in his life.

He decided to walk to Nicola's flat in Ashmill Street, telling himself he'd nothing to lose if no one let him in. Things couldn't be any worse than they already were. It occurred to him that he had no one to talk to, no one to confide in. There was only Nicola, and perhaps even she wouldn't speak to him.

He walked through Church Street market, where the traders were dismantling the stalls. Farther up on Lisson Grove, the man with the antiques shop was removing his chairs and tables from the pavement and closing up for the night.

By now it was early evening, and once off the main streets, few people were about. Carl turned down the street by the fish-and-chips

shop. Nicola knew, he said to himself. She was the only one other than Dermot who knew; she had heard his account of what had happened, she *knew*. Surely now she would be over her initial shock and horror and would be able to give him some sympathy, tell him what to do.

The Victorian terraced house where she lived was one of a long row and must have been ugly and shabby even when it was first built. It looked empty, as if all the girls were out somewhere; with friends, maybe, or boyfriends, having coffee or a drink or at the cinema. Nicola wouldn't be there, he accepted this, but one of the others might know where she was. He rang the bell, the top bell for the top floor, then rang it again.

The window above him opened and Nicola put her head out.

"Let me in, Nic. Please."

She smiled her beautiful Nicola smile. "I'm coming down."

It wasn't all right, it couldn't be that, but it was better. He knew it was better when, as soon as she had let him in and closed the front door, she took him in her arms and hugged him tightly. He felt like a small child whose mother had been cross with him for some misdemeanour, but had now forgiven him and loved him again as she used to.

THEY WENT TO bed. It was Judy's bedroom, which Nicola was sharing as a temporary measure. It had one tiny window offering what Nicola described rather sardonically as "a magnificent view of the Marylebone Road." The bed was a single, with a camp bed beside it. They slept, and when they woke up, Nicola produced a bottle of port she had bought at a fete in the village where she had spent the previous weekend.

"It's not me giving Stacey the stuff, is it? It's selling it. That's the problem you've got with it."

Nicola agreed. "It wouldn't be so bad if you hadn't sold it. What's Dermot going to do? Or what do you think he's going to do?"

He told her about the rent. The newspapers, maybe the police, Stacey's relatives. "He calls them 'her loved ones.'"

They heard the front door close and a set of footsteps on the stairs.

"We'd better get up and go," Nicola said.

So she was coming home with him. For a moment Carl was almost happy.

Out in the street, she asked him again what he thought Dermot was going to do. "Would it be so bad if he did go to Stacey's relatives, or even the newspapers? You keep saying that giving her the pills wasn't against the law."

"Having sex with your friend's wife isn't against the law, but you still don't want it known."

"But let's say you tell Dermot you want the rent and he says OK, you can have it, and the consequence is that he starts telling people—newspapers, police, whatever. Can't you face up to it? The police caution you—isn't that the worst that can happen? You just tell everyone it's not against the law, and in time it'll blow over."

Carl was silent. Then he said slowly, "I know it's not against the law, but the national press—the print media, don't they call it that?—will get hold of it from the *Ham and High* and the *Paddington Express*, and they will say exactly what they like about me. I guess the broadsheets like the *Guardian* and the *Independent* may not be that interested—or they may be, but not in a loud, screaming-headline way. That'll be for the *Sun* and the *Mail*. And they'll run great big headlines in—oh, I don't know, seventy- or eighty-point typeface, and they can do it because all their readers will want to know about an author selling what the paper will call poison to a poor, desperate actress who's so overweight people laugh at her."

"You've really thought about this, haven't you? You've sort of constructed it. Look, let's go and eat somewhere and forget about this for an evening and a night."

Very out of character, he threw his arms round her and said loudly so that people stared, "Oh, Nic, it's so good, it's so lovely to have you back."

12

WALKING SYBIL SOAMES home from church on Sunday morning was possibly (or *arguably*, as journalists wrote every day in newspapers) the most fateful thing Dermot had ever done in his life. He didn't know this, of course. He didn't arrange it. It happened, that was all.

Sybil shook hands with the vicar and he was the next to do so. They walked down the path from St. Mary's, Paddington Green, one after the other and came out together in Venice Walk.

"Are you going my way?" he said.

Because she didn't know what to say, a situation Sybil often found herself in, she blushed. "I don't know."

"Where do you live?"

"Jerome Crescent. It's sort of Rossmore Road."

He said no more. He didn't find her attractive. To be attractive, a woman had to look like Angelina Jolie or Caroline the vet: tall, thin as a reed, long-necked, with full lips, dark red hair piled on top of her head. If Dermot had met Sybil Soames anywhere but in church, she might never have become his girlfriend. Sitting next to her by chance in the third pew from the front at St. Mary's made speaking to her, and at their fourth meeting asking her out, respectable.

Dermot had little experience of going out with women, and most

of that was with his mother in Skegness, or one of his aunts, who lived next door to his mother. But somehow he could tell that Sybil would not be particular or exacting. She was not good-looking, nor, from the conversation they had had (mostly about the hymns they had sung that morning), particularly intelligent. Perhaps the most attractive thing about her was the admiration she clearly had for him. They talked about the vicar, whose gender Sybil approved of, and Dermot told her he thought women in the clergy was a mistake, while making them bishops was the beginning of the end of Anglicanism in this country.

"Don't you like women, then?" said Sybil.

"Of course I do. In their place."

He could educate her, he thought. He told her where he worked, making his position at the pet clinic rather more elevated than it was. She seemed to think he must be a vet and he said nothing to correct her. Would she meet him next day for coffee in the Café Rouge in Clifton Road? he wondered. A lot of girls would have asked why not a drink or dinner, but he knew she wouldn't. She was innocent enough to ask him if he was sure he wanted her to meet him.

"I asked you, didn't I?"

"I just wanted to check."

"One p.m. OK?"

No, she couldn't do that. She'd be at work. She looked almost triumphant, as if she'd known he hadn't meant it.

"OK, make it the evening."

He didn't care what her work was; she would tell him this when they met. And she was bound to be early, probably ten to seven rather than seven.

He was right. When he arrived at Café Rouge the next evening at five past seven, she was sitting at one of their outside tables. He talked to her about the animal patients at the clinic, describing dog diseases and dog surgery. Her parents, with whom she lived, had two dogs and she didn't much like them. Animals smelt, she said,

and made a mess. She preferred a clean house and would like one of her own but she'd never afford it. She said this with some passion. He realised he had no need to make another date, but only said he would see her in church on Sunday. Things could go on from there.

"Why don't you grow your hair?" he said. "It would look a lot better."

He knew she would. He'd get to work on her clothes next. Maybe persuade her to lose a bit of weight. After all, people were going to see her with him.

LIZZIE WAS GOING to visit Dermot at the Sutherland Pet Clinic. She remembered Stacey once telling her that her aunt Yvonne took her cat there for its injections. She'd also worked out that Gervaise, who'd taken her number but not yet called her, might still be living at home, if he hadn't already gone travelling.

When she had handed over to its parent the last of what the head teacher called "the kiddiwinks," Lizzie got on her bus in the middle bit, which you were not supposed to do because if you were lucky, the driver wouldn't see you and you could get away without having a ticket or a pass. This worked well if you were going no more than two stops. But Lizzie was going a lot farther, and the driver was leaning out of his window shaking his fist at her as she tripped lightly down Sutherland Avenue.

Dermot was happy to talk to her when he learned that she knew Carl and had been one of Stacey's closest friends. He told her about Stacey's aunt, Mrs. Weatherspoon, whose son and daughter both lived with her in her mansion at Swiss Cottage.

"Poor Stacey left her apartment in Primrose Hill to her aunt, as I expect you know. I shouldn't say it, but it doesn't seem quite fair, does it? 'To him that hath shall be given and from him that hath not everything shall be taken away, even that which he hath.'"

"Is that right?" Lizzie had no idea what he meant and didn't care. "You know, Stacey once gave me her aunt's phone number, but I've mislaid it. Would you let me have it?"

"I couldn't do that," said Dermot in unctuous tones. "But I could give her yours and ask her to call you."

She's already got it, or her son has, thought Lizzie. But in a piece of luck at that moment the vet called out to Dermot to come and give her a hand with Dusky. "Excuse me," said Dermot.

By another piece of luck, he had also left Yvonne Weatherspoon's details on the computer. Lizzie, popping behind the counter, committed landline and mobile numbers to her excellent memory, then, on the principle of better safe than sorry, exited the file and quickly afterwards the clinic.

Back in Kilburn by six, a good time to phone anyone, Lizzie was soon speaking to Gervaise Weatherspoon, who answered his mother's phone.

"I'm so glad to have caught you," Lizzie said. "I was hoping we might have a talk before you go on your trip. About the apartment in Pinetree Court, I mean."

"Oh, yes?"

"It's just an idea I had. I don't want to talk about it on the phone."

He sounded strangely hostile. "Where did you want to talk about it then?"

"I thought perhaps in the apartment?"

"OK. Tomorrow morning? Ten a.m.? I'll be there."

THE FIRST TIME Lizzie had seen Gervaise, she had been dressed in jeans and a sweatshirt. The idea would be to create a glamorous image today, so she put on the green suit she had worn for that evening visit to her parents. Getting on the bus in Kilburn High Road, she presented her pass this time and settled into her seat, conscious that she was the best-dressed woman there. Not that there

was much competition from this bunch, who looked as if they were all off to clean out someone's drains.

She was five minutes late, but Gervaise wasn't there. Irritated, she waited outside Stacey's front door and wondered what she would do if he didn't come. But he did, arriving just as she was making her contingency plans, and let them both in.

Inside, he looked her up and down. "That thing you're wearing looks exactly like one Stacey had in her slimmer days."

"Does it? Well, it isn't hers. Stacey was never as thin as me."

He laughed. "Don't you girls ever watch films from the fifties? All the women in them are what you call fat. Marilyn Monroe was a size sixteen."

Lizzie didn't say anything. She wondered what he was trying to prove. "When are you going to wherever it is? Thailand, was it?"

He seemed to find that funny too. "Cambodia and Laos. Next week. Why?"

"Well, I thought you might want someone to look after the place while you're away. I mean, live here, keep it clean. I wouldn't want paying."

His apparently irrepressible laughter was bubbling up again. "I don't suppose you would. I don't suppose you'd want to pay me either." He made no answer to her offer, but strolled into the bedroom. Lizzie followed him. He opened the wardrobe doors and peered inside. She was conscious once again of how good-looking he was. "I wonder what happened to Stacey's clothes. There's not much here."

Apart from the green suit and a few other items, they were all in Lizzie's cupboards in Kilburn. She had an answer for him. "Someone must have taken them to that designer-seconds shop in Lauderdale Road."

"Ah, of course." He looked at his watch. No one else of his age that Lizzie knew had a watch. They all told the time on their mobiles or iPads. "I have an appointment in St. James's in half an hour, so I'm afraid we must terminate this interview. It's been delightful."

Lizzie had lost all her confidence and now felt small and inferior, but she had not entirely lost her nerve. "Well, can I stay here while you're away?"

"Oh, didn't I say? Of course you can. We'll keep in touch while I'm in Cambodia." There was no invitation to have a drink or even dinner before he left; no laughter this time, only a broad smile. "I won't need to give you a key, I'm sure you've got one already."

She nodded in stupefied silence.

"I'll leave you a phone number."

Would you be able to call a mobile number in Cambodia? Lizzie wondered. Gervaise produced a receipt from his pocket and wrote in pencil on the back of it what was obviously a landline number. She put it in her handbag.

Once he had gone, and she had helped herself to a long draught of tequila for what her grandmother would have called medicinal purposes, she made a survey of the flat. Since Gervaise hadn't checked what was in the place apart from the absence of clothes, she would be able to help herself to whatever she wanted. The days of getting into people's flats or houses and taking some small item away with her seemed long past.

The bathroom was still crowded with makeup and perfume, most of it barely used. She would have all that. The Roberts radio wouldn't be missed, she thought, nor would the nearly new camera. Was there anything in the flat she could sell? Maybe what her mother quaintly called cutlery? But no. She had never stooped to stealing and she mustn't start now.

After another swig of tequila, she went downstairs to tell the concierge that she was looking after the flat for the next—how long? She didn't know; say, eight weeks? But Gervaise had already given the concierge the news, and it seemed not to have gone down well. The man scowled behind the black-framed sunglasses he wore, which seemed a strange choice as it had come on to rain and the sky was dark.

13

IT WAS A little late in the day to take a bus to Hampstead Heath, Tom Milsom thought, but now that it was light for sixteen hours of the day, he hadn't noticed it was nearly five when he left home. Still, his favourite bus, the number 6, had taken him to the stop outside the Tesco in Clifton Road and the flower shop, and there he got on the single-decker 46, which took him to Fitzjohn's Avenue.

The houses up here were huge four-storey places, most of them sheltered and veiled by tall creeper-hung trees. Tom wondered if just one family or even a couple lived in them, or were they divided into flats? *Flats* wasn't a suitable word. You would have to call them *apartments* and the houses *mansions*. Although quite-heavy traffic filled the road, the whole area was oddly silent. Few people were about, and no young ones. Tom saw a youngish woman in high heels taking a dog out for its walk, a dog you couldn't mistake for a mongrel or a crossbreed, it was so unmistakably pedigree, with its slender, elegant shape, sleek cream-coloured fur, and legs rather like its owner's. The collar it wore was black leather studded with green and blue jewels.

This was a safe, quiet bus, his fellow passengers mostly middle-aged and elderly women, all middle-class and with shopping bags. Working women would have shrieked, or at any rate gasped, when the bus driver had to stamp on his brakes and judder to a stop as

a teenager in a long, scarlet sports car charged across Nutley Terrace right in front of him, yet these women barely reacted. Tom got out by Hampstead station, which he remembered was the deepest belowground in the London underground system—or was that Highgate? Hampstead was pretty. That was a word a man should never use, he thought as he walked down Rosslyn Hill, except perhaps about a girl. A thin drizzle was falling.

Should he try to find the house where Keats had lived? There seemed little point when all he knew about Keats was a poem about a knight-at-arms and a woman who had no mercy that Tom had had to learn at school. Anyway, he didn't know whether the house was in Downshire Hill or in Keats Grove, where it ought to be, and he didn't want to show his ignorance by asking. He could have some tea instead. Perhaps he ought to buy something, a little present for Dorothy, and what better place than Hampstead? It was a bit ridiculous, for he was hardly on holiday, but he bought it just the same, a book of notelets, one for every day of the year, with *Hampstead Queen of the Hills* printed on it in Gothic lettering. He had a cup of tea and a millionaire's macaroon before going off to find the bus home.

The kind of people who made trouble on buses were not to be found in Hampstead. The Hampstead sort all had valid passes, plenty of silver coins should the pass have mysteriously become obsolete, and a driving licence for ID. Tom had all this, and the bus he was getting on was the prestigious 24, which plied between Hampstead Heath and Victoria, taking in Camden Town and Westminster on its way.

He got on and sat in a small, single seat tucked away behind the driver's cab. The girl who followed him, instead of touching her pass to the reader as he had done, turned away and got on halfway down, after Tom's daughter's fashion. He waited for her to go up to the driver and either present her pass or put down the requisite two pounds forty. Neither happened. Should he approach the driver himself and tell him? Or hand the girl the coins, which he had? But she was on her phone, talking to someone with whom she appeared on intimate terms.

Tom felt indignant. How dare she impose on what the government called "the hardworking taxpayer" and have a free ride? Walking up the bus, he said, "Excuse me," into the driver's window. The entire lower floor of the bus had stopped talking and was paying him close attention. He dropped his voice to a whisper. The driver said the girl probably hadn't got a pass or any spare money. He seemed displeased, not grateful and friendly as Tom felt the driver should have been. Wondering if this would produce a warmer response, Tom laid down the two-pound coin and the two twenties.

"What's that for?" said the driver. "Her? Cash payments stopped last month. By law."

The girl was still on her mobile, talking in a rather indignant way, and when the driver pulled the bus to the kerb and stopped, Tom began to feel nervous. Whatever happened next, he would be drawn into it. Standing up, he watched the doors at the front of the bus come open, muttered, "Got to get off," and jumped out onto the pavement. He looked back over his shoulder. The driver and the girl appeared to be in a fierce argument as Tom walked away down the hill.

He wasn't sure what to do. It was a long walk from here to Willesden, and bad enough to the number 6 route. He didn't even know which way the number 6 went between Clifton Road and Willesden Green. Perhaps he should make for the Beatles' place in—what was it?—Abbey Road. The bus he had got off passed him, sending spray up from the water in the gutter. It wasn't exactly dark yet, but getting that way.

He was almost at the next bus stop by now. The best thing would be to wait there, as by now he had no idea where he was. People were waiting for the next 24: two young men, no more than boys. One of them said to him, "Got a ciggie, Granddad?"

Tom wanted to ask him how he dared call him that, but he was frightened. "I don't smoke," he muttered.

The other one said, "Don't you lie to me," and grabbed him by the shoulders, shaking him.

Tom made a whimpering sound. He was released so violently that

he staggered. The one who had asked him for a cigarette pushed himself in front of him and punched him hard in the stomach, a blow powerful enough to knock him over. He fell to the ground, doubled up. The two men kicked him onto a patch of grass under a tree and, as the 24 bus came, ran away.

IN FALCON MEWS, something crashed onto the floor from the flat above. It must have been heavy, a saucepan or a bucket. The sound it made reverberated through the house, followed by footsteps running down the stairs and the front door slamming.

The noise went on like this every day, only stopping when Dermot went to work. Carl knew it must be deliberate, intended to annoy him. It had started about the time the August rent was due but never came. The noise varied: a crash made by something dropped, doors slamming, the piercing growl of an electric drill, the hammering of a nail into the wall, the TV on full, the radio playing hymns—and all the doors up there wide-open.

The houses in Falcon Mews were Victorian jerry-built with thin walls and not very substantial floors, so that every sound echoed and trembled. When the noise first began, Carl had been irritated by it. Now it had started to frighten him. Could the neighbours hear it, the Pembrokes on the left side, Elinor Jackson on the right? They hadn't complained to him, but then he hadn't complained to Dermot either. He and Dermot barely spoke to each other anymore. Dermot no longer knocked on one of the doors in Carl's part of the house to make some fatuous remark. Instead he ran faster than ever down the stairs and burst out into the street, banging the front door behind him.

While Nicola was at home, the noise stopped altogether. This behaviour on Dermot's part was so transparent, so obvious, that Carl found it almost incredible. Now, if he told her his tenant made a deliberate racket simply to annoy him, she wouldn't believe it. He had told her, though, and she had begun to treat him as if he were

imagining the bangs and crashes and might be hearing things as a result of the nervous state he had worked himself into.

"I've got a couple of weeks' holiday owing to me," she said. "Why shouldn't we go away somewhere? It would be good for you."

"I can't afford it. Well, I can now, but I soon won't be able to if I don't get any rent."

That only led to her giving him the advice she always gave him. "Tell him you must have the rent and let him . . . well, do his worst. No one can charge you with anything. You won't go to prison. Tell him to go ahead and talk to these people and the newspapers, and once you've done it, you'll feel a great relief and we'll go to Cornwall or Guernsey or somewhere."

Dermot was out. The house was silent. It was Sunday, so he was probably in church, but he would soon be back and the noise would start again.

"I can't," Carl said. "I mean that literally. I can't do it. I can't allow him to shame me. And yet it's such a little thing, isn't it? Sometimes I dream he's dead, and when I wake up and he's not . . . I lie there and hear him drop something, or his telly comes on, and I know he's alive and there's nothing I can do."

Nicola was looking at him in horror. "Oh, Carl, sweetheart."

The front door opened and closed softly and Dermot's footsteps tiptoed up the stairs. Carl put his head in his hands.

"Let's hope this has taught you that riding around to dodgy places on buses isn't a good idea," said Dot Milsom.

"Oh, Mum, Hampstead's not a dodgy place." Lizzie was more shocked by this description of London's loveliest suburb than by her father's experience.

"On your own too," said Dot. "I did offer to come with you, you'll remember."

"You're not old enough." Tom laughed at his own wit. "It's not

the kind of thing that happens more than once, anyway. It looks to me like the girl I reported to the bus driver phoned her boyfriend, and it was him waiting to clobber me."

A passerby had found him struggling to get up and called an ambulance, which took him to St. Mary's Hospital, where he was treated for various cuts and bruises. It was discovered that no ribs were broken, but he was kept in overnight and allowed home next morning. For now he could just about walk with someone holding his arm.

Lizzie had come with her mother to see him in hospital and had told her parents in great detail about what she called her new job, looking after her friend Stacey's state-of-the-art apartment in Primrose Hill. Tom again thought about his daughter's flat in Kilburn. But his thoughts were mostly on his recent ordeal. The breezy attitude he adopted as he recounted his encounter with the two young men, and that he continued with the police officer who called to ask him what had happened, was a show of bravado and not what he really felt.

Some would say it was his own fault, provoking that girl by shopping her to the driver. But wasn't that the duty of a good citizen? I wouldn't do it again, though, he thought. I'd lie low. But even making this resolve failed to give him confidence. He postponed the idea of getting on the number 82 bus, which had been his next project. Instead, now that his bruises were getting better, his headache from hitting his head when they kicked him over gone, he planned to take himself up to Edgware or Harrow at the end of the week.

But when Thursday came—Friday was the day planned for this excursion—he went to bed dreading the next morning and found it impossible to sleep. He lay awake tossing and turning and only fell asleep at 5:00 a.m., to be jerked awake by a dream, not about an assault in Haverstock Hill but a car crash in Willesden Lane.

At breakfast, he told Dorothy he wouldn't be taking a bus ride that day.

"Very wise," she said. "You can come with me to have a look at Lizzie's lovely apartment."

14

Elizabeth Holbrook had divorced her husband after fifteen months of marriage and was now living in her mother's house.

"I suppose you'll revert to your maiden name," said Yvonne Weatherspoon.

"How ridiculous is that? Maiden name indeed. Anyway, I won't. I always hated being called Weatherspoon. I more or less got married to get Leo's name."

"It's nice to have you back," said her mother insincerely. "You're not thinking of moving into a place of your own?"

"If that was what you wanted, you might have given Stacey's flat to me instead of Gervaise."

In fact, Elizabeth had no real quarrel with the way things had turned out. Her mother had five bedrooms, a self-contained flat in the basement, a cleaner every morning, and two cars. The only drawback to the house in Swiss Cottage was that cat. Elizabeth had attempted in the past to show Sophie who was boss, but never stood a chance. Their first—and almost their last—encounter had been when Elizabeth had roughly removed her from the seat of an armchair, and Sophie had turned on her, teeth bared, claws out, and

inflicted some nasty wounds before returning to her favourite spot. These days they gave each other a wide berth.

DAYS PASSED AND no rent had appeared. Carl hadn't expected it, but he was still angry and miserable. He also knew that Dermot was playing some sort of complicated game, for after a week or two, the noise had stopped. Even the front door was closed silently. It was so quiet that there might have been no tenant on the top floor if Carl had not occasionally seen Dermot walking down Falcon Mews, on his way to or from work or leaving for church. Then, in the middle of the next week, something made of metal—a watering can, perhaps—was dropped and crashed resoundingly, bouncing across the floor above. Because he was no longer used to it and had believed the noise had come to an end, Carl shivered and actually cried out.

There was no more noise that day, but it left him trembling. Nicola was due home at six thirty, but he couldn't bear to wait that long, not so much because he wanted her company as out of terror that the dropping of things was due to start again.

When he phoned her, she said she had the afternoon off and would come home in an hour's time. Having her here would be wonderful, were it not for the fact that she would constantly urge him to stand up to Dermot and demand the rent. But Carl had to have her here for this coming weekend. He couldn't live without her. He had done no work for weeks now. The book was a dead loss, not a book at all, for he had destroyed all of it, even the plan and the notes he had made before he started. He had never wanted a real job, but now he wished he had one. It would get him out of the house. He read in the paper and saw on the television that jobs were hard to get. It was hopeless for him even to look for employment.

On Friday afternoon, on his way back to work, Dermot knocked on Carl's living-room door.

Carl was asleep. He got off the sofa and opened the door. "Yes, what is it?"

"Just to ask you if it'd be all right to use the garden sometimes, sit out there, I mean. I've got a couple of deck chairs."

"That would mean coming through my kitchen."

"That's right. OK with you?" Implicit in the enquiry was *it had better be.* "'A garden is a lovesome thing, God wot.'"

Carl shrugged, nodded, shut the door. He wondered why he ever spoke politely to Dermot. Why even answer him? Silence would be best, but he knew he wouldn't keep silent. Was it because he clung to some hopeless hope that Dermot would relent, that he would say he hadn't meant it, it was a try-on, and now, soon, he would pay the rent as he had always known he must?

When Nicola came in from work, Carl was waiting for her, sitting on the front step, maybe just to escape from breathing the same air as Dermot. Money was short. The lack of it was beginning to make itself felt in a serious way, and Carl couldn't admit this to Nicola. Even though he had grown up in a world where women were becoming increasingly equal to men, where equality was the subject of almost daily TV programmes and constant newspaper features, he had still absorbed enough of a male-supremacy culture to believe that, if he were to mention his financial crisis, Nicola would think he was asking her for a loan or even a gift. And she would press him again to confront his tenant.

ON SUNDAY, THEY watched from a window as Dermot went to church. Like churchgoers in times gone by, he carried a prayer book. They had talked about Dermot for half the night, what he would do if crossed, and what the consequences would be. They did make love, at just before three, and afterwards fell into a heavy sleep until nearly ten. Saturday's rain had stopped during the night. The sun was out, the wind had dropped, and Mr. Kaleejah was taking his

dog for its morning walk. It always walked along in a docile way, pausing sometimes to look up at Mr. Kaleejah and wag its tail. Carl had never heard it bark.

"He'll bring his deck chairs through the kitchen to the back door," said Carl. "Why deck chairs? One for him, and who's the other for? Perhaps he's got friends, but I've never seen them. The next thing will be he'll want to take over one of my rooms. He's got a living room, a kitchen, a bathroom, and a bedroom. Maybe he wants another bedroom? He could take over my second bedroom. Why not? I can't stop him."

"Yes, you can, Carl. He can tell his story to anyone he likes. How do you know they'll even care? They'll probably say, so what? If they're even interested, they'll google it and see that what you did wasn't against the law. Tell him you want the rent and if he says no, you'll evict him. That's what anyone else would do."

She made it sound so simple, Carl thought. He watched Dermot turn the corner into Castellain Road and disappear. Carl put his head in his hands, a frequent gesture with him these days.

The day continued fine, becoming sunnier and warmer. "Let's go out for lunch," said Nicola cheerfully, though she felt anything but cheerful.

"I can't afford it."

"Well, I can. You'll have to face up to that, Carl. When you do what I suggest, you'll have some money and you'll feel much better because things won't be as bad as you think. Probably they won't be bad at all. Come on, we'll go out, and we won't be here to see Dermot come back."

So they went round to the Café Rouge, ate fish cakes and chips and lemon tart and drank a lot of red wine. "You'll think I'm crazy," said Carl, "but I don't want to go back there. I can't bear to be under the same roof as him."

"I live there too, you know. When you tell him to do his worst, I'll be with you. We'll confront him together."

The sun was hot and the house warm and stuffy when they got home. Nicola went upstairs and looked out the bedroom window. She called Carl. "You're not going to like this, but you'd better see it."

No one had attended to the garden since Carl's father had died; in fact, since long before that. Where the lawn had been, the grass had grown tall and turned to hay, and the flowerbeds were dense with stinging nettles three feet tall. Two deck chairs covered in red-and-blue-striped canvas had been put up among the hay, and in them sat Dermot and a rather large young woman with shaggy, dark hair wearing a dirndl skirt and peasant blouse.

Carl made a sound like a howl of agony. "Who's that woman?"

"His girlfriend, I should think."

"He hasn't got a girlfriend."

"Well, he has now."

A VISIT FROM her parents was not to be welcomed by Lizzie. Usually, that was. Now, however, in possession of Stacey's beautiful flat, she felt very different. Not just on account of the decor and furnishings, but because quite a lot of exotic drink still remained from Stacey's store, as well as tins of the sort of biscuits and snacks that went well with drink.

Tom and Dot had been in the flat no more than ten minutes, had examined the large refrigerator, the freezer, and the washing machine and dryer, as well as the living-room and bedroom furnishings and the two flatscreen televisions, when they were plied with dry oloroso and tequila sunrises. Conversation concentrated on Tom's recovery from his assault on Haverstock Hill. Lizzie, who didn't take admonition well herself, told him how careful he must be in future, and to be sure to take his mobile with him and phone her or her mother at the least sign of danger. Dot agreed, but added that it was useless to say anything as Tom never did what he was told.

Advice, in any case, was unnecessary. Dot and Lizzie both thought privately that Tom had given up his exploration of London on buses. It had, in their opinion, been ridiculous and had, fortunately, and without too much harm being done, been ended by the Haverstock Hill attack. Both Dot and Lizzie were now putting their minds to some alternative hobby for him and already had ideas: golf, for instance, though Willesden was a long way from a golf course; the Willesden cycling club, though Tom didn't possess a bicycle, and anyway, look how many cyclists got knocked down by lorries; dog walking, which, considering they had no dog, was never taken seriously. None of these options was mentioned to Tom.

UP TO NOW, Tom Milsom had led a calm, steady, peaceable life. His job had been largely trouble-free. His wife loved and respected him, or seemed to. His daughter—well, she took his money, he thought bitterly, and for a flat she no longer even lived in. What did they think of him, the pair of them, for giving up an interest he had plainly enjoyed because two boys had hit him? Part of him never wanted to get on a bus again, even though it was not the buses' fault. In fact, he had not even been *on* a bus when the boys had attacked him. This line of reasoning sent him out of the house—though perhaps it was more the result of Dorothy plying the vacuum cleaner round the armchair he was sitting in.

He walked about a mile, thinking it was good for him, then got on the number 139 bus. Only then did it occur to him that he should have looked at London Bus Routes online. Perhaps when he got to Baker Street he could find a number 1. Something about a bus numbered 1 was fascinating, intriguing. It ought to be the best of all London buses. He asked the driver, who told him to stay on till Waterloo and pick up the number 1 there, which would take him to Bermondsey and Canada Water. Relaxing in the back of the 139

once more—several seats were empty—Tom felt enormously better. He had always wondered what Canada Water was like, what Canada Water *was*, and now he would find out.

The sun was shining; it would be light for hours. Nothing was going to happen today or on the days to come. The trouble with those two boys had been no more than a nasty incident. Luckily he hadn't been much hurt and all was going to be well.

15

Nicola wanted to protect Carl from Dermot, but she didn't tell Carl this. No matter how far emancipation had progressed towards equality, a woman might tell a man she wanted to care for him but she could not admit to him that she wanted to defend him from another man. Anyway, she seldom saw Dermot. If she heard him on the stairs, she kept inside the living room until the front door closed. They had met only once recently, in the hallway, she going out and he coming in, he from the pet clinic and carrying shopping, she on her way to buy something for an evening meal.

"You're living here full-time again now, are you?" he had asked. That enquiry could be put several ways, and Dermot's phrasing was rather accusatory, the implication being that she shouldn't have been.

She would have liked to ask him if he had any objection, but Carl's fear of Dermot was beginning to affect her too. "I am, yes."

He shook his head, the kind of gesture that implied wonder more than disapproval. "As I always say, it takes all sorts to make a world."

She said nothing about it to Carl. When she got back with the two ready meals and a bottle of rosé, her anger, which had been considerable, had died down. Dermot was upstairs but silent apart from a burst of "Amazing Grace" when he briefly opened his front door.

Next day was Saturday, the weather improved, and he was out in the garden with the two deck chairs, though only one was occupied. He must have sneaked—as Carl put it—through the kitchen with them while Carl and Nicola were out.

"You'll have to tell him you don't want him in the garden," said Nicola. They were in the bedroom, looking down on the top of Dermot's head.

Carl didn't say anything.

"You'll have to, Carl. This is only the thin end of the wedge."

"I've already told him he can use the garden."

"Don't you think that if he was going to tell anyone—I mean about selling that stuff to Stacey—"

"I know what you mean. I think about it every day. It haunts me. I know what you were going to say. That if he was going to tell the newspapers or her aunt or her cousins or *anyone*, he'd have done it by now. But why would he? He has the perfect arrangement. He could tell them tomorrow or next week. It's not something that gets easier for me, is it? The newspapers will send someone around here to interview me. He's biding his time, as he might say. He's waiting for someone or something to trigger it, and me telling him he can't sit out in my garden might be just the trigger he needs."

The weather went on being nice, and Dermot sat out in the garden again the next day. Carl and Nicola knew he would because he left the deck chairs out overnight. This, Carl said, was the thickening end of the wedge, or was it the further thinning? Dermot had gone to church, carrying his *Alternative Service Book*. Carl, like many atheists, disapproved of that work, preferring the *Book of Common Prayer*, and would have liked to say so scathingly to Dermot but was afraid. His tenant—could you describe someone as a tenant when he paid no rent?—returned at eleven thirty with the fat, dark girl. They sat in the garden for an hour, then the deck chairs were vacated and soon a strong smell of curry permeated the house.

Carl and Nicola went out. They had a drink in the Prince Alfred around the corner. It was a fine old pub, much loved by Nicola and once loved by Carl. He loved it no longer; he loved nothing.

"Except you," he said. "I love you a lot. I really love you, but how can I marry you?" He had never before mentioned marriage. "This torment will go on for ever, for the rest of my life. I know it sounds mad, but it's true. I shall live in this house or another house and he will be there with me, wherever it is. He will never go and I can't get rid of him. Sometimes I think I'll kill myself."

WEEKS HAD PASSED since Yvonne Weatherspoon had been to the pet clinic. Sophie was well and no injections were due, but a new event had taken place in the Weatherspoon household. Elizabeth had occasionally opened the French windows for the cat to go out in the evenings, and Sophie had stayed out until dawn, squealing under Yvonne's bedroom window to be let in. This truancy had badly frightened Yvonne, and she was even more distressed when she saw that Sophie had a wound on her neck and a triangle of furry skin nipped from one of her ears. She had plainly been fighting with the Bengal next door.

"This is what happens when you have your children home to live," Yvonne told Dermot the next morning, referring of course to Elizabeth, not Sophie.

"You wouldn't be without her," said Dermot in a sentimental tone.

"There's no question of that. Will Caroline be able to see me? Well, see *her*, poor darling."

"I expect we can fit you in. Sophie will have to have intravenous antibiotics." Dermot liked to display medical knowledge picked up from Caroline, Darren, and Melissa without actually knowing anything about it.

"I should have phoned first. I know that." Yvonne brought her face close to his across the desktop. "But you see, if I did that, I thought you'd say no, maybe say there was no room for us."

"Not this time." Dermot smiled his toothy, yellow smile. "Now here's Melissa come for you. I'm afraid Caroline's out on a call."

Left alone, and with no other pet owners due until the afternoon, he let his mind wander to Stacey Warren and the pills that Carl had given—no, sold—her. He mustn't tell, he knew that beyond a doubt. It would be different if Carl had demanded the rent and threatened eviction, but it was unlikely that he would do that as he was too frightened.

No one had ever been afraid of Dermot before, or not to this degree, and it gratified him to have caused someone this amount of fear without violence or even the threat of it. A shame really that he couldn't have it both ways: not tell Stacey's aunt or cousins, say not a word to the *Ham and High*, but drop a hint just the same to Carl as to how near to danger he had come and would come again. Of course the game would have to end at some point. He had no intention of being evicted. He would have to quietly resume paying rent. But not now. Not for a long time. For now he would keep the money, keep the fear up, and keep Carl exactly where he wanted him.

Yvonne came back into reception with Sophie wearing a wide, white collar designed to prevent her claws from tearing at her wound. In this purpose it was already failing.

"I shall have to have a taxi back," said Yvonne. "I had to have one here. I couldn't have Sophie with me loose in the car."

Dermot would have told her it was against the law anyway, but he had told her that on numerous previous occasions. He called a taxi for her. "It'll be up to fifteen minutes."

This was an opportunity too perfect to ignore. True, Sophie was whimpering, but this place reverberated and echoed to the cries and growls of animals. Yvonne was sitting now, murmuring soft words to the cat. "You must be missing your niece, Mrs. Weatherspoon." Dermot broached the subject with extreme politeness.

Yvonne looked surprised. "Yes, well, of course. It was very sad."

"Indeed it was. More than that. Tragic really. Drugs are everywhere these days, aren't they?"

The cat, satisfied that the torture was over and might not recur, had fallen asleep. Yvonne sighed, shook her head. "I'm glad to say neither of my children ever took them."

Dermot didn't believe her. "You're lucky." He saw the taxi arrive. "It's worse, I would think, when someone one trusts—a so-called friend—gives or even sells such horrible substances to one's loved one."

The seed was planted. Yvonne smiled vaguely, said he was right, and allowed him to carry cat and cat box out onto the pavement. She would remember what he had said, he thought, but he had given nothing away. If things continued as they were, he need reveal no more.

Meanwhile, Sybil had become quite a useful tool. She liked sitting in the garden, as her parents had nothing like it in Jerome Crescent. From what he gathered, Jerome Crescent had nothing much that Sybil liked. The previous Sunday, as they'd walked back together to Falcon Mews, she'd asked him if she could do some weeding. She put her request humbly and with a lot of excuses because she was afraid of offending him.

"Good idea."

"You won't have to ask Mr. Martin, will you?" She always called Carl Mr. Martin.

"Good gracious, no. We're the best of pals. He'll be grateful."

So while Dermot slumbered gently in his deck chair the following Sunday afternoon, placing the *Observer* open on his face to protect it from the sun just as his grandfather used to do, Sybil pulled up nettles, campions, and docks and dug out their roots with a trowel.

From the bedroom window, Carl looked down on them. Getting your garden weeded wasn't exactly something you could object to. But surely they could have asked? Besides, Dermot's taking what he would undoubtedly call a liberty would just lead to another. First the deck chairs; now that girl was digging up Carl's garden. What

would be next? He had suggested to Nicola that Dermot's next move would be to take over one of Carl's own rooms. No doubt that would soon happen.

But something else did. Not a takeover, but an interference in his personal life.

"Been wining and dining, have you?"

Carl and Nicola had just come in from dinner in Camden with Carl's mother, Una. Carl didn't reply and expected Dermot to go upstairs.

But his tenant said, "Could I come in for a minute? I've got something I want to say to you."

Taking over the second bedroom, Carl thought, that was what it would be. He opened the living-room door and Nicola went through to the kitchen. "These things are always awkward, aren't they?" Dermot smiled with his lips closed. "But I'm not easily embarrassed."

"What did you want to say?"

Nicola had come back into the room. She had a glass of water in her hand.

"Well, it's unfortunate, but it's something that must be said. You were living alone when I first came here, Carl, but now you're living with this—this young lady. Miss Townsend. This isn't right. It is in fact far from right. I'm not old-fashioned, I'm a progressive kind of cove, but there I draw the line. I don't call it living in sin, that would be to go too far, but it is—to put it plainly—wrong. Now I'm sure you'll agree with me when you think about it."

Nicola drank the water, all of it down at one gulp. She said afterwards that now she knew the meaning of *stupefied*.

"How about you living with that woman you bring to the house? That's different, is it?" Carl asked.

"Ah, very different, Carl. We don't live together, you see. I have just come back from taking Sybil home to her parents in Jerome Crescent." Dermot nodded sagely. "Well, I've said my piece, got it off my chest, and I suggest that when you think about it, you'll find I'm right."

16

"WHERE'S JEROME CRESCENT?"

It was three fifteen in the morning and Carl hadn't slept at all. Nicola was fast asleep, but she woke up when he asked the question a second time and even more loudly.

She turned over in bed. "What?"

"That woman Sybil lives there."

"Carl, I have to go to work in the morning."

"I don't know why I'm asking. It doesn't matter. Go back to sleep."

He thought he would never sleep again. He lay there for a little while, maybe ten minutes, then got up and went down to the kitchen. The house was as silent as if it had been a cottage in a country lane.

Upstairs, two floors up, Dermot would be asleep, deeply asleep in bed, without worries, at peace. He probably drank cocoa or Ovaltine at bedtime, and the mug it had been in would be on his bedside table. There would be a bin for the washing in his room, and before he went to bed he would drop his clothes in it. Things would be like that every night, night after night, unchanging, on and on, while he, Carl, wandered wakeful around the house, growing poorer and poorer, eventually going on the dole or benefits or whatever it was called. For him things would never change, but they would change

for Dermot, who would marry that Sybil and have children with her. He'd get a better job, flourish, and one day seek Carl out, and he would be a wretched, broken creature in rags, in a shabby, dirty room, and Dermot would offer to buy the house from him. Offer him half the price the other houses in Falcon Mews fetched because he could. . . .

You must stop this, he told himself, you will drive yourself mad. But what did you do when you were caught in a trap as he was? You had to decide which was worse (or better): to be utterly disgraced, your name all over the papers, your writing career ruined, to be interviewed and photographed as the man who'd sold poison to an unsuspecting young girl and brought about her death; or to escape that by giving up all you possessed, your only means of making a living. He couldn't see a way out. It was one or the other.

He went into the living room, took a bottle of gin, the only spirits he had, and swigged what remained of it, about a glassful. As he swallowed it, he thought, I am mad, I am crazy, I shall be ill, and he lay down on Dad's sofa, staring at the ceiling and breathing like someone who had run a race. If he ever had another book published and it was ever reviewed, the journalist would refer to him as "the disgraced author Carl Martin."

The gin had its effect, swinging the room around, deadening him, knocking him unconscious. Nicola found him four hours later and lay down beside him, holding him in her arms.

Old Albert Weatherspoon, who was Elizabeth and Gervaise's grandfather, used to say that two women could never share a kitchen. It was just one of his many misogynistic maxims, and Elizabeth would have been the first to rise up in wrath at such sexism, along with that of his other sayings, such as that women made bad drivers. But having lived at home with her mother for a couple of months, she was ready to admit that two women could never share a house.

"If you'd known that Gervaise wasn't going to live in Pinetree Court but was going to announce plans to go off to Cambodia, would you have given the flat to me instead of him?"

"You'd got a home and a husband. How was I to know that you and Leo would split up? There was no warning."

"How could there be a warning? When you're in a relationship, you don't tell everyone that although things are all right now, they may go wrong in a couple of months' time, do you?"

"I don't know. I haven't lived like you do, jumping about from one man to another."

"I can't stay here, I do know that. We have a row every day. And as for that cat, I'd drown it if I could get near it without being torn to pieces."

"Don't you lay a finger on my sweet lamb." Yvonne stood up, quivering. "You can do as you like with the flat. I don't want it. But I don't want any trouble. Remember that." She considered for a moment. "I'd be quite pleased if you could get rid of that Lizzie woman. Milsom, she's called. I know she was a friend of Stacey, but it can't be right that she's still living there. It was your brother who told her she could. Amazing what a pretty face can do, isn't it?"

"Pretty? I don't think so."

YVONNE WAS ALMOST as anxious to get rid of Elizabeth as Elizabeth was to move. Although Sophie was obviously capable of defending herself, Yvonne was afraid her daughter might find a way of doing the cat real harm. Both Elizabeth and Sophie were free to wander about the house at night, and Yvonne began having bad dreams of her daughter's putting poison in the cat's dish.

So Yvonne went to Pinetree Court to speak to the concierge. He knew who she was and would have much preferred her as the occupant of the flat. As far as he was concerned, she was the owner of what he called "the property," and the sooner she moved in,

the better. Yvonne could understand this. A handsome, obviously wealthy woman in the prime of life—she would never call herself middle-aged—was a more suitable occupant than a twenty-four-year-old. That it would actually be her daughter who would be living there wasn't his business, she thought. She would like the lock changed—could he arrange that? Of course she understood that changing the locks on the entrance to the whole block would not be possible.

"I'll do what I can," said the concierge. "It may take a few days."

MRS. WEATHERSPOON PHONED Lizzie and asked her to vacate the flat on the following day, as her daughter would be moving in and the lock would be changed. Lizzie put up a weak defence that she was here at Gervaise's invitation, and Yvonne told her not to be silly. It was five in the afternoon and Lizzie had just returned from play school. She poured herself a large vodka and orange—the first of a new bottle—and decided that there was nothing for it but to get out the next day.

Swithin Campbell, her phone said, ringing musically. "Come out with me tonight, Liz? I'll call for you at seven."

It gave her little time to get ready, but five minutes would have been enough. She rushed into the bedroom and got into a bright red bra and pants and Stacey's black dress with the white lace panel down the front. Jo Malone's pomegranate noir was sprayed down her cleavage. She slid her feet into Stacey's most uncomfortable shoes, the red ones with the four-inch heels. By the time she was sitting down again, finishing off the vodka, the doorbell was ringing.

It wasn't Swithin. The man at the door told Lizzie he was Mr. Newman's driver, sent to fetch her. Mr. Newman was waiting outside in the car.

Swithin wasn't called Newman but Campbell, but Lizzie didn't

think this important. Newman was probably his business partner or something.

He stepped inside, and Lizzie felt something rammed into her spine and let out a shriek that no one was around to hear. He showed her the gun, then replaced it on her spine. "We're going to walk downstairs, you first."

Of course she did, trembling by now. The gun wasn't real. It was a toy that the driver had borrowed from his five-year-old nephew, but Lizzie didn't know that. It felt and looked like a gun. They walked past the concierge's office and out into Primrose Hill Road. A car was there, but the man in it was someone Lizzie had never before seen, a big redhead in a leather coat and ragged jeans. The driver bundled her into the back.

Lizzie was so frightened she couldn't speak. She tried to, stammering and hesitating and gasping, but no real words came out. She wanted to ask her abductors where they were taking her, but it was useless to try. The redhead held her hands behind her back and put what felt like handcuffs on her wrists while the other man told her to bite on something he held across her mouth. She had seen this done on TV but had never thought how horrible it must feel, the bandage or scarf or whatever it was tied so tightly that it felt as if it must split her lips. The driver gave her a great shove so that she fell across the backseat with no hands free to struggle or defend herself.

The redheaded man took the gun from the driver, thrust it into her ribs, and they were off. Few people were about, but even if the street had been crowded, Lizzie realised that people didn't look into parked cars, or moving cars for that matter. Not being able to use her hands made her into a disabled creature. It was the worst part of it. The gag was horrible, but only because it hurt, not because it made it impossible to utter a sound. She hadn't been able to speak before it went on, and somehow she knew she wouldn't be able to speak now even if they took it off. Would they remove the gag and

the handcuffs when they got her to where they were taking her? If they didn't, the time might come when she wouldn't be able to go on breathing just through her nose. The thought of this made her give a little whimper, and the redhead hissed at her, "Shut the fuck up."

Like most Londoners, the only part of London Lizzie really knew was the bit round where she lived, in her case the area between Willesden and the Marylebone Road. They seemed quickly to have left that behind. Swithin would be ringing her doorbell now. Would he raise the alarm? Unlikely. A kind of fog spread across Lizzie's brain, although she was fully conscious, and she began to cry, tears falling down her cheeks onto the stretchy cotton stuff of the gag.

17

"I KNOW WHAT you're going to say," said Carl. "I know it by heart. So don't bother. I could recite it. You don't have to say it."

They were in Carl's bedroom on a Sunday afternoon, and Nicola had brought them two mugs of tea. Hers was half-drunk, his untouched. Down below the window Sybil Soames was chopping down stinging nettles with shears while Dermot sat in one of the deck chairs reading what Nicola thought might be the parish magazine.

"I wouldn't put it past him to ask me to buy a lawn mower."

"You have only to say no."

"Look, the rent was due weeks ago, but it didn't come, and it won't. It won't come at all, will it? It will never come. At least he pays his gas and electricity bills, but he soon won't, you'll see. He'll ask me a favour, and the favour will be that I take on those bills."

"Aren't you going to drink your tea?"

"No, I'm fucking not going to drink my tea." He rolled over and put his arms round her. "I'm sorry. I shouldn't talk to you like that."

It was a beautiful day. They walked across to Regent's Park, where it seemed the whole of London—except for those in Hyde, St. James's, and Green Parks among others—were gathered, lying

on the grass, playing ball games, eating and drinking, admiring the rose garden. The sun was hot, the leaves were green. Nature proclaimed that the winter had been mild and wet and the spring and summer warmer than usual.

"Suppose he starts rearranging my private life?" said Carl. "What if he tells me that if you continue to live with me, he'll have to tell the Weatherspoon woman what I did? If he asks for the other bedroom, the one next to mine? What do I do then? I can't say no, can I?"

Nicola sighed. "Carl, you know what I'll say to that."

EVEN FOR A local weekly paper, the *Paddington Express* had a small circulation. But the current issue was selling better than any other had for years. It led with the photograph of Stacey Warren that had previously appeared in the *Evening Standard* and various other dailies. The text surrounding it told that Stacey had obtained her dinitrophenol not online but by purchase from "an unknown source."

Dermot was given a copy of the newspaper by Sybil, who knew nothing of the DNP story but wanted Dermot to see an ad for a secondhand bed to replace the broken-down one that had been Carl's father's. Carl's tenant, if such he still was, carefully left the newspaper on the table that was the only piece of furniture in the hallway of Carl's house on Falcon Mews.

The account in the *Paddington Express* didn't say anything new. But Carl, who found the newspaper where Dermot intended him to find it, lead story headline uppermost, read everything into it that wasn't in fact there. He felt as though he was about to faint, though he had never fainted in his life. There was nowhere to sit down. He staggered dizzily into the living room and subsided into an armchair. Nicola had gone to work, as had Dermot.

Reason was disappearing. Carl was past the stage of looking calmly at the situation; long past. The sanity he clung to was that he knew he was being irrational. He knew that what Nicola said was

true and that a rational person would do what she kept telling him to do. But with his increasing disgust at Dermot had come fear, and fear was now changing into terror. He was beginning to imagine horrible actions Dermot might take against him. This newspaper account was the beginning of them, for he had no doubt Dermot had fed the story to the *Paddington Express*. Probably even now he was passing the insinuations on to the *Evening Standard* or tomorrow's *Mail*. No imagining was needed for the takeover of his garden, the dropping and noisy shifting of pieces of furniture, the banging of doors and the spurts of music that gushed out for five minutes at a time when the front door to the top-floor flat was opened.

Carl had found that going out and walking, especially in green places and under the heavy-hanging foliage of trees, was somehow remedial. He could tell himself that whatever happened at home, however much Dermot tightened the screw and in so doing deprived him of every penny of his income, he would still have his health and strength and these green trees to walk under and lawns to look at. His walk this morning took him across Maida Vale and a little way down Lisson Grove in the direction of Rossmore Road. If he continued along Rossmore Road, he would come out onto Park Road and from there onto the Outer Circle of Regent's Park. Plenty of greenery in there, great trees densely in leaf and shrubs in pink and white flower.

As he walked along Rossmore Road, a sign pointing to Jerome Crescent reminded him of something. Of course—Dermot's girlfriend, Sybil Soames, lived there with her parents. He turned into Jerome Crescent, where trees grew on a triangle of green grass, and decided to sit down there and wait for Sybil. She would come; she would be bound to come this way on her way home for her lunch. Somehow he knew she was the kind of girl—an only child sheltered and protected by her working-class parents—who would go shopping arm in arm with her mother on Saturday mornings, and on weekdays always go home for her lunch, which she would call din-

ner. Dermot, with his quaint, outdated morality, would have had no difficulty in persuading her to go along with his wish for a chaste relationship. Carl asked himself why he wanted to talk to her—why he wanted to see her even—but came up with no answer.

She did come, but took a long time about it. He saw recognition and something that might have been fear in her eyes. She would have avoided him, turned off the path across the green, but for his saying, "Sybil."

On his feet now, he stood in front of her. "Sybil, I've been waiting for you."

"Is something wrong? Is he ill?"

You know what he's doing to me, don't you? Carl wanted to say. You know he's stopped paying me rent, he's taking over the house, he'll force me into one room and then out altogether. But confronted by Sybil, poor ignorant creature that she was, he couldn't do it. "It's nothing. I just went for a walk and then I remembered you lived down here." In a low, weak voice, quite wrong for such a cheerful remark, he said, "It's a beautiful day."

"I'd better get on home. My mum'll be worrying."

He watched her cross the road and turn into a doorway. Slowly making his way back up Lisson Grove, leaving behind all these pastel-painted blocks of flats and their green gardens, he realised again what he dreaded most in Dermot's threats. It wasn't the loss of income. It was the humiliation he feared. He couldn't live with the shame.

18

A T LEAST SHE could see. They had deprived her of speech and to a great extent of movement, but neither of the men who had abducted Lizzie had blindfolded her, so she was able to lift her head high enough to see some street signs.

When—if—someone came to rescue her, they would want those sorts of clues to where she was. The car had gone over one of the river bridges and, for a moment, had drawn alongside a number 36 bus going north in the opposite direction. Lizzie thought fleetingly of her dad: Could he be on the bus on his way back to Mamhead Drive? What would happen if he chanced to look over at the car and saw her—his only daughter—on the backseat, bound and gagged? But the traffic lights changed, and the bus moved on, and there was no help for her, no possibility of rescue. As her eyes filled once more with tears, she struggled to read the names of the places she was passing before, finally, the driver turned into an alley.

It occurred to Lizzie that these two men weren't good criminals. They had the right sort of language and did the right sort of things, like putting on the gag and the handcuffs. But professional kidnappers, real criminals, wouldn't have left her eyes uncovered, they wouldn't have left her able to see everywhere they were taking

her. Such as the lane off Abbotswood Road where they were now, and the alley with its row of lockup garages.

The driver must have used a remote, for the door of number 5 went up. Inside, the garage was empty and she could see there was no other way in or out of it. Lizzie thought they might speak to her now, but they didn't. They got out of the car, the driver first, then the redhead. Then she remembered a film she had seen of someone's dying from being left in a car in a garage with carbon monoxide exuding from somewhere and poisoning them. Crying out or just crying was no use. She watched them moving out of the garage, leaving her inside the car, noting the height and size of them, their hair. And she thought of Swithin.

The garage door went down and closed, and deep darkness descended. When thinking about what to expect, Lizzie had forgotten darkness. She had forgotten air too. But they must not want her to die because the driver had left his door open a little way and the engine was turned off.

They would be back. They must be back.

UPSTAIRS ON THE number 36 bus, heading north, Tom was thinking about his daughter. He'd long hoped for a change in her lifestyle and character, and now he clung to small steps towards improvement. She needed to find a nice young man with a job. Not a good job, not yet, that would be too much to ask in this day and age, but a man with a job in an office nine till five, and preferably Lizzie at home cooking his dinner. These flights of fancy continued until the bus reached Queen's Park and Tom got off to wait for one to take him to Willesden.

When the bus had dropped him at the end of Mamhead Drive and he was in the house, he learned from Dot that Lizzie was expected to supper. Also coming, though not exactly invited, was Eddy Burton, from next door. His parents had moved in a month ago, and his

mother was going out for the evening and had asked Dorothy if she would be kind enough to give him dinner. Tom thought feeding a man of twenty-eight who wasn't disabled or with learning difficulties was taking spoiling to an absurd extent. Surely Dot couldn't be matchmaking? Tom felt rather cross. He wanted to see his daughter on her own.

He didn't know how many times he had said to Lizzie that punctuality was the politeness of princes, yet still it was never any good expecting her at a specific time. He wondered if Prince Charles was punctual. He must be, with dozens of people fussing around to make sure he was on time for all those engagements. The Milsoms regularly ate at seven, and Lizzie was a Milsom, who knew their ways if anyone did.

Eddy had arrived early, bringing his pug with him, an uninvited guest, and had already got through a liberal helping of wine, pushing the empty glass into a prominent position where his hostess couldn't fail to see it. The pug, whose name was Brutus, ran around the room, leaping onto laps and licking faces. Dot refilled Eddy's glass, and Tom's. Clicking her tongue, not at all pleased, she phoned Lizzie's mobile.

The only answer she got was that the call had been transferred to a number consisting of about fifteen digits.

"She's forgotten," said Tom. "Or she's out with some bloke."

Eddy looked embarrassed. He had been giving his hosts his dog's complicated life history, too complicated considering the animal was only eight months old, and both Tom and Dot were trying not to show their boredom.

"I suppose we'd better eat," said Dorothy, and persuaded Eddy to shut the dog in the kitchen.

The doorbell rang in the middle of their dessert, lemon meringue pie. Tom was sure it must be Lizzie and went to answer it with "Lost your key, have you?" on his lips.

The roving fishmonger was on the doorstep, asking if Tom wanted some beautiful cod fresh out of the Atlantic that morning.

Dorothy phoned Lizzie again later, but again the voicemail was transferred to that long number. Both she and Tom thought this meant that Lizzie had either gone home with the man she was no doubt out with or had turned off her phone. They disliked the idea of her spending the night with a man, but they never said so, not even to each other. It was what girls did these days, and nothing was to be done about it.

South of the river, Redhead and the squat, little man who had been the driver came into the garage, switched a light on, and opened the nearside rear door of the car. Lizzie heard Redhead call the other man Scotty and thought how stupid he must be to reveal his name to her. Then, with a sob, she understood that he might do this if he didn't care if she knew his name. He didn't care because he meant to kill her.

Redhead got in the driving seat while Scotty got in the back with her. When he undid the gag, Lizzie had a strange feeling in her mouth and throat. It was like a block on her voice so that all she could do, no matter how she tried, was grunt and gasp like an animal.

"Gone loco," said Scotty.

"Good. Don't want her screaming the fucking place down."

The clock on the dashboard had showed Lizzie that it was a quarter past three in the morning. Redhead reversed the car out of the garage and into Abbotswood Road. In silence, Lizzie laid her head back against the upholstery.

Fear of urinating was keeping her silent and tense. She contracted her muscles as if they were fists closing tightly. It was called a sphincter, she thought; this was what kept her bladder holding it in. If her urine leaked out of her in front of them, she thought she would die. Tears trickled from her eyes. If only the water from her eyes would take some of the water that wanted to pour out of her bladder. Was that the way it worked? Redhead was turning the car

into a row of marked-out parking places at the foot of a squalid-looking block of social housing. She had no idea where they were. She didn't care, concentrating only on holding her sphincter tight shut.

No one was about. Redhead and Scotty took her inside and up a flight of stone stairs, holding her between them. If someone had followed them, he or she would have seen the handcuffs still on Lizzie's wrists. No one was there to see.

Let into a flat by Scotty, she said, "Toilet," and Redhead pushed her through a door, slamming it behind her. The relief was so great, the *joy*, that for a moment she was almost happy, taking great breaths, indifferent to her cuffed hands, leaning her upper body forward to press onto her knees.

Scotty was outside the door, but even so she couldn't have gone anywhere. If your hands were tied behind your back, it was as bad as tying your feet, worse maybe. Scotty walked her into a living room, holding her shoulders. Redhead was in there, talking on his phone. He put it down when he saw her. Had he been talking to her parents?

"They haven't got any money," Lizzie said.

"What you on about?" Scotty pushed her down onto a battered and ragged couch. "He was talking to his husband."

So they were gay. Or Redhead was. And likely Scotty too. This comforted her. All the time she'd been in that car in the garage, she'd feared that one or both of them would rape her. Gay men wouldn't. "What are you going to do with me?"

"You know something?" said Redhead. "We're like the filth, we ask the questions, not you. You shut the fuck up."

He produced a mobile phone and dropped it in her lap. He seemed to have forgotten she couldn't use it without her hands. Leaning towards her, his face close to hers and his breath smelling of curry, he said, "Tell me your mum's number."

"I don't know what it is."

Of course he didn't believe her. They gave her two pills after that, capsules really, half-red and half-green. Redhead held her down on the couch while Scotty forced the red-and-green things into her mouth, sitting on her legs and holding her lips crammed together with both hands. She swallowed them in saliva, not daring to hold them in her mouth.

Lizzie thought she would have a few minutes to take in the room in all its squalid detail, note that outside it was now getting light, but unconsciousness was coming fast. She just had time to wonder why Redhead had asked for her mum's phone number, and not her mum and dad's, when a black door slammed over her eyes and she passed out.

19

Tom and Dot were vaguely concerned that they had still not heard from Lizzie, but they had become used to her disappearing for days on end, only to find that she hadn't really disappeared, just gone off to lead her own life. And she was of course a young woman in her twenties, not a teenager any longer.

Tom had observed, with interest, that when your child is living in the parental home, you worry when she is out in the evening after eleven, say. You are worried sick if she is still out after midnight. You watch the clock and pace and open the front door every ten minutes to try to spot her coming down the street. Sleep is out of the question. But when she is no longer living at home, although you know she goes out in the evenings just as much, stays out just as late, if not later, you scarcely worry at all. You go to bed and sleep. You wake up in the morning and have no doubt—if you even think about it—that she came in at midnight or one or two, safe and sound. Why was this? Why did you worry when she was living with you but not when she wasn't? He had asked other parents about this, and they all felt the same.

"She probably got the wrong day and thinks she's due here to supper on Friday rather than last night," he said to Dot. "She'll turn up."

LIZZIE AWOKE TO broad daylight. It hadn't been a natural awakening. One of them—Scotty, she thought—had shaken her while the other pressed an ice-cold rag against her face. It felt as if it had been in the freezer.

"We want a phone number," Redhead said.

"But I haven't got my bag. I haven't got my phone. How can I have a number?"

"You've got a memory, haven't you? You know your own mum's number."

What had her mother to do with anything, Lizzie thought, and why would she give these obviously violent men her parents' number? "I don't know," she lied. "I don't know. I can't remember."

Her voice was breaking again. She tried to say she couldn't think, but the words wouldn't come. Scotty slapped her face hard and she burst into howls. Her hands were shaking in the cuffs, which were wet with sweat. Yvonne, she thought suddenly. She took deep breaths in and out as slowly as she could as she thought about Stacey's beautiful flat, and how unfair it was that Yvonne, who had her own mansion in Swiss Cottage, had inherited this too.

No, she decided in a fit of spite, she wouldn't give Scotty and Redhead her mum's number; she'd give them Yvonne's instead. She knew her telephone number too and could almost visualise it from when she'd seen it on the pet-clinic computer screen that day. Closing her eyes and concentrating hard, she recited the number to her captors.

A LITTLE PATH runs down from Lisson Grove, a shortcut into the pink- and green- and blue-painted blocks that fill the area north of Rossmore Road. Nicola and Carl had walked through the Church Street market, bought some fruit and a couple of avocados, which Carl put in his backpack.

Nicola was surprised to see the antique shops at the other end of Church Street. She had never before been there and wanted to go into every shop. They held no interest for Carl, but once inside, the various vases and urns and small pieces of furniture caught his attention, even distracting him momentarily from his general despair. A chess set with half the big chessmen carved from golden wood and the other half from white attracted him so much that if he'd had the money, he would have bought it. The cost would have been beyond his means at any time.

Nicola fell in love, as she put it, with a green goose in a shop called Tony's Treasury. The ornament, of no possible use, had its charm, being made of pottery, green with white edges to each of its feathers and a purple head with red wattles and beak. It was big, rotund, the size of a football, and heavy to lift.

"It would look lovely on your hall table," she said. "I'll buy it for you."

Impossible to say he didn't want it and equally impossible to get up much enthusiasm. He didn't ask how much it was but found out when he saw her hand the shop owner two twenty-pound notes and a ten. The goose was so heavy he had to carry it in his backpack with the groceries.

They crossed Lisson Grove and he led the way down the little path that ultimately brought them into Jerome Crescent. These streets here, Carl thought, could aptly be called respectable. They were clean, the buildings in a good state of decoration, and the postcode one of the most prestigious in London. No one called the blocks council flats anymore—it would have been politically incorrect—but that was what they were.

"Up there is where Sybil Soames lives." It was the first thing Carl had said to her since they left the antiques shop. "That bastard's girlfriend. Those flats that are painted green, that's where she lives with her mum and dad."

Nicola followed his gaze. She took in the bicycle on the balcony

and the net curtains. "You only call them that because you're a snob. You'd call them her mother and father if you didn't despise them."

He said nothing. He was looking at the yellow nasturtiums in a flowerbed, the scaffolding on the block opposite the green one, and the stack of bricks on the pathway. The goose in the backpack weighed heavily on his shoulders.

"Why did we come here?" she asked.

"Something seems to draw me to this place. I can't get away from him, you see. And he's here. He may be up there now. I dream about him. I don't want to let him out of my sight and yet I hate him. I loathe him."

"Oh, Carl." She took his arm, held it, and clutched his hand. "What shall we do?"

"What you want me to do I can't do. I never will. Come on. Let's go home."

As they walked back to Falcon Mews, along the sunlit streets, under the green trees, Carl became increasingly agitated, uttering angry denunciations of Dermot, cursing him, going over once again, twice, three times, what had happened and what his tenant had done.

NICOLA KEPT SILENT; she had nothing to say because she had said it all. Now she was thinking what she must do. Should she force Carl to take some drastic step, perhaps? Leave the house in Falcon Mews, rent a room for both of them, find himself a regular day job? Or should she abandon him, leave him behind? She thought, I used to love him—do I still love him? He hardly speaks but to rage against Dermot. He sleeps a little, dreams violently, cries out, and sits up fighting against something that isn't there. I would be better without him, but would he be better without me? She didn't know the answer.

How pretty Falcon Mews was on a sunny day. The little houses

were all of different shapes and heights, their roofs of grey slate or red tile, their windows diamond-paned or plate glass in white frames, some walls covered in variegated ivy or long-leaved clematis. Flowers were everywhere, sprays and bunches of them hanging on the climbers amid festoons of dark green leaves. It was all so lovely, a beautiful place to live and be happy in. They went into the house, into the dim silence. Carl put the food and drink into the fridge, took the backpack upstairs, and dropped it on the bedroom floor.

Nicola was looking out of the kitchen window into the back garden, where she could see Dermot in one of the deck chairs reading a magazine. Sybil had acquired a pair of lawn trimmers and was cutting the edges, where the grass met the flowerbeds where the nettles used to be. She was the kind of woman, Nicola thought, who always had to be doing something: weeding, cutting, chopping, cooking, cleaning—a gift to a man. Carl was silent now, but when he saw those two, as he must sooner or later, he would start his agonised complaints again. She couldn't leave him, nor could she put up with him much longer.

Suppose she did what Dermot hadn't yet done and might never do? Only she and he knew the truth of what had happened on the day Carl sold the DNP to Stacey Warren. If she told the whole story to a newspaper, and if, say, the *Paddington Express* used it and passed it to the *Evening Standard*, it would be in the public domain—wasn't that what they called it?—just as much as if Dermot had told them. Dermot wouldn't have been responsible for its appearance, she would, but the effect would be the same. Dermot would no longer have anything to hold over Carl. His inverted blackmail would no longer work. He would therefore be obliged to pay Carl's rent once more or leave. Also, Carl might demand rent arrears and surely get them. Once that had been done, he could evict Dermot.

And what of her? She would have to tell Carl that she had— well, betrayed him. He might never want to see her again, but as

things were, she couldn't continue with him like this. She went to the fridge and opened the still-rather-warm white wine they had bought in Church Street—well, not *they*; *she* had bought it. Carl had almost run out of money.

She poured the wine and carried in the glasses and found Carl at the back window, looking through a barrier of leaves and branches and privet bushes at Sybil chopping away at the lawn edge and Dermot apparently sleeping in his deck chair.

Carl took the glass and gulped down half of its contents, the way he always drank these days. Nicola drank more slowly, studying the man she still loved, wondering what she should do.

20

Dermot wasn't in love with Sybil, but aspects of her pleased
him very much. She reminded him of his mother, always
busy, never sitting down for long except in church. A woman should
have a faith, he thought now; women needed religion more than
men. She spent a lot of time in his flat but he hardly ever saw her
relax. Washing machines, microwaves, and freezers held no attrac-
tion for her. "Made for lazy people" was how she described them.
When she had finished doing his washing by hand and putting up
a line to peg it out on, she settled down with his mending. Even
his mother no longer mended socks or sewed on buttons, though
he remembered her doing his father's darning when Dermot was
a little boy. Sybil cooked his dinner on Saturdays and Sundays too,
the old-fashioned food he liked: roast beef and Yorkshire pudding
and shepherd's pie. Until now he had never thought about getting
married, but that might have been because he had never met a girl
he could contemplate marrying.

One thing he particularly liked about Sybil was that she had
never shown any sexual interest in him. He had started kissing her
because that was what you did with a girl, but only on the cheek.
He also held hands with her, and she seemed to like it. He didn't
know, because he had never put it to the test, how having sexual

relations would be with her or anyone else. But he was convinced he would only be able to perform this duty if they were married. Then it would be all right. But it would be far from all right and would fail if he attempted it before marriage, because that would be immoral.

He was thinking along these lines and resolving to ask Sybil to marry him when Yvonne Weatherspoon walked into the pet clinic with Sophie in her cat box.

"I haven't got an appointment, I know," she said quickly. "There's nothing really wrong with her, but I thought maybe Caroline would give her her injections, you know, for worms and fleas and whatever, even though it's a few weeks early."

"Maybe Melissa can, I'll enquire." Dermot did and got an exasperated agreement. Yvonne was one of their more demanding clients. She needed more attention than Sophie.

Yvonne took Sophie out of the box and held her in her arms, closely snuggled.

"Better not," said Dermot. "We had a cat escape last week when a client opened the door—no more than an inch or two, but you know what cats are."

Yes, she knew what cats were: highly intelligent, beautiful, and good. Reluctantly, Yvonne put Sophie back in the box. "Nasty Dermot's a real spoilsport. We need our cuddles, don't we?"

Dermot was still thinking about what form the question he planned to ask Sybil should take. He wouldn't be asking her yet; it was Tuesday, and they only met at the weekends and on Friday evenings. They had discovered quite early in their relationship that they were in perfect agreement on this subject. Both worked hard, went to bed early, and got up early. Otherwise, how could they do their jobs properly? That was what weekends were for, relaxing (in his case) or catching up on all the domestic tasks that needed to be done (in hers). Yes, he thought, she would make him a good wife. A good old-fashioned wife, none of your postimpressionist feminist partners, or whatever they called them. Would he have to buy her a

ring? That was something to give some thought to. They could live in the flat for the first few years, then maybe he could buy a house in Winchmore Hill or Oakwood.

NICOLA HAD FOUND a website for the *Paddington Express*. It had offices in Eastbourne Terrace, walking distance from Falcon Mews. With all the contact information in hand, her plan of action seemed real. She would go there and ask to see the editor (or news editor or features editor), and she or he would be interested, record what Nicola had to say, and perhaps take it down in shorthand as well. Did people still use shorthand? They would ask if they could send a photographer round. They would find out that Carl didn't know she was telling them what he had done. It wasn't as simple as it had seemed at first. It now appeared almost treacherous. If she did this, she would lose him. This must be the end.

Perhaps she wouldn't have to do it herself. Or not do it in person. She could send an anonymous letter. Nicola marvelled that she, who was surely an honest, decent sort, should even contemplate such a thing. Perhaps honest, decent people imagined this kind of behaviour, but they didn't carry it out. Of course they didn't. When the time came, she would go herself and be straightforward and truthful. There was nothing else for it. The only question was when.

YVONNE WEATHERSPOON ARRANGED the white-chocolate-coated, circular shortbread biscuits she knew she shouldn't eat, and therefore restricted herself to one a day, on an oval china plate. She put the plate on a tray with the coffeepot and two cups, the jug of semi-skimmed milk, and the two sachets of sugar substitute. The thin milk and thinner little packets were to make up for the biscuits.

Yvonne was setting the tray on the table by the open French windows when the landline rang. She picked it up.

A coarse voice, quite a rough male voice, said, "Mrs. Weatherspoon? Mrs. Yvonne Weatherspoon?"

"Yes?"

"We've got your daughter. She's OK at present, and you can have her back"—the man paused to speak to someone—"for a lot of money."

Yvonne laughed. "That's very funny, as my daughter is sitting here beside me. You can speak to her if you like."

The phone was abruptly cut off.

Yvonne and Elizabeth agreed on few things, but this was one of them. They both laughed, Elizabeth hysterically, Yvonne with more restraint. "Do you think we should tell the police?"

"I don't think so," Elizabeth said. "Let sleeping cops lie."

21

"**A**RE YOU GOING to set me free now?" Lizzie asked, using a phrase she had learned from a TV drama about royalty in the thirteenth century.

Scotty and Redhead looked a bit rattled, she thought, as though their plan hadn't gone entirely as they had expected.

"Why would we do that? That wasn't your mum, just as you must have known it wouldn't be." Redhead fetched her a mug of water. "We're going to have to move you, so we're going to give you enough pills to knock you out for twenty-four hours." A faint smile crossed his face. "Don't say we don't look after you."

"Would you put the cuffs on my hands in front?" she asked, feeling alarmed. "Please."

But the handcuffs remained where they were, and soon the two men appeared to be ready to leave, Redhead with a suitcase and a big holdall, and Scotty with a bottle that must contain the sleeping pills. He shook not two but three of them into his hand and signed to her to put her head back and open her mouth.

What's the maximum safe dose? Lizzie wondered, but she opened her mouth and swallowed the pills, washing them down with the rest of the water in the mug.

They walked her downstairs, both supporting her, talking as they went, grumbling about who they had thought she was, and what they were going to do with her now.

The car was in a side entrance outside a back door. Consciousness was going and Lizzie stumbled down the last few steps, wondering vaguely what time it was, early or late, as blackness and oblivion descended.

WHEN SHE CAME round, to use her father's phrase, her hands were shackled in front and cable had been tightly tied round her feet.

While captive, she was learning things. When you feel comfortable in your body, most of the time you're barely aware of having a body. But when part of it is tied up, hands together and feet together, you feel stiff and then you start to ache. You wonder if this is what it will be like when you're old. Recovering consciousness, you don't feel wide-awake quickly; for a long time you feel weak and feeble and vague and the room swims around you.

To keep her weight down, Lizzie had eaten sparingly for months, years really, so she had got used to small meals and hadn't often felt hungry. But she had in the past eaten something every day and had never felt like this. Her hunger was a devouring presence. Although she knew it was a stupid thing to do, she couldn't stop herself imagining her mother's cooking, so that she actually saw before her eyes her famous lemon meringue pie, the glistening leg of lamb surrounded by potatoes roasted in goose fat, the apple tart with its latticed lid. She had never known what it meant to have your mouth water. Now she did.

It amazed her that she could do without a bath or a shower. She was still wearing the same clothes she had worn when Scotty and Redhead took her away, and inside Stacey's black dress with the white lace panel, filthy now and torn, her body smelled like a sick dog and her hair as if it had been buried in dusty earth. But all this

worried her less than she would ever have expected. If she smelt bad, so did Redhead and Scotty.

In this new place, she was left alone, drugged, given water when she woke but no food apart from a piece of white bread from a sliced loaf and a hunk of cheese in the morning and the evening. One of them took her to the bathroom when they brought the bread and slammed the door on her, waiting outside. She had to shuffle along slowly because of the rope tied around her ankles. They no longer spoke to her.

She had no idea of how much time had passed when they took her downstairs again, put her in the car, and drove her through dark, winding streets to a new prison.

THE PREVIOUS YEAR, in late July, when school was finished and the little ones were supervised by volunteer mothers, Lizzie had gone off somewhere on a holiday with a friend or friends. Or she said she had, but you never knew when she was telling the truth and when she was not.

These were Tom's thoughts, not Dot's. Tom no longer believed much of what Lizzie said, while Dot always had faith in her daughter. More than this, though, she trusted and believed in what her husband said. If Tom said Lizzie was somewhere on the Mediterranean, or in Cornwall, that was where she was. While it annoyed Tom that his daughter would disappear somewhere with friends and not tell him or her mother where she was, it upset Dorothy.

"She's an adult," he said. "She has her own life."

"I knew you'd say that. Of course you're right, but I think she could ring us. It's not much to ask."

"You've never asked her, though, have you? Maybe you should. I doubt it'll make any difference, but it would set your mind at rest—in the future. To know where she was."

"Oh, it is at rest. I'm not worried, I'm cross."

But she was worried, and so was he. They might have confided in each other, but they never did that. Each pretended that Lizzie must be safe somewhere and fine. Unpleasant things happened to young girls every day, the newspapers said so, but they did their best to dismiss this thought. Nothing nasty could ever happen to their Lizzie.

22

I T HAD BECOME an obsession. Carl understood that his behaviour was just as much that of a fanatical lover as of a fixated hater. He followed Dermot with his eyes whenever he had the opportunity, listened for what he could hear of him, outside the door at the top of the stairs: his music, his footsteps, and his words on the phone or when he spoke to Sybil Soames. When Dermot approached the door, Carl ran down the top flight of stairs to hide in his own bedroom.

At first he did this only while Nicola was at work, but gradually he came hardly to care at all. Anyway, she knew. She had told him what he should do, but now she had stopped; telling him, she said, was useless. Probably the time was coming when she would give up on him and leave. He wouldn't care. Sometimes he thought he wouldn't even notice.

Once or twice he had followed Dermot to work. If Dermot had turned round and seen him, he wouldn't have cared, but he didn't turn round. Carl watched as Dermot went into the pet clinic by a back door. Then the clinic lights came on and Carl walked away.

He had also begun to follow Dermot to Sybil's parents' house when he walked her home in the evenings. Occasionally, if it was raining or chilly, Dermot called a taxi for her. He could easily afford

taxis now, Carl thought bitterly. But mostly Dermot set off with Sybil at about nine thirty in the evening. They held hands. Or rather, Dermot held her hand. She wouldn't have dared take his, Carl thought.

Their walk took about twenty minutes and they always went the same way: down Castellain Road, into Clifton Gardens and across Maida Vale into St. John's Wood Road to Lisson Grove. They kept always to those same wide roads and never took the shortcut along the canal path. Although it was lit, it was much darker along there, a lovers' walk under the trees. Did Dermot avoid it with Sybil for that reason? Because it was somehow intimate, sheltered, a place for kissing?

On the way back though, Dermot did go that way. After he had kissed Sybil's cheek, watched her go into the flats, waved once, he turned round and took the little path that went over the canal bridge and led along the dark water. He walked slowly, pausing to look down on to the glassy canal.

Carl watched from the other side of Lisson Grove. When he was at university, he had belonged to the drama society, and the high spot of his second year had been their performance of *Measure for Measure*. A line came back to him, a phrase really, "the duke of dark corners." Dermot looked like that, with his round shoulders and long, thin neck; almost a mediaeval figure, dressed in a dark jacket, black jeans tucked into black boots. Under the bridge at Lisson Grove and under the bridge at Aberdeen Place were dark corners, footpaths melting into blackness.

If Carl wondered about Dermot, why he always walked to Jerome Crescent the way he did and returned along the towpath, Carl also wondered at himself. What made him follow Dermot? What did he get out of it? He didn't know. He just had a compulsion to do it.

Nicola had gone back to her old flat and the girls for the night, and he was sitting in his bedroom in the dark when he heard Dermot come in. These days he seldom thought about anything but Dermot, and sometimes Sybil, but pushing his backpack into a cor-

ner with his foot, he noticed that Nicola hadn't taken the goose out to put it on the hall table.

Sunday, and Dermot had come back from church with Sybil and a crowd of other people. Carl, watching from upstairs, saw him unlock the front door and welcome them all in. It was another fine day, clouds across the blue sky but plenty of sunshine too. Two women were among them apart from Sybil, and all wore bright floral dresses. Sybil's had a pattern on it of pink cabbage roses on a black background. The door shut with a bang.

Nicola was out, at a brunch with two of her ex-flatmates. He had forgotten to mention the goose. Never mind. It wasn't important. Nothing was but Dermot and maybe money.

He went into his bedroom and looked out of the window, hoping that Dermot and his guests wouldn't go into the garden. No one was out there, but as he turned away, he heard a commotion from downstairs as they all burst out among the flowers. Gusts of laughter drifted up. Sybil appeared with the trolley that had been Carl's father's, loaded with bottles and cans and plates of food and packets of crisps. Everyone started eating and drinking. Sybil was walking among them holding up her left hand for them to see something. Someone said, "I know you'll be very happy." Not *I hope*, but *I know*.

It was an engagement party. Carl felt sick. He fell back into a chair. "Don't let him see you," he said aloud, then whispered it. "Don't let him see you, he'll ask you down. He'll tell you his news and ask you to join them."

Quietly, as if they were all listening for him to make a move, he crept into the bathroom and drank from the cold tap above the sink.

Nicola had said nothing about coming back that evening, but he expected her. Even if those people were still in the garden, still eat-

ing and drinking, her return would be a comfort. He would ask her about the goose—did she really want it? He didn't care if the hall table had an ornament or not.

He had eaten no lunch, had eaten nothing, and no wine was in the house. In the kitchen was half a loaf of bread and a piece of cheese left over from last evening's dinner. He lay on the bed and fell asleep, overcome with despair. At some point in the afternoon or early evening—it was still light—he was awakened by the party guests going home. They weren't especially noisy, he had to admit that, but the slightest sound would have disturbed him. He got up and watched them go.

The sky had clouded over and a wind got up. The tree branches in Falcon Mews swayed and all the leaves fluttered. A blackbird was singing somewhere and a magpie making its repetitive squawk. He searched for his phone, but it had run out of charge. If Nicola didn't come, bringing food, he would have to go out and buy himself something to eat. Though it was Sunday, all the shops round here stayed open till late.

He picked up the backpack, and its weight told him the goose was still inside. He'd take it back to Tony's Treasury, he decided, and see what Tony would give him for it.

He heard Dermot's footsteps on the stairs, and Sybil's. He wouldn't be walking her home yet but maybe taking her out to dinner. Some snack at one of the cafés on the Edgware Road, Carl thought contemptuously. This would be an evening when he wouldn't follow them. Nicola had left some money in a jacket pocket: a twenty-pound note and five-pound coins. He wrote on an orange Post-it he took from a pad in the other pocket, *Borrowed £25. XX.* That would be enough to get something to eat in case Tony refused to buy back the green goose.

Dermot and Sybil had disappeared when Carl came out into the mews. No one was about except for Mr. Kaleejah and his dog. He took that dog out three or four times a day. It was carrying a rubber

bone in its mouth. Carl walked along Sutherland Avenue and across Maida Vale into Hall Road, and from there into Lisson Grove, where a crowd was coming out of the Roman Catholic church. The Tesco in Church Street would still be open. But Tony's Treasury wasn't. Carl hadn't anticipated this. That Tony might refuse to take the goose back, yes, that was possible, but not for his shop to be closed. The Tesco was open, though, and still had a couple of Sunday papers on the rack outside. He bought a loaf of bread, a piece of cheddar, a bar of chocolate, and a half bottle of rosé, using the money he'd taken from Nicola.

Carl wanted to avoid seeing Dermot. He didn't think Dermot would be near the canal, but when he and Sybil had eaten they would walk back to Jerome Crescent via the little path that ran from Lisson Grove. So Carl followed a route that was new to him, into Lisson Green where the canal came out from under the Aberdeen Place bridge. The water was dark here, the path along the bank deserted. He also noticed that you could see the path from Lisson Grove, and see too where the canal disappeared under the next bridge on its way through Regent's Park.

He sat down on a wooden bench and ate some bread and cheese. He was surprised to find how hungry he was. The path continued to be deserted. After a while, he made his way into Paveley Street. There, looking for a path out, he saw Dermot and Sybil up ahead in Jerome Crescent, entering the block where Sybil lived. Going to continue the engagement celebrations, Carl thought bitterly.

Lights were on in a couple of windows in Sybil's block. Carl sat down on the stack of bricks. He didn't know why. He certainly wasn't waiting for Dermot. He didn't understand what brought him here so regularly to watch what Dermot did, what they both did, as if they were fascinating people whose activities were of enormous interest, rather than the reverse.

Carl got up and walked round the block, round Jerome Crescent and back. As he watched, a light in one of the windows went

out, then the other one. He moved into deep shadow as Dermot appeared at the entrance, then emerged into the half-light and crossed the street towards him.

"Hello there. What brings you here?" Dermot sounded surprised.

"I've got something to show you," Carl said. "I've brought you a present."

"That's awfully decent of you," said Dermot, like a public-school boy of a hundred years ago. "For my engagement, is it?"

"That's right." Carl suddenly decided to give him the goose. He didn't know why he'd said he had a present. Just an odd impulse. He bent over the backpack and started unzipping it. For a brief moment while Dermot watched, anticipating his present, Carl began taking the goose out, then abruptly he lifted the backpack as high as he could and brought it down hard on Dermot's head. He was taller than Dermot, and there was a crunch of bone.

Dermot uttered a long, dull groan. It was the only sound he made as he slumped over onto the pavement.

Careful not to touch Dermot, Carl bent over him to see whether he was still breathing. He didn't appear to be. Then Carl picked up the bag. He couldn't see any blood. Perhaps it was too dark, or there wasn't any. He hoisted the backpack onto his shoulders and for some reason looked at the windows that had been lit up. Both were still in darkness, though he fancied he saw a faint flicker of movement behind the higher one. He thought, Why did I never think of doing this before? For months I've been desperate to get rid of this awful threat, this burden. He felt no guilt, no regret. He felt relief.

He walked away and up the path into Lisson Grove. It was as well the backpack was on his back because his hands were shaking so much as to be useless for carrying anything. He climbed up the hill past the Catholic church, turned into Lodge Road, and walked along beside the high walls above the railway line. Walking was

automatic, his legs carrying him mechanically towards a safer place. A single cyclist rode past him and up to cross Park Road. Carl went across the road after him and down a path into the green, the trees, the dense leafiness that clustered and shivered in the rising wind along the canal bank. The water was black and still and shiny.

He hoisted the backpack off his shoulders, unzipped it, and lifted out the green goose. Something dark was on his hands, but whether it was blood or not, he couldn't tell. He looked about him into the trees above, the leaves making a soft whispering sound. The screen of branches that hid the road running alongside Regent's Park was dense and dark. The man on the bike had disappeared, was no doubt far away now, heading for Primrose Hill or Camden Town. Carl knelt down on the canal bank and dropped the backpack into the water. It floated for a few moments, then sank with a sucking, glugging sound.

He remained on his knees for perhaps two minutes holding the goose, then got to his feet with difficulty, like an old man, feeling about him in vain for something to hold on to. Carrying the goose under one arm, he started to walk back. He climbed up into Park Road and thought, without quite knowing why, that it would be better to go back along the St. John's Wood Road rather than Lodge Road.

It started to rain, a drizzle at first, blown about by the wind, but soon it changed to a great storm. Good, Carl thought, it would wash Dermot's blood off him, although he was pretty sure what little there was had been on the backpack. He could feel the rain lashing against him, and streaming down his back and legs. It changed him from being mildly warm to a sudden, sharp cold, and a huge weariness took hold of him, an exhaustion so powerful that he stumbled as he walked.

The rain had driven home those people who had been in the streets. Sutherland Avenue was deserted, apart from the Tesco supermarket, where cars still came and went, skidding through pud-

dles. Turning into Castellain Road and staggering to the corner of the mews, he found himself dreading that Dermot might be there, waiting inside the front door to make some fatuous remark. Then he remembered.

No Dermot. Never again. But Nicola was there, opening the door just as he reached out with his key. She took one look at his sodden clothes and without asking him why he was carrying her green goose, put her arms round him, and pulled him inside.

23

THEY WERE GOING to move Lizzie again. For some reason they were in a hurry and packing stuff into bags and boxes, and they'd forgotten to give her the pills. It wasn't much help—her hands were still shackled and her ankles tied—but at least her head was clear. She thought, They'll remember in a minute and then they'll drug me, but it seemed they thought she'd had the pills, for they dragged her down the stairs, clutching her arms painfully and roughly, and bundled her into the backseat of their car. It was broad daylight, but nobody was nearby. Had anybody seen her, they would have thought she was just another drunken woman and would have taken little notice.

She didn't know where they were taking her, only that it was like countryside here, with broad areas of grass and big trees. She didn't recognise it, but they must have thought she did, because Redhead pulled to the side of the road and stopped, and Scotty got into the back and tied a scarf round her eyes. The smell of him so close was bad, but she must smell as foul, for while she could still see, she saw him flinch away from her.

Now that her head was clear, Lizzie considered her position, and not for the first time. Could Swithin Campbell be behind her abduction? she wondered. Was that even his real name? She'd invited him

into Stacey's flat, had wanted him to think she was well-off. Could he and Redhead and Scotty have mistaken her for Yvonne's daughter, another Elizabeth? Now that they all knew she wasn't the Elizabeth they'd supposed her to be, what was going to happen to her?

They drove on, through open spaces or streets, she could no longer tell. They were all out of the car and halfway up a path when she thought she had a chance of escape, but her ankles were still tied and the single, hobbled step she took resulted in her sprawling. Redhead picked her up with rough hands and, once they were inside a door, slapped her face on both cheeks painfully. The scarf was pulled off and she was dragged upstairs to a single room at the top.

Most people of Lizzie's age would not have been able to identify the type of dwelling she was in. They would have known it was old and small, and that was about it. She hardly knew why she bothered to amass all this stuff in her head. Why did she care? Perhaps she thought it might be useful to know once she got out of here. If she got out.

She got off the bed where they had dumped her and, wide-awake for the first time since she had become their prisoner, stumbled across to the window.

She was in the kind of cottage her grandmother had lived in. Such small, terraced or sometimes semidetached houses are to be found in every London suburb, tucked away among blocks of flats, tall Victorian terraces, and large single houses. A few are still occupied by a solitary elderly resident; others have been bought by young couples who have smartened them up and filled them with the latest equipment.

This cottage, Lizzie saw, had been lived in by someone of her grandmother's generation. She could tell by the single bed and its eiderdown, the two little armchairs with cushions on their seats shaped like doughnuts, and the twenty or thirty tiny ornaments on the mantelpiece: china dogs, a brass bell, two framed photographs, and a number of unidentifiable objects. She thought this old lady—

for it was surely a woman—must have died and left the house to a relation, perhaps Redhead's or Scotty's mother, and that was how they had possession of it.

The window was large, far too large for the cottage, and although it had been put in perhaps only ten years previously, the frame looked jerry-built and rotten. The curtains, pink roses on a blue-and-green background, were drawn, and Lizzie pulled them back so that she looked out on what seemed to be a public park. She could, she realised, be anywhere south of the river Thames, a vast area of London she barely knew. Below her were tall trees, smaller trees and bushes, tennis courts, paths winding among flowerbeds, people strolling. Birds in the trees, English ones, and those green parakeets that were English now, having come here to live and settled down happily.

She thought, feeling happier suddenly, Tomorrow they will let me go. I know it, but I don't know how I do. She sat down in one of the little armchairs and swung her bound legs up onto the other chair. It is almost as easy to untie a knot in a rope with cuffed hands as with free ones, and she had this one undone in seconds. Someone would be bound to come in, so she sat where she was with the rope tied loosely round her ankles and waited. Someone did come, Redhead, with a plate of chips and a can of Diet Coke. He didn't speak as he took off her cuffs, allowing her to eat, and he didn't even glance at her ankles.

As he was leaving, she said, "Where's the bathroom?"

"Downstairs. I'm not taking you."

Once she would have argued, pleaded, even cried. Not now. She thought of the old woman who had lived here, waited till Redhead had gone, and looked under the bed. It was there, a china chamber pot, as she had once heard someone call it. She would have to use it and, worse, leave it for one of them to empty. The alternative was to pour the contents out the window. People used to do that, she had read in a social-history book, in the days when there was no plumbing.

Revelling in having her hands free for the first time in days, she used the pot and pushed it back under the bed, so as not to have to see it. Then she lay down under the eiderdown and thought about the old and the poor who had not so long ago used chamber pots and carried big pottery jugs of hot water to fill bowls for washing in. It was the first time she had thought about something other than herself and her plight. For some unaccountable reason, going to bed with an almost-empty stomach on top of a pot full of urine in a stuffy room no longer seemed a dreadful fate. It would pass, she knew; it would soon end.

IT MUST HAVE been four or five in the morning when the crash woke her. Outside it was getting light, and a large pane from the window in her room had been smashed. Most of it was lying in shards on her bed.

Lizzie got up and put on her shoes before making her way to the window, glass crunching under her feet. Standing there looking down, she heard thuds and bangs as Scotty and Redhead ran downstairs. Seconds later they both appeared carrying bags and hoisting backpacks and ran up the street in search of their car. They were abandoning her.

What had caused the crash? Had someone fired a gun at the window? Had something exploded? Scotty and Redhead evidently thought so. Lizzie knew she must leave as quickly as she could in spite of the early hour, in spite of Stacey's soiled black-and-white dress. She opened the door of the wardrobe—on the off chance, her grandmother would have said. Nothing was inside but a padded jacket, shiny, purple, but not dirty. It could have belonged to any-one, but no matter. She put it on.

Only then did she remember she had no money, no bus or tube pass, no credit card. But she didn't care. Freedom was the main thing, and she had freedom. She went downstairs. The front door

was open, and out in the street there was no one but a young man pulling a case on wheels along a path in the park. It didn't matter which way she walked, though it made sense to go in the opposite direction from Scotty and Redhead.

She saw what must have caused her smashed window. The biggest pigeon she had ever seen had flown straight into the glass and lay dead, a shining mass of blue and green and gold and brown feathers, on the pavement.

"Oh, poor bird," said Lizzie aloud, tears in her eyes. She bent down and picked up the dead pigeon and laid it on the grass just inside the park gate, covering it as best she could with leaves.

She walked along painfully in Stacey's ridiculous high heels and read on a street name the postcode SE13. Beyond its being southeast London, she had no idea where that was. There might be a tube station, though, and there would certainly be buses, but neither would be of any use to her with no pass and no cards and no money.

What she could do came to her quite suddenly, and she thought what a fool she had been not to have thought of it before. The sole form of transport you paid for only at the end of the journey was a taxi.

24

T OM AND DOT were still trying not to feel anxious about Lizzie.

Dot believed that Lizzie must be somewhere on holiday. Cornwall was a likely choice because Lizzie knew someone whose parents lived there. Tom fixed on Barcelona. It was popular with young people; indeed, he'd read that visitor numbers—formerly about a million a year—had increased sevenfold in recent years. But another day had come and brought no Lizzie with it.

They got up an hour or so later than usual on weekend mornings, having always done so when Tom worked, so Dot was standing at their bedroom window at twenty past eight on Sunday morning, drawing back the curtains, when a black cab pulled up outside their gate. A girl she didn't at first recognise got out of it and ran up the path. She was young, with straggly, caramel-blond hair, and a short black-and-white dress covered by a cheap, shiny padded jacket probably bought from a market stall. Even from this distance she looked dirty, very dirty.

It was Lizzie.

Tom was sitting up in bed, drinking the tea Dot had brought him. "Our daughter is at the front door," Dot told him, and then,

using a phrase popular with her own mother, "She looks as if she's been pulled through a hedge backwards."

The door was opened to admit a Lizzie even dirtier than she had looked from upstairs. "Mum, can you pay the man? It's a terrible lot but I haven't any money."

"How much?"

"Thirty-five pounds."

"I don't believe it," said Dot, who did.

In the house, Lizzie said she'd pay her back but was first going to have a bath and wash her hair. Dot didn't ask her where she had been or why she was dirty and without money. As for Lizzie, she wasn't sure what she would tell her parents about what had happened to her.

Lying in the bath, she decided. If she told her parents the truth, they would only make a fuss. Without a doubt, they would want to inform the police. She would be asked awkward questions that she might struggle to answer, such as why was she living in Stacey's flat, drinking her drink, wearing her clothes? She couldn't also help feeling a little complicit in her own abduction: Had she not wanted people to believe she was someone else; someone a lot wealthier than she actually was? Now, she just wanted to be left in peace to live her own life and forget the whole awful episode.

In the steaming-hot bathroom she shuddered, ducked her head under the water, and massaged in the shampoo. No, what she wanted most to do was dry her hair and put on some makeup. She knew that her mum had kept some of her old clothes, so she should be able to find something clean to wear. She'd go out and enjoy her freedom, maybe go for a walk around Willesden, or follow her father's example and have a bus ride.

Never explain was a good way to live, she decided, getting out of the bath. It would be far easier for all concerned if no one knew where she had been these past few days.

Picking up the disgusting black-and-white dress, she rolled it into a ball, determined to drop it into the first litter bin she came to.

He wouldn't tell anyone, Carl decided, falling asleep as soon as he got into bed and sleeping soundly all night.

No dreams came, no sudden awakenings to horrid realisation, no remembering in the warm darkness what had happened. When he'd got in the previous night, Nicola had brought him a glass of water and some sort of hot drink, but he hadn't touched either of them. When he woke, he had no idea of the time except that it must be morning, maybe early morning, though it might have been light for hours.

The silence was broken by the ringing of the doorbell, Dermot's bell, as audible down here as in the upstairs flat. He wouldn't answer it; he was sure he couldn't speak of Dermot, might never speak of him again. The bell rang once more, and this time Nicola went to the door. She had left the bedroom door open, so he could hear what she said.

"He lives in the top flat. You should go upstairs and ring at the door that's facing you."

It must be the police. Of course. Someone had found Dermot's body, established where he lived, and had come here to ask about him, to tell his wife or girlfriend or parents or whichever of his people lived in Falcon Mews. Carl heard their feet on the stairs, then Dermot's doorbell ringing, and turned over to bury his face in the pillow. He remembered a favourite saying of Dermot's that was supposed to be funny: "No answer was the stern reply."

Nicola had a clear, rather beautiful speaking voice, and he heard her telling the police officers that Dermot might have gone early to work, told them about the pet clinic and where it was. After some conversation, Nicola said, "Oh, no!" and he knew they must have told her Dermot was dead.

They left. He heard the front door close, and Nicola came into the bedroom.

"I heard," he said, his voice sounding dulled and broken as anyone would say it should have done.

"They don't know how it happened. Or they didn't say. They didn't say anything about foul play. That's the term, isn't it?"

"Newspapers' term, I expect."

"He was found in Jerome Crescent. It's a shock, I must say. Sudden death is always a shock, isn't it, even if you didn't much like the dead person? I must go to work now, but I expect they'll come back, they'll want to search the place, or they will if his death was suspicious. You'll talk to them? You know more about Dermot than anyone, I should think."

He listened to her going, her high heels on the stairs, the pause while she picked up her bag, the creak the front door made and the click as she closed it as softly as she could behind her.

It must be Monday morning, Carl supposed. He got up and walked into the shower, not waiting for the water to heat up but stepping into it and shivering at its cold touch. Jeans, sweatshirt, trainers. All much as usual, though it wasn't as usual, was it? Eating was impossible. He would never eat anything again. Stretched out on his father's sofa, he wondered why he always thought of this piece of furniture as Dad's. Almost everything in the house had been his father's, yet he never thought of the tables and chairs and beds as his, only this sofa. The police would know by now that Dermot had been killed, that his death had not been an accident. *Murdered* why don't you say? he thought. You mustn't say it, though, when they come and talk to you. You must just answer what they ask.

His throat was parched and his mouth dry, no matter how much water he drank. There must be some reason for that but he didn't know what it was. He waited a long time for the police. Perhaps they would never come. Perhaps they thought Dermot had been killed in a road accident and they were searching for the driver of

the car that hit him. Such a thing could hardly happen in narrow, bendy Jerome Crescent.

The police arrived at ten to one, when Carl had almost given them up. He had to tell himself as he was walking towards the front door not to speak to them unless they spoke to him, not to express any opinions about Dermot, not to ask questions; above all, not to speak of murder, or of Dermot as "the murdered man."

They told him rather baldly what had happened. They asked only one question, and that was whether they could go into Dermot's flat. No reason was given. If he were an innocent man, nothing more than Dermot's landlord, would he ask if they had seen Miss Soames? Did they know he had a fiancée? Did she know what had happened? Oh, yes, they would take care of notifying her, said the older man. Carl gave them a key and they went upstairs.

Carl hadn't given a thought to Sybil until now. Picturing her hearing the news, understanding that the man she was going to marry had been killed in the street, more or less outside her own home, would be what the newspapers would call "a devastating blow." Poor Sybil. Perhaps she had loved Dermot, been in love with him, and now this had happened. Don't be a fool, Carl told himself. Pull yourself together.

The police came back downstairs. The younger one was carrying a briefcase, and it seemed to Carl to have more in it than when they had gone up. Papers, certificates, records of something or other? Of no interest to him, nothing to do with him, nothing to incriminate him. The older one said it might be helpful to have Carl's phone number in case they needed to get in touch, and Carl gave it to him. He saw them out, went into the living room, and sat down. From what he had read and seen, he might have expected them to ask where he had been the previous evening, but they hadn't asked. They must believe that the only connection between him and Dermot was the usual relationship between landlord and tenant: remote, a matter of business—one paid the rent, the other

received it. Of course it hadn't been like that, but how would they know?

Lying on the sofa in the living room, he had nothing to do, almost nothing to think about. But after a time, his mind filled with scenes of the previous evening, of the dark waters of the canal and his backpack floating, then sinking with that queer sucking sound, and of the fat, round goose as green as the grass and the oak leaves, sitting on the hall table, quietly mocking him.

25

Nicola came home early, just after five, bringing with her the *Evening Standard*. Carl had no desire to read the details, but he looked at the picture of Dermot—when he was alive, of course; there was no picture of him dead—and read the story to please Nicola.

She wanted to talk about what had happened, as more or less everyone in Maida Vale would now be discussing the case. Why would anyone kill Dermot? Money was the general consensus, or even to steal his phone. Was his phone missing? The newspaper didn't say. Someone with a lively imagination suggested that a former lover of Sybil Soames's, jealous of this new fiancé, had done it. Several residents of Falcon Mews who had never spoken to Carl before approached him in the street when he and Nicola went out to eat, to express their amazement, disgust, horror, or disbelief. What a shock it must have been for him and the young lady, said Mr. Kaleejah, walking his dog for the third time that day. Nothing like this had ever happened before in the vicinity of Elgin Avenue, said someone else. That it hadn't been anywhere near Elgin Avenue, Carl didn't say. He smiled and nodded. Nicola shook her head and thanked them for their concern.

They walked to the Canal Café on the Edgware Road and ate

fish and chips and drank lager. Soon, thought Carl, when I find a new tenant, I'll have money to pay for things myself.

Two DAYS PASSED and the police didn't return. Nor did they phone. The only caller was Sybil. Carl wasn't particularly surprised by this visit, though he hadn't exactly expected to see her. What astonished him was her appearance. She was dressed in deep mourning: long black skirt, big black shoulder bag, high-necked black blouse, and black jacket, her head wrapped in a black scarf like a Muslim woman. He knew he ought to say how sorry he was for her loss, and he did say it, hesitating over the words, almost stammering.

She came into the hallway. "Yes, it's been terrible for me. I shall never get over it."

He thought he should ask her to sit down, offer her something to drink, remembering that she wouldn't touch alcohol. But the need to offer her a seat and a glass of orange juice failed to arise as she walked straight upstairs and, with the key Dermot must have given her, let herself into the top flat. She had come for some of her things she had left behind, Carl supposed. Nothing could be more likely, seeing that she had spent day after day here with Dermot. And sure enough, after about ten minutes she came back down the stairs, the black bag stuffed with what appeared to be heavy objects. Opening the door, she said to him—oddly, he thought—that he hadn't seen the last of her.

Carl couldn't help thinking that her words might have been Dermot's.

LIZZIE HAD MANAGED to pass the whole day of her return without telling her parents about her abduction, and she was sure she had done the right thing. Now she had to figure out what to tell the school where she worked. She probably no longer had a job. She didn't much care. No way could she tell them the truth.

She phoned Stacey's apartment in Pinetree Court on the land-line. The phone was answered by Elizabeth Weatherspoon. Had she already moved in? When Lizzie asked if she could come round and collect her handbag, which she had left there some days previously, Elizabeth said it was with the concierge. If Lizzie wanted it—she spoke as if the matter was in doubt—she could pick it up from his office.

Lizzie got a cool reception from the concierge, but she also got the bag. Her phone was still in it, and the key to her own flat, and possibly what money she had, though she couldn't remember how much this should be.

She returned to the flat in Iverson Road, and while she was resolving not to go near her parents until she absolutely had to, in case they asked her more questions about her disappearance, her mother phoned. "Eddy next door," as he was usually referred to by the Milsoms, had a virus and was bedbound. The pug too was ill, and Eddy's mother wanted it taken to the vet.

"Why doesn't she take it then?"

"She says she can't leave Eddy."

"He's not a baby, he's a grown man," said Lizzie.

"It's not what I say, it's what she says. Your father's gone some-where on the number seven bus, and I've got an appointment with the dentist."

"Tell me you're not expecting me to take the bloody dog to the vet?"

"That silly Eddy's in an awful state. Eva said he was crying."

So Lizzie got on the number 6 bus and, with an ill grace, picked up Brutus the pug from her parents' neighbours. "I've made an appointment with someone. I don't know who, since the tragedy, but it'll be all right," said Eddy's mother.

Lizzie didn't know what she was talking about.

"I won't ask you in to see Eddy in case he's infectious. I've booked a taxi for you and Brutus."

The taxi came and Lizzie got in with the dog in a rather grand basket.

At the Sutherland Pet Clinic, Melissa the vet was sitting at the reception desk, looking harassed.

"Where's the man who used to work here?" Lizzie asked.

"Dermot? Didn't you know? It was a shocking thing: he was murdered."

Lizzie didn't know what to say.

"It's awful, isn't it?" Melissa continued. "It seems callous to talk about it so soon, but we're desperate for someone to take his place. If you hear of anyone, you'll let us know, won't you?"

Melissa took Brutus into the surgery and Lizzie waited in reception. It wasn't her first visit to the clinic—she had of course been there before to talk to Dermot and get hold of the Weatherspoons' phone number, but on that occasion she had taken little notice of the room. It was rather nice, she thought now, quiet, and different from what she would have expected in that it didn't smell of dog. The swivel chair drawn up to the counter and the computer she was already familiar with. One of those water dispensers was in the corner of the room, surely for people, not dogs. Up on the wall was a photograph of the current Pet of the Month, a Great Dane who had jumped into the Regent's Park lake to rescue a child's teddy bear. Quite a pleasant place to work, thought Lizzie, not to be compared to running around for half the afternoon after a bunch of five-year-olds, which she seriously didn't want to do anymore.

Melissa came back with Brutus and told Lizzie she had given him antibiotics and to keep him warm.

"This job. I mean the job that Dermot had . . ." Lizzie hesitated. "I mean, I don't want to be pushy, but could I have it?"

"Well, I don't know. I don't know what Caroline would say."

Lying came naturally to Lizzie. "I've had two jobs working as a veterinarian's receptionist, one in London and the other in"—she thought rapidly—"Peterborough. I know all about it."

"Could you come back at three? Caroline will be free then to talk to you."

Lizzie phoned for a taxi, planning the reference she would have to forge, signing it with a name she could easily get off the Internet. How on earth did people manage to live at all in the days before the World Wide Web?

She went back to the clinic at three, walking from Iverson Road. Not having written it down, she had forgotten the name of the place she had said she had worked at—somewhere beginning with a *P*, she thought. Portsmouth, Pontypridd, Penge? Never mind, Caroline didn't care and didn't ask. She read the letter of recommendation Lizzie had forged and asked when she could start. Lizzie said how about tomorrow? So much for the school and having to fabricate excuses for her absence.

Walking home, she met her father getting off a bus and told him that the pet clinic had headhunted her.

Headhunted women don't need their fathers to pay half their rent, Tom thought hopefully. But Lizzie said nothing about financial independence, only that she'd had a long day and needed to put her feet up.

26

I N THE DAYS following the murder, Carl thought of almost nothing else. Only a psychopath or a hit man or perhaps a soldier in battle could kill someone and put the killing out of his mind. He had hated Dermot but just the same found it impossible to be sanguine about the murder. A much more satisfactory solution to the problem would have been Dermot's removing himself to a different address, or his getting married and buying a flat somewhere with Sybil. Carl found himself close to resenting that Dermot had brought his death on himself by his stupid inverted blackmail. A strange thought it was, that Dermot had directly courted murder by refusing to pay his rent. But Carl still couldn't stop thinking about it all the time and every day.

Nicola, who knew the murder preyed on his mind, told him he must get over it. "You're not involved. I wouldn't say you ought to be glad. Of course not. But it has taken a weight off your mind. It's removed a worry."

"I wouldn't want to think like that," he said, conscious of outrageous hypocrisy. "It must be wrong in anyone's philosophy to feel relief at someone's death, especially death by violence."

That night he had the first of his dreams. He could hear a moaning from upstairs that grew in volume and suddenly broke off. He

climbed the stairs, a slow climb, his steps made sluggish by some unseen force, but he reached the top at last and made his way into the living room. All was silent. Dermot lay on the floor, his face and head a bloody mass of torn flesh and broken bones. Carl tried to cry out, but only a whimpering sound came. He was sitting up in bed when he woke and the whimpering went on. Nicola was asking him what was wrong. He didn't answer her.

He forced himself to lie down and breathe steadily. She reached out and took hold of his hand. He thought, I killed someone. I murdered a man. That's something that will never go away. It will be with me for ever, for the rest of my life and beyond, if there is a beyond. Nothing I can do will ever get rid of it because I did it and it is written in my past.

DERMOT'S FUNERAL TOOK place at one of the churches he had attended. The first Carl knew of it was when Sybil brought two older women to the house and rang the doorbell.

"I could have let us in," she said. "I've got Carl's key, but I didn't want to be rude."

She didn't introduce the women. The one that looked a lot like Dermot said, "Pleased to meet you. I'm Dermot's mum, and this is his auntie. I should say, I *was* his mum. We'll go upstairs and help clean out his clothes and bits and pieces if you've no objection."

They were exactly as Carl would have expected Dermot's mother and aunt to be, both short and squat, wearing black straw hats and black coats. Sybil was dressed in the same black clothes she had worn when she called round last time; no hat, just a black head scarf tied under her chin. They went upstairs and stayed there for over an hour.

Carl could not possibly relax while they were in the house, but was relaxation ever to be thought of now? He faced the horrible truth that the mother of the man he had murdered was in

his house, was upstairs. It was both unbelievable and true. He had returned to pacing, to walking up and down, opening doors and closing them, sitting down and getting up and pacing again, the way he had done when he first realised how Dermot intended to withhold the rent.

When they came down, should he make them tea, or at least offer it? he wondered. The thought of sitting down with them and talking about Dermot—what else could they talk about?—was so dreadful that he gasped aloud. He went out into the hall when he heard their feet on the stairs. They were all carrying bags that must have been Dermot's, and the bags were stuffed full of the bits and pieces Dermot's mother had talked about. Carl wondered if much of it was his property, as almost all the furnishing of the flat had been, all of it inherited from his father. But he didn't care.

Dermot's mother expressed his own desire precisely: "We'll go and leave you in peace."

The aunt said, "It was nice to meet you."

Sybil, nodding as if to confirm this meaningless statement, added, "See you soon."

From the window he watched them make their way along Falcon Mews in the direction of the tube station, or perhaps a bus. They had shown no overt grief, no horror at what had happened, only a dull acceptance. Carl felt sick. He asked himself if there would be any further developments, any more visits, police enquiries, relatives or friends of Dermot's turning up. If so, it must be faced, and it was nothing compared to what Carl had been through these past months.

You're free now, he told himself, You didn't mean to kill him, not at first, and when you did, no one saw you or connected you with his death. It's all over. Hold on to that.

Nicola came home earlier than usual, carrying two bags full of food: a roast chicken, a selection of cheeses from the local delicatessen, white grapes, a mango and a large pineapple, and the ingredi-

ents for a special kind of salad. The wine she had bought was being sent, she said, but for one bottle of rosé, which she had with her.

"I'll soon have money," Carl said. "Just wait a couple of weeks and then I'll advertise the flat. There's such a demand round here that it'll go at once."

She put her arms round him. "There's no hurry, sweetheart. Wait a little. It will look rather . . . well, not like you or me, come to that . . . grasping. We could go away somewhere first. You're in need of a holiday and I've got a couple of weeks owing."

He wanted to tell her not to remind him he had no work and no money, but he restrained himself. Maybe he could start writing again soon. "We'll see. What I'd like to do would be to go out to eat—to celebrate."

She pulled away and stared at him. "Celebrate what?"

"I don't know why I said that. I wasn't thinking." He started to tell her about the visit that afternoon of Dermot's mother and aunt. "I think they live up north somewhere. They were going to take huge carrier bags full of bric-a-brac on the train."

"I'm sure you were nice to them, Carl," she said, but her tone was that of someone who believed the reverse was true.

It was scarcely a quarrel, but it left him feeling sore and resentful. Nicola put away the food and drink she had bought and opened the wine, still cold from the chill cabinet of the shop. They sat side by side on the sofa and she said, "Let's go to one of those boat cafés on the canal. That wouldn't trouble your conscience so much because they're cheap."

The phone rang. He knew it must be his mother because no one else used the landline. Her astonishment and horror at Dermot's murder had already been voiced. This time she wanted to tell him about his grandmother's shingles. Carl made appropriate noises.

"Now, darling, the most important thing: I've got a tenant for your flat. Aren't I clever? An estate agent, that's me, and I don't charge a fee."

"No, Mum, not yet, it's too soon. I mean, thanks, it's brilliant, but I don't want to let it yet."

"But why not, darling? You're in need of the rent, aren't you? You told me you were."

"Of course I am. But I can wait a few weeks. You haven't told this person they can have it, have you?"

"No, of course not. And by the way, it's horrible the way you use a plural when you mean a singular. It's not just you, it's everyone under thirty, and a lot over."

"Sorry, Mum. I'll try not to, but I can't promise."

Nicola asked what that was about. He told her. "You were quite right to say no. Let's go out, shall we?"

They had another glass of the rosé first. Nicola's approval was nice, but still he asked himself why he had turned down his mother's offer.

"Why was I right to say no?" he asked Nicola as they walked down the mews. "I'm beginning to think I shouldn't have."

"It shows respect for Dermot. I know he treated you badly, but he had such a horrible death. Any decent person would feel pity and—well, indignation. You didn't want another tenant in there yet; you wanted to wait."

Carl said nothing. It didn't matter if he waited, say, a couple of weeks.

THERE WAS NO sign of Sybil the next day. Carl hoped that she might have gone away on holiday with her parents, although the season appeared to be over, and most people were back at work.

While Nicola was having a shower in his bathroom, he went upstairs to use the bathroom that had been Dermot's and found the place full of what Sybil would call "toiletries." These bottles and jars were the sort that came from back-street pharmacies or the soap-and-shampoo department of a supermarket. She might not want

them but she need not think she could dump them on him. He was thinking how he must tell her to take them away when he realised he had no phone number for her, and although he knew where she lived, no email or postal address.

Just as he was deciding he must go to Jerome Crescent and put a note through her door, he heard her footsteps on the stairs. But now that his chance had come, he felt rather awkward telling her he had had a shower in the bathroom that had been Dermot's. He waited, listening, and when he heard her leave, he felt sure she wouldn't come back again. She would have completed whatever tasks had brought her back to Dermot's rooms. He went upstairs and found the bathroom just as it had been. Full of her things. What did it matter that a few jars of bath oil and sachets of cheap shampoo were left behind? Leave it a day or two and then he would throw them all away.

Carl found that he was becoming acutely aware of Sybil's presence, though he didn't know how. On Saturday evening, Nicola asked him how he knew Sybil was in the house, and he couldn't tell her, he just knew. Nicola had heard nothing. She conceded he had been right when she saw Sybil walking down the mews next morning on her way to church, prayer book in hand. She had clearly spent the night upstairs. It was another fine, sunny day, and Carl and Nicola went to Hampstead Heath, Carl painfully conscious that every item of food and every drop of drink they bought was still purchased with Nicola's money.

That kind of one-sided spending looked to be coming to an end on Monday morning, however, when the post brought a letter from Carl's agent telling him that a short story Carl had written three years before, and forgotten about, was to be read on radio, for which he would be paid a hundred pounds.

Susanna apologised for the smallness of the sum, but it felt like a fortune to Carl. Income from his writing, recognition of his talent! A happy start to the day, it seemed, not to be spoilt by the sound of

Sybil's feet in heavy shoes marching about on the top floor. So she hadn't gone. She had spent two nights up there. It was time to tell her to leave, and to take her pots and jars with her. He went upstairs and knocked on the door.

She looked at him, unsmiling, as if she had never before seen him. He noticed that it wasn't shoes she was wearing, but heavy brown leather boots.

"What was it you wanted?"

Not to be left on the doorstep, he thought. "Can I come in?"

"If you want."

He stepped over the threshold. She left the door open. She was still in the mourning clothes that were perhaps to become a permanency.

"I'd like you to take your things out of the bathroom. When you go home."

"I'm going out now. I've got to go to work."

"Yes, of course. But later on you must come back here and take your stuff."

She nodded, a meaningless gesture. "Dermot told me when we first started courting that we would live here together."

Courting: the word shocked him rather than the content of what she said. He had never before heard anyone use it. "Yes, it's very sad what happened. I'll see you later."

From his front window he watched her go. In her walk was a familiarity with her surroundings that made her look as if she had lived here all her life. He realised he didn't know where she worked or what she did: Why should he know or care? She would be gone by the end of today and he would never have to see her again.

Sybil returned from work before Nicola did. Carl wouldn't have known this if he hadn't been watching for her. He went out into the hall just as she had her heavily booted right foot on the lowest stair.

"Sybil?" Had he ever before called her by what she would no doubt refer to as her Christian name? "You'll be going home this evening, I assume. Don't forget to take your stuff from the bathroom."

In a calm, straightforward tone she said, "This is my home. This is where I live."

"No, no." Nervous as he was, he had to treat her as if she were simple. That was a word his father had used, one that predated political correctness. "You live with your parents in Jerome Crescent. Now give me my key. You won't need it again."

"I live here. I must go up now. I've things to see to."

"No, Sybil. I'm very sorry about Dermot, but I shall have a new tenant coming in. That's why you need to go. That's why I need the key."

"I'm the new tenant. I told you Dermot said I was to live here." Suddenly her voice took on the tone of an ordinary, determined woman who knew exactly what she was doing and saying. "I have to hold on to the key. I'm taking over my fiancé's tenancy."

He said nothing. To think that he had believed her naïve, an ignorant fool. He went into the bathroom and threw up. Because he had eaten nothing all day, he vomited only yellow liquid.

He was still in the bathroom when Nicola came home. He had reached a stage where he had to remind himself that she didn't know he had killed Dermot. Sometimes, when he thought about it, he seemed to remember telling her, and her forgiving him or overlooking it or something.

She doesn't know. Hold on to that, he told himself. But I can tell her about Sybil, what Sybil said. I must ask her what to do. "Sybil is here. She says she's the new tenant. She won't give me the key."

"She must. Tell her you'll get the police to put her out."

"I couldn't do that."

"Then I will."

"No." The idea of the police coming meant only one thing

to him: Dermot's murder. They would be in the house and they would know what had happened to the previous tenant. They would become suspicious. "No, Nic. We can't do that. Would it be too bad to have her as the new tenant? I mean, she'd be steady and quiet and regular in her habits—I know I sound like an old-time landlady— and she wouldn't make trouble."

"I'm not hearing this."

"Yes, you are, you are. I'm saying let's have Sybil as the new ten- ant. It would make things easy. There'd be money coming in. She'd be on her own. She wouldn't bring men home."

"What's happened to you, Carl? You're young. You don't talk and think like that." In a scathing tone she said, *"She wouldn't bring men home. She wouldn't make trouble, she'd be quiet and steady."* Nicola didn't wait for his defence. "What's got into you? You have to turn her out, and do it now. She can go back to her parents'. I don't want her here. We'll find someone else."

He spoke to Nicola in a tone he had never thought possible. "This is my house. I decide about tenants, not you."

She didn't argue. Her face went white. "I'm sorry. Let her stay. I just hope you won't regret it."

She had said *you*, not *we*. Whatever happens now, Carl thought, this is the beginning of the end for us.

27

Most of the pet owners at the clinic accepted Lizzie without question. One of the few exceptions was Yvonne Weatherspoon, who had known Lizzie when she'd been a friend of Stacey's. Yvonne hadn't much liked Lizzie then, and she didn't seem to like her now.

"Where's Dermot?"

Lizzie didn't know what to say. Surely Yvonne knew? It had been all over the papers and even on the London regional news. "Didn't you see it on TV?"

"What do you mean, on TV?"

"Well, he was murdered. It was on TV and in all the papers. They still haven't got anyone for it."

"I saw about *that* Dermot, but I didn't connect it with *our* Dermot. My God, what a dreadful thing. I'm really shocked." Yvonne pointed to the occupant of the cat box. "Sophie knows. You can tell, can't you? It's been a shock to her as well, poor angel." Yvonne mouthed kisses to the cat through the bars of the carrier. "A nasty animal from down the hill has scratched her and I think it's got infected. I do hope Caroline can see her. I think she's got a temperature."

Caroline could see her this time and would keep her in to operate on the abscess. Perhaps Mrs. Weatherspoon would like to leave

her here and come back for her at four? *Like* was not the word, but Yvonne had to agree.

They closed the clinic for an hour at lunchtime, and Lizzie went across the street to the Sutherland Café for a sandwich and a Diet Coke. She still found it hard to sit quietly on her own. Her mind played nasty tricks, returning to the horrific days she so much wanted to forget.

When she'd first got home, she had thought about phoning Swithin Campbell and confronting him with her suspicions that he'd been in cahoots with Scotty and Redhead. But what would happen if he was dangerous? It might be better to leave things as they were, with Scotty and Redhead as far away from her as possible.

If only she had someone clever to advise her.

BACK AT THE pet clinic, nothing much happened until four o'clock. In the operating theatre, a small room in the back, Caroline lanced Sophie's abscess and laid her comfortably in her cat carrier to sleep until Yvonne Weatherspoon came for her. But at five past four it was Yvonne's son who called at the clinic.

"Hi, Gervaise." Lizzie was surprised and pleased to see him. He must have cancelled his trip to Cambodia or wherever it was. Or perhaps he just hadn't left yet.

"Well, if it isn't little Lizzie. What are you doing here?"

"I work here."

"Do you really? My mother didn't say." Caroline came out with the cat, still asleep in her carrier. "Can I pay with a credit card?"

"Sure you can. That'll be a hundred and eighty pounds."

"I'll have to get that back from my mum." He looked at Lizzie again. "Lizzie, I owe you an apology."

"Do you? Whatever for?"

He slipped his card into the machine. "Last time I saw you, I said you could stay in Stacey's flat while I was away. But then my sister wanted to live there, and you must have had to move out."

"I did. But that's all in the past now." What he'd said had given her an idea. "Can I ask you something?"

"Sure you can."

"I need some advice."

Gervaise looked interested, as Lizzie had thought he might. "OK. Shall we meet in the café opposite after you finish here? Let me get this animal home first."

NEXT MORNING CARL watched Sybil in the garden before she went to work, pulling up the few weeds she had allowed to take root there, cutting off the dead heads from flowers he didn't know the names of.

She probably worked as someone's cleaner, he thought. That was what she looked like. Perhaps she would clean for him. Maybe she could do decorating as well as gardening. It began to appear as if he had done rather well in not getting rid of her.

He must get her a rent book, something he had never done for Dermot. It would be more businesslike. He'd draw up another contract and have Nicola witness it. He had hoped to raise the rent this time, but now he realised he could hardly do that. Sybil wouldn't earn that much; maybe ten pounds an hour was what he had heard cleaners' wages amounted to. No, keep the rent to what Dermot had paid—or hadn't paid in recent months.

He sat down at the laptop and contrived a sort of contract for Sybil Soames to pay Carl Martin one thousand two hundred pounds per calendar month—a good touch that, *calendar month*—for a one-bedroom apartment at 11 Falcon Mews, London W9. He'd arrange the signing down here in his living room. When Nicola came home from work, she usually went straight upstairs to their bedroom to change into jeans and a tee-shirt, and after that he and Sybil would sign the document.

He asked himself why he was treating the process with such weight

and formality. Dermot's contract had never been handled like this. His mother had told him he could now get much more than twelve hundred a month, but he had said no, and she had supposed he was being generous, that asking more would be greedy. No one could know—no one would ever know—that he shuddered whenever he thought of profiting from the death of a man he had murdered.

Sybil came back at five. Her shoes made a flapping sound as she walked upstairs. A bit less than an hour later Nicola arrived, carrying a basket of strawberries, a carton of cream, and a bunch of pink and purple flowers she said were zinnias. Carl showed her the contract.

She nodded. "You're still going through with this, then?"

"You agreed it was a good idea."

"I don't think so, Carl. As you said, it wasn't for me to agree or disagree. It's your house."

"Well, will you witness Sybil and me signing this contract?"

"If that's what you want."

She went up to their bedroom to change. The beginning of the end for them, he had thought their argument was. But it had passed, and perhaps the end wouldn't happen. He hoped not. He picked up the phone and called Dermot's number. He couldn't yet think of it as Sybil's.

"Can't you come up here?" she said.

"I suppose so. If you like."

Passing his bedroom door on the way, he called out to Nicola that he would want her up in Sybil's flat in a few minutes and would shout for her. It was a hot day, and a thick, humid warmth had risen to the landing. Sweat broke out on his face, on his upper lip, as he climbed the stairs. He had a strong, quite unreasonable feeling of impending doom.

Sybil opened the door before he got there and was standing just inside. She was wearing a pale pink dress with blue and green geometric shapes all over it, which left her arms and shoulders bare.

"It's very hot up here," he said when he was in the even more stifling atmosphere of the living room. "Don't you want to open the windows?"

"I never open windows. It lets insects in."

By now, he was bathed in sweat. "May I sit down?"

"Be my guest."

Ridiculous, he thought. I *am* her guest. He unfolded the sheet of paper on which he had typed the contract and laid it on the round table. She remained standing. "I have the rent contract. Would you like to read it?"

She didn't sit down, but just glanced at the contract. "I don't need to read it. I told you I'm living here. Dermot said I should."

"Yes, perhaps. But you still have to pay me rent."

She shook her head vigourously. "I don't pay rent. Why should I? I already said I'm living here."

The perspiration was dripping down his face like tears. "I don't think you understand. If you have rooms in someone else's property, you have to pay for it. You have to pay by the week or month. That's what this paper is about. I'll call Nicola in to witness it, if you know what that means, and then you sign and I sign and she sees us do that and she signs. OK?"

"No. It's not OK. I haven't got the money. I work in Lidl on the checkout."

"Well, I'm sorry, but that means you'll have to go. You can't stay here without paying rent."

That awful shaking of the head began again. "I'm staying here like Dermot did. He never paid rent, not a penny, and I'm not either. This is my home now."

"No, it's not, Sybil. If you don't go, I shall have to fetch the police to put you out."

She took a step towards him and a cunning look spread across her face. Deceit was in it, and a half smile. "I saw you hit Dermot with that bag you carry. It must have had something heavy in it. I

was in my bedroom and I saw you from the window. He just lay there. I went to bed. He was still there in the morning. I went out there at five and saw him. You killed him like a killer on TV."

Carl stared at her.

"I'll tell the police if you make me leave. I didn't go to them before as I've always wanted somewhere to live that's not with my parents, but couldn't afford it. Now I have this place, and I don't have to pay any rent at all."

An analogy people made when something bad had happened was to say it was a nightmare. Carl's bad thing was worse than a nightmare, a conjuring of horror only bearable if he knew he would wake up.

He lacked the strength to speak and she saw this. She was watching him closely, not quite with a smile but with a calm, satisfied look. "I'll keep it nice. I'll pay for the electric and the gas, no need to worry about that. And I'll do the garden for free, it won't cost you."

Still Carl couldn't speak. He got up and walked out, stumbling a little. Nicola was downstairs, doing something in the kitchen, preparing a meal perhaps. The flowers she had bought were in a vase on the living-room windowsill, pink and mauve, stiff-petalled daisies. In films when someone was in a rage or despair or the kind of situation Carl was in now, he—it was always a man—would pick up the vase of flowers and smash it against the wall. Carl stared at the vase, then lay down on the floor and buried his face in his hands. Nicola came in with the strawberries in a bowl and a jug of cream.

"Oh, Carl, sweetheart, what's wrong?"

He lifted his head, then struggled to his feet. He couldn't tell her. He couldn't tell her he was a murderer. He couldn't tell her anything.

28

I T WAS STILL warm outside when Lizzie left the clinic, and people were sitting at the tables outside the café, Gervaise among them. She sat down next to him.

"What would you like? Coffee? Tea?"

"Do you think they have—well, alcohol?"

"In this country," he said, "I doubt if there's anywhere they don't."

They did. She asked for white wine, not particular about what sort. His having a cup of tea seemed to her a reproach. She would have much preferred him to have wine too.

"You wanted to ask my advice. What about?"

"Well, it happened a week ago but I haven't said a word to anyone. I nearly told my parents, and then I thought they'd tell the police and the police would ask me questions—the sort of questions I shouldn't want to answer."

"What would those sort of questions be, then?"

"Oh, well, never mind. Nothing important. Shall I tell you what happened?"

"That's the point of all this, isn't it?"

She began to tell him the story, starting with her meeting the so-called Swithin Campbell and his arrangement to call for her while she was staying in Pinetree Court. She told him she was sure

171

Swithin had thought she was rich and had put Scotty and Redhead up to abducting her. "Didn't your mother tell you that a man called her to demand a ransom for her daughter?"

"Should she have told me?" Gervaise looked almost amused.

"I thought she might, but they got it wrong. We are both called Elizabeth, you see, and they thought I was the rich one. They took me to various places, handcuffed me and put a gag on my mouth. I don't know where I was, it was nowhere I knew. They fed me on bread and water like in a prison, they moved me about and took me down to south London. It was while I was there that a beautiful, enormous pigeon flew into the window and smashed a pane, and the horrible men who were holding me ran away and left me. I suppose they believed it was the police breaking in. I got out and got a taxi back to my parents. There, now you know."

Lizzie took a large and satisfying draught of her wine. The girl who had served them had brought two chocolates on a glass dish to go with their drinks, and she took one. "What do you think I should do?"

"I remember when we were children and your parents lived near Stacey's parents in Willesden. Do you remember that?"

"Of course I do, but what's it got to do with anything?"

"You used to come round to Stacey's to play, and you used to tell the most enormous whoppers. That's the name they gave to lies in those days. Do you remember that too?"

"I don't know what you mean."

"Yes, you do, Lizzie. I was visiting once and your dad came to fetch you, and I heard him ask Stacey's mother, like it was a sort of joke, if you'd, I quote, been up to your usual tricks of telling porkies. There are a lot of words in the English language for telling lies."

"I wasn't telling lies. Not now. It's all true." Lizzie remembered how afraid she'd been.

"Anyone who didn't know you might believe that tale, especially if you left out the bit about the miraculous bird." He paused and

smiled at her. "Just a piece of advice. After all, that's what you asked for. Next time you tell that story, leave out the bird." He went inside to pay the bill.

Lizzie got up and walked in the other direction, up to Maida Vale. She'd never liked that family; it wasn't just Yvonne Weatherspoon, they were all the same. To be honest with herself, she had only asked Mr. Clever Gervaise for advice because she fancied him.

Well, that was the end of that. If nobody would believe her, she might as well put the whole experience out of her head. It had all been a mistake, not meant for her. She had thought she might warn the other Elizabeth about those two men, but now she didn't care. Elizabeth Weatherspoon would just have to look out for herself.

Meanwhile she, Lizzie, had a date that evening with a nice man who'd asked her out when he'd brought his basenji to the clinic. Only for a drink, but perhaps it would lead to greater things. While she waited for the number 98 bus, she thought about which of Stacey's clothes she should wear for the evening.

Tom was also on a bus—the number 18—and also giving some thought to a serious subject. The evening before, he and Dot had been to a birthday party, his sister Wendy's, and there Wendy's next-door neighbour had listened with interest to Tom's account of his bus rides and asked him why he didn't write a book about them. If Tom had only known, Trevor Vincent made that enquiry of everyone who talked to him at any length about any hobby or pursuit. He did so not because he cared or knew anything about the particular topic, but because he had no other conversation.

"Do you think I could?" Tom had asked.

"Have you got a computer or a tablet or whatever?"

"Of course I have. Shall I give it a go?

"You do that." Trevor Vincent then moved off to find his wife and go home.

Tom thought little more about the suggestion that evening, but next day the conversation came back to him. Well, why not? Describing today's adventure might provide the opening of such a book, the incident in Harlesden High Street, for instance, when those Chinese people had refused to get off the bus when told to do so because they had no passes but only offered cash. The driver had tried to turn them off but they had sat in the vacant seats playing some strange musical instruments Tom had never before seen. A huge, burly man (not Chinese) had joined them and also refused to get off the bus when the police came and told them to. Tom had had to get off himself then, sad not to see the outcome. That could all go in his book. He might start it tomorrow.

THE BASENJI MAN, whose name was Adam Yates, took Lizzie to something more like a wine bar than a pub. He seemed quite overcome by Stacey's beautiful cream-coloured dress and jacket, though Lizzie thought it was a bit over-the-top for the Unicorn Lounge. She was hungry and enthusiastically responded to Adam's suggestion that they have dinner in the Unicorn's rather beautiful dining area. Lizzie had a principle that if a restaurant, no matter how grand and expensive, had an illustrated menu—coloured photos of chicken tikka and fish pie—she would refuse to eat there. There was nothing of that sort here. The food was civilised and delicious, the experience quite unlike that dreadful evening with the awful Swithin Campbell and his boring talk. Adam made no suggestion of coming in when he took her home, but kissed her lightly on the cheek and went to catch the 82 bus.

Next morning he phoned. He had tickets for a concert. A famous orchestra from Hungary was playing Mozart and Respighi and would she come with him on Friday? She accepted, already plan-

ning to wear the green suit with the pearls. Lizzie had never heard of Respighi, but what was Google for but to help out in situations like this?

To Lizzie, designated future tasks loomed large. She anticipated little pleasure in completing the task Caroline had set for her: to carry all the items that had once belonged to Dermot to Carl Martin's house in Falcon Mews. Unless, of course, Carl might invite her in. She was curious to see what his place looked like. He probably wouldn't even recognise her, it had been so long since they had seen each other in their school days; they both had been close to Stacey. It wasn't far to the mews that linked Sutherland Avenue to Castellain Road. Dermot was said to have walked it, there and back, every day, but Lizzie didn't fancy the walk at all.

While Caroline was busy removing a nail from a cocker spaniel's pad, Darren was out on a call, and Melissa was carrying out a routine examination of Spots the dalmatian, Lizzie had a look inside the storage cupboard, largely to assess the weight of the late Dermot's property. A pair of sheepskin gloves, a framed photograph of a dark girl with a fat face and heavy shoulders, two broken mobile phones, an ancient Bible, three box files, a hardcover London atlas, two notebooks, and a box of paper fasteners all added up to considerable weight. She decided that she'd postpone the task till the following week.

29

S YBIL'S PARENTS PAID her a visit at the flat in Falcon Mews on a dreary Sunday. It was late morning, and the streets were deserted; those few people who were out carried umbrellas. Rain, torrential rain, had begun at nine and looked as though it would continue. A worse day for rain couldn't have been thought of, for it was the second and most important day of the local carnival, and the sound of it, though a little subdued, could be heard from Falcon Mews, a throb, a beat, muffled cries and shouts and music.

Carl saw Mr. and Mrs. Soames arrive. He guessed who they were, for who else could they be? Mrs. Soames looked much like her daughter, or her daughter looked much like her. The parents came along the mews under a single, large black umbrella, which they only folded up when Sybil answered the door.

"She'll want me to meet them," Carl said to Nicola. "You'll see. Maybe they'll have tea first and then she'll bring them down here and present them to me."

"Does it matter?"

"Well, insofar as nothing matters anymore, no, it doesn't."

"Carl, what's wrong? Why does nothing matter? If you don't want Sybil living here, why did you say she could?"

"I can't answer that, Nic. I will never be able to answer that. I

would if I could, but you have to take it from me that it's impossible. She's here forever or until she chooses to go."

Nicola turned away and looked out the window at the ceaseless rain, at Mr. Kaleejah, at his dog trotting along, ignoring the water underfoot and the water descending from the low, grey clouds. "What's that dog called? Do you know?"

"I don't know and I don't give a shit."

Nicola walked out of the room without a word.

For a while Carl had convinced himself that what he had done was not important. But gradually guilt and shame had arrived, as well as not so much a fear of discovery as a fear of some kind of retribution for his wickedness. He knew now that his action, irrespective of Dermot's own wrongdoing, would always be with him, day after day, year after year. In the unlikely, indeed impossible, event of his confessing his crime, asking for forgiveness, walking into the police station, and telling whoever was there that he had killed a man, would his fear go away? When his guilt was known, when everyone knew, perhaps he would no longer be haunted by it. But it was with him now and inhabited his body the way his heart did. It slept with him and woke with him, it lived with him like an organ. It would never leave.

He tried to deflect himself from this wretched reverie by thinking of practical things; for instance, getting some sort of job. He should never have set forth in life thinking he could live on his writing. He'd relied on renting out his property for his livelihood, and this was no longer possible. A tenant, and now that tenant's ghastly successor, had found a way to deprive him of his rent while enjoying all the benefits of a home in one of the best parts of London.

If Dermot knew from beyond the grave what Sybil was doing, would he be proud of her? And what could Carl do now? A philosophy degree was training for nothing. But that was the qualification he had; it must be a start. He could perhaps take a teacher-training course, teach English.

Footsteps sounded heavily on the stairs and Sybil called out, "Hi

there, Carl." She had recently stopped calling him Mr. Martin. Perhaps she thought her new status as a permanent householder made her his equal. "Can I bring my mum and dad in to make your acquaintance?"

He would have liked to tell her to go to hell, never to speak to him again, but he got up and opened the door. One thing particularly struck him about the couple at the foot of the stairs. They were nervous. Of him, or of Sybil?

"These are my mum and dad. They're called Cliff and Carol. This is Mr. Martin."

Carol Soames said she was pleased to meet him.

Cliff Soames said nothing for a moment but looked around the room apparently without approval. "You own this place, do you?" He fixed Carl with a stare.

"I told you he did, Dad."

"Let's hear what he has to say for himself. Belongs to you, does it? A young man like you?"

"Yes."

"Sybil says your dad left it to you. A whole house to do as you like with. That true?"

Carl hated this man's attitude. Whatever hold Sybil had over him, he wasn't obliged to take this. "Yes, I can do with it as I like, and one of the things I'm going to do is turn you out of it. Now. Get out and take your fat wife with you."

Immediately he said it, Carl regretted that *fat*. "Go on, leave," he continued, not touching Cliff but pushing Carol out of the room. "Get out now. I never want to see you here again."

They hurried out quickly, clearly in shock at Carl's anger. Sybil stared at him. "Don't think that bothered me. I don't care if I never see them again." She lumbered up the stairs without another word.

Nicola had heard it all, coming silently from the kitchen and standing in the doorway. "You were very rude, but you managed to stop the lecture he was going to give you on capitalism versus anarchy."

"Maybe."

"Shall we go out, do something? It's brightening up. At any rate, the rain's stopped."

"All right," Carl said, still in the same gloomy, downcast tone. "I've got no money. Where can you go and what can you do without money?"

"In a week's time you'll get the rent."

As they walked along the mews, Carl began to consider, not for the first time, what he could or should tell Nicola. But as before, he had no answer that was both a reason for no money coming in, such as Sybil's being unable to afford the rent, and, far more difficult to explain, for his tolerating this void like some sort of rich philanthropist. No one would believe such a tale, and certainly not Nicola, who knew him so well, who knew he disliked Sybil, who knew how totally strapped for cash he was.

He said to her suddenly, "Is there anything I can do to make money quickly? I mean, get a job tomorrow or very soon that would bring me in, say, a hundred and fifty pounds a week?"

"Oh, Carl, you don't know much about wages, do you? How could you? But you don't have to. You'll get twelve hundred pounds next week."

He would have to tell her the truth. But the truth was so terrible that he would lose her. If she wouldn't tolerate his selling a drug to Stacey, how could he expect her to accept that he had killed a man? And what would she *do* about it? Force him to go to the police? But would it take much forcing?

"Where are we going?" he asked.

"Where would you like to go?"

"A pub. To have a drink, something strong. I need it."

THEY WENT TO the Carpenters' Arms in Lauderdale Road, where they met the local bookshop owner, Will Finsford, and his girl-friend, Corinne. The girls kissed, delighted to see each other. It was

still only midday, but Will plied them with wine that Nicola firmly and effectively, and Carl feebly and in vain, refused.

It had been several months since they had seen one another. Corinne and Will sympathised with Carl over Dermot's death as if his tenant had been a friend and wanted to know if they had found someone new to occupy the top floor. Carl, his head feeling muzzy with alcohol already, was looking at Nicola as she spoke. Nothing compared to beauty like hers: those soft but classical features, those dazzling eyes, and the blondness of her—the pale, glossy hair and the slightly darker, more golden eyebrows. More than her physical beauty, there was her essential goodness. It would all be taken from him when he told her what he had done. As he must, as he had to, in the next few days. She had left him before. Of course she had come back. But she wouldn't come back this time.

Nicola was telling the others about Sybil Soames's taking over the tenancy, but she said nothing about Carl's reaction to Sybil's appearance and manner. So lovely herself, Nicola spoke of other women as if they were equally beautiful and gentle.

When Carl's glass was empty, she took one of his hands and whispered to him that it was time to go. She had already got a promise from Corinne that she would phone to accept one of the dates Nicola had given them to come over. Outside the rain had cleared, and the sky was a cloudless blue. Carl had scarcely said a word for the past hour, but now he began on his current favourite subject, his inability to pay for anything and the shame this brought him. The shops of Sutherland Avenue and Clifton Road often had notices in their windows offering work for supermarket staff or restaurant waiters. He would have to apply for such a job. Maybe tomorrow.

They had reached the Rembrandt Gardens, overhung by broad-leaved trees. Nicola sat down on a wooden seat and motioned to him to sit beside her. The seat overlooked a part of the canal where it widened into a lake with an island in its centre clustered over by waterbirds. Nicola knew that Carl wouldn't take kindly to her tell-

ing him he had neither the experience nor the patience for manual work; instead, intent on cheering him up, she reminded him that next week he would have an envelope with twelve hundred pounds from Sybil.

He turned his eyes from the island and the birds and looked at her. "I won't get it. It won't come. Let's go home."

Nicola felt near to tears. Whatever was the matter with Carl now? What did he mean about the rent's not coming in? Surely Sybil would pay. Was it the book he was unable to get on with? Was it simply the presence of Sybil in his house?

It wasn't far to Falcon Mews. When they entered the house, there was no sign of Sybil and no sound from upstairs.

"Shall we have a cup of tea? I've got some of those nice biscuits you like, the round, white-chocolate ones."

She made the tea, set out the white biscuits. They sat down on Dad's sofa. On the walk back, Carl had decided: he would tell her that he'd killed Dermot. But sitting beside her now, looking at her, so beautiful and loving, he knew it was impossible. He couldn't even pretend it had happened by accident. He could invent nothing to account for his lifting up that bag with its green pottery contents and bringing it down on Dermot's head.

"You were going to tell me why you fear Sybil won't pay the rent next week. You were, weren't you?"

"She thinks I killed Dermot and she says she'll tell the police she saw me do it if I make her pay. That's what it amounts to," Carl said in a single breath.

Nicola looked shocked. "She *can't*. She's out of her mind. She can't think that way. Where does she get such an idea? To suspect you of all people, a gentle person like you, of doing such a thing."

He said nothing for a moment. He was wondering what she would say if he told her the truth.

"Of course the poor woman's mentally ill. But to accuse you with her insane belief? Why didn't you tell me before?"

"I don't know. But now you can see why I can't risk her going to the police with this story."

"But it isn't true, Carl. They wouldn't believe her. You'd tell them the truth and then ask her to get out of this house. You would find someone else for the flat."

"Nic, my sweetheart, I can't do that. Leave it now. You know what the situation is. Wait till tomorrow or Wednesday, say, and if the rent comes, we'll know she's thought better of her accusation and all is well."

But all would not be well. He knew that. Strangely, for he had always believed that telling a lie, and as monstrous a lie as this one, could never make you feel better, this one did.

30

O N MONDAY—A dry day apart from the inevitable occasional showers—Tom set off on a trip to Leyton Green on the number 55. He picked it up at Oxford Circus, having got there on his favourite number 6 from Willesden. The number 55 proceeded through Holborn and Clerkenwell to Shoreditch. Tom hardly knew these places and found them shabbier than he expected, with the exception of Shoreditch, which had been much smartened up and seemingly filled with trendy shops and restaurants.

The bus might be full of schoolchildren in an hour's time, but now it was half-empty. From the laughter and shouting, a lot of young people appeared to be upstairs, but Tom never now went to the upper deck; he preferred to be downstairs at the front on the right, where his fellow travellers were mostly women and a few girls.

One young man did get on, though, as the bus moved into Hackney; or Tom thought it must be Hackney. To find his bearings when in an unfamiliar district, he usually looked at the newsagents' shop fronts or a post office or a police station where lettering over the front entrances told the observer that this was Clapton News or Islington Central Post Office. But he saw no clues of that sort as the bus proceeded along wide streets and shabby, narrow ones, heading for where he had no idea.

The young man who had got on at the possible beginnings of Hackney stayed downstairs and settled himself on the left-hand side in a seat next to the window. Tom had expected him to go to the upper deck, but he hadn't. Black-haired, beardless, and with very white skin, he carried on his back what Tom would have called a satchel. He kept it on his back as the bus went on into what a post-office sign told Tom was Clapton.

At the next stop, a crowd of women and children got on and the young man got off. Most of the mothers and children went upstairs, and those who remained went to the back of the bus, where you could sit facing each other. Tom then saw that the young man had left his bag behind, on the floor, pushed into the corner. It no longer looked like a simple satchel but rather more threatening—a container for something dangerous. It would be hard to say what suggested this; it might only have been that its shape gave the impression of having something heavy and metallic inside. A heavy metal zip went all the way round it. Tom didn't like the look of it at all.

He went up to the driver and told him about the bag, told him about the young man who had got off, leaving it behind.

"It'll go to the lost-property department," said the driver.

"Yes, but that won't be for several hours. It ought to be dealt with now."

"I tell you what. I'll have it taken off and left in the garage when we get to Leyton Green."

With that Tom was expected to be satisfied. But he wasn't. He admitted afterwards that he had been thinking of his own skin just as much as the children eating ice-cream cornets in the back-seats of the bus, and the noisy young people upstairs. He didn't select the place where he got off with the bag; it just happened to be beside a patch of open space, where people were strolling about under the trees and someone was picking chrysanthemums. Tom had once told a woman to leave the flowers alone and got a mouthful of abuse.

He carried the heavy bag up to the railings and set it down on the pavement. Things happened fast after that. He was a little way away from it, back at the bus stop reading the timetable up on the post, when with a huge, blinding flash and a roar, the sinister black bag exploded.

When Tom came to, he was lying on the pavement and a woman and a small boy were beside him, both prone. The woman was bleeding, Tom couldn't see where from, only that she was alive. The boy struggled to sit up, then get to his feet. Blood was pouring from his left arm.

Tom felt for his mobile phone, but it wasn't needed; he could see three other people on their phones. Somewhere a siren was braying. It seemed to belong to an ambulance that roared to a halt at the bus stop. The paramedics tumbled out. Tom was amazed by the speed with which they had got there, and then by the arrival of a second ambulance, and one police car after another. Holding on to the bus-stop pole for the support he suddenly needed, he watched the police holding the uninjured people back from the place where the bomb had gone off; the place where he'd put it. The woman and the boy with the bleeding arm were already being loaded onto stretchers. He looked away as another woman on a stretcher was covered with a white sheet, which meant death.

A paramedic was telling him he must get into the proffered wheelchair and be taken to hospital when a policeman interrupted them and asked him if he had seen what had happened.

"He's a hero," said the woman who'd been with the small boy. "I saw him carry that bomb thing off the bus. He saved all the people on the bus."

Tom was dreadfully embarrassed.

"Is that a fact, sir?" said the policeman.

"Well, yes. I suppose so. I'm not a hero, though. I'm going to get on the next bus."

"Not yet," said a paramedic. "Your leg is bleeding and your right

arm doesn't look too good. Come along, into the chair, and we'll get you seen to."

So the wheelchair was unfolded and Tom was put into it much against his will. Sitting down, he could see a wound in his knee and blood leaking from his arm. The paramedic, pushing him to the second ambulance, said, "You were very brave. If that had gone off a couple of minutes sooner, it'd have blown you to kingdom come."

Lifted into the ambulance, Tom looked back at the scene. Most of the people had been picked up from the pavement, but signs of them remained, blood lying in shallow pools. He wanted to go home.

31

"ONE GOOD THING has come out of it, though," said Dot Milsom on the phone. "This ghastly bomb has put an end to all his junketing about on buses."

"You ought to be proud of him." Lizzie was still at an age to enjoy setting her parents against each other. "He was amazing. A hero—that's what people are saying about him. Where is he now?"

"He was brought home last night. I suppose you'll come over and see him?"

"I will tomorrow. I have a dinner date tonight. Say hello to him for me."

"I know it's trendy to say that, but wouldn't it be a lot nicer to send your love?"

But Lizzie had put the phone down.

Adam Yates, her basenji date from the clinic, had been to the Iverson Road flat several times by now. He said he liked it, and that she was lucky to have a self-contained place of her own. He owned a flat in Tufnell Park, and although he made little of it, he couldn't disguise its considerable size and pleasant, leafy location. This evening, she thought, he would come back with her, and this time—would he stay?

In half an hour's time he was calling for her and they were going

to the Tricycle Theatre, just down the road. You didn't dress up for the Tricycle, but it wasn't jeans and Primark tee-shirt wear either, so Lizzie put on her best black trousers and a white shirt with a cardigan. Reviewing her conversation with her mother, she liked the idea of inviting Adam to one of her family dinners, but first she must take all that stuff belonging to Dermot McKinnon to his old flat in Falcon Mews. Perhaps she could do it one night next week, before she went to visit her parents?

The front doorbell rang absolutely on time. No previous boyfriend had ever been so punctual. The trouble was that she still felt fearful when someone rang the bell, after what had happened with Redhead and Scotty.

As she went to answer the door, she thought, I'll tell Adam how I feel and then tell him the whole story. He won't be like Gervaise Weatherspoon; he'll believe me.

CARL SLEPT WELL that night but awoke next morning to a weight of dread that shaped itself into sickness. He could eat nothing, drink nothing, not even coffee. He waited for Sybil's footsteps on the stairs, holding his breath. They sounded, a heavy clumping, and then came the front door's banging with more of a crash than usual.

Nicola went to work. She'd told him she would be late home because she was going out in the evening with two of her old flatmates, and the boyfriend of one of them. Carl had been asked but he had said no, he was sorry but he didn't feel up to it. She said good-bye to him that morning with more than usual tenderness and love, and he was sure this was due to that convincing lie he had told. Perhaps he should lie to her more? But, no, he had only a few hours left if he was to do what he meant to do. And he must.

Sybil was asking to die as Dermot had, another thing the two had in common: a propensity to invite their own death. But this death couldn't come from the stairs or a fall from a window. Instead, some

impulse sent him up to the bathroom and the store of alternative medicines his father had accumulated.

The fifty capsules of the DNP that Stacey had not purchased were in the front of the cabinet and behind them too was the powder-to-liquid variety in sachets. It said on the box that the sachets should be dissolved in water and then drunk down. This was what Carl was looking for. Offering Sybil the DNP powder would be no more murder than selling DNP to Stacey had been. The last thing he had wanted was to kill Stacey, but he wanted this concoction to kill Sybil.

But had Sybil read the coroner's report in the newspaper? Would she know about DNP? Probably not. Sybil didn't impress Carl as the type who would read much of any newspapers, including the tabloids.

Carl took the box of sachets down to the kitchen, opened one, and dropped the contents into a glass of water. It turned bright yellow. This, he told himself, was just a trial run: now he knew how it reacted. He found a leaflet inside the box, which stated that DNP was for rapid weight loss. That it was a dangerous drug, likely to cause death if taken in large quantities, was mentioned at the end in small print. The only difficulty now, he thought, was how to get Sybil to take it.

If Nicola came upon it, she would know what it was. She must never see it. But she wouldn't be home this evening before about ten, and by that time the deed could be done. Sybil would arrive home between five thirty and six, and he must catch her in the hallway and make some friendly overture to her, using Nicola's absence as his reason for such unlikely behaviour.

At lunchtime he went out. Nicola had left him some money, a twenty-pound note, and although he knew she had meant it for food, he spent it on two bottles of wine and fed himself from the fridge, bread that he toasted and the end of a piece of cheese. Before Sybil was due home, he placed a couple of DNP sachets on the hall

table on top of the leaflet on which he stood the glass he had used. She came in at ten minutes to six, and ten minutes later he found her standing over the table, reading the leaflet. His heart thumped.

"I'm glad I've caught you. I wanted to ask you in for a drink; it doesn't have to be alcohol. Nicola's away for the evening, you see, and I wanted some company."

She looked him in the face, puzzled. "Well, OK, I don't mind."

"I thought it would be a good idea for us to try to be friends. I know we haven't been on very good terms, but that ought to change, don't you think?"

Astonishingly, she seemed to believe him. "I'll just go up and leave my stuff."

He went back into the living room, but came out after a minute to see if she had taken the sachets on the table. She hadn't. Would she ask him about them? He could only wait and see.

She returned more quickly than he expected, having changed her tee-shirt and cardigan for a fussy pink blouse with a frill round the neck and her boots for court shoes from which her feet bulged. Was she trying to look attractive for him? He found that disgusting. He offered her Nicola's breakfast orange juice; it was all he had of the soft-drink kind.

"You're having wine, aren't you? I'll have some of that," she said, evidently not as abstemious as Dermot had been.

Carl handed her a glass of the pinot grigio he had bought that afternoon.

She took it without a word, then said, "Haven't you got any nibbles?"

"I'm afraid not."

"You want to get some in. I shouldn't have them, though. I don't want to put on any more weight."

Again he felt that thump of the heart. Should he mention the sachets and the leaflet in the hall? Better not. "Snacks between meals aren't a good idea." He could hardly believe he had uttered

such a sentence. "Are you on a diet?" was the nearest he would get to touching on the substance and the directions in the hallway.

"I like my food too much for that." She drank a long draught of her wine. "Does wine put weight on you?"

"I don't know, Sybil."

"Give me a fill-up, will you?" He did, willingly, now that he could sense the question that was coming. "What's that stuff out in the hallway?"

He wouldn't offer it to her. "I don't know. Nicola left it there."

"I'd better go up now. I've got my tea to get."

Not *dinner* or *supper*, but *tea*. Nicola would call him a snob, and maybe he was. He stood up to see her out, then went back into the room and listened. She had come back down the stairs and was just outside the door. He heard a little sound, a click as of glass tapping on a hard surface, then footsteps on the stairs again.

Waiting for the footfalls to fade up the stairs was the longest he had ever waited for anything in his life, yet it could only have endured for a minute at the most. Then he went outside.

The sachets, leaflet, and glass had gone from the table.

32

THAT NIGHT, CARL made himself scrambled egg on one slice of toast and a can of baked beans on the other. Another bottle of wine remained and a small amount in the bottle he and Sybil had been drinking from. He sat there and listened, though for what he didn't know. A scream? A groan? A stumbling down the stairs? There was silence, a silence that endured for long, slow minutes that seemed like hours. Just before ten, Nicola came home. It occurred to him that he shouldn't have told Sybil that it was Nicola who had put the sachets and the leaflet in the hallway. But surely Sybil wouldn't mention this to Nicola. Sybil never spoke to her. Still, it was a small, niggling worry.

Next day, Sybil went to work, and Carl realised that while he'd been tormenting himself the previous evening, speculating about her brewing up that yellow drink and suffering, perhaps on the verge of death, she had been passing a pleasant few hours.

Her morning departure coincided with Nicola's, and they set off together, sharing an umbrella. They might have been friends, once schoolfellows, chatting away and smiling. Is she telling Nic now? Carl thought. Is she explaining how she took the sachets without permission, just picked them up from the hall table? Why had he been such a fool as to give Sybil that explanation for their presence?

He had still done nothing about a job, so in an effort to put that right and to put Sybil out of his mind, he went into the delicatessen, which was advertising for an assistant. When the manager heard Carl had no training and no experience, he said he was afraid not. Carl went into the hand car wash, which hadn't advertised, and asked if they wanted anyone. They told him they might in November; men didn't want to work outside in the winter months, so he could come back then. He had plundered Nicola's housekeeping tin so had enough for coffee and even for a sparse lunch.

Sybil came home at five, which was early for her. Watching her from the ground-floor window, he seemed to see purpose in her heavy tread, as if, on her journey home, she had decided on some particular step to take. She was lost to his sight as she let herself into the house.

Nothing happened. Carl made himself a cup of tea, which if taken without milk was the cheapest thing he could drink. Why had Sybil come home early? Perhaps she'd said she wasn't well. A girl behind the checkout at Lidl couldn't just take a couple of hours off by making an excuse about a delivery or someone's reading the meter. But it didn't matter: she was home, and it must be to take the DNP.

It occurred to Carl then how significant DNP had been in his life, first leading to Dermot's behaviour, his blackmail, and his death; now ridding him, he hoped, of Dermot's blackmailing girlfriend. He sat downstairs on Dad's sofa, listening, though for what he didn't know.

All he heard was his phone ringing. Nicola. "A girl I know at work has two tickets for the cinema. Her friend who was going with her can't, so she's offered it to me. It's for *Before I Go to Sleep*. I won't be late."

He was glad she wouldn't be there. There might just be silence. On the other hand, there might be shouting or screaming. Sybil might come down complaining of pain or crying. The first symptom would be sweating. Her temperature could go up to thirty-six

degrees Celsius. She wouldn't have taken the stuff upstairs with her if she didn't mean at least to try it, he thought. And you couldn't just try DNP; it was all or nothing. He must wait.

Feeling the way he did, tense, slightly sick, screwed up, he couldn't contemplate eating anything. Drink, yes, a whole bottle of wine was awaiting him. *Screw your courage to the sticking place*, he thought, *and we'll not fail.* That was what Lady Macbeth said to Macbeth, Macbeth, who was going to do murder. Like him. He fetched the wine, opened it, and drank a whole glass straight down.

There was still no sound from upstairs.

LIZZIE WAS SITTING outside a restaurant in Clifton Road, reading the *Evening Standard*. Its front page featured what it called the Bus Bomb, and her father's part in it.

Like all the other newspapers of the day, the *Standard* was also calling him a hero, the brave man who had carried a ticking bomb off the 55 bus to comparative safety. None of the other papers had mentioned ticking, but all had run the photo of the now-famous Thomas Milsom, described (inaccurately) as a press photographer. The "happily married bus rider" and his "beautiful daughter, Elizabeth" lived (again inaccurately) in a "fine detached home" in northwest London. Mr. Milsom, known to his many friends as Tom, would certainly receive an award for bravery, and possibly an OBE from the Queen. On an inside page was another photo of Tom, with Lizzie and Dot this time, and a picture of the roadway where the bomb had gone off and of the injured being taken away on stretchers.

Feeling pleased for her dad, and even more pleased with her own coverage, Lizzie drank her coffee and ate the chocolate biscuit that came with it. She picked up the large plastic carrier containing the late Dermot McKinnon's property and hoisted its straps onto her shoulder. It was ten to seven. Leaving the *Evening Standard* on the table, she went inside to pay.

The girl behind the till also had a *Standard* and did a double take. "That's you! That's your dad! You must be so proud of him."

IT FELT TO Lizzie quite a long walk to Falcon Mews, especially as she was carrying a heavy bag and wearing high heels. Adam phoned when she was in Castellain Road. He'd finished the work he was doing and said he would come and meet her. "Amazing about your dad. It's been all over the papers. There's a picture of you, too."

Lizzie said she'd seen it and told him the number of the mews house where she'd be.

Five minutes later, she was ringing the doorbell.

CARL PUT THE television on and caught the Bus Bomb story. He seemed to remember that man Milsom from years ago; he'd been at school with his daughter, Carl thought. Impossible to concentrate, though. He switched it off and went back to where he had been sitting for the past half hour, almost at the top of the upper flight of stairs, as near as he could to the top flat. He had been rewarded by sounds. Not loud sounds; in fact, sounds that could hardly be identified, grunts really, and sighs, nothing more than that. He noticed that Sybil's front door was slightly open.

The doorbell's ringing shocked him; it made him furiously angry. It seldom happened, and when it did, it was like an insult, an intrusion and an assault. Who dared come here, and *now*? It rang again.

He ran downstairs to answer it. He needed to get rid of whoever it was. He opened the door, flinging it back. "Yes? What is it?"

A girl stood outside, a girl who seemed vaguely familiar. "Hi, Carl, long time no see. I've brought some stuff from the pet clinic that belonged to Dermot McKinnon. I believe he lived in the top flat? We didn't know where else to take it." She stepped in, swinging a large bag, before he could stop her.

"You can't go up!" he shouted.

But she was already on the stairs, and he could only have stopped her now by seizing hold of her. A shrill cry came from behind the half-open door on the top floor, followed by a hoarse sobbing.

Lizzie ran up another four or five steps, stopped, and called, "What's that? What's going on up there?"

"Not your business," Carl said, adding absurdly, "You're trespassing!"

Lizzie dropped the bag and flung open the door. A girl of about her own age was rolling on the floor, sweating so much that her face and arms looked as if they'd been dipped in water. Vomit splashed the rug and soaked the armchair she had tumbled out of.

A quick memory of how she had failed to do anything when she was herself threatened came back to Lizzie. She hesitated no longer but took her mobile out of her coat pocket and dialled the emergency number. "Ambulance," she shouted. "Eleven Falcon Mews, West Nine."

She thought of Carl, how they'd been to school together and that he'd been a friend of Stacey's. He didn't seem to recognise her, and she wasn't going to remind him, especially not now.

He had disappeared downstairs, and a good thing too. She knelt down beside the girl and told her it was all right, help was coming. They'd take her to hospital, St. Mary's probably.

"What's your name?"

"Sybil." It came out as a choked whisper.

"I can hear the ambulance now."

I've learned from what happened with Scotty and Redhead, Lizzie thought. Once I'd have been in a real panic, but not now. I'm stronger now.

"Don't leave me," sobbed Sybil.

"I have to let them in, but I'll be right back."

Running down the stairs, Lizzie flung open the front door as the ambulance came howling round the mews. A man and a woman jumped out and ran across the cobbles carrying what looked like a stretcher.

"Upstairs!" cried Lizzie.

She went into the living room, where Carl lay facedown on a sofa. In the kitchen she poured a glass of water and drank it down. "What did you do to her, you bastard?" she said as she passed him on her way back. Upstairs, the paramedics had laid Sybil on the stretcher and were covering her with a white blanket.

"You'll be OK now," Lizzie said. "You're safe."

She went back downstairs, and out the front door. Carl needed to stop her, explain. But Adam was coming along the mews, and when he saw her, he put out his arms. Lizzie went into them and he hugged her tightly.

"Can we get away from here?" she said. "I really don't want to stay here a moment longer. It brings back too many memories of something bad that happened to me. I'll explain. It's time I explained."

They held hands down Castellain Road. "Oh, dear," she said after a while, "I haven't a clue what I did with Dermot's stuff. I must have dropped it."

"I'm sure it doesn't matter at all. It's just so great to be walking down the street with you."

33

THE BATTERY OF Carl's mobile phone appeared to have gone
flat. Nicola tried the landline, but no one answered. Leaving
a message when all you wanted to say was that you hadn't liked the
film and left early was pointless. The ambulance that passed her
bus on the way home she didn't connect with Falcon Mews. Why
should she? By now it was growing dark, but no lights were on in
number 11. On the front path someone had dropped a crumpled
tissue, and farther along a ballpoint pen. The front door had been
left on the latch. Balancing her shopping, she pushed it open, went
in, and called, "Carl?"

No answer. He wasn't in the living room or the kitchen or
upstairs, and the front door of Sybil's flat stood wide-open. Indoors
it seemed stuffy and close, oppressive. Feeling deeply uneasy, Nicola
put the hallway light on, opened the front door, and stood on the
step. Light poured out, filling the little front garden. Mr. Kaleejah
and Elinor Jackson from next door came out simultaneously to ask
if anything was wrong.

"I see the ambulance," said Mr. Kaleejah, "and I think someone is
taken ill, someone has an accident."

Elinor's partner came out to join her. They suggested Nicola
come into their house, offered a drink. Had she called the police?

Nicola said no to everything, thanks but no. She had to be indoors, she said, in case the phone rang. Mr. Kaleejah's dog threw back its head and started howling, not a bark but a wolflike howl.

Back inside, Nicola put a light on in the living room and saw something move in a dark corner. She nearly screamed but controlled herself by clasping her hand over her mouth. She sat down on Dad's sofa, got up again, said, "What are you doing?" and then, when there was no answer, "What's going on?"

"Why have you come here?"

"Carl? Tell me what's going on. There was an ambulance. What's happened?"

He was silent for so long she thought he wasn't going to speak to her. Then at last he said in a voice she barely recognised, "Sybil. They took her away."

"What's happened to her?"

She was looking at a man she wouldn't have recognised but for his voice. She thought of people she'd read about whose hair turned white overnight from shock. That could happen to Carl; it looked as if it would, though she had never believed it possible.

"You must sit down. And I will tell you. She took poison. Someone came to the house and found her and called an ambulance."

"What do you mean?"

"I've been in her flat. There's sick all over the place. She nearly died; she probably is dead now."

"What poison?" said Nicola in a voice that didn't sound like her own.

"I don't know. It doesn't matter."

"I am going to look."

"No, don't. Don't. It's not your business."

But she was on the stairs. He followed her, clambering up, too weak to do anything but crawl. The big room where Sybil had sweated and struggled stank of vomit. Carl crept across the floor on all fours, making whimpering sounds. Clearly, he thought, the

paramedics must have taken away with them the sachets that had contained the DNP.

Nicola covered her nose with a handful of tissues from her bag. "It was that same stuff you sold to Stacey, wasn't it?"

"She got it herself online," he muttered.

"No. No, Carl. You gave it to her. I saw it in our bathroom, a powder in sachets it was. I don't suppose you sold it this time. Let's go downstairs. I can't stand this smell." At the foot, she sat on the bottom stair. "Whatever she held over you, whatever Dermot did, I don't want to know. I'm frightened of you, Carl."

He went past her and stood holding on to the table. He noticed how she flinched. "There's nothing to be frightened of. I'll tell you everything. I won't keep anything back."

"You've killed her, haven't you? I never thought I would say that to anyone. It's the most terrible thing anyone can say." Nicola got up and pulled her coat round her as if she were cold. Her face was white and her hands shook. "I can't stay here with you."

"Don't leave me. Please don't leave me."

He took hold of her by the shoulders and pulled her to him. Any other girl, he thought later, would have kicked out at him, fought him. Nicola let herself go limp in his arms, then gently slipped out of them, putting out her hand to open the front door. He stepped back in a kind of shame.

"Let me go, Carl," she said in her clear, resounding voice. "Let me go."

She stepped out into the dark. It had rained since she came back, and the darkness was shiny with yellow light on wet cobbles and silvery slates.

He ran after her, calling to her to come back. But when she turned the corner into Castellain Road, he gave up. Moaning softly, whimpering, he sat down on a front step and put his head in his hands.

34

H E LAY AWAKE for hours, aware that things always appeared
so much worse at night. The knowledge that these fears and
horrors would surely shrink away in the morning, assuming their
natural size, did nothing to calm him. He tossed and turned, thinking of Sybil dead in a mortuary somewhere and, uselessly, point-
lessly, of the mess and filth upstairs, the room that smelt so bad
that Nicola had had to leave it behind and run away. At about three,
before it began to get light, he fell asleep and went on sleeping until
sunshine streaming in woke him up.

Only then did the horrid sequence of events come back to him,
gradually, one at a time, until he was overwhelmed by fear and a
physical pain that squeezed his stomach like a griping indigestion
and doubled him up. He was frightened to lie there, twisted up,
and forced himself onto the floor, a severely painful cramp in both
legs. The sound he heard he couldn't identify; it seemed to him the
strangest sound he had ever heard, until at last he recognised it as
the phone, the landline. He let it ring until it seemed to get tired
and stopped. The ensuing silence was so beautiful—he told himself
it was beautiful—that he thought if losing his hearing would bring
this blissful nothingness, he would welcome deafness.

In the sweet quiet he got onto all fours, then hoisted himself to his

feet. It took a little while. He made his way slowly into the kitchen. The first thing he saw was the shopping bag Nicola had brought in with her the previous evening. Inside were apples, a cut loaf, sliced cheese, a half litre of milk, two tins of sardines, and six large eggs. He pulled out the crust end of the loaf, laid a slice of cheddar on it, and sat on a stool to eat. He ripped the top off the milk container and took a deep swig, the first milk, he thought, he had drunk since he was a child. It was ten past eleven. Now that he was fully awake, he felt much better and stronger. The woman was dead. She had killed herself just as Stacey had killed herself, from vanity, from a willingness to do anything fast and easy to achieve weight loss, even if that anything was suicidal. Of course she hadn't known that, the poor foolish creature; she hadn't been the sort of woman who read labels with cautionary advice.

He knew he must, at any rate superficially, clean up that top flat and went upstairs, carrying a bucket with him. The smell in the room wasn't nearly as bad as Nicola had said. A slightly sour whiff, that was all. He filled the bucket with hot, soapy water from the kitchen and scraped the vomit off the rugs and cushions before deciding to put the cushions in a plastic bag and then in the rubbish bin by the back gate. The stains left behind on the various textiles he scrubbed with a brush he found under the sink. It wasn't all that long a job once he got down to it, and by midday the task was completed. Only then, when evidence of what had happened had been removed, did he realise what Sybil's death meant: the life of the second unwelcome occupant of the top flat at 11 Falcon Mews was over.

"It seems to be a fine day," he said aloud. "I shall make myself some lunch—two eggs, I think, and a piece of toast—and then I'll go out and walk up to my mother's. I'll borrow enough money from her to tide me over until I can get a tenant set up in the top flat. It shouldn't take long."

He broke the two eggs into a bowl, beat them with a fork, scrambled the mixture in a saucepan, and made the toast. His lunch was almost eaten when the doorbell rang. It made him jump. He told

himself not to be stupid, that there was no need to answer it. But when the bell rang again, he went to the door.

Sybil's father stood outside. He was carrying a suitcase. No doubt he had come to tell Carl what he already knew: Sybil was dead.

"You'd better come in."

"I won't stop. Sybil's back with us now. The hospital sent her home this morning. I've come for her things."

Was this how it felt when you knew you were going to faint? Carl clutched hold of the tabletop.

Cliff Soames came in, slamming the door behind him. "They got most of that stuff out of her. They said she'll be OK now, but she'll not be coming back here. Not ever. Her mum's looking after her, won't let her out of her sight. She won't think of leaving us again. I'll go up and put her things in the case."

Carl went into the living room and sat on Dad's sofa as Cliff Soames's words sank in. Sybil wasn't coming back here, Sybil wasn't dead; they didn't all die, the people who took DNP, not the ones who were careful. He began to shake, his hands trembling, the muscles in his legs jumping.

The suitcase Cliff had brought, now full, bumped down the stairs. He left it in the hall, took a step into the room. "Sybil wants to stay alive." His tone was ominous. "You'll never set eyes on her again. Does she owe you any rent?"

Carl didn't know what to say. The real sum she owed he was afraid to put into words, but the temptation to say something, to name a small figure, was too great to resist.

"Eighty pounds," he said, and stupidly, "if you can see your way . . ."

Cliff Soames pulled a wad of notes out of his pocket, handed them over, and said he'd like a receipt. "The rents you people charge. I've read about you in the papers, greedy, grasping buggers. I hope it chokes you."

Carl wrote a receipt for eighty pounds and handed it over in silence. When the front door slammed, he watched Cliff stagger

down the street with the heavy bag. His first task, he thought, would be to spend some of the money he was still clutching on a couple of bottles of wine, and perhaps a bottle of something stronger.

IT WAS SATURDAY, it had to be. Carl's priority was to look at accommodation wanted online and pick one or two people who seemed likely. But there were hundreds—probably thousands—all wanting somewhere to live in central London. Investigating these things brought it home to you how desperate the housing situation was.

He soon saw that the place he had to offer, a self-contained top floor of a mews house in Maida Vale, was about as desirable as you could get, and the rent he had asked (though scarcely ever succeeded in getting) had been derisory. This would have to be revised. Within ten minutes he had increased it considerably and had arranged for three applicants to come round later: a couple at two, a single man at four, and a woman at six. What to do if he liked the first ones he didn't yet know. He would give it some thought.

After a shot of vodka and a glass of pinot grigio, he began looking through his part of the house for Nicola's property. She must have left a lot of things behind, he thought: clothes, maybe jewellery, though she hadn't much, makeup and perfume (to which the same applied), books, CDs, and DVDs. But she hadn't—just a bit of underwear, a grey dress and a red dress for work, and jeans and sweaters or tee-shirts for the weekends. The grey dress was still in the wardrobe and so was a pair of jeans and a blue-and-white-patterned top he had always liked. It gave him a pang to look at it; it was as if she had died.

The doorbell rang while he was wondering what to do next. It was Mr. and Mrs. Crowhurst, right on time. They looked young, about his own age or younger. The rent he was asking—the new rent—seemed not to put them off. They walked around the rooms, Mrs. Crowhurst sniffing the air in the living room rather suspi-

ciously but making no comment. Could they use the garden? Carl remembered last time and said no, he was afraid not. Mr. Crowhurst said they were called Jason and Chloe but had said they were Mr. and Mrs. because married people sounded more respectable.

"Aren't you married, then?"

"Oh, yes, we're married all right." They held out their left hands to show their wedding rings. "We'll call you and let you know."

"I've got two more people coming, one at four and one at six, so don't be too long about it." Carl had never felt so powerful, monarch of all he surveyed, as Dermot might have said.

The next possible tenant came at ten past four. He was old enough to be the Crowhursts' father, tall, grey haired, wearing a suit. His name was Andrew Page, and whether he was married didn't come into it. He agreed to the rent, didn't ask about the use of the garden, but said he would like to move in as soon as possible. Something about him reminded Carl of Dermot. He said he had one more applicant to see, and Mr. Page was to call later.

When the phone rang at five, Carl thought it must be Andrew Page, but a man called Harry said he was a friend of Nicola's and would like to come round in his jalopy and pick up her stuff. Now, if poss. Carl said the following day would be more convenient, but that didn't suit Harry.

"It must be now or never," said Harry.

Harry seemed unlike any possible friend of Nicola's. He wore a paint-stained tracksuit and had a big, bushy beard as well as shoulder-length hair. It was as well, Carl thought, that Nicola wasn't clothes conscious, for Harry had brought only two large, whitish pillowcases to put everything in. This he accomplished in about five minutes, before hurling the pillowcases into the back of the van and driving off much faster, Carl thought, than anyone had ever before sped along the cobbles. He had tried to persuade Harry to take Nicola's green goose with him, but Harry had looked at it and shaken his head. So there it sat on the hall table, a silent and reproachful

reminder of everything that had happened to Carl during the past few months.

Immediately after the van departed, a small woman who introduced herself as Mrs. Hamilton drove up in a silver Lexus. Before she had even entered the house she was back in the car and driving away, once Carl had told her no off-street parking was available at 11 Falcon Mews.

Andrew Page returned in a taxi just before eight. "Turned up like a bad penny," he said, which was so like Dermot that it made Carl shudder.

"Changed your mind, have you?" Carl said, almost hoping that he had. But Andrew Page hadn't. He simply wanted to know that nothing had happened to keep him from the tenancy. Nothing had, Carl said rather reluctantly.

"I'd like to come back tomorrow with my solicitor to sign the contract. Oh, and pay the deposit. Best to have things all open and aboveboard, don't you think?"

Carl had never heard of anyone's having a solicitor present for such a transaction, but he didn't know much about letting property. He had certainly made a mess of it last time. It seemed amazing to him too that this man wanted to give him a deposit without even being asked for it. While the taxi waited, they arranged for him to return at 6:00 p.m. the following day with Mr. Lucas Partridge, LLB.

Throughout the rest of the evening, Carl repeated to himself the two clichés Andrew Page had uttered, Dermot-like. What did it matter? He intended to avoid speaking to him as much as possible during his tenancy. The money was good and would keep on coming—without hindrance, without blackmail.

"WHAT WOULD YOU DO," said Adam, "if you recognised someone you'd seen doing something weird and you thought he might have committed a crime?" He and Lizzie were walking along the canal

towpath between Cunningham Place and Lisson Green. It was a fine, clear evening.

"What d'you mean by weird?"

"Sit down a minute."

They sat on a seat on the bank. "The guy who used to do your job at the pet place—what was he called?"

"Dermot McKinnon. He was murdered."

"I know he was. It happened in a street called Jerome something. Jerome Crescent, I think. They never found who did it." Adam paused. "At approximately that time, I'm not exactly sure of the date, I was on my way to drinks with a friend at a pub in Camden and was cycling along the path where we are now and under the bridge on Park Road until I was on the edge of the park, and this guy was on the opposite bank with a big backpack. It was getting dark and he didn't see me."

"What guy, Adam?"

"The man whose house you took McKinnon's stuff to. He was standing at the door when I met you in the street that day. He's the man I saw with the backpack. I watched him from the bank through the trees. I know he didn't see me. I was fascinated. He squatted down, undid the bag, and took a big, heavy thing out of it. Then I saw him throw the bag into the canal, but not the heavy object, which he sort of cradled in his arms. It was all very odd."

"Oh my God."

"I hadn't given it much thought until recently. At the time, I didn't know who he was, certainly didn't know there was any connection between him and the man who was murdered. So it gave me quite a shock to recognise him."

"Carl Martin?"

"Yes. And he and Dermot McKinnon lived in the same house. It's an odd coincidence, don't you think?"

35

T HE DEPOSIT, REFUNDABLE on the termination of the tenancy, was so welcome to Carl, and so unexpected, he could
scarcely believe it even when the cheque for two thousand pounds
was put into his hand. Mr. Partridge, the solicitor, seemed to find
nothing strange in this transaction. That Carl had prepared no contract between landlord and tenant caused some shaking of his head,
but no great harm was done as on Page's instructions he had created one himself. All of it looked favourable to Carl, another cause
of wonderment, so that he felt he must be living in a happy dream.
He half expected to wake up and find himself back in the real world
without money, food, or any sort of security.

The contract was signed and witnessed. If it was agreeable to
Mr. Martin, as his new tenant insisted on calling him, Andrew Page
would move in the next day. He would bring some small items of
furniture, if that was all right with Mr. Martin. Carl, still dazed from
the windfall and promises of further cash, said it was fine. When the
two men had gone, he looked hard at the cheque. It really was for
two thousand pounds. It was funny that he now had all this money
but not a single note or coin and wouldn't have until he cashed the
cheque in the morning.

He would have liked to celebrate by going to the Summerhouse

restaurant nearby, or the newly opened Crocker's Folly, and treating himself to oysters and steak and a bottle of champagne. Then he remembered his credit card, which hadn't been used for months— he hadn't dared to use it; he couldn't now recall where he had put it. It took him half an hour before he located it in the pocket of a jacket he never wore.

It was dinnertime, precisely seven thirty. He strolled along Sutherland Avenue and across the Edgware Road into Aberdeen Place. Crocker's Folly was grand outside, and its greatly refurbished interior pretty and elegant. They had no oysters, but steak and champagne were no problem. It was so long since Carl had drunk champagne that he had forgotten what it tasted like. He wasn't going to gobble his food, but ate it leisurely, sipping the champagne and savouring the sautéed potatoes. He had moved from this delicious first course on to a confection of three kinds of chocolate and Cornish ice cream before allowing himself to think about his life and what was happening to it.

Maybe Nicola would come back now that he had a new tenant and money, though money had never attracted her. He could see his friends again, phone them, visit them, and ask them over. He would resume the abandoned novel; he would find that writing afforded him the pleasure it once had, he would find inspiration. His worries were all past and he must take care not to create new ones by getting on overly friendly terms with Andrew Page. Perhaps "Mr. Martin" and "Mr. Page" was the best policy, so there would be no need for invitations to drinks or even cups of tea.

He had begun the walk back to Falcon Mews when thoughts of Dermot McKinnon came into his mind. Surely now that his new life was taking shape, the memory of Dermot would fade. There could be no pity, no regret. What Carl had done had been close to an accident, in that he had hardly known what was happening until it was all over. In a year's time, after a year of enjoying the new tenant, with his formal ways and cold correctness, Carl would

have ceased altogether to remember Dermot and certainly wouldn't blame himself in any way for his death.

"ARE YOU GOING to do anything about it?"

"I don't know," Adam said.

He and Lizzie were alone in the reception area of the Sutherland Pet Clinic. The clinic was closed, but one patient, a King Charles spaniel, and its owner remained. They were in Caroline's examination room, where the dog, Louis Quatorze, was receiving immunisation. "I could go to the police, I know that. I would tell them what I've told you: that at what I think was roughly the time of the murder, I believe I saw Carl Martin holding the instrument he'd used to kill Dermot McKinnon."

"Are you going to go to the police?"

Adam sighed. "I saw a man drop something into the canal where it goes into Regent's Park. I didn't come forward earlier because I didn't think any more of it till I went to pick you up in Falcon Mews and that same man—no doubt about that—came out of the house onto the front steps. You told me that Dermot McKinnon had also lived there, in the top flat. It doesn't amount to much, does it?"

Before Lizzie could reply, Caroline emerged with Louis Quatorze and his owner. Lizzie presented the owner with the bill and patted Louis on the head. She and Adam left at the same time as the dog and his owner, leaving Caroline to lock up.

"Do you really think he might have killed Dermot?" Lizzie remembered the callous way Carl had behaved when Sybil had been so ill upstairs. But still, could he have committed murder?

"I don't know, Lizzie. Let's go to the Prince Alfred pub and have a drink. It's too cold to be outside."

In the pub, Lizzie sat at one of the little tables and Adam fetched two glasses of white wine. "What I'd like would be to talk to Carl about it," he said. "Find out how he reacts. I'd like to know his state of mind."

"Well, you are training to be a psychologist."

Adam laughed. "I've got a psychology degree, but that's about it. You know, I'd just like to see him. I think I'd tell him I don't intend to go to the police, but when I've heard him out—if he consents to speak to me—I'll tell him he should go to them himself."

"What—and confess?"

"That would be the general idea."

"But people don't do that, Adam. Not voluntarily. And what happens if he gets violent? If you're right and he did kill Dermot, what's to stop him killing again?"

36

The previous winter had not been cold. It had been wet instead, and if you lived near the Thames or in the Somerset Levels, you stood a serious chance of being flooded. This year the warm weather had gone on and on, but as autumn turned into winter, sharp cold began. London was always the mildest part of the United Kingdom, and the cold started in Maida Vale rather later than elsewhere. But by the end of November in Falcon Mews, frost was glittering on the bushes that lined the cobbled street, and silvering the bare branches of the trees.

In number 11, the central heating, which hadn't been put to the test the previous year, was soon needed and found wanting. At least in Carl's opinion. At the top of the house, in the tenant's domain, there were no complaints, but one evening Carl happened to be in the hall when Andrew Page came in with two large electric heaters he fetched from the back of a taxi.

"I'm a bit of a chilly mortal," he said by way of explanation. "I'm sure the heating's adequate."

The heaters were taken upstairs, and as always, Andrew Page's front door was closed silently. Carl's only way of knowing if his tenant was in was to go out into the street or the back garden and look up to see if a light was on behind the top windows. Even that

was hardly a sure guide, as people all too often went out leaving lights on, and Andrew Page might be one of them. But Carl had no desire to know. Everyone had television, so presumably Andrew had. Most had a radio or music player or both, so no doubt he had one of those too. But if he did, no sound was ever heard from the top-floor rooms. No running water, nothing dropped on the floor, no click of a switch, no phone ringing, no computer coming on. Andrew Page seemed to live in utter silence. In that respect, in *all* respects, he was the ideal tenant. The rent was received without fail in Carl's bank account on the last day of every month. Carl sometimes thought Andrew Page was too good to be true, but he told himself that he felt that way because until recently the people he had come across had been—not to put too fine a point on it—degenerate bastards.

All was well in Carl's life, except for the loss of Nicola. He'd discovered that she no longer lived in Ashmill Street, which meant that she had got herself other accommodation, and he could only find out where this was by calling her office at the Department of Health. In other words by calling her, and he shied away from doing that. He had to face it. If she wanted to see him, to be with him again, she would phone him. He remembered their parting, and that man coming round in his "jalopy" to collect her things. Walking past a mirror, the only one in the house outside the bathroom, he stopped and made himself smile into it. As he feared, his smile had become a facial distortion, like a mask or a gargoyle, with no warmth or friendliness in it.

In the mornings and sometimes in the evenings he worked on his novel, mechanically, almost automatically, typing words that all meant something, describing events or people or actions. Remembering Raymond Chandler's advice to authors that, when at a loss, they should have a man come into a room with a gun, Carl introduced violence to liven up his story. Then, when he had almost decided to abandon the novel and accept that he was to be a one-

book author, Andrew Page came down the stairs and, instead of leaving the house, tapped on Carl's living-room door.

Carl had been sitting at the laptop, his hands idle, staring at the blank screen with its green hill far away. He called out for Andrew to come in.

He entered the room holding a copy of *Death's Door*. "Sorry to disturb you, but I was hoping you'd sign this. I bought it this afternoon in that little bookshop round the corner."

Only Carl's publisher and a friend of his publisher's had ever put this request to him before.

"Of course I will." Carl wondered if the smile with which he agreed looked as sinister and forced as the toothy grimace he had an hour before achieved in the mirror. If it did, it had no adverse effect on Andrew Page, who handed over the book open at the title page, and Carl signed it. Some instinct from the past must have inspired him, for, repeating the grim smile, he asked his tenant to stay for a while and have a drink. These days the flat was always well stocked with wine and spirits.

"Thanks. I'd like to."

Carl produced gin and a bottle of tonic, white wine, and a couple of cans of lager, all of it suitably chilled. He was already regretting his offer, not because he cared how much Andrew Page consumed, but for want of knowing what to talk about. In fact, it was easy, because the hitherto silent Andrew did most of the talking. He turned out to be a trainee solicitor with a law degree, soon approaching the end of his two-year articles. This, Carl thought, probably accounted for his bringing a solicitor along with him for the signing and witnessing of the contract. Andrew Page explained that both his mother and father were solicitors, and his older brother was a barrister. He moved on to say how lucky he was to have found this flat in this nice street and how much he liked living here. He was engaged and intended to marry as soon as he qualified. He seemed to believe that Carl was a successful author with

RuthRendell

several bestselling books behind him, and Carl was on the point of
denying this when the phone rang.

It was a man called Adam Yates, whom Carl had never heard of.
He had a nice voice, civilised and educated, which meant nothing.
"You know my girlfriend, Lizzie Milsom."

Did he? The name seemed familiar. A school friend, he thought.
Back when he and Stacey were children. All so long ago.

"I won't keep you," said Adam Yates. "I just want to talk with you
for a few minutes. I could come round about eight."

Could he put it off till tomorrow? Carl wondered. But if he did,
he would worry all night and half the next day. He suggested nine.

Adam Yates said nine would be fine.

Carl put the phone down and apologised to Andrew Page. They
talked a little longer. Carl's guest refused another drink but, as he
was leaving, said, "If I can be of any assistance, please feel free to
ask me. I've been thinking for a long time now that you might need
help." He let himself out, closing the door behind him. Carl felt
rather humiliated. And worried. Had his troubles, or the memory of
them, shown so plainly, and not just in his rictus smile?

He had two hours to wait for Adam Yates, whoever he was. A
friend of Lizzie Milsom's, he had said. Adam Yates would come and
talk to him about whatever it was. But the phone call had trans-
ported him back to the foodless life of the previous summer, the
time when more and more drink was needed and eating was impossible. He wanted nothing to eat now, but to drink another glass
of wine would be stupid, especially considering the three he had
already had with Andrew. He needed to be able to defend himself.

Defend? There was nothing this man could accuse Carl of or
suggest he had done wrong; nothing, surely, that would call forth a
defence.

At ten to nine, Carl went upstairs and stationed himself at the
window that looked onto the mews. Would Adam Yates come in
a car? Or by taxi? If he was a Londoner, he would more likely

arrive on foot. Carl sat in darkness and watched by the light of the streetlamp that was outside Mr. Kaleejah's. The mews was deserted, lights on in most of the houses. It was a fine night, the moon not yet risen but a single star showing, bright and steady. The pole star? Carl kept his eyes on his watch. At one minute to nine, Mr. Kaleejah came out of his front door with his dog on a lead and its rubber bone in its mouth. Slowly and purposely they set off in the Castellain Road direction. On the dot of nine, a man of about Carl's own age appeared at the other end of the mews. Carl went downstairs to answer the door, feeling sick for the first time in months. He was back in that state he recognised as perpetual anxiety.

He opened the door and the man he had seen from the window said, "Adam Yates."

Carl nodded. He stepped back and Adam Yates came in. He was a little taller than Carl, his dark hair cut short, clean shaven so closely as somehow to have an official look. To Carl, Yates's appearance and his neat jacket and matching trousers suggested a detective inspector in a TV serial. He followed Carl into the living room and was offered a drink.

"This isn't a social call. It won't take long."

Carl, retreating into his old world of fear and dread, was longing for a drink. Two bottles of wine, one white and the other rosé, stood on the table by Dad's sofa. His craving was strong, but not strong enough to break through the inhibition that competed with it. He told Adam to sit down and sat down himself on the sofa, as if the proximity of the bottles could be a comfort. In fact, the reverse was true.

"What do you want to say to me?"

"The event that I want to talk about happened last September. By the canal."

I knew it, Carl thought. Another blackmailer. How could he have believed he was safe, that everything was all right, that there was nothing more to fear? He nodded, moving his head slowly. "Can I have a drink?"

"If you need it. I see you do."

Carl filled a glass from the sauvignon bottle. The wine had grown warm, but that was unimportant. It had never been so much needed or tasted so good.

"I was on the canal bank, up among the trees. I saw you come along the bank below me, kneel down, and take a heavy object out of your backpack, which you then dropped into the canal. Of course I wondered why, but I didn't put it together with the murder of Dermot McKinnon. I didn't even hear about the murder until some time later. I didn't know you had any connection to Dermot until I came to Falcon Mews to meet Lizzie and I saw you come out of your front door."

Carl said nothing. There was no point. This man, who looked like a detective but obviously wasn't, knew everything. Carl swallowed half the contents of the wineglass.

"I wanted to tell you that I know what you've done."

Carl sat back, his mind clear suddenly. "Well, don't think you're alone. Dermot McKinnon knew about the first girl who died, and blackmailed me by withholding the rent. After he was dead, his girlfriend came to live here and blackmailed me again by withholding the rent. You can't aim to do that because you don't pay me rent."

Adam seemed surprised by this. "You've had a bad time," he said reasonably.

"Worse even than all this: my girlfriend guessed what had happened and left me. I've got a good tenant for the top flat now, but maybe he'll leave when you tell your story, because I'm not paying you blackmail money. I've had enough of that. I'm not paying you to keep silent. I'm not handing over to you the rent my tenant pays or letting you live in part of the house rent-free."

"I'm not asking you to let me live in your house. I haven't asked for anything." He refilled Carl's glass. "I don't even want wine from you."

This made Carl wince. The man was so calm. So quietly condemning. "What's the point of all this then?"

"I just wanted you to know that I know." Adam leaned forward, his voice still reasonable, soothing even. "What I'd really like is for you to go to the police and confess what you did. You'd not have any worries then. It would all be over. You'd go to prison, but confessing would shorten your sentence."

For a moment Carl felt an immense burden lift from his shoulders as he considered a life free from anxiety and fear. But then reality came crashing back. "Why should I? I've got a peaceful life now. I've enough to live on, everything's worked out for me. Why the hell should I confess?"

"Because I know. And you know that I know. Look, I'm not interested in retribution or punishment. I promise you I will never tell a soul, and I keep my promises. But why would you believe me? In fact, I can see right now by the look on your face that you don't."

Adam got up. "I'll give your kind regards to Lizzie, shall I? She says you were at school together, but I'm sure you remembered that when she came round with Dermot's things." He turned and looked at Carl. "I can see you're suffering, but there is a way to end this, and you know what that is."

37

O F COURSE HE didn't believe what Adam Yates had said. You don't believe someone who makes a promise and then says he doesn't break them. Anyone can say that. After sleeping well for weeks, Carl lay awake that night. He thought of everything Adam had said, repeated it over and over, considered the man's promise and dismissed it. He would tell. The police would put it all together. It was only a matter of time.

But the weeks went by, and then months. Andrew Page continued to pay the rent on the last day of each month. Mr. Kaleejah continued to take his dog out three or four times a day, and Carl's neighbours said good morning and hi and how are you when they encountered him.

One fine day Nicola came round. By that time he was drinking again, and as heavily as he had done in the days after Sybil had returned to her parents. Nicola refused a drink but asked if she could make herself a cup of tea. She made the tea and produced the white-chocolate biscuits he had always liked but hadn't eaten since she had left him. She told him she had met someone else, was living with him. They were getting married soon. Nothing was said about Dermot or Sybil or Stacey, and nothing about money. Nicola left after half an hour.

Carl watched her from the window, keeping his eyes on her until she had turned out of the mews into Sutherland Avenue. All the time she was with him, he had been drinking, no longer bothering to hide his habit from visitors and friends. Of all of them, only his mother reproached him for drinking so much. Nicola had said nothing. From her face, he thought he could see that she no longer cared.

Now that she was gone, he opened his third bottle of wine of the day and poured himself a large glass. The stronger kinds of alcohol, the whisky and gin and vodka, sent him to sleep quite quickly, but wine only made him feel rather dazed; as if nothing mattered much. It took away for a time the damning sentences that kept repeating in his head: *You murdered Dermot, you killed him,* and Adam Yates's *There is a way to end this, and you know what that is.* The words combined to make a kind of mantra.

Nearly a year had passed since Dermot's death, six months since Adam Yates had come to tell him what he knew. Carl kept up his habit of walking and now roamed farther and over larger areas, covering Regent's Park and exploring Primrose Hill. Breakfast started with a large glass of wine, a tumbler not a wineglass, which was refilled, so that when he began on his walk, he was dizzy with drink and had to sit down on a roadside seat, sometimes to fall asleep. He had ceased to write anything. The few attempts he had made to start something new he gave up after a paragraph or two. The rent continued to come in, though, and even after he had settled his utilities bills and the council tax and his small amount of income tax, the money mounted up.

Still, he bought the cheapest wine because there was no point in buying the expensive stuff. He drank it without tasting it, swallowing it fast to bring a few hours' oblivion, and grew even thinner. His mother, whom he occasionally saw because, despairing of his visiting her, she came to visit him, told him that he looked more like his father than ever. For the first time in months he looked in the mirror and saw a skeletal man with staring eyes and protruding bones.

Increasingly now his thoughts were centred not on Dermot's murder but on Adam Yates's knowledge of it. Few people visited him, and those who did were postmen or someone come to read a meter. He fancied that they stared at the scanty beard he had grown, and his emaciated body.

For a long time after Adam's visit, Carl was sure that every ring on the doorbell must be the police. Of course Adam would have reported him, Carl told himself. Of course Adam would; his promise meant nothing.

Carl spent whole days thinking of nothing but Adam, about what he'd said, and the soothing tone of his voice when he'd told Carl that his worries could soon be over. He thought too of what must happen next, of the step that must be taken to restore the peace of mind he'd had before he crashed the green goose down on Dermot's head. He had dreams about that earlier time, and although he knew he had been in a perpetual anxiety and bitter regret, he looked back on it now as calm and carefree.

Adam Yates had been right: if Carl wanted that peaceful life back again, there was only one way to do it.

"He's a very serious young man," said Dot Milsom. "He acts more like a man twice his age."

"Who does?" Tom asked.

"Lizzie's young man, Adam."

"He's a cut above any boyfriend she's ever had." Tom looked up from his newspaper. "And very clever. Quite nice too, don't you think? At least he's got some manners."

Tom, who had given up his joyriding on buses—as Dot called it—in favour of a modified form of motorbike tracking on a ploughed field, turned to the crime pages and gave a low whistle.

"What is it, Tom?"

"Wasn't Lizzie at school with a boy called Carl Martin?"

Dot nodded. "What's he done?"

"He appears to have confessed to murder. Remember that chap who was hit over the head in Jerome Crescent? Well, that was Carl. Who did it, I mean. It says here that he walked into a police station and confessed. Imagine doing that!"

"I'd be too scared."

Tom shook his head, more in sorrow than anger. "It wouldn't be as scary as not confessing. It might even be a comfort. Think what it must have been like to have that on his conscience." Tom put his newspaper down and leaned back in his chair. "And now, now it's all over."

About the Author

Ruth Rendell (1930–2015) was an exceptional crime writer and will be remembered as a legend in her own lifetime. Her groundbreaking debut novel, *From Doon with Death*, was first published in 1964 and introduced readers to her enduring and popular detective, Inspector Reginald Wexford.

With worldwide sales of approximately 20 million copies, Rendell was a regular *Sunday Times* bestseller. Her sixty bestselling novels include police procedurals, some of which have been successfully adapted for TV, stand-alone psychological mysteries, and a third strand of crime novels under the pseudonym Barbara Vine.

Rendell won numerous awards, including the *Sunday Times* Literary Award in 1990. In 1996 she was awarded the CBE and in 1997 became a Life Peer. In 1991 she was awarded the Crime Writers' Association Cartier Diamond Dagger for sustained excellence in crime writing.